THE
AMISH
SEAMSTRESS

Books by Mindy Starns Clark and Leslie Gould

THE WOMEN OF LANCASTER COUNTY SERIES

The Amish Midwife
▶ http://bit.ly/AmishMidwife

The Amish Nanny
▶ http://bit.ly/AmishNanny

The Amish Bride
▶ http://bit.ly/AmishBride

The Amish Seamstress
▶ http://bit.ly/AmishSeamstress

• • •

Other Fiction by Mindy Starns Clark

THE MILLION DOLLAR MYSTERIES

A Penny for Your Thoughts
Don't Take Any Wooden Nickels
A Dime a Dozen
A Quarter for a Kiss
The Buck Stops Here

A SMART CHICK MYSTERY

The Trouble with Tulip
Blind Dates Can Be Murder
Elementary, My Dear Watkins

STANDALONE MYSTERIES

Whispers of the Bayou
Shadows of Lancaster County
Under the Cajun Moon
Secrets of Harmony Grove
Echoes of Titanic

THE
AMISH
SEAMSTRESS

MINDY STARNS CLARK
LESLIE GOULD

HARVEST HOUSE PUBLISHERS
EUGENE, OREGON

Scripture verses are taken from the

Holy Bible, New International Version®, NIV®. Copyright © 1973, 1978, 1984, 2011, by Biblica, Inc.™ Used by permission of Zondervan. All rights reserved worldwide. www.zondervan.com

King James Version of the Bible

Cover by Garborg Design Works, Savage, Minnesota

Cover photos © Chris Garborg

The authors are represented by MacGregor Literary, Inc. of Hillsboro, Oregon.

THE AMISH SEAMSTRESS
Copyright © 2013 by Mindy Starns Clark and Leslie Gould
Published by Harvest House Publishers
Eugene, Oregon 97402
www.harvesthousepublishers.com

Library of Congress Cataloging-in-Publication Data
   Clark, Mindy Starns.
   The Amish seamstress / Mindy Starns Clark and Leslie Gould.
        pages cm. — (The Women of Lancaster County Series ; Book 4)

   ISBN 978-0-7369-2626-3 (pbk.)
   ISBN 978-0-7369-4171-6 (eBook)

   1. Amish—Fiction. 2. Women dressmakers—Fiction. 3. Lancaster County (Pa.)—Fiction.
   I. Gould, Leslie, 1962- II. Title.
   PS3603.L366A87 2013
   813'.6—dc23

                                                                          2013012257

Printed in the United States of America

13 14 15 16 17 18 19 20 21 / LB-CD / 10 9 8 7 6 5 4 3 2 1

Mindy:
For my niece Gabriella Rose Clark,
who is a ray of sunshine in my life,
and
Leslie:
For my father, Bruce Egger,
a gentle man who still stands for those in need.

"I lift up my eyes to the mountains—
where does my help come from?
My help comes from the LORD,
the Maker of heaven and earth."
PSALM 121:1-2

ACKNOWLEDGMENTS

Mindy thanks

My husband, John, who never ceases to amaze me with the depths of his love, care, and support. Truly, I couldn't do it without him.

Our daughters, Emily and Lauren, who are always there for me—and who were especially helpful on this one.

Jonathon Stutzman, for information about cameras and filming, especially in an academic setting; Kim Alexis and Ron Duguay, for help with hockey lingo.

Leslie thanks

My husband, Peter, and our children, Kaleb, Taylor, Hana, and Thao, for their support and ongoing practical help. Laurie Snyder for all of her encouragement through this process. And Mary Hake for always answering my questions about Anabaptists with such grace and love.

Jeff Kitson, executive director of the Nappanee, Indiana, Chamber of Commerce, for his assistance and direction; the many good people of Elkhart County that I encountered while researching this story; and the staff of the Menno-Hof Amish/Mennonite Information Center in Shipshewana, Indiana, for an outstanding experience.

Mindy and Leslie thank

Our agent, Chip MacGregor, for his vision for this series; our editor, Kim Moore, for her dedication to our stories; and the exceptional folks at Harvest House Publishers for giving such care and attention to every detail of the publishing process.

Also, thanks to Dave Siegrist for his expertise; the Mennonite Information Center in Lancaster, Pennsylvania, for their invaluable resources; Erik Wesner, author of amishamerica.com, for his insightful view of the Amish; and Richard A. Stevick for his book *Growing up Amish: The Teenage Years*. For more information about Native Americans in Lancaster County, we recommend *A Clash of Cultures: Native Americans and Colonialism in Lancaster County, Pennsylvania*, by Darvin L. Martin.

ONE

Was that Zed, already?

The generator powering my sewing machine was right outside the window, and it was so loud I couldn't hear much, but I felt sure I was picking up the sound of his voice coming from the kitchen.

Smiling, I finished the seam, cut the threads, and carefully folded up the half-finished dress I'd been working on. Then I stood and slid open the window, leaned down, and turned the generator off. In the looming silence that followed, the noises of the household came through to my little side room much more clearly. Sure enough, it was Zed, and though I couldn't make out the words he was saying, his familiar tones were warm and sweet as always.

I pulled down the screen and hurriedly straightened my work area so we could be on our way. Though it was a hot August afternoon I grabbed my wrap, knowing the temperature might drop if we were still out in the woods when the sun began to go down. I did a quick check in the mirror on my way out of the room and saw that my hair was a mess. Brown strands hung loose and framed my face, as usual, thanks to the busy morning I'd spent in a caregiving class at a local nursing home, followed by several hardworking hours here at the sewing machine at home. I made a halfhearted attempt to smooth everything back down before moving into the hallway. At least my *kapp* was still on straight.

Zed had told me to wear shoes I didn't mind getting "disgustingly muddy," so I paused to slide my feet into the giant pair of work boots I had put there earlier. You would think with so many siblings—nine total, five of us still living at home—that I could have come up with a decent pair of boots, yet the only thing I'd been able to find that wasn't currently in use were these pontoon boats that once belonged to my much-larger-footed older brother Melvin.

Feeling ridiculous, I clomped into the kitchen. Zed was leaning against the counter near the door, his frame lanky and long, and his blond bangs hanging nearly to his eyes. When he saw me, he stood up straight and gave me a broad smile. His smile was so big, in fact, that at first I thought he was reacting to the sight of me in these stupid boots. But then I realized it wasn't that. Something was up, something much more exciting than just a friendly late afternoon hike between friends.

I looked at him questioningly, expecting him to explain, but instead he just gave me a wink and returned his focus to my mother. She was at the counter, helping my youngest brother, six-year-old Thomas, drop spoonfuls of biscuit dough onto a cookie sheet. Clearly, whatever Zed was beaming about, he wanted to wait to tell me in private.

Despite my curiosity, I knew it would be rude to rush out, so I forced myself to relax and tune into their conversation. *Mamm* was in the middle of giving Zed some advice—no surprise there. He would be leaving for college at the end of the week, and every time she'd seen him lately, she had taken it upon herself to relay some point of encouragement or word of warning. Not that she had ever been to college herself, of course. We were Amish, not Mennonite like him. But Peggy Mueller was a sharp, no-nonsense woman who had always seemed to have a clear picture of what the outside world offered, both the positive and the negative. At the moment she was going through a mental checklist, asking if he had remembered to pack this and that.

"Oh, and of course," she added, "don't forget to bring along a list of everyone's addresses and some stamps so you can stay in touch."

"Yes ma'am. I have the stamps already, and some stationery my mom gave me."

"*Gut.*"

"No need for a list of addresses, though. Just about everybody is already in the contacts app on my cell phone."

My mother seemed neither embarrassed at her lack of knowledge about the current technology nor impressed that Zed was in possession of it. "Imagine that." Turning back to Thomas, she tilted the bowl as he spooned out the last bit of dough. I watched them both for a moment, thinking what a lovely, homey scene they made.

Thomas was as cute as a button as always, his round cheeks dusted white with flour as he worked. Beside him, *Mamm* was the very picture of patient, maternal efficiency.

She was a little shorter than I and nearly as slim, despite having given birth to children. She looked younger than her age, especially considering that her oldest child, my sister Sadie, was twenty-eight. *Mamm* had a way about her—an independence I didn't see in many of the other mothers in our community. She was also, quite frankly, beautiful. Her large brown eyes were full of life, and her dark brown hair, without a streak of gray, contrasted with her clear, creamy skin. The funny thing was, she'd passed on her eyes, hair, and skin to me. I just didn't wear them all as well as she, I felt sure.

"So where are you two off to this afternoon?" she asked, glancing our way.

"We're going out near the old Conestoga Indian Town," Zed replied. "I want to show Izzy a potential shooting location for my next film." He was an aspiring filmmaker, something my family tolerated but didn't understand in the least.

Mamm had just picked up the cookie sheet, but she paused, her eyes wide. "Your *next* film? But you just finished the last one. Can't you take a break from all of that before you start again?"

"Oh, c'mon," he teased, "that's like saying…" His voice trailed off as he glanced around the room, his eyes finally landing on me. Then he looked back at my mother. "Well, you've pretty much finished raising Izzy here. Didn't you want take a break from all that mothering before you moved on to the others and started again?" With that, he stepped forward and mussed the hair on Thomas's head.

I knew Zed was just kidding around, but I stiffened, holding my breath until my mother laughed in response.

"Point taken," she replied, clucking her tongue at his audacity as she slid the biscuits into the oven and closed the door. Somehow Zed could always get away with saying things to her no one else ever could.

Certainly, with ten kids *Mamm* had done her share of mothering— and she wasn't finished yet. At six, Thomas was the youngest, but there was also Stephen, who was eleven. I was nineteen and the oldest still living at home, but I wasn't much help to her as my time was mostly spent sewing and caregiving. My younger sisters, Linda and Tabitha, were both home as well, and though Linda frequently pitched in around here, Tabitha was gone a lot, working for another family as a mother's helper.

As for our older siblings, Matthew, Mark, Becky, and Sadie were all happily married and living in homes of their own. Only Melvin was single, but he lived across the county, where he worked as a farmhand.

Now I watched as *Mamm* wiped little Thomas' cheeks clean with her apron and then directed him to wash the dough from his hands.

"Go out and check with your *daed*," she added, "to see if he needs any help in the barn until supper's ready."

"Okay!" He climbed down from his perch atop the tall stool and went to the sink. When I was his age, I would have been expected to stick around and help clean up the mess we'd made from all that cooking first, but it was different for boys.

As Thomas washed his hands, I looked to Zed, ready to go, but his eyes were still on my mom. When it came to the topic of making movies, the man had a one-track mind. "You know, even if I did want a break from filming—which I don't—I'm leaving for school in four days, so there's no time to lose. I want to do as much location scouting as I can before I go because I won't have another chance until I get back here at Thanksgiving."

Thanksgiving. Three whole months away. I tried not to think of how empty my life would be between now and then as I absently watched my little brother rinse the soap from his fingers.

"Most people don't realize how much prep work goes into making a movie," Zed continued as Thomas turned off the faucet and raced through the mudroom and out the back door, banging it loudly, without even stopping to dry his hands. The screen door fell shut behind him with a *thwack*, one tiny wet handprint glistening on the wooden frame.

"Oh?" my mother asked, but I could tell her focus had shifted to the mess their meal preparations had left behind.

"Filming won't start till next summer, but I'll need the time between now and then to plot out and write and storyboard the whole thing. The sooner I have an idea of my location options, the easier that process will be."

My mother turned to him, one eyebrow raised. "Seems to me that your time in Indiana should be devoted to your studies, not to getting ready for some movie you won't even start filming for months. Don't forget, Zed, academically speaking, Goshen may be far more demanding than you're used to here."

She was right about that last part. Since graduating from high school two years ago, Zed had been attending a local community college in Lancaster, where he had cruised through almost every class with straight A's across the board. But now he was off to Indiana, where he would be entering Goshen College as a junior and would spend the next two years finishing out his degree in communications. Fortunately, he was a super smart guy and totally up to the challenge, but I had a feeling this new school was going to require a far more balanced effort than was his norm. Not that he was lazy by any means. He just tended to focus on his film classes and little else.

On the other hand, Zed was being himself. When it came to creativity, he could be as obsessed as I was. Filming wasn't my area, but sewing and embroidery and other handwork were. Far too often I would ignore more important tasks that needed doing in order to press on with some creation that consumed my every thought. This tendency drove my parents crazy, but sometimes I just couldn't seem to help myself.

"Fortunately, this film preparation stuff *is* for a class," he said to *Mamm*, interrupting my thoughts. "Two classes, actually. This semester I have scriptwriting, and in the spring I'll take storyboarding. So I'll be able to do both—course work and prep work for my new film—at the same time."

He grinned, but she just shook her head in bewilderment. As world savvy as she was overall, my *mamm* had trouble understanding how someone could make an entire college career out of moviemaking. In fact, on her scale of useful occupations for a grown man to have, I felt sure that "film director" fell somewhere near the bottom, right between "hairdresser" and "videogame designer." In her life, at least, there simply wasn't any point.

"Speaking of location scouting," I blurted out, "we need to get going while we still have some sunlight. Oh, and we may be a few hours, so don't hold supper for me." With a surge of guilt, I added, "Though I can do these dishes for you when I get back, if you want."

"We'll see," she said, her hands on hips as she surveyed the pile. No doubt, every single item would be washed and dried and put away before Zed and I even reached our destination. "You two have fun."

Smiling, I headed outside, grateful she and my *daed* both seemed to understand the depth of my friendship with Zed. Better than that, they accommodated it, even if he was Mennonite, not Amish, and a college student besides. As families went, I was usually the odd one out around here—a square peg to the round holes that were my parents and siblings—but at least they respected my judgment enough to give me this.

Of course, once the day came that my *rumpspringa* ended and I joined the Amish church, I wouldn't be able to hop in a car and just run off with some guy for a few hours, even if he was a trusted family friend. But for now they took such things in stride, and I appreciated it more than they knew.

Zed and I headed toward his banged-up old red Saab, which was waiting in its usual spot in the driveway. As we climbed inside, I noticed that mysterious gleam had returned to his eye, but I didn't ask what it was about. I knew he would tell me in his own good time.

Soon we were out on the road, zipping up and down hills, past farms and fields and houses, and he was telling me all about his plans for this next movie he would be making. He'd recently won a big contest for his last film, and that success made him eager to plunge into the creative process yet again.

I couldn't blame him. I felt the same way. I had made most of the costumes for the reenactment portion of that film and would do so again for this one. It had been such a thrill to work with Zed like that, even if I hadn't understood a lot about the specifics of moviemaking. Before agreeing to help, I had read his script, so I knew going in that the story would be respectful of the Amish, which I appreciated—and which no doubt went a long way in convincing the bishop to approve my association with the project.

But beyond that, I had never even *seen* a movie, much less helped out somebody who was making one. Of course, when Zed was in high school, I'd seen him working on the computer plenty of times, editing the little films he'd made with his cell phone. But in college it was different, starting with the big, fancy camera and lights and things he was allowed to check out from the media lab for his film project. I had found the process fascinating—and the final result incredibly satisfying.

In the end, the film he made was wonderful—so wonderful, in fact, that the professor of his community college film class had encouraged Zed to enter it into the Pennsylvania Film Festival's "New Voices" contest once the semester was over. That was where he had won not just one but two big prizes.

The movie had focused on one of Zed's ancestors, an artist and woodcarver named Abraham Sommers who had lived in Switzerland back in the 1700s. The story was all about the legacy of that man's Christian faith, symbolized by three beautiful carved wooden boxes made by his own hands, and how that faith had been passed down through the generations all the way to today, just as those boxes had been passed down.

Thinking of it now, I found myself overwhelmed with emotion. I turned away and gazed out at acres of cornstalks swaying in the breeze, a surge of sadness filling my throat. I knew this feeling wasn't so much about Zed's touching movie as it was the fact that he was leaving in just a few days. I took a deep breath and held it in for a long moment. As I let it out, I wished for the millionth time he wasn't leaving at all.

I understood why he wanted to go off to school—why he practically had to, given his field of interest—and I knew how blessed he was that a Mennonite college even offered film classes. Still, the selfish part of me yearned to hear him say that he'd changed his mind and decided to stick around Lancaster County forever.

Oh, how I would miss him!

"You okay, Iz?" he asked, sensing my distress.

Turning back, I gave him an encouraging smile. "I was just thinking how…different it'll be not having you around anymore."

"Different as in sad? Or different as in better?"

I smiled, forcing away any tears. "Different as in I sure hope Thanksgiving gets here soon, because I'm going to go nuts without my best friend around."

To my surprise, he didn't make a joke or say something sarcastic. He just swallowed hard and nodded.

"I'll miss you too," he replied softly. "More than you can imagine."

We were quiet the rest of the way, but it was a comfortable silence, borne from four years of close friendship. I hoped that friendship would continue to endure despite the impending distance between us and the diverging trajectories of our lives.

Once we reached our destination, he parked along the side of the road near the head of a hiking trail, and a few moments later we were trooping down that path into the woods. Even though it hadn't rained for several weeks and most of the walk was dry, it became quite muddy in places, just as he'd warned, probably thanks to a spring or two that bubbled up from the ground along the way. At the worst parts, my big boots made a moist sucking sound with almost every step.

Zed talked nonstop as we went, going on and on about the story for his new movie and the various scenes he wanted to film here, but I wasn't really listening. My mind tended to wander in and out no matter the situation, but now I was starting to feel even less focused than usual. What was the matter with me today? Perhaps it wasn't just my growing sadness about Zed's departure but the realization of how different his world was going to be from mine from now on.

Here in Lancaster County, the ways he and I lived were fairly similar, despite the fact that I was Amish and he was Mennonite. Zed's mother, Marta Bayer, was Mennonite and had been for years, but she'd been raised in an Amish home, so she'd always cooked lots of Amish foods, taught her kids the language of Pennsylvania Dutch, and in many ways emulated an existence more Amish than Mennonite.

Of course, as a Mennonite Zed had access to some things I didn't, such as electricity and a car and a computer. But in many other ways his life-style was still quite Plain. Most importantly, he and I held the same core beliefs about God and His Son, about how being Christlike meant living simply and humbly, in full submission and surrender.

Once Zed went off to college, however, the Amish influences around him would be far less pervasive. At least he would be at a Christian school, but Goshen wasn't the only college in the area. Who knew what sorts of temptations awaited off campus in town or at some of the secular schools nearby? My mind filled with images of sleazy bars, wild parties, and coeds in tight tops and short skirts. Even if Zed was living and studying in a Christian environment, could he remain the same, solid, faithful guy he'd always been once he had that much freedom—and no one from home to see what he may or may not be doing?

"Okay, Izzy, here we are," he said now, oblivious to the scowl that had formed on my face. He bent down to pass beneath a low-hanging branch and then turned to hold it out of the way for me as I moved forward.

My scowl fading, I looked up and couldn't help but notice how tall he was getting these days. Tall and handsome and sweet. No doubt some beautiful college girl would try to nab him within weeks—if not days—of his arrival at Goshen.

We moved forward, side by side, to where the path opened up into a broad clearing, and then we came to a stop.

"What do you think?" he asked as he made a sweeping motion with his arm.

In the distance I could see what looked like the remains of a couple of old log cabins. One was missing a roof, the other an entire wall, but the parts still there looked utterly authentic.

"Don't you think this could serve as our little cluster of Amish homes?"

I hesitated, wishing I had paid more attention to what he'd been say-ing about the film itself. I knew it would focus on an historical topic, but beyond that I couldn't recall what that topic was or even the era it would be in.

"You do you understand what I was saying about selective framing, right?" he asked, taking my confused silence for reticence.

I cleared my throat, embarrassed to admit that no, I didn't understand what he'd been saying, but only because I hadn't been listening. "Tell me again now that we're here."

With a nod he moved forward, clomping another ten feet or so toward the ramshackle structures and then coming to a stop. "It's simple, really." He held his arms out in front of him, making an *L* shape with the thumb and forefinger of each hand, and then moving the *L*s together to form a square. "Even though the cabins are in pretty rough condition, what I'm saying is that we can make them seem intact with some simple camerawork."

"We can?"

"Yeah. Pretend this is the camera lens," he said of the square, "and that the frame includes only what you can see through here."

I walked over to him and peered out toward the cabins through his fingers.

"Now, move me so that the top of the frame is aligned just above the door on that first cabin."

Placing a hand on his upper arm, I did as he said, surprised at the hardness of the muscle I could feel through the fabric of his sleeve as I pressed his arm downward. Zed was so lanky and tall—and his life so cerebral and sedentary compared to most of the men I knew—that I'd never thought of him as being muscular before. But now I realized he must have bulked up during his summers of physical labor at the Gundys' nursery business and over Christmas breaks on their tree farm. I felt bad I hadn't noticed that until now.

Once I got his hands into place, I again leaned in close, viewing the scene as he had instructed and trying not to think about the enticing scent of sandalwood that wafted from him. Was that aftershave? Cologne? Had he always smelled like that?

"See?" he whispered, tilting his head down toward mine so he could look through his hands with me. "If the lens never goes higher than this, the viewer won't even know that building doesn't have a roof."

Unable to speak, I simply nodded, aware not just of his scent and his build but of the heat that radiated from his chest and arms. Suddenly, I wanted to be in those arms. Wrapped in them. Pressed against him. Our hearts beating in tandem.

His attention was still on the cabins, but mine was on him. What was going on with me? I had known this guy for years, ever since we were little kids. We hadn't always been close, but the year we were both fifteen, I had been hired as a caretaker for his dying father, and we had come to know each other well. Almost immediately our friendship moved into a romance, one that was all-consuming. But then my parents sat me down and expressed their concerns—that we were too young, that he was Mennonite and not Amish—so out of respect for them, Zed and I had agreed to cool things down and keep our relationship purely platonic after that. It took some time, but eventually I really did grow to think of him as a brother. To my relief, when I later explained that to my parents, they took me at my word and had trusted us to keep it that way ever since.

Now here I was, no longer a child of fifteen, seeing this man in a way I hadn't in several years—as a love interest, not just a friend. We were so much alike, he and I, and so very compatible. As my mother liked to say, Zed was just so *easy*, so loveable. A truly good guy to the core. Our relationship had only grown stronger since, and I enjoyed and appreciated him more than just about any other person on earth. In every sense of the word, he was my best friend.

But was he just a friend? Or something more? At the moment I wasn't sure. For some reason, I found myself wanting to embrace him—but not like a hug between buddies. With shocking clarity, I realized that the embrace I yearned for was the *romantic* kind. I wanted to be held—tightly—by this tall and sweet and handsome man, to be taken into his loving arms. *Just* friends?

Not hardly.

Stunned, I stepped back and turned away, hoping that the range of emotions I was feeling hadn't shown on my face—or that if they had, he hadn't noticed.

"I'm going to take a closer look," I mumbled, and then I began walking as quickly as I could toward the cabins. With each step, a new truth pounded in my head like a drum.

I didn't just love my best friend Zed.

I was *in love* with him too.

Two

Somehow I managed to get through the next hour without Zed noticing anything was wrong. But something *was* wrong. My whole world had shifted on its axis in a single moment. I simply couldn't be in love with Zed Bayer for so many reasons...

First of all, we were now *buddies*, not lovers. Could I honestly kiss someone who was like a brother to me?

Second, the two of us couldn't marry unless one of us converted to the other's faith. Was either one of us likely to do something that drastic?

Third, he no longer had any interest in me that way. What if I told him how I felt and it became such an issue that it ended up destroying our relationship? I couldn't bear to lose Zed from my life, to risk our friendship for the sake of a romance, no matter how wonderful that romance could be.

My mind continued to swirl around such thoughts all Tuesday night and into Wednesday. But I knew I would be seeing him again on Thursday afternoon when we were going location scouting again, so I made it my goal to have composed myself by the time he came to pick me up.

Sure enough, when he returned for our second jaunt of the week, I managed to greet him and get out of the house without feeling or acting weird. I wasn't sure if I'd be able to keep my composure for several hours, but I would do the best I could.

Soon we were off, barreling down the road toward our destination. This time our mission was to figure out which one of several different covered bridges would work best for a certain scene he wanted to film. I reminded him that he had access to a covered bridge right by his house, but he simply rolled his eyes and said, "That one's too cramped to pull off an arc shot." I didn't know what an arc shot was, nor did I care. I was content to simply be a part of the process.

Ten minutes into the drive, I was still maintaining my composure, at least on the outside, but then it struck me that *Zed* was the one acting odd. He gave me a quick glance when we were stopped at a red light, and in that one look I realized he had an excited gleam in his eye—the same gleam he'd had on Tuesday. But I'd become so worked up over my feelings for him that I'd forgotten all about it.

"Okay, come on out with it," I said.

"Out with what?"

"With whatever it is that has you grinning like a fool."

His grin widened further as he gestured toward the console between us. I looked down and saw several pieces of paper rolled into a cylinder, sitting in the cup holder.

"What is it?"

"My score sheets finally came. I've had them since Tuesday, but I didn't say anything then because I was out of toner. I wanted to print them out and show them to you, not just tell you about them."

The light turned green and he continued on again.

"Wow. I knew *something* was going on."

Ever since the film festival, he'd been extremely eager for the score sheets to come in, but I hadn't really understood why. Three weeks ago, a film Zed made in school had won two different awards at the Pennsylvania Film Festival. That had been cause enough for celebration, especially given that those awards included a generous endowment to be used toward making another film. But it seemed to me that he had been even more eager for the arrival of the judges' review sheets than he had been for the custom engraved trophies.

"You don't seem all that excited," he said, sounding almost hurt.

"I don't get the importance, I guess." I reached for the pages and pulled them from the holder. "I mean, you already know the judges loved your movie. They loved it enough to make you the winner, for goodness' sake. Why do you need to see the individual scores?"

"Because the judges don't just write a total. They also rate the film's individual components—cinematography, casting, pacing, things like that. And they add actual comments too, not just numbers. I've been dying to see every score and read each word."

I raised my eyebrows. "So you can hear firsthand about all the things you did right?" That sounded prideful to me.

Zed laughed. "No, silly. So I can hear firsthand about all the things I could have done *better.*"

Of course. I should have known. Zed was the least prideful person I'd ever met.

"Okay, that makes sense," I replied as I unrolled the papers and smoothed them across my lap.

Flipping through the pages, I saw three identical forms, each with the name of Zed's film, *The Carving of a Legacy*, printed across the top. Various scores were all over the pages, but at the bottom right was a box where each judge had written in his or her total score. In Zed's case, it looked as though the totals were 97, 99, and 94. Averaged together, they represented the highest in his division, History and Heritage, which had made him the winner.

The focus of the film festival had been Pennsylvania, but the categories had been wide ranging, bringing in submissions on everything from *Endangered Birds of the Poconos* to *Falling for Frank Lloyd Wright's Falling Water* to *Business and Industry in Pittsburgh*. First prize for each category had been a thousand dollars, but then Zed had also won one of the festival's biggest awards for Most Promising New Director. The two prizes added together had brought him to a total endowment of $5000, to be held and distributed through his college, as needed, for production costs on his next Pennsylvania-themed film.

My parents thought it was a shame he wasn't free to spend that money however he wanted, but I was secretly glad. If a check had just been handed over to him, then his mother would probably have absorbed it into the household budget as she had his earnings from the past few summers he'd spent working for his cousin Will's nursery and Christmas tree farm. This way, Zed's first official film creation had earned him the right to fund another, bigger, and better creation with every cent of his winnings.

Taking a deep breath, I lifted the first form and studied it more closely. Right away, I could see how he would find these score sheets helpful—just as I'd found helpful the weekly reviews I'd been getting at the caregiving course I was taking. "Izzy, you're great with the elderly, and they absolutely adore you," my teacher would say. "But you need to work more with the Hoyer lift. And your time management skills are still weak."

For Zed, the critiques I held in my hand were all about his abilities with the various elements of filmmaking, and from what I could see, he was best in the areas of pacing, editing, and storytelling, His weaknesses mostly had to do with mechanical issues and cinematography. *This film clearly shows a need for more technical mastery,* one judge had summarized, *but the clarity of theme, the innovative juxtaposition of images, and the gracefulness of the story's progression more than compensate. Well done! Am eager to see more from this promising young director.*

"Wow, Zed." I glanced up at him. "This is really something."

He tapped out a rhythm on the steering wheel with finger and thumb. "Keep reading. I'm not the only one the judges had an opinion on, you know."

"No?"

He smiled but did not reply, so I returned my attention to the pages in my lap and continued. I finally spotted what he was talking about under the section labeled "Costuming and Set Design." He'd been given a nine out of ten, and beside that the judge had scribbled out the words, *Except for several of the fabric choices, the film exhibits amazing accuracy with both current and historical Amish clothing styles.*

"Nine is good?" I asked, wishing it had been a ten.

"Are you kidding? That's nearly a perfect score!"

I knew I shouldn't, but I couldn't help feeling just a little bit proud of myself. "Okay," I said with a smile. "Then nine it is. You can thank me later."

He shook his head. "Sorry, but I only have Ms. Wabbim to thank."

We both laughed at the private joke. I had made most of the costumes for the film, but modesty had prevented me from allowing my name to appear in the credits. Zed insisted on honoring my efforts somehow, so in the end, he had listed the film's costumer as "Ms. Wabbim"—a code he'd come up with for "My Secret Weapon and Best Buddy Izzy Mueller."

Thinking of that now, I faltered a bit, and I had to cover by clearing my throat and looking out the passenger window. His best *buddy*. Me. Only now I was in love with him.

What was I going to do?

Taking a deep breath, I pushed such thoughts from my mind and focused on the pages in my lap.

"There's only one problem," he said. "What are we going to do someday when one of our movies wins an Academy Award for best costume design, and we have to admit there is no Ms. Wabbim?"

I smiled, secretly thrilled to hear how he he'd so easily tossed out a "someday" for us, not to mention that he'd called it "our movies" rather than just his. Did he really see it that way? Did he plan on bringing me in on his creative projects from now on? Did he hope we would always be as close as we were now—or possibly even closer?

"I guess we'll have to hire a stand-in to accept the award for you," he said, answering his own question.

"So you think this little ol' Amish girl has a future as a costumer for the Hollywood elite?"

"You bet. Stick with me, kid, and I'll take you places."

I laughed. "Stick with *me*, and you'll end up with the slowest seamstress in history."

"You pulled it off for this film."

"Yeah, but it wasn't easy. I'm so slow at handwork. *Mamm* says that's why I could never make a living with my sewing, because I daydream too much."

Zed shook his head. "She's wrong. You are kind of slow, but that's because you're a perfectionist. And that's a *good* thing, Iz. For my purposes, at least."

I shrugged, not so sure he was right. Either way, it was why I had enrolled in the caregiving course, so I could stop having to try so hard to make money with my fabric goods and instead earn a more consistent income as a caregiver for the elderly. I truly enjoyed spending time with older folks, and the fact that sometimes I was able to do embroidery and other handwork when just sitting and talking with them made the job even better, as it allowed me to kill two birds with one stone.

At one point, I had thought I would teach prior to marriage, but all it took to rid me of that notion was the week I'd spent last year helping out my sister Becky when her co-teacher was home sick. I was only there to assist, but it hadn't taken long for me to see that teaching would not be the right job for me. Between my tendency to daydream and my inability to focus, I found the whole experience overwhelming and exhausting. Sitting quietly with my handwork, chatting with old folks, was much more my style.

"I mean it, Iz," he said, his expression serious. "You are so gifted. And you have no idea how much I appreciate your help with the film."

"I do know, Zed. You've only said it about a billion times."

He shrugged. "Yeah, but here's what I haven't said enough: It's not just that you pitched in to help, it's that you brought such an amazing skill set into the mix with you. In fact, I think you're about the most talented person I know."

"Besides yourself, you mean?" I teased, heat rising in my face.

"Goes without saying," he replied, not missing a beat.

We shared a grin, but I knew my skin had to be redder than his car. I wasn't used to compliments, not even from him.

And I totally didn't know how to handle the sudden pounding of my heart when he looked my way.

Fortunately, we were nearing our destination, so his attention was on his driving and figuring out the safest place to pull over onto the side of the road.

"Anyway, these score sheets really are great. Thanks for sharing them with me." I rolled them up and returned them to the cup holder.

As he pulled to a stop and turned off the car, I gazed out at the beautiful covered bridge in front of us and smiled. Even if we were still just friends at this point, I couldn't imagine there being anyone on earth I would rather go location shopping with than him.

The next morning the entire lecture session of my caregiving training was lost on me. I couldn't stop thinking about Zed. In fact, since he'd brought me home last night, I hadn't been able to get him out of my mind. Now I was sitting in the back row of the conference room with nine other students, none of whom were Plain, and trying to pretend I was actually listening to our teacher. At least we only had one week of training left and then our exam. After that I would be an official, certified caregiver and wouldn't have to endure any more long, boring lectures when my mind was so utterly distracted.

"Izzy?"

My thoughts were interrupted by the instructor, Patricia, who had obviously just asked me a question. Now she was just waiting for my answer, staring at me from the front of the room, her reading glasses pushed on top of her head, her gray hair pulled away from her face.

"Yes?" I sat up a little straighter.

"I asked why it's important to promote independence in your elderly patients. Just give us one reason out of many."

I took a deep breath. I'd read about this the night before as I did my homework—although I'd been obsessing about Zed then too. I took a guess. "To help keep the patient's frustration level as low as possible?"

Patricia pursed her lips together and then said, "Good," as if surprised I was able to come up with an answer. Then she continued on with the lecture. "The more helpless the patient feels, the more likely they are to react, including aggressively. It's in everyone's best interest to encourage independence…"

I took notes in my spiral notebook as she spoke, trying my best to keep my focus on the lecture, but soon I was doodling, first drawing lines, then circles, and then a heart and wondering if or when I should tell Zed how I felt about him, that I was in love with him.

I added a face, arms, and legs to the heart and then drew on an eighteenth-century Plain dress before adding a cabin as a backdrop. I couldn't get over how well he had done on his first film. He certainly had a lot of talent and drive. I was so proud of him, but I couldn't help but envy him a bit as well, even though I knew it was wrong. It wasn't the filmmaking I envied, nor even that he was able to go college and I wasn't. What I wanted was to be as sure about my path in life as he was—and had always been—about his.

Since the day we met, he had known what he wanted to do, and he'd been willing to learn and grow in whatever ways it would take to make that happen. I, conversely, had never been that sure about anything, except maybe my friendship with him. And my love for my grandmother, who died when I was little. Otherwise, my entire life had been without purpose or direction.

A loud bang from the front of the room startled me. The instructor had dropped a large, hardcover book. She bent down to pick it up, and as she returned to a standing position, she locked eyes with me. For a moment I wondered if she'd dropped the book on purpose.

I returned my pencil to where I'd stopped taking notes.

She continued talking. "The patient's safety is always of the highest concern and you must closely supervise…"

Maybe I wasn't in love with Zed. Maybe I only felt as if I was because he'd be leaving for college the next day and because, above all, I was going to miss him terribly. I blinked back a tear and stared at my open notebook, realizing I'd stopped listening again.

"And that is, of course, one of the biggest benefits of working with the elderly," Patricia said, though I'd missed the first part of her thought and hadn't a clue what she meant.

What I liked most about working with the elderly was hearing their stories. Just yesterday morning I had been taking care of Phyllis, my favorite patient here at the nursing facility, and listening to her talk about being a girl in New York City and going with her grandmother to something called the Russian Tea Room. Phyllis was in her late seventies now but still quite capable, and as we talked I suggested she stand at the mirror and brush her own hair while I cleaned her dentures. So, *ya*, I guess I did promote independence, even if I wasn't a firm sort of person by nature.

The instructor clicked the remote to her computer and a slide of a patient chart flashed on the screen. "When you're doing home health care, you'll need to assess your client." She clicked the remote a second time. "Start with a questionnaire for the patient and family members."

I wrote down *questionnaire*.

"Encourage them to be as honest as possible."

As honest as possible. I swallowed, trying to rid myself of the lump that had just formed. Even if I did love Zed—and I couldn't think what else this overwhelming feeling was—I couldn't be honest with him. It would ruin our friendship. It would *end* our friendship. I blinked away another tear.

"Izzy, do you have a question?"

Startled, I quickly shook my head.

Thankfully someone else did, although I didn't hear exactly what it was because I was placing my pencil back on my paper. Next to *questionnaire*, I wrote, *encourage honest answers.*

I'd never been kissed by anyone. Would kissing Zed be like kissing a buddy? Realizing I'd just made a face, I stopped immediately and quickly looked at the instructor. She hadn't noticed.

No, kissing Zed would not be like kissing an old friend, not the way I felt three days ago. Not the way I'd felt last night. Not the way, if I was honest with myself, I was feeling right now.

I'd never even wanted someone to kiss me.

Until now.

A noise in the hall distracted me for a moment, but then I focused on Patricia again.

She said, "When you're developing short term goals…" I wrote that down but obviously I'd missed something.

I looked up at the screen. There was a new slide with the title *Goal Setting.*

The instructor continued. "Encourage the patient to pursue a hobby— either an old one or a new one. For example, they may no longer be able to travel, but perhaps they can write about their experiences or tell someone who can write them down. Telling stories often becomes therapeutic for patients…"

I wrote that down too. Which brought me back to thinking about Zed. That's what he did. He told stories. On film. And he had such a gift for it too.

Then there was his cute smile. His kind heart. The way he brushed the blond bangs from his eyes when he was feeling self-conscious.

No, if he ever kissed me, it wouldn't feel like a buddy's kiss at all.

Somehow I made it through the rest of the lecture without Patricia calling on me again or challenging my attentiveness. I tried to stay focused, but it was so hard with Zed competing for my thoughts.

As she wound things down up front, it struck me that it was a good thing I'd always been a voracious reader, because otherwise there was a chance I could have ended up being somewhat ignorant and uninformed. I'd never been able to concentrate in classrooms and hadn't picked up much knowledge that way, even as a child. But perhaps, over the years, those gaps had been filled by my addiction to books of all kinds—history, fiction, biographies, and more. And Zed was so smart that I was often expanding my repertoire of reading just to keep up with him.

After the class ended, I followed the other students out of the conference room, down the hall, and through the breezeway to the skilled nursing facility where we did our clinical training. We'd already learned the basics—feeding, dressing, and all the other stuff my fellow students seemed to balk at but I didn't mind.

In the first few weeks, we'd been working alongside certified assistants, but now, as the course neared the end, we were on our own as much as possible in caring for the patients.

I went to Phyllis's room first but didn't find her there. She was probably down at the craft room. She had some shoulder problems but was still able to design, cut, and paste—which she loved to do. I'd seen some of the handmade cards she'd constructed, and they were clever. Phyllis had worked as an attorney, and I couldn't imagine she had much time for card making back then, but she seemed to enjoy it now.

She had lived in Manhattan much of her life, and she had stylish gray hair and dressed in classy sports suits. Her only child, a son, lived near Lancaster, and she'd told me that was how she'd come to the area ten years before.

I stopped at the end of the bed of Phyllis's roommate, Marguerite, who had just had her eighty-ninth birthday. She was also a dear, but she could no longer communicate, poor thing. According to Phyllis, Marguerite had grown up in France but had married a U.S. soldier at the end of World War II and moved here to the States with him. Though she'd spoken English almost exclusively after that, nowadays, whenever she said something, it was in French, and usually just a syllable or two. How I longed to hear her stories! I could only imagine what she would tell me if she could.

Her children, grandchildren, and even great-grandchildren visited her regularly, all calling her Mimi. She smiled and seemed to remember them, although it was hard to tell for sure.

Phyllis had taken Mimi under her wing and would ring for help anytime she thought the older woman needed anything, often in the middle of the night, I was told.

After I greeted Mimi, who was immobile, I turned her to check for bedsores. Thankfully, there were none. Next I helped the patients of mine who ate lunch in the dining hall get there, wheeling some and walking alongside others. Phyllis hadn't come out of the craft room yet, but I knew the staff person in charge of that area would wheel her to the dining room when she was ready.

After I'd settled my mobile patients, I collected Mimi's tray from the kitchen and returned to her room to feed her. Getting enough nutrition down her was a challenge. Today she had beef-and-barely soup, creamed spinach, and custard. I raised her bed to a sitting position and began. I knew it took me longer to feed Mimi than it took the other caregivers. They seemed to be able to shovel in the food quickly, wipe her mouth, and then give her another spoonful.

I couldn't do that. For one thing, Mimi seemed fascinated by me. Perhaps it was my *kapp* or my Plain dress, but she couldn't take her eyes off me and always chewed and swallowed more slowly for me than the others. Because she couldn't tell me her stories, I'd been telling her mine— or, more accurately, the stories my grandmother had passed down to me about her childhood during the depression and as a teenager during World War II. I wanted Mimi to be able to compare her experiences with someone in the U.S., a Plain someone and conscientious objector at that.

After I finished feeding her, I had two more patients who were also bedridden. Of course, I took too long with them as well, and by the time I finished, it was nearly time for my break. Before I took it, I stopped by Phyllis's room again, hoping to tell her hello, but she still wasn't there.

Mimi was sound asleep, her feet sticking out of her covers, so I pulled the blanket down over them as I thought about Phyllis. I decided her son must have taken her out for lunch. I knew how much she loved those dates with him.

For the next hour, even though I should have gone to the break room to eat my own lunch, I hurried from patient to patient, seeing to all of their needs. To be honest, my mind continued to fall on Zed, but the urgency of finding another blanket, fluffing a pillow, or changing a spilled-upon shirt pulled me back to the present much faster than my instructor's lecture had. All in all, I felt pleased with how little I was thinking about him as the day progressed.

When I returned to Phyllis and Mimi's room again, Phyllis still hadn't appeared but Mimi was awake. I raised her bed and opened the curtain to the sunshine out in the courtyard. She smiled sweetly.

On my way out of the room, I nearly collided in the hall with the shift supervisor. After apologizing, I said, "I hope Phyllis gets back before I leave."

The supervisor's face froze.

Alarmed, I asked, "What is it?" I feared my favorite patient had been transferred to another facility. Although that didn't make sense. Her things were still in the room.

"No one told you?" the woman stammered, holding a clipboard to her chest.

I shook my head, studying her expression as the realization slowly dawned. Phyllis hadn't been transferred.

She had died.

I tried to take a breath but couldn't. I gasped, an odd groan coming from my throat. Perhaps I looked as if I might faint, because the supervisor grasped my elbow to steady me. Another noise erupted from me, this one sounding like a cow lost in the woods.

From where we stood, I could see into Phyllis's room, to the empty but perfectly made bed. I forced my eyes toward sweet Mimi instead. She smiled and gave me a little wave, her faded eyes lighting up as best they could.

How could I not have known?

"Phyllis passed," the supervisor whispered to me.

I returned my gaze to her face. "But why? How?"

She shrugged. "I know she seemed fairly healthy, but she did have a heart condition. It finally caught up with her, I imagine. That's my best guess, anyway."

"When?" I managed to rasp. "When did it happen?"

"This morning, around ten."

Around ten. My mind raced. At ten, I'd still been in class, taking notes, or trying to. More likely I'd been thinking about Zed.

I felt weak, as though I might pass out.

The strange thing was, I wasn't even sure why. I had really liked Phyllis and cared about her, but it wasn't as if we had ties outside of this place. I had known her for all of three weeks, yet now the news of her death was hitting me as hard as if she had been one of my own beloved relatives.

The supervisor, Heather, must have sensed the depth of my reaction, because she gripped my elbow more tightly. "I know it's hard when your first patient dies—"

At that the tears started, followed by an outright sob.

"But you'll be done with your coursework in a week anyway," she added softly in an attempt to make me feel better.

I wiped my eyes, saying, "I just didn't expect her to die." Another round of sobs overtook me.

"I know, Izzy. But it happens in this work all the time. If you can handle that, well..." Her voice trailed off, and then she added, "You learn to expect it, even in the healthy ones. That's part of what being a professional caregiver is all about."

Our very first lesson in the program had been on being a professional—and right now I was being the exact opposite of that. "I'm s-sorry," I stammered.

"It's all right. Go to the break room for a few minutes, get ahold of yourself, and then finish out your shift."

With a nod I made my way down the hallway, shielding my face with one hand as I continued to cry. Instead of going to the break room, where I was bound to run into someone, I headed for the double doors to the breezeway, aiming for the conference room, expecting it to be empty.

As I opened the door, a realization overcame me. Obviously, I wasn't made for caregiving. Another sob erupted from me as I staggered through the door, only to come face-to-face with my instructor.

With a look of dismay on her face, Patricia said, "For heaven's sake, Izzy, what happened?"

I managed to respond that Phyllis had died.

"Oh, dear," she said, putting her arm around me. "And you're taking it this hard?"

I nodded. "I don't know why," I sniffled.

"Sit down. I'll get you some water."

As she left the room, I put my head in my hands. I wanted to call *Daed* and ask him to come get me. There was no reason to finish the training. What if Mimi died next? I couldn't take that, I really couldn't.

Patricia returned with a bottle of water and asked if it was my first time to be close with someone who died.

"I took care of a man several years ago who lost his life to cancer." Zed's father, Freddy, to be exact. I hadn't actually been present when he'd passed, but then again, I hadn't been present when Phyllis had either. Another sob caught me by surprise.

I put my head back in my hands.

Concern filled Patricia's voice as she patted my back. "What can I do for you?"

I took a raggedy breath. "Could I use your phone?"

"Of course," she said, digging in the pocket of her smock and then handing me her cell.

As I dialed the number of our phone, located in the barn around the corner from where *Daed* did his woodworking, I prayed he wasn't using one of his power machines so he would be able hear it.

It rang and rang, ten times. Thinking the answering machine was about to come on, I began to ready myself to leave a message when a boy's voice said, "Hello?"

"Stephen?"

I could barely hear my brother as he said, "*Ya.*" He was eleven and home from school already.

"Go get *Daed.*"

I held the phone to my ear for what seemed like an eternity. Finally, Patricia said, "Izzy, I can take you home if you want."

I shook my head. That was the last thing I wanted.

Finally *Daed* came on the line and I told him I needed a ride earlier than expected. The care center was only a few miles from our house. He'd been transporting me both ways each day.

In a soft voice he asked, "So soon?" Then, intuitive as ever, his voice became even quieter as he added, "Izzy, what happened?"

I swallowed hard, fearing another sob was going to escape. "I'll tell you when you pick me up."

I handed Patricia back her phone. "*Danke*," I said, my face growing warm as I realized my mistake. "I mean, thank you."

"Of course," she said. "The weekend will do you good. Everything will look better on Monday."

I hiccupped as I shook my head. "I'm withdrawing from the program."

"Why would you do that? You only have a week left."

"I'm not meant for this sort of work."

"Izzy, every person in the medical field, whether an aide or a doctor, has a story about when they felt incompetent."

I shook my head.

It seemed as if she might roll her eyes but then she didn't. "Think about it," she said, her voice kinder. "Then come by Monday morning—either way—and talk with me."

I nodded, but I knew I wouldn't. I thanked her again and said I needed some fresh air. Leaving my uneaten lunch behind in the break room—content to abandon it rather than risk having to explain myself anymore—I went outside to wait for *Daed*.

THREE

*D*aed's reaction to my description of what happened was a simple, "I see." Then we rode in silence.

His calm response convicted me of just how badly I'd overreacted. The whole story sounded ridiculous. I knew people died, especially in care homes. Especially when they were old.

I shifted on the bench, trying to get comfortable in the heat.

I'd only been fifteen when I cared for Zed's father, Freddy, through the final stages of his battle with cancer. I fixed meals, washed clothes, and helped him manage his medication when Marta was busy with her midwife appointments or off delivering babies and Zed was at school. It wasn't until Freddy's very last day that he needed help with his personal care—and Zed's sister, Ella, and his mother, Marta, were there for that. Marta was with Freddy when he passed.

In the end, their family dynamic worked, but it was complicated, and I often wondered if that had something to do Zed's heightened interest in stories. His origins were different than most people's. Twenty years ago, his father had had an affair with a young woman and gotten her pregnant. Marta had found out about it, but amazingly, in response she asked if she and Freddy could take in the baby and raise it together—despite the fact that it was the product of her husband's affair with someone else. The birth mother had agreed to the plan, and once baby Zed was born, Marta had adopted him.

The birth mother went on with her life. She eventually married and had several more children, though she ended up dying at a young age due to a previously undetected heart condition. Meanwhile, Freddy abandoned Marta, Ella, and Zed and moved away. Marta had soldiered on alone.

Then, four years ago, Freddy showed up again in Lancaster, more than a decade after he'd left, ill physically but in other ways far healthier than he'd ever been. After a lifetime of alcoholism, he was finally clean and sober, in recovery, and deeply repentant for all of his past transgressions. Amazingly, Marta and Zed both forgave him, reconciled with him, and then cared for him as he was dying. Even Ella ended up patching things up with him at the very end.

All along I knew Freddy would die—he had stomach cancer—and the prognosis was never good. Zed and I became friends as I cared for his father. And although I'd liked Freddy well enough, and I missed him once he was gone, I hadn't been traumatized by his death.

Clearly I'd reacted to Freddy's death in a professional way. So why the outburst over Phyllis's today?

Daed began whistling as he turned off the main road and onto the one that led to our farm. A hot breeze rustled the leaves of the cornstalks, our one cash crop. Harvest, however, was still a month away.

I leaned back against the seat, willing myself not to think about money. My plan had been to get a job as a caregiver and contribute my checks to the household budget. But now I'd have to take in more sewing, which meant I'd need to work faster to make up for it. I could at least try to be professional at that.

Patricia had asked if I'd had anyone close to me die. Why hadn't I mentioned *Mammi* Nettie? She was *Daed*'s mother and had lived with us when I was little, sleeping in the downstairs bedroom next to what was now my sewing room.

I took another raggedy breath. *Daed* glanced my way. "Are you all right?"

I nodded, but I wasn't. Not at all. Another sob rose up from deep within me. I loved spending time with *Mammi* Nettie, listening to her stories and brushing her hair.

Mamm and *Daed* didn't have much time for her with all their other responsibilities, but every day, both before and after school and again at bedtime, I'd sit beside her and soak up everything she said.

When I was nine years old, I'd hurried into her room one morning before school, and she wasn't there. *Mamm*, who was fixing breakfast, came into the room after me.

"She's gone," my mother had said, taking my hand and guiding me back into the hall.

"Where?"

"She passed late last night after you went to sleep. The undertaker came around ten."

Sadie and Becky both stared at me from the kitchen—none of it seemed to be a surprise to them. Perhaps they had still been up last night when it happened, or maybe *Mamm* had already told them.

I pulled away from my mother and stumbled back into *Mammi* Nettie's room, throwing myself across her bed.

Mamm sat down beside me for a few minutes and rubbed my back. After a while she said, "You girls go finish breakfast," and I realized Sadie and Becky were standing in the doorway, staring at me.

When we all sat down to eat, I seemed to be the only one upset about *Mammi* Nettie's passing. *Daed* said it was her time. It was as if he and *Mamm* and my older siblings had expected it and my younger ones didn't care. No one else seemed to be mourning. That caused me to flee the table, once again in tears.

Now, all these years later, I wasn't sure if I was crying for *Mammi* Nettie or for Phyllis—or entirely for myself—but another sob welled up in me as the horse slowed for the hairpin turn near our house.

Daed reached over for my hand, took it, and squeezed. "Izzy—"

"I'm all right," I stammered, but I wasn't. It seemed Phyllis's death had tapped a deep well of grief inside of me, one fed all those years ago by my grandmother's death. I hadn't expected that Phyllis would die either. But when she wasn't there, why hadn't I asked someone? Had I been so engrossed in my thoughts of Zed that I hadn't thought to? Or was I that unobservant? Or simply in denial? No matter which it had been, none of those traits bode well for a caregiver.

One of my worst qualities was my absentmindedness. How I could totally lose myself in my thoughts and not even notice what was going on right in front of my nose? Cleary I was unfit to be a caregiver at all.

I sobbed again. This time *Daed* didn't respond.

Ahead, our two-story house rose above the green sea of cornstalks. The afternoon sun glinted off the silo. A flock of starlings swooped toward the barn.

I hiccupped and turned toward him, swiping at my eyes. "Would you tell *Mamm* what happened?"

He shook his head. "You need to."

"She's not going to be happy with me."

He didn't respond. She'd been so set on me being a teacher. Then she'd adjusted her thinking to me being a caregiver. Now I'd have to convince her I could make it as a seamstress. And I already knew her opinion on that occupation, that I was far too slow to make a living at it.

Mamm stood at the island in the kitchen, rolling meatballs and pursing her lips as I told her what happened. Then she looked over my head at *Daed* and returned to her work without saying a word. For once I longed for her practical advice, for some word of encouragement to keep me going. She wasn't a bad *mamm*. She just wasn't the sweet, nurturing type I sometimes needed. I knew how constantly frustrated she remained with me. If only shaping me could be as easy for her as molding meatballs for supper.

I excused myself to my sewing room, but when I reached the hallway, she called my name. Still expecting a wise word, I turned around in anticipation.

She plopped the next meatball onto the sheet. "Don't forget that Zed is coming for supper. He'll be here in an hour."

I sighed, glad I would be seeing him tonight but sad for the reason why. He was leaving for college tomorrow and this was his farewell supper with us. Because of his mother's busy clinic schedule today, she'd had her big meal with him the night before.

Thankful that I had the next hour of sewing to distract me, I continued on toward my workroom, an enclosed sunporch at the back of the house. It was hot in the summer and cold in the winter, and no one but me wanted to spend time in it. It was where I did my reading and handwork and where I wrote in my journal. Where, when *Mamm* let me, I would dream a day away doing mending and sewing and my embroidery.

I was sliding open the window to turn on the generator outside when I heard the front door open and close. It was my younger sister Linda, who called out to *Mamm* that she would be in the kitchen in a minute to help. She was fifteen and our mother's second pair of hands around the house.

Leaning out from the window, I flipped the switch on the generator, and as it roared to life I slid the window closed again and sat down at my sewing machine.

I heard a knock at my door and looked up to see Linda standing there, smiling. "Zed will be here soon," she said.

"*Ya*, I know."

She crossed her arms. "Gee, try not to sound so overjoyed."

"It's not that," I said. I let out a breath. "I quit the caregiving program this afternoon."

I should have known she wouldn't be sympathetic.

"Izzy, what's wrong with you?" She unfolded her arms and dropped them to her sides. I wasn't surprised by her exasperation. If it hadn't been her chastising me, it would have been one of my older sisters once they found out.

"It…it just wasn't right for me."

"Nothing's right for you," she muttered as she left the doorway and headed down the hall.

"Except for Zed," I whispered. "Zed is right for me."

I felt so spent, I was certain I couldn't cry any more if I wanted to. I'd planned to sew for the next hour, but instead I stared out the window at the gigantic sunflowers in our garden, swaying wildly, too heavy for their stalks, and at the rabbit that darted around their bases, upsetting their balance. Then, once Stephen began to chase the little creature, I watched it race to the edge of the cornfield, backtrack in confusion, and then make one final push and disappear along the ground among the stalks.

I had no idea what I was watching or what I was even thinking when I realized Linda called my name sometime later. I pushed away from my machine.

"Izzy!" she yelled again.

"Coming," I said, expecting I needed to set the table.

"Zed's here!"

Oh, goodness. Where had the time gone? I surged to my feet, upsetting my chair and then righting it quickly. By the time I reached the hallway, he stood under the archway to the living room.

Linda swerved down the hall, back to the kitchen, as Zed stepped toward me. "What's wrong?"

I hadn't even cleaned up after my crying jag. "Nothing. Give me just a minute."

After washing my face and hands, I ventured back out to the living room.

Zed sat on the couch looking at a library book with Thomas. *Mamm* was setting the table and said, without looking at me, "Supper's ready. Thomas, go call Stephen and *Daed.*"

I'd hoped to talk with Zed before we ate, but there wouldn't be time. As we moved toward the dining table, he glanced at me, a questioning look on his face. "What is it? Problems in class?"

"I'll tell you later," I said, as quietly as I could.

Somehow I got through the meal, thankful that no one brought up the subject of what had happened at school today. Either *Mamm* had told Linda not to bring it up or else she knew well enough to leave it alone. Thomas and Stephen would never have thought to ask about my schooling anyway.

Soon the conversation fell to Zed's trip to Indiana in the morning. "I'm hoping my Saab will make it," he told us as he reached for another helping of mashed potatoes.

"I heard one time that red cars are pulled over more often than others," *Daed* replied. "Do you think that's true?"

Zed laughed. "I might get pulled over for going too slow, but never for speeding. Not in that old thing. My bigger concern is for next semester. Indiana is one thing, but making it all the way across the country is something else."

I looked at him, my eyebrows raised.

"Oh, right, I haven't told you my big news yet." He gave me an excited smile and then directed it toward the others around the table as he announced, "I may have a chance to spend spring semester in Los Angeles at a film school. Goshen has an arrangement with..."

He continued talking but I stopped listening. California? My Zed hoped to study filmmaking in Los Angeles? That was even farther away than Indiana! I shivered, realizing that, *ya*, I was excited for him but overcome with grief for myself. I truly was losing my best friend.

Stephen started talking about chasing the rabbit back into the corn. *Daed* shook his head, saying he hoped warrens of them weren't in the field. Then Thomas wanted to know what a warren was, and the topic of conversation shifted far away from Zed and his future.

When the meal was over, I stood to clear the table.

"Linda and I will see to cleaning up," *Mamm* said. "I know Zed has to leave soon."

"Are you sure?"

She gave me a how-silly-can-you-be look. She was right. I'd never insisted on cleaning up before.

I turned toward Zed. "Want to take a walk?"

He nodded. I led the way out the front door with him behind me. He caught up with me on the porch and then we went down the steps side by side.

"To the overlook?" he asked.

"*Ya*," I answered. It was our favorite spot, about a half mile away and above a creek bed, with amazing sunsets on clear nights, like tonight.

We turned on our country road the opposite way of town and walked along the narrow shoulder. When the house was out of sight, Zed asked, "So what happened today?"

I told him the whole story, barely pausing to breathe, telling him all about Phyllis and the connection I'd finally made between her death and *Mammi* Nettie's.

"Of course you would react that way."

I sighed. "But I made a complete fool of myself."

"Oh, Izzy. You're too hard on yourself. The fact you're able to show your emotions is one of the best things about you."

"*Danke*, but I don't think you're going to like what I have to say next."

"I doubt that," he answered. When I didn't jump right in, he said, "Try me."

Increasing my stride, without even meaning to, I blurted out, rather loudly, "I quit the program."

He didn't respond.

"See—"

"Why?" His voice wasn't accusatory, only curious.

I tried to explain as best I could, but my reasons sounded silly and unfounded, even to me.

"Didn't they prepare you to deal with death in your coursework?"

I shook my head. "Not yet, anyway."

He reached for my hand. "Do you think it would have made a difference if they had?"

I thought about that for a minute, relishing the feel of my hand in his. He'd never done that before. Finally, I answered him, saying, "Maybe a little, but in the long run, no. There will always be people who die unexpectedly, and I'll never be prepared for it. Someone in my family will die again some day, maybe unexpectedly, and I'll have to deal with that, but why would I subject myself to that all the time as part of my job?"

He nodded sympathetically and squeezed my hand, sending a shiver up my spine. "I understand. You must have felt so shocked and helpless. I wish I could have been there with you."

"*Danke*," I whispered, encouraged by his kindness. "You know what the worst of it was? The supervisor and my instructor thought—actually, they both implied—that I needed to get over it right then."

Zed squeezed my hand again. "That's just wrong."

A buggy approached from behind us and Zed let go of my hand.

Grateful for his quick thinking—I wouldn't want anyone to spread rumors—I stepped ahead so we were single file until the buggy passed.

Once it did, Zed caught up with me and stated, "But I'd hate for you to stop caregiving."

I must have bristled just a little.

"Now hear me out," he said. "You have a gift, Iz. It was evident when my father was ill. I've seen it in the way you interact with my grandmother. The reason you hurt so much is because you *care* so much." He paused for a moment and then said, "It would be a shame for you not to take care of others."

"But I couldn't bear to lose another patient." I knew my words came out as a wail, even though I didn't intend that.

"That's how you feel right now, but give it time. Think about it. You might change your mind."

A moment later he led the way off the road to the shortcut through a neighbor's field. We kept to the fence line, again walking single file, until we reached the viewpoint.

Below, the creek was an end-of-the-season trickle and the marshy area on each side was browning, but the field of alfalfa across the way was a mesmerizing emerald green.

The sun had started to set, a ball of orange sending streamers of pink and yellow across the sky just above the horizon. I wished Zed would take my hand again, and not just to comfort me this time.

It dawned on me, as the sun sank farther, that perhaps Zed loved me too—but he didn't know it yet. As much as I wanted to reveal my feelings for him, I knew I needed to hold my tongue and bide my time. He had to be the one to say it first. I knew him so well, enough to know he had to come to the truth of our relationship on his own, without any prompting from me.

We stood there as dusk fell and then the sun set completely, in those few fast moments when day passes to night. In no time hundreds of fireflies ascended from the marshy area below, dancing in the darkness, flitting up around us, swarming this way and that, blinking on and off. There were always a few here at dusk, but now it seemed as though hundreds, if not thousands, were all about us. I gasped in delight and Zed even jumped around a little.

"This is amazing! Absolutely incredible. If only I could film it!"

I told myself that this many fireflies had to be some sort of omen—an indication about the brightness of our future. I hugged myself in anticipation. But then the fireflies began to fade away again, one by one, until only a few flickers remained.

Facing the inevitable, I asked him, my tone as effortless as I could make it, "What will you do when all of those college girls start taking an interest in you?"

"I'll just have to suffer through it, I suppose," he responded with a leering grin.

I'd half intended it as a joke, but he was only half kidding in return. It was clear he looked forward to dating while away at college, dating girls who weren't me.

I wanted to throw my arms around him and tell him, *No! Don't go out with anyone else! You should be mine and mine alone!* But of course I didn't. Instead, thankful that the darkness hid my sorrow, I said, "We should head back."

He pulled out his phone and clicked on his flashlight app. As he aimed it at the ground in front of us, we walked back along the fence line and then down the highway, going single file in the darkness. I was relieved he left me to my own thoughts.

When we reached the house, we went in for him to tell my parents goodbye, and then I walked him to his car. After this, I knew I wouldn't see him until Thanksgiving break. That was much too far from now.

He gave me a half hug, really hardly one at all, and said he'd write. I told him I'd write him back. Then he paused for just a moment as if he had more to say. Instead, he climbed into the car and started the engine.

As Zed backed around, I stepped on our lawn and watched. Behind me, the screen door banged and footsteps fell on the porch. I waved as he drove past. He grinned and waved in return, but for once his smile didn't warm my heart. Instead, it practically broke it.

As I headed up to the porch, I made out two figures along the rail. My *mamm* and *daed*. My mother reached me first and put her arms around me—a rare move for her, indeed. *Daed* joined us, standing on my other side, and together the three of us watched until the red taillights of Zed's car disappeared around the hairpin curve.

They were being so kind that I had to wonder if the two of them had picked up on the shift in my feelings for Zed. Did they know I loved him this way? I doubted it. After all, considering the history here, that would be a very big deal indeed. Thinking of that long-ago conversation when they shared their concerns about my relationship with Zed, I knew one thing had changed and one had not: We were certainly old enough now to embark on a romance, but I was still Amish and he was still Mennonite. As far as I could see, that issue was never going to go away.

"It's been a long day," I said softly. "I'm going up to bed."

They nodded in unison, pulling away from me and letting me go into the house first.

I headed straight upstairs, undressed, and crawled under the covers as quickly as I could, willing the tears not to come. But of course they did. I cried again for *Mammi* Nettie. And for Phyllis.

But mostly I cried for myself. Because I was pretty sure I'd just said goodbye, forever, to the only man I would ever love.

FOUR

I never returned to the care center as my teacher Patricia had requested,
though I did call and leave her a message, saying I appreciated all she'd
taught me, but I really was withdrawing from the course just as I had told
her I would the day Phyllis died.

After that, as the heat of August turned into a long Indian summer, I
focused almost solely on my sewing and handwork. All through September a numbing loneliness was my constant companion as I holed up in
my little room and hid from the world. Daily, I prayed that God would
help me hold my feelings for Zed Bayer in check until the time was right.
It turned out that was easier said than done.

Zed and I corresponded on a regular basis, and though I lived for every
new letter that came, I also wondered if, in a way, such constant communications were only making things worse. His letters were serious and
funny, wise and wacky all at the same time. They were my lifeline, and I
found them both entertaining and encouraging. On the other hand, each
new note from him served as a reminder of all we shared, how much I
loved him, and how very far away he was.

At least we could connect on our joint project, the research and preparation for his new film. He was so excited about it—and I was still so

clueless about what he had in mind—that finally I asked him to describe the film in detail, laying it all out for me on paper. His response, a letter that came just a week later, was classic Zed.

> Izzy Bear,
>
> Great idea, making me put this into words. Okay. Here goes.
>
> EXT. A COVERED BRIDGE. LONG SHOT. DUSK.
>
> What? Not in script form, you say? Okay, sorry about that.
>
> In regular people speak, here's the basic premise, but keep in mind that I still have a lot more research to do. For now, though, this is what I know.
>
> Back in the 1700s, there was an Indian tribe living near Lancaster, called the Conestoga. They lived on land reserved for them in a treaty decades before, by William Penn. But slowly, as more and more settlers came to the area, that land was being encroached upon and taken from them.
>
> The Conestoga were a peaceful tribe, but of course not all Indian tribes in the region were. In fact, there was a lot of bad blood on both sides—Indians and settlers—especially once the French and Indian War started.
>
> Anyway, fast-forward, and it's 1763 and the F&IW has ended but people are still really worked up about the "Indian problem." The poor Conestoga stayed out of it, but you know how that goes, guilt by association, etc.
>
> Okay, so people start getting really aggravated with all Indians in general until they finally form an angry mob, led by a man from the town of Paxtang. Soon, there are like 250 of these creeps, and they were well on their way to becoming full-throttle vigilantes. They even get a nickname, the "Paxton Boys."
>
> So then one day the Paxton Boys come down to our region, ride into the Conestoga camp, and kill every

member of the tribe who was there. They don't just kill them, either. They're brutal and destructive, like the Hulk on steroids—well, we won't go into that. Regardless, these Paxton guys are so worked up by then that when they learn some of the Conestoga hadn't been home the day of the massacre, managed to squeak by, and are now huddled together in Lancaster, they ride right into town and massacre them too. Essentially, the Paxton Boys wiped the Conestogas from the face of the earth.

What does all of this have to do with me, you ask? I'll tell ya. I know for a fact that my nine-greats-grandfather, Hubert Lantz, lived in the area at the time and was a friend of the Conestoga Indians. Many of the Plain people here were sympathetic to their cause and horrified at what their fellow settlers had done, my NGGH (Nine-Greats-Grandpa Hubert) included.

Once the massacre was over, a lot of people started writing about what had happened, publically, like hashing it out in the press. People took sides. NGGH, of course, stood on the side of the Conestoga. He even wrote a pamphlet himself, condemning the massacre, and my family still has one, a copy of which is enclosed. As you'll see when you read it, his pamphlet is my inspiration for the film. (Sorry about that. I meant to give it to you before I left for school but forgot.)

Anyway, that's your history lesson for today. What do you think? I want to make a film about NGGH, the Conestoga, the Paxton Boys, and the massacre. (Though I'll keep it G-rated, I promise. No red-colored corn syrup on my movie set!) Of course, I still need to verify the historical facts of the matter and also find more info on NGGH so I can flesh things out.

As you and I learned a few years ago when we were doing that genealogy project, this was the same settlement your people lived in for a while as well, so feel free to dig up some of your own roots. Maybe your ancestors and my ancestors were friends. Get me some names,

and I would be happy to make them actual characters in
the film.

Gotta run for now. My roomie is practicing his trumpet,
and if I don't get out of here soon, somebody's going to
be wearing a new trumpet hat.

Zed

I was glad to get the full rundown on the film, and he was right. This
story could be very compelling. The key was in tracking down more facts
about his ancestors—and mine.

Once I'd read his letter through twice, I set it aside and focused on
the photocopies of the pamphlet he had included. There were four pages,
typeset in an old-fashioned style, with the title, *The Paxton Dilemma*, and
under that the name of the author, *Hubert Lantz*, followed by the year,
1764.

I thought I would hang on to every word, but it was very dry and hard
to get through, full of old-fashioned terms and phrases, and I ended up
merely skimming it instead. At first, more than anything else, it seemed
to be a commentary on the political situation at the time, a condemnation
of government officials who claimed to be pacifists yet repeatedly chan-
neled funds to be used in "meeting the needs of defense." The author's
words were eloquent and his argument well laid out, but I couldn't see
how any of this had inspired Zed to make a movie about it—until I got
to the last page. There, the author finally shifted from the political to the
personal as he described his own relationship with the locally-based Conestoga Indians.

> *That I would call them brethren, and Christian brethren*
> *at that, is no mere generality. The Conestoga were, in word*
> *and deed, wholly and completely given over to the serving*
> *and worship of our Lord Jesus Christ. In the days following*
> *the massacre, my entire community mourned the loss of these*
> *fellow Christians.*
>
> *To my dismay, however, now that the massacre is nearly*
> *ten months hence, I find this is no longer the case. There are*

> *some with whom I have worshipped, shoulder to shoulder,*
> *and indeed considered the dearest of friends, who have begun*
> *to change their position of late. They refuse to acknowledge a*
> *previous fellowship with the Conestoga, and in fact now en-*
> *dorse the actions of the Paxton Boys. These heretics call them-*
> *selves A___sh, but their words do not support nor promote*
> *A___sh beliefs and practices.*
>
>   *May we all pray for the souls of these lost sheep who have*
> *wandered from the fold, that they may eventually come to see*
> *the error of their ways. May it happen before they are cast out*
> *entirely and forced to begin anew without benefit of commu-*
> *nity, fellowship, or God's blessing on their endeavors.*

The pamphlet ended there. I reread that final section again, trying to understand. I knew it wasn't unusual back then for certain institutions, people's names, and even denominations to be somewhat obscured in print, but there was no doubt this man was talking about his fellow Amish. It sounded to me as though rifts were within the community, and that some members had begun to take a very non-Amish stance in the wake of the massacre.

Putting the pamphlet aside, I wrote Zed back right away, asking questions about his research and providing a few ideas of my own about how I could see the story playing out. I also told him I thought the subject was compelling, but that we needed way more information on Hubert Lantz, the "heretics" to which he referred, and the true facts behind whatever had made him make public what should have been a confidential matter, handled within the privacy of the church.

I ended my letter with more general fare. It was a gloomy Friday afternoon when even my sewing wasn't going well, and I was feeling especially down. Soon I found myself bemoaning my situation in full. I poured out a litany of complaints—everything from the constant drone of the generator that powered my machine, to the continued scorn of my mother, to the endless stretch of days that lay between now and Thanksgiving.

My dour mood must have come through in my words, because Zed responded quickly with a shorter but more somber note than usual, expressing concern at what he said sounded like a case of the "days-are-getting-shorter blues" combined with "extreme Zed withdrawals."

If he only knew.

He prescribed a program of frequent walks in the sunshine, saying it really was humanly possible "to be more than ten feet from your sewing machine and still manage to survive." I smiled, even as his concern brought tears to my eyes. He ended the note with bit of a pep talk, saying:

> All kidding aside, I'm challenging you to push yourself beyond where you think you can go. Though you may not see it, you have an incredible inner strength and grace. It's time for you to draw on that. Start pushing, Iz. Push yourself hard, and let God take it from there.
>
> Yours,
> Zed

I wasn't sure what he meant, but I tucked it away as food for thought. As the sun of September left, replaced by the gray days of October, which brought rain and then more rain, I realized I couldn't put off leaving the house any longer. One especially dismal Monday morning, I decided it was past time for me to push myself and deliver the work I'd finished to my cousin Susie's shop. Otherwise, I'd have no money to show for my efforts at all.

She'd been having great success selling my work and had left several phone messages requesting more. I'd asked *Daed* to do the delivery for me, but he'd refused, saying it was my responsibility.

I hitched the horse to the buggy, hunkering down in my cape as I did, and sped as quickly as I could into downtown Bird-in-Hand. The stop would be quick and efficient. Susie never had time to talk much, which was fine with me, and Mondays were probably extra busy. With my recent withdrawal from all but the most necessary of events, I already found myself the topic of too much conversation. I didn't want to add any fuel to the gossip.

Once I arrived, I tied my horse to the hitching post out front, flung the waterproof blanket over her back and secured it underneath, grabbed my bag of goods, and dashed up the stairs to the shop. I pushed against the door but it didn't budge. I pushed again. Then I saw the sign. It simply read "Shut" with no time posted as to when Susie would return.

I knocked. And then knocked again, louder. Susie didn't come to the door. It wasn't as if she were expecting me, but I sure didn't want to have to come back. The last thing I felt like doing was to make the effort again tomorrow.

Pulling my cape tight against the rain, I knocked a third time, hoping she didn't plan to close the shop for good.

Susie had been a widow and single mother for five years, supporting her two children with the shop until she remarried last year to a nice man named Carl. I stepped from the stoop toward my buggy. My horse bobbed her head, as if thanking me for being ready to go so soon.

But then I turned and went around back, to where Susie's house sat behind the shop, on the other side of a narrow alleyway.

A soggy orange maple leaf fell through the air in front of me, then another. I slung my bag over my shoulder and then caught the third leaf dancing down, chased by the rain. I twirled the stem through my fingers, sending a splattering of water into the air, as I skirted along the lawn to the alley.

I looked both ways and was halfway across when I spotted a car parked in Susie's driveway—an old Toyota. I dropped the leaf, sure the vehicle belonged to Marta Bayer, Zed's mother.

I didn't want to see Marta. She was always so perceptive, and I couldn't bear the thought of her picking up on my feelings for her son. Turning abruptly, I hurried back toward the street.

"Izzy?"

I ducked my head against the rain and powered on as if I hadn't heard.

"Izzy? Is that you?" It was Marta sure enough, her concerned tone cutting through the storm.

Next Susie's sweet voice called out, "I was hoping you'd stop by soon!"

Torn between fleeing and turning, I froze.

"Izzy?" Marta's voice was growing closer. "Are you all right?"

Footsteps fell behind me and then suddenly the rain stopped. I glanced upward. An umbrella hovered over my head. I turned.

"Come on back to Susie's," Marta said. "She has something to ask you. And you have work for her, *ya?*"

I nodded.

Marta, holding the umbrella with one hand and her midwifery bag with the other, nodded toward the house and then started walking. The umbrella bumped against my head, forcing me along too. Maybe the topic of Zed would never come up.

We crossed the alley together as we moved toward the brick house, which was small for an Amish home but with two stories and a small garage to the side. I couldn't imagine why Marta would be here, and then it struck me. Susie must be in a family way.

She stood on her small front porch under the overhang, her purple dress a contrast to the white wood-framed door. She was probably close to thirty, just over a decade older than me, but she looked much younger than that with her round face, light blond hair, and bright blue eyes. It appeared that her apron jutted out a little, but it was hard to tell. I quickly diverted my eyes to the soggy roses clinging to the trellis on her right.

"Just the person I wanted to see," Susie said. "I have a question for you."

I forced a smile as I made eye contact.

"In fact, Marta and I were just talking about you."

I cringed.

Marta's voice was so low I was sure only I could hear her. "It was all good, believe me." She stopped as we reached the stoop but still held the umbrella above my head. "Come see me sometime," she said in a normal tone. "I've missed you."

I smiled, a little warily I'm afraid, and nodded, thankful she hadn't mentioned the three messages she'd left for me that I hadn't returned. I imagined Marta was lonely with Zed gone to college and Ella married and living in Indiana. Marta's little cottage, her nest, must have seemed awfully empty with both children off on their own.

I waved goodbye and then she turned to go as I followed Susie into her house.

"I need to get over to the shop, but I wanted to ask you about something first."

Susie pulled her cape from a peg on the wall as she and I hovered there by the back door.

Tilting my head, I hoped she meant to ask for even more of my handwork—though she already had me working quite a few hours each day. I nodded in encouragement.

"Marta said you're a caregiver."

My eyes must have shown my dismay at her question because she added, "*Ya*, she also said you had a recent problem, but you are very good at it."

I wasn't sure how to respond. I wondered if Zed had told Marta about my episode at the care center and what an impact it had had on me, or if she'd heard about it elsewhere. It didn't matter. The whole county probably knew—and had since the day odd little Izzy Mueller had an emotional breakdown over the death of an old woman she hardly even knew.

"Izzy?"

I blinked and managed to ask, "Why would you need a caregiver?" Her children were in school and in perfect health. Her new husband was robust and strong, working as a blacksmith nearby. Her parents lived across the county near several of their other children. Then it hit me— something was wrong with her. With her pregnancy. "Oh, dear," I said. "Should you sit down and put your feet up?"

"Whatever for?" She swung her cape over her shoulders.

"Well, because the baby—" My face grew warm.

She shook her head quickly. "I'm fine. I need someone to help with Verna."

"Verna? You mean Verna Westler?"

Susie nodded. "I guess you haven't heard. We moved her in here with us."

I smiled, a warm feeling filling me despite my trepidation at the thought of caregiving again. I loved my great-*aenti* Verna and always had. My maternal grandmother's sister, Verna had been the only one of her siblings never to marry. Instead, she had lived out her life on her brother's farm, still sprightly and sharp minded even in her advanced age.

"She's not ill, is she?" I asked as Susie's words registered.

"No, she's fine. I promise."

"So why is she here? I thought I heard that Rod and Ruth Ann were moving in with her at the farm."

"They did. Rod bought the place from his *daed*, and though he and Ruth Ann were fine with having Verna stay on, once the baby came…" Susie's voice trailed off and then she shrugged. "Well, you know how sensitive some old folks can be to every little sound. The babe's a bit colicky, and, well, it just felt as if our home might be a better place for Verna, at least for now." As an afterthought, she added, "Verna's wonderful with older kids. Just not…newborns."

I nodded, not stating the obvious, that with Susie's pregnancy, in about four or five months Verna might end up wanting to relocate elsewhere yet again. Older Amish women never seemed to be bothered by crying babies, but Verna had never had any children of her own, so maybe her reluctance was somewhat understandable.

"Anyway," Susie continued, "though the move here has worked out quite well, I really think she ought to have someone around in the mornings. She naps in the afternoons, and then the children get home. But she could use some company—and a helping hand—when I'm working in the shop and she's back here all alone. I was thinking about eight a.m. to one p.m., Monday through Friday."

I stood there for a moment, considering her words, until she interrupted me to add, "Also, I was thinking how handy it would be to have you here, near the shop, so you could meet some of my customers from time to time, and maybe take special orders in person. There has been a lot of interest in your work, you know."

"There has?"

She smiled. "Don't look so surprised. You're a very talented young woman, Izzy, and people notice. The next time it comes up, think how great it would be if you could just pop into the store for a few minutes to say hello, answer their questions, and take their requests yourself if they have any. I can almost guarantee it would boost sales."

She was probably right about that, and I was willing to do whatever it took to bring in more money for my cloth goods, but I was still so torn. On the one hand, I dearly loved Verna and would be thrilled to have more time with her. On the other hand, I really didn't want to care for someone who was terminal again.

"You're sure there's nothing seriously wrong with her?" I asked, hating myself even as I asked.

"Just old age. See for yourself."

I squinted through the dimness and was surprised to see a person two rooms away, a tiny figure wrapped in a dark quilt, sleeping in a chair in the corner of the living room.

"Oh!" I cried, hoping she hadn't been able to hear any of our conversation from all the way in there.

Susie and I moved through the kitchen and dining room, and as we stepped into the living room, the old woman raised her head. I realized she hadn't been asleep after all; she was reading. Her thin, gray hair, poking out from under her *kapp*, matched her eyes, which locked on mine through the small lenses of her glasses.

Susie gave her hand a squeeze and said, "Look who's here. It's Izzy, Peggy's girl."

Verna's face broke into a smile. She dropped the book onto her lap and then reached for me. I slipped my hand between both of hers.

"Izzy," she said, her voice practically purring. "It's so good to see you. Thank you for stopping by."

Her features shone and her eyes sparkled, twin circles of blue in a soft round face etched with smile lines.

Still, as bright as her features shone, the rainy day had cast a pall through the rest of the room. Everything was in order and clean, of course, but the house was old, probably close to two hundred years, and the windows were small and the glass warped. The wood floors had grayed with time, and the sofa and straight-back chairs in the living room were worn.

"She's thinking about coming regularly," Susie said to Verna.

I took a deep breath, but the older woman didn't seem to notice my reaction. "Oh, goodness. I've been praying for some company during the day. That would mean so much to me."

"Maybe," I said, not wanting to get her hopes up. "I'd like to, but I am awfully busy with the handwork I'm doing for Susie's shop."

"Bring it along and work on it here," Verna said. "Although I can't do much myself anymore, I'd love to see what you're doing."

I glanced at Susie.

"How about if Izzy and I talk some more?" she said to Verna, and then, catching my eye, she nodded toward the front door. "Right now we need to go over to the shop and look at her things."

Verna squeezed my hand and let me go. Shifting in her chair as she did sent the quilt and the book tumbling to the floor.

I picked up the quilt and quickly repositioned it, tucking the soft fabric in around her legs.

Then I knelt for the book, which had slid under her chair. *Colonial Pennsylvania.* It looked ancient with a torn cover, yellow pages, and a binding that was falling apart.

I handed it to her. "It was my father's," Verna said. "I love history."

"So do I." I grinned.

"Izzy?" Susie was at the front door now.

"Coming." I patted Verna's hand. "I'll see you soon."

"That would be lovely."

Even if I ended up not taking on the job, I decided I would at least stop by now and then, especially when I made deliveries to the shop.

I followed Susie back into the rain, holding my bag of handwork under my cape to keep it dry. We scurried across the alley and then ducked under the grape arbor, heavy with vines, to the back of her shop. She opened the door quickly and ushered me inside.

Before even taking off her cape, she hurried to the front, unlocked the door, and flipped the sign.

When she returned to the counter, she said, "What do you have for me today?"

I began pulling out what I'd made, starting with white doilies crocheted with red and green edges.

Susie fingered one of the doilies. "Nice," she said. I was always sur-prised *Englisch* customers bought them. Didn't they have a *grossmammi* or a favorite aunt who gave them doilies at Christmas? Susie had assured me most people who weren't Plain didn't, but I couldn't fathom that.

Next I pulled out four linen placemats, each embroidered with a scene from one of the four seasons, and then a table runner that included all four scenes. Her customers bought plenty of quilted placemats and table runners from her, but many liked the more delicate work I did, which was a mix of sewing and embroidery and crocheting. At least, that's what Susie said.

"I'm trying to increase my inventory for Christmas," she said now, running her hand over the winter scene. Simple figures, embroidered in white against red fabric, skated across a pond. "Can you make more of these?"

"*Ya.* I'll get started this afternoon."

She swung her cape from her shoulders and went over to the peg by the back door to hang it up. She straightened her *kapp* and then turned toward me again. "If you agree to sit with Verna, you really can do your work while you're here. Mostly she needs someone to visit with her. And fix her lunch. And read to her when her eyes tire."

That seemed simple enough—as long as she didn't die on me.

"She'll bend your ear with stories from the olden days," Susie continued, "and talk of all the sewing she did through the years, but she's awfully sweet." Both topics sounded good to me. Maybe she could help fill in some of the blanks on our ancestors for Zed's film. After all, Verna and I traced back to them through the same family line.

Thinking of Zed brought to mind the words in his letter: *Start pushing, Iz. Push yourself hard, and let God take it from there.*

Perhaps he was right. If I didn't take this job with Verna, was I denying God a chance to work in my life? And in hers?

I looked at Susie. "Do you mind if I go back and talk with *Aenti* Verna a little more before I decide?"

She was across the room now, hanging the runner across a long wooden rod. "Go ahead, but let me know your decision soon, okay?"

"Of course."

I picked up my empty bag and hurried toward the back door, bracing myself to go out into the storm again just as the front door opened. Three *Englisch* women wearing raincoats bustled in as I made my escape.

Moments later I was in Susie's house, calling out another hello to Verna.

Her voice sounded relieved. "You came back."

"*Ya.*" I kicked off my shoes this time, set them neatly against the wall, and then headed through the dining room and into the living room, taking the chair to her right. "I'm all done with Susie, but I don't have to rush right out just yet. I thought we could chat for a bit. How are you?"

We launched into conversation, catching up on ourselves, other family members, and her transition to this house. After a while, we moved onto the topic of Susie's store out front and the items I was making for her.

"She said you worked as a seamstress through the years too," I told Verna, but she shook her head.

"Not really. I did do a lot of sewing—that was my job for each of the families who lived with me at the old place. I've always enjoyed it. But I never took in any extra work from the outside."

"To be honest, I wish it were that way for me too. I'm rather slow, and it's hard to keep up."

"At least you're young, I'm sure you do fine."

Giving her a smile, I settled more deeply into the chair. Soon the conversation turned to our mutual love of history, and that led to our own family's history. When I told her I wanted to trace all the way back to some of our ancestors from the 1700s, her face lit up and she said she would be happy to help. Verna was my grandmother Delva's sister, and she said if it was the maternal line I was interested in—which it was—then she might even have some old family papers from that era. I was ecstatic to hear that.

We kept talking for at least an hour, until I finally remembered my poor horse hitched outside of Susie's shop in the pouring rain. Feeling horrible, I told Verna a hasty goodbye. Assuring her I would come back soon, I flung my cape back over my shoulders and hurried into the kitchen and out the door. I dashed across the alley, trying to dodge the rain, and burst through the back door of the shop, calling out Susie's name as I did.

But then I froze. The three *Englisch* women were still there, looking at my runner.

"Here's Izzy." Susie scooted toward me. "They've been admiring your work."

"Thank you," I managed to say.

"We're all putting in special orders," a woman with dark short hair said.

"Thank you," I said again. The woman smiled and then joined her friends across the shop.

"You're going to be busy." Susie held a notebook and a pen in her hands.

I smiled. "Doubly so, it seems."

"Oh?"

I glanced at the women, who were busy admiring some fabric dolls and said, "I'd love to sit with Verna." I took a deep breath and then low-ered my voice. "As long as you're sure she doesn't have any serious health problems."

"Well, high blood pressure. Edema. And her balance isn't good." Susie picked up the doilies and headed for the shelf under the window.

"But no cancer? Or heart disease?" I took a deep breath. "Nothing fatal?"

Susie shook her head as she arranged the doilies.

"Then I'll take the job."

Susie's head shot up as a smile spread across her face. "Are you sure?"

"Positive. When do I start?"

"My parents will be visiting tomorrow, so how about the day after. Nine sharp?"

"Perfect," I answered.

Susie hugged a doily to her chest. "*Danke!*"

"I'll see you Wednesday," I said and then smiled at the *Englisch* women on my way to the front door.

"Bring your handwork," Susie said. "To fill your orders."

I waved in acknowledgment. "See you then," I called out as I opened the door and dashed out to the buggy.

When the horse and I were both ready to go home, I decided to turn left and left again, circling around through the alley on my way. As I did, I couldn't help but grin at the sight of the face in the window of Susie's house on my right. Verna was still sitting in her chair, but now she was smiling back at me, her hand raised in a wave, as I went past.

Day after tomorrow I'd start my new job. I was sure it would all work out. At least my loneliness, for the first time in over a month, had lifted.

Somewhat, anyway.

FIVE

To my surprise, *Mamm* wasn't too happy about my big news. She didn't say much that night, but she finally weighed in the next day as we were peeling apples for applesauce.

"I think you need to focus on your long-range plans instead of jumping from one job to another." She spun the silver handle of the apple peeler as she spoke. "It's time to settle down, choose a path, and stick to it."

I sighed.

"You were finally starting to get up to speed with your sewing and actually see some profit. Now you're going to drop that and move on to this…" She shook her head. "Izzy, how long do you think this new caregiving job will last? A week? A month?"

My face grew warm. "As long as they need me, I suppose. And I can do my handwork at the same time as the caregiving." Her frown remained fixed, so I added, "Verna is your aunt, *Mamm*. I thought you'd be pleased."

She pulled the apple off the spindle and plunked it on the corer, jerking down the lever. "Of course I'm pleased, for her sake. But what I am concerned about is what happened at school. Who's to say you won't get hysterical again?"

I grabbed another apple from the pile I'd washed and slid it onto the spikes of the peeler. "That was because a patient *died*. My favorite patient. *Aenti* Verna isn't even ill."

"Izzy, she's ninety-one. Just because she's not ill now doesn't mean she's going to live all that much longer. Life comes to end; that's a fact. You can't just fall apart when things get hard." *Mamm* dropped the apple slices into the pot on the stove.

"I won't," I muttered.

"Pardon?" Her voice rang out over the clatter of the peeler.

"I'll be fine," I answered, keeping my tone respectful. "I know the realities of life and death. Last time just took me by surprise, is all."

Mamm harrumphed but didn't speak.

"Besides, Verna's going to help me with some family research about our ancestors who came to America back in the 1700s. I need that information for Zed's script."

Mamm looked my way, one eyebrow raised.

"For his next film," I added, trying not to sound as aggravated as I felt. She pulled off the peeled apple and I replaced it with another. "We talked about this, remember? He's going to focus on the Conestoga Indians and the local Plain folks who befriended them. He's basing it on the story of one of his own ancestors. And if I can get him enough info, he said he would put some of ours in there as well."

Now it was *Mamm*'s turn to sigh. She just didn't get it.

Most of the people in our community loved to think and talk about history, but my mother didn't, not even history related directly to her. Her parents died before she married, and she didn't have much of a relationship with her older sisters, so maybe she preferred to forget about the past—or at least her own past—and just focus on the present.

She'd cared for my *Daed*'s parents when they were old, but she hadn't particularly wanted to hear all about their lives prior to then, either. She was kind to them, but *I* had been the one who had spent hours listening to *Mammi* Nettie's stories. Though I was quite young then, I'd found them fascinating. Looking back, I wished I'd written down all that she'd told me. I hadn't realized that whole histories could disappear when the people who knew them passed away. *Daed* seemed to value that kind of thing somewhat, at least more than *Mamm* did, but I knew we ought to take care, lest our pasts were slowly erased with every new death of a loved one.

Mamm and I finished with the apples in silence, and then I rinsed my hands at the sink. I stepped toward the doorway to leave the room just as Thomas rushed in from outside, his hands covered with dirt.

"Wash, wash, wash!" *Mamm* ordered, pointing toward the mudroom. "And take your boots off! Then tell me what you want."

Thomas obeyed but called out over his shoulder. "*Daed* needs help, but I'm not big enough."

The rain had put off the corn harvest, so *Daed* had been using the time to build a woodworking shop in the barn.

"You go, Izzy."

I must have made a face.

Mamm rubbed the back of her wrist across her forehead. "You've been moping around long enough. If you're able to get a job outside the home, you're able to start helping around here more too."

I bristled but didn't respond. I hadn't been moping. I'd been distracted and introspective, that was all.

Thomas slipped back by me in his stocking feet, sliding on the linoleum. Oh, to be six again. He had no idea how wonderful his life was.

I put my bag in my little room and then headed toward the back door to help *Daed*, catching Thomas's sweet voice chattering away to *Mamm* as I slipped outside. I pulled the hood of my cape atop my head and dashed down the brick path.

The young mother Tabitha worked for needed extra help for a short time, so *Mamm* had sent Linda for the week. Stephen was in school, which left Thomas and me around the house during the day. At age six he should have started school, but he'd been sick a lot as a baby with ear infections, which had impacted his hearing and delayed his development. *Mamm* said another year at home would have him ready for next fall.

She always talked about how quickly the chicks flew, but with Thomas so young, it would be a long time before my parents had an empty nest—if ever. In fact, I was pretty sure I'd end up an old maid, living here with *Mamm* and *Daed* for the rest of their days.

She wouldn't like that one bit.

It wasn't that she wasn't a good *mamm*. She really was. She cared for us, each of us, meticulously. Her house sparkled. She worked tirelessly from dawn to nightfall to keep us clothed, fed, and scrubbed. She tended the garden, canned, shopped, and cooked. Sewed, mended, and laundered. Swept, mopped, and dusted.

She loved each of us deeply, I knew, even if she didn't show it with affection very often or words of endearment. We could tell by what she did for us, by the look in her eyes, by the way she instructed us.

She was efficient and no-nonsense. She did her work quickly and properly. She was all action.

But she and I were as different as could be. I thought about something long and hard before I took action. That wasn't her way, so she didn't value it in me.

Daed did his work well too, but differently than *Mamm*. He was slow and methodical, focusing on craftsmanship and quality. I knew it irked her how long it took him to finish a project, but I also knew she was proud of the end result.

I was far more like my *daed*, except I wanted to talk through what I was contemplating with someone. I wanted a sympathetic ear and words of encouragement. I wanted someone to bounce ideas around with. I wanted Zed.

I stumbled on the path, catching myself before I fell, and then once I reached the barn, I pushed the door open with more force than needed.

Daed was building his shop in the back, and I made my way there over the concrete floor, inhaling the scent of pine as I went.

My father stood by the window, staring out over the field of corn.

"*Daed?*"

It took a moment for him to turn toward me.

"I came to help."

He smiled and nodded toward a wall frame lying on its side. It was huge. No wonder Thomas had been too small to assist him.

"Get that end," *Daed* said. He was dividing the area in half so he had a shop on one side and a place to do his finishing work on the other. He was a carpenter, but because he hadn't had much to do on building sites lately, he was trying to get more business going on his own by making tables, all sizes, including big ones for Amish families. He'd filled several orders as wedding presents over the last year and hoped to get more.

I grabbed the two-by-four, lifted at the same time *Daed* did, and then scooted the frame into place. He grabbed a mallet from the workbench and tapped his side into place. Then he worked his way toward me, tapping along.

"I got a new job," I said.

"Oh?"

He kept slowly tapping as I explained the situation to him.

"Well, good," he said when I'd finished. "It sounds like you'll be a big help to Susie. And I know how fond Verna is of you."

"I'll be able to keep doing the handwork while I'm there. In fact, Susie asked specifically that I keep doing it. She's getting lots of orders for my stuff."

"Sounds like a win-win situation, as long as you don't let it go to your head."

I nodded.

"Things are coming together, *ya*?" He stopped tapping and stepped back, sliding the mallet into his tool belt. "Next you'll join the church. Then find the right husband."

"*Daed*," I said, wanting him to stop.

He looped his thumbs into his suspenders. "You know what I want more than anything is for all of my children to be hard workers, serve the community, and join the church."

I nodded again. We all knew that. *Daed* didn't talk a lot, but he'd made his wishes clear through the years. "You know I'll join the church," I said. "But the marrying part is up to God, not me."

"Izzy, God has someone planned for you. Wait and see."

When I didn't respond he said, "Let me know when it's time to eat."

The next morning Stephen and I headed out together. I was going to drop him off at school and then go straight to Susie's. Stephen, an exact replica of *Daed* minus the beard and a foot of height, sat silently, watching the fields go by.

The rain had let up, finally. Both of my parents had seemed in a good mood this morning. *Mamm* and Thomas were going to help *Daed* out in the field with the harvest. I imagined, if I didn't have a new job, they would have dragged me out there too. There was nothing I disliked more than fieldwork. The forecast was for three days of sunshine—just enough time to get the harvest done.

I left Stephen at the schoolhouse and continued on toward Susie's. I had my handwork beside me in my bag, plus a collection of history books, mostly ones Zed had loaned me over the summer. He had said I was free to keep them while he was gone, and I thought Verna might enjoy them too.

Thinking of Verna, I really did hope she would be able to fill in some of the blanks for me in our family's history. Remembering the book I'd seen her reading the day before, I wondered what others she might have, and if any of them had illustrations showing what people wore back in the mid-1700s. I knew it would be a while yet before Zed finished the script and locked in his character list so I could get started on the costumes, but I couldn't wait. My heart raced at the very thought.

I turned off the highway by Susie's shop and pulled around to the alley. A few minutes later, after I'd unhitched my horse and put her in the small pasture with Susie's gelding, I hurried up the steps to the house, my things in tow.

I'd barely rapped on the door once when I heard Verna call out, "Come in." I stepped into the kitchen, shed my cape, slipped off my shoes, and started toward the living room.

"Over here." Verna was on the sofa, wrapped in a quilt again, reading the same book.

"Anything new?" I joked.

She shook her head and smiled at me.

I asked if there was anything she needed, tea or another blanket or whatever, but she said no, just the company would be lovely.

Happy to oblige, I sat down on the other side of the couch from her, and after just a few minutes of simple conversation, I decided to ask her about the parts of our family history that would be relevant to the topic of Zed's film.

"I've been thinking about our ancestors who first came to America," I told her. "The ones who would have been around in the 1700s. Well, more specifically, in 1763."

She tilted her head. "Oh? Why these particular ancestors?"

I hesitated, wondering how to put it and hoping she wouldn't find the idea of my involvement with filmmaking offensive or improper. Then I realized that the subject might go over better if I started by telling her who was at the helm.

"You know Marta Bayer, right?"

"Of course. She was just here the other day looking after Susie."

I nodded. "Do you know her son, Zed?"

Verna thought for a moment. "A tall, handsome young man? Blond hair that hangs too low over his eyes?"

I chuckled. "That's him."

"Oh, I'd like to take a pair of scissors to those bangs of his. But otherwise he's a lovely boy. Sweet, handsome, well mannered—and quite intelligent, from what I understand."

"Quite. He's in college out in Indiana right now, where he's studying film."

"Film?"

"He wants to become a movie director." I went on to explain about how he won the two awards at the recent film festival and how his next movie was going to focus on either his ancestors or ours, both of whom came to America on the same ship and settled in the Lancaster County area. "He wants me to get some details about my people from back then so he can work them into the script. Meanwhile, I'll start researching the types of clothes they would have worn and make the costumes."

That seemed to give her pause. "All by yourself?"

I shrugged. "Filming won't begin till next June, so as long as I can get started on them by the end of the year, I should be able to finish in plenty of time."

Verna nodded, and then after a long moment, she glanced around and then said, "I saw a movie once."

My eyebrows shot up.

She leaned forward and lowered her voice. "Don't ever tell a soul," she whispered, "but when I was in my thirties, a few of the women in my sewing circle and I snuck off to a theater in Harrisburg to watch *Ben Hur.*"

I gasped. "No way!"

She nodded again, a sheepish grin spreading across her face. "One of the Mennonites in the group had a car. I knew I shouldn't go with them, but I'd already read the book and simply couldn't imagine God would count it as a sin for me to see the film. Of course, I felt so guilty about it afterward that I made a full confession to the bishop. More than anything, he just seemed to think it was funny. He didn't even have me confess to the congregation. He just said not to do it again."

"And did you?"

"No. I felt guilty enough the first time."

I sat back in my chair, in that moment loving Verna more than I ever had. "Wow," I said, shaking my head. "Did you get popcorn? Zed says people always get popcorn at theaters."

"Oh, goodness, I don't remember."

"What did you think of the movie?"

Her face colored. "There were not enough clothes on some of those actors and actresses, but when the resurrection scene came, oh my…" Her eyes lit up as her voice trailed off in wonder.

I gazed at her for a long moment, and it struck me how glad I was she'd chosen to share this secret with me. I hoped to hear many more of her stories in the days to come.

We took a break for some coffee in the kitchen, but soon we were back on the couch and again onto the subject of Zed's film as I sewed. I was explaining that his primary interest was in the demise of the local Conestoga Indians. Verna seemed familiar with the story, but I reiterated the high points, that in 1763 a group called the Paxton Boys brutally murdered the entire Conestoga tribe, even though they had been peacefully coexisting with the settlers in this area for years.

"Zed hopes to tell the story of the Plain people who lived nearby and how they reacted to the massacre," I said. "As pacifists, you'd think the Anabaptists would have been quite vocal in the Conestogas' defense.

Some were, of course, but he says that many sat quietly by and let it happen without speaking up at all."

The crease in Verna's worried forehead only deepened.

"What is it?" I asked, afraid I had said too much.

She glanced away and then back at my face. "I'll tell you, but you're not going to like it."

I tilted my head, curious. "What?"

"It's rather hard to explain," she said, one hand flitting nervously to her collar.

"Take your time."

Verna thought for a moment and then finally said, "I'm already aware of everything you've described. But have you ever heard of the War of Words?"

I shook my head.

"It began soon after the attack on the Conestogas," Verna went on, not waiting for an answer. "Benjamin Franklin started it, actually, by publishing an account of the entire massacre and condemning the men who had carried it out."

"Oh, that. Right. Zed said everybody started hashing it out in the press."

"Exactly. Soon all sorts of people were jumping into the fray, publishing this and that, and basically fighting with each other about what had happened via the written word."

I nodded, my own brow furrowed as I waited for her to get to the point.

"People made pamphlets to present their positions—saying 'The Paxton Boys were murderers' to 'The Paxton Boys were fully justified,' and everything in between."

"That makes sense with what I already know because that's how Zed got the idea for the film in the first place. His nine-greats-grandfather published an essay about the injustice of the massacre. Zed has a copy of it, but it raises more questions than it answers. From what I read, it sounds as though some members of the local Amish community took a very un-Amish stance on the situation back then and actually endorsed the massacre."

"Well, dear, I hate to tell you this, but…"

Verna's expression grew quite miserable and her voice trailed off. I squinted at her, waiting, until she met my gaze. "The folks who did that were *our* ancestors."

"What do you mean?"

"I mean our ancestors were not in support of the Indians. They condemned the Indians and supported what the Paxton Boys had done."

My mouth fell open. "You can't be serious."

She nodded.

"But they were *Amish*. How could an Amish person ever endorse violence, much less violence directed at innocent people?" My mind was reeling.

"I'm unclear as to the details, but I'm certain several members of the family took that stance. Something about the Indians being the aggressors and not living peacefully with the settlers. In fact, they were almost excommunicated because of their position."

"How do you know this?"

She shrugged. "Family lore, mostly."

I set aside my handwork and leaned forward, resting my elbows on my knees. "Is there any proof?"

Verna pursed her lips together and thought for a moment. "Some sort of church document about the situation is supposed to exist, though I don't recall actually seeing such a thing. As I said, they wrote some pamphlets back then in favor of the massacre."

My heart fell. "Do you have any of those?"

"I don't think so." She was lost in thought for a long moment and then said, "I may have some other things from back then, though. Over the years I ended up with most of the family papers, at least what no one else wanted."

"Yes, you mentioned that…"

"Oh, that's right. I brought several boxes with me when I moved in. They're in my room." She gestured toward the hallway.

My pulse surged with anticipation until she added, "I also left a couple of boxes and a trunk at the farm."

I folded my hands together, trying not to sound desperate. "Could we get them too?"

"There may be no need. Why don't we go through the boxes I brought with me first? If we don't find anything, then we can look into getting the others."

Leaning back against the couch, I exhaled. There were times, no matter how much I loved history, that it scared me. This was one of those times.

My ancestors—my *Amish* ancestors—had condoned a massacre? I couldn't fathom it. Obviously, my time with Verna was going to take me far beyond just learning family history and researching costumes for a film. It seemed we would be going much deeper than that, perhaps all the way to something I'd rather not have learned at all.

Six

As soon as I arrived at Susie's the next day, I spotted a square pine box, about the size of an apple crate, on the floor next to the couch where Verna sat.

"Is that what I think it is?" Part of me felt apprehensive, as if that box might contain some facts that would best remain buried. On the other hand, I'd spent a lot of time the night before thinking about the situation and praying on it, and this morning I'd decided that, either way, I wanted to know the full story. As I hung up my cape and put my handwork bag on the floor below it, a verse from the book of Luke came to mind, *For nothing is secret, that shall not be made manifest; neither any thing hid, that shall not be known and come abroad.* Perhaps it was time for us to make some very old truths manifest at last.

While I got settled, Verna explained that Susie's husband had carried one of her boxes of old papers to the living room the night before.

"Tell me again where you got all of this?" I sat down on the edge of the couch and studied the box, wondering if it would take a crowbar to get the lid off.

Verna tucked her quilt around her legs. "Every few generations, someone in the family has taken charge of keeping the family papers. Years ago, it was my grandmother, my mother's mother. When she died, it was all passed down to me." She glanced up at me, a gleam in her eye. "Given your interest, Izzy, and considering I don't have any children, I think perhaps you should be the next person to take it all on once I die."

I couldn't help but be flattered by her suggestion, nor could I help being distraught at her mentioning the possibility of her death. Taking a deep breath, I reminded myself of my promise to my *mamm* to keep my feelings in check.

"My grandmother had inherited all the papers from *her* grandmother, who had been a real pack rat." Her eyes fell to the box, and mine couldn't help but follow. "A lot of it wasn't important and was purged at the time, but I still think my grandmother should have thrown out even more. Much chaff is among this wheat, I'm afraid."

I reached out to run a hand across the smooth wood of the lid. "Do you think any of those pamphlets our ancestors wrote about the Paxton Boys and the massacre are in here?"

"Not that I recall specifically, but I know there is something somewhere that has to do with Indians. It's hard to remember because I haven't gone through everything in full since my grandmother died. And that was a long, long time ago." She exhaled slowly. "Unfortunately, there's no real organization to this stuff. It might take some doing to find what we're looking for—and, like I said, most of it we won't need at all."

"That's okay," I said, growing more eager to get started. "We'll just keep digging till we find what we're looking for."

"Exactly." Verna smiled. "Let's go item by item, and we'll see what's there." She nodded to me sweetly. "You may have the honors."

The lid was on tight, but I jiggled it a bit and finally managed to pull it open. Old papers filled the interior of the box to the brim. With a glance at Verna, I inhaled deeply as I picked up the first slip and squinted at the faded script, written in longhand.

It looked like a receipt for a trade, dated 1939—one mule exchanged for two hundred pounds of grain. I showed it to Verna, and she chuckled.

"It must have been an old mule."

Smiling, I placed that piece of paper on the floor next to the box and reached for another. This one was just a grocery list, and a short one at that: "Sugar, salt, and baking powder." I read it to Verna and asked if it was important.

"Goodness, no, throw it out. See what I mean?"

I crumbled the paper into a ball and tossed it toward the wastebasket at the end of the couch. We kept going, but unfortunately, for a while at least, it was much of the same. Half of it ended up in the trash, and after a while Verna apologized.

"I guess it's been a long time since I went through this stuff and tried to do a little paring down myself. For all I know, there's nothing else of worth in this whole box."

"At least some of these papers are really interesting," I said, trying to make her feel better even as my own heart sank.

We kept going, though the task remained fairly tedious. A receipt for some lumber, dated 1946. A ration card, from 1942. A doctor's bill, from 1927.

"Oh, my," she said, holding out her hand to see it. "That was the year my sister Delva was born—your grandmother. Our *mamm* had a few problems that time and *Daed* had to go for help. I was five, but I can remember the two of them, *Daed* and the doctor, bursting in through the front door just in time. In fact, that's probably my earliest memory."

I nodded, grateful for that bit of information. Delva Westler, my mother's mother, had survived being born and gone on to live into her early sixties. I wasn't sure exactly when she died, but I knew it was before *Mamm* was married and long before I was born. How fascinating now to see the receipt for the cost of her birth.

We kept going. Things soon grew tedious again, but I finally perked up when I came upon an old report card from 1943. It was made from heavy paper, but instead of being preprinted, all of the lines had been drawn with a pencil and probably a ruler. The ink of the lines and the grades was faded, but some of it was still readable. I couldn't quite make out the name at the top, though I did see that it contained mostly C's and D's.

"Any idea whose report card this was?" I asked, handing it over to Verna.

She took a long look, her eyes growing moist even as she smiled. "Judging by the grades, this belonged to my younger brother, Raymond," she said, then she dabbed at her eyes with a handkerchief. "He was smart but hated school. It bored him to death."

Verna began telling a story about Raymond, and I kept going as she talked, placing the card in the keeper pile and moving on to the next scrap of paper.

We continued, breaking for lunch, and then worked for another hour afterward, until it was time for Verna to rest and for me to be on my way. There were a few more inches of papers to go, but I couldn't help but assume they would all be from the wrong period. So far there hadn't been anything prior to the early 1900s, and definitely nothing about the Paxton Boys or the Conestoga Indian Massacre.

I tried to hide my frustration, but I'd never been very good at pretending, and I'm afraid Verna picked up on my feelings. "Don't fret, dear. We simply started in the wrong place," she said. "We'll soon figure out which box holds the papers from the 1700s."

I nodded, giving her a smile. As I put on my cape and grabbed my handwork bag, that I hadn't even opened, Verna promised to have Carl carry the remaining boxes from her room before I returned.

"It's in there somewhere. Don't you worry," she said.

Feeling encouraged, I told her goodbye and that I would see her in the morning. On the way home, as I mulled over what we'd found, I realized I'd hardly thought about Zed all day. Spending time with Verna really was the best thing for me, even if her old family papers had been a bit disappointing so far.

When I arrived the next day, three more boxes lined the area in front of the couch. My trepidation from the day before was gone, and in its place was only enthusiasm. Clapping my hands together, I said, "This is like Christmas!" It wasn't that we had lavish celebrations, but it was one of our most anticipated days of the year—and this moment was every bit as exciting as that.

Verna sat in her regular place, a wide grin on her sweet face. "I think first we should do a quick inventory of each box and decide where to start. Judging by the dates of all of yesterday's papers, I have a feeling this stuff may be grouped somewhat by time period. Perhaps one of these holds mostly older fare."

I quickly hung up my cape. This time I hadn't bothered to bring my handwork. I'd worked late the night before to make up for the lost time yesterday and planned on doing the same tonight.

Two of these boxes were made from wood like the first one, but the other was just cardboard. I opened it first, suspecting its contents would be more recent. I held up a copy of the *Budget*. "Hmm…1983."

Verna laughed. "Goodness, why would I have saved that?"

She probably had a good reason at the time. The next item was an old pattern for an apron, and then there was one for a *kapp*.

We worked our way down another inch or two, and then finally Verna said, "Push that box aside. We don't need to bother with it."

I agreed and did as I was told, prying the top off of the pine box closest to me. I took the first item out. It was a death notice from 1957, cut out from the *Budget*, for a Raymond Westler. He'd only been twenty-five.

I swallowed hard as I handed the yellowed clipping to Verna. "Was this your younger brother? The one who hated school?"

Her eyes pooled with tears as she read it. "Raymond and I were so close, just a year and a half apart in age and for many years inseparable. His buggy was hit by a truck." She returned the clipping back to me.

"I'm sorry," I said. I couldn't imagine the heartache of that.

She pulled out a handkerchief and dabbed at her eyes. "There I go again, getting all emotional. There's no reason to, really. I'm not long for this world myself…"

I reached over and patted her hand, trying not to shudder at her words. When it seemed she'd recovered, I scooted back to the box, sure it contained, like the box from yesterday, documents from the more recent past.

It did at first, but after going just an inch or so down, I found some things that were much older. A cemetery listing, from 1802. A tax assessment, from 1862. A list of supplies dated by hand as 1767.

Finally, my pulse surging, I noticed one thing that looked like a handmade envelope, with writing on one side. The creases were so worn that the packet was falling apart. I held it toward the light from the window and struggled to read the faded ink.

"Is that a letter?" Verna asked. "Who's it to?"

"I think it's addressed to a Bernard...something with a *V*, Conestoga Township, Commonwealth of Pennsylvania."

"Oh, goodness. Bernard. He's one of the ones we've been looking for. If I'm not mistaken, he and his wife lived here during the time you're interested in. They came over on the *Virtuous Grace*."

Sucking in a breath, I carefully opened the packet and removed a single page of handwritten text on old, old paper. A letter.

It was dated February 25, 1764, and was written in a feminine hand. My heart racing in excitement, I read it out loud to Verna:

> *Dear Papa,*
>
> *At long last we have arrived safe and sound. The relentless rain made stretches of the GWR muddy and full of ruts, but still our dispositions remained positive. Though our guide was rough and unrefined, the rivers high, and some of the mountain passes quite steep, the terrain was magnificent, and the forests we traveled through were straight from the pages of a fairy tale.*
>
> *Despite the fact that we are not Moravian, your gracious friend and his community here have welcomed us with open arms. We are grateful for their kind hearts and generosity during this time of unrest. Br. Gunter's orchard is less mature than those at home in the North, but with a greater variety. The fruit will do fine here for a while, I feel sure.*
>
> *The good Lord has been with us every step of the way, and for that we are very grateful. Please keep us informed of any developments.*
>
> *I have never been more sure of anything in my life, nor has Gorg. We hope you are feeling the same.*
>
> *Your loving daughter,*
> *Abigail*

I handed the letter to Verna and she read it silently. Then she handed it back to me and I reread it again, taking in every word.

"Do you remember seeing this?" I asked her.

She shrugged. "Not necessarily, though I do recall seeing the name Abigail on something else, something printed."

I glanced toward the box, hoping it was filled with more treasures like this.

"What do *you* make of it?" Verna asked.

"Well." I took a deep breath and studied the page in front of me. "I'm not sure. It's fascinating, of course, but I wish I knew more of what she was talking about."

I sat back and looked at the page again, trying to decide what we did know. For starters, the date was fairly significant. I glanced at Verna. "The Conestoga Massacre happened in December 1763, and this was written about two months after that. I have to wonder if by 'this time of unrest,' that's what she's referring to. The Indian conflict and the war of words, as you called it."

Verna squinted through the lenses of her glasses. "But it sounds as though she's writing from somewhere else. The Indian conflict happened here in Pennsylvania."

I shook my head. "Obviously, this letter is about a trip. My guess is that she and this Gorg person had been here but then traveled away. What's the GWR?"

Verna thought for a moment. "Some kind of travel route, I suppose? A roadway of some kind?"

"GWR," I mused. "The Georgia–West Virginia Route?"

"The George Washington Roadway?"

We considered the date and decided it would probably be a bit premature to name a road for a man who hadn't yet risen to his full prominence. Still, the GWR had to be some kind of road.

"She mentions a Moravian," Verna said, turning to look at the shelves along the wall where she kept her history books. "I seem to recall something about the Moravians..." She rose and moved over to the books, tilting her head to scan the spines.

I returned my attention to the letter. "Do you recognize the name Gorg?"

"No, but if he's also an ancestor, I probably knew who he was at some point." She turned and looked at me, an idea alight in her eye. "The old family Bible, of course. It's on the table in my room."

"You want me to get it?"

"Please. Second door on the right." She plucked a book off the shelf, and as I headed down the hallway, she shuffled back over to her chair.

Verna's bedroom was sparsely furnished with a single bed, a bureau, and a table by the window, on which was a brush, a bottle of lotion, and a massive black Bible. I carefully picked up the Bible, noticing that its cover was old and brittle, and hurried back to the living room. When I got there, though, Verna had the history book open on her lap and seemed to want to show me something first, so I set the Bible aside for a moment and gave her my attention.

"I thought so," she told me, placing her finger on the page.

Leaning forward, I read the heading she indicated, *The Moravians Venture Out from Bethlehem.*

"This whole chapter is about the Moravians," she explained, "and their migration from Pennsylvania down to North Carolina in the mid-1700s."

"North Carolina? Do you think Abigail would have traveled from here to all the way down there?"

"Well, I wasn't so sure at first, until I read this third paragraph."

Curious, I skimmed the words she indicated, which were about a group of Moravian brothers of varying skills and professions who had traveled together to North Carolina in 1733 to establish a new settlement there. That was interesting, but I couldn't figure out what had Verna so pleased until I got to the end. It said:

> *They followed the Great Wagon Road, which was a main route of travel for southbound settlers of the era. Starting at the port of Philadelphia, the roadway passed through Lancaster and York, Pennsylvania, down through the Shenandoah Valley, at that time ending around what is now Salem, North Carolina. Over the coming years, the Great Wagon Road would continue to expand and eventually provided passage all the way to Augusta, Georgia.*

I looked at Verna, my eyes wide. "The GWR in her letter is the 'Great Wagon Road.'"

We shared a grin. I couldn't believe we had found the answer to at least one of our questions so quickly.

After that, she put the book away and asked for the Bible, so I handed it to her. She struggled to balance it on her lap as she opened it, so I scooted in beside her and steadied the book.

"Is this the Westler family Bible?"

She shook her head. "No, this came from my mother's side. In fact, it was first owned by my great-great-grandmother and was passed down to my grandmother and then my mother and then me." She smiled. "Which is a good thing, because the Westlers didn't immigrate to this area until the mid-1800s. My maternal line goes much further back."

I felt tingles run down my spine. Her maternal line was mine as well.

She flipped through several pages at the front until she came to a family tree. It was a chart of sorts, with printed blank boxes that had been filled in by hand. "As you can see, my great-great-grandmother did a good job of cataloging her forebears, and my great-grandmother and grandmother added to that, but eventually they ran out of room."

I nodded, my eyes taking in the various handwritings of the script. Sure enough, the tree went on for several pages and was full to the end.

She flipped back to the first page of the family tree. "Here we go. Look! Does that say Bernard?"

She pointed to a box near the top. I leaned forward, squinting. "I think so. Looks like Bernard...Vogel. Yes! I thought it was a *V* on the envelope."

"Vogel," she repeated, deep in thought. "I was right. Bernard Vogel and his wife were the ones who came over from Europe on the *Virtuous Grace*. They settled in the area in—" She lifted the Bible, which wobbled a little, closer to her face and peered through her glasses. "Actually, this doesn't say. But look at this. Here's the name Abigail! Abigail was his daughter."

Verna and I grinned at each other.

"So this letter was written from daughter to father," I said. "Abigail to Bernard. That makes sense. I would touch base with my *daed* if I went on a trip."

Leaning toward the Bible, which we'd left open on the coffee table, I studied the line in the chart that had her name on it. The handwriting was deeply slanted and hard to read, but it looked as though she was born in 1743, and in the box for her spouse had been written in the name Gorg Bontrager.

I shivered at this connection to the past, astounded that it had been this easy. Zed and I could definitely put a character named Bernard Vogel in his movie. And if I could learn more about Abigail and Gorg, maybe they could go in it too.

My excitement at the thought soon faded into sadness as I remembered what Verna had told me, that we had ancestors from that time who were Paxton Boys sympathizers. Abigail and Gorg, and Bernard for that matter, could have been the ones she meant.

Abigail had several brothers listed, and for some reason I really wanted it to be one of them instead. Something about reading Abigail's letter made me feel close to her. I couldn't imagine an obedient daughter who kept her disposition positive despite the hardships of Colonial travel could be the kind of person to endorse violence.

I asked Verna where I might find pen and paper and then settled back down next to her and began carefully recording all the names from the Bible, from Abigail on down, going through all three pages. When I reached the end, Verna helped me take it from there, and we filled in the remaining generations, including my grandmother, Delva, my *mamm*, Peggy, and then me, Isabel Mueller.

I counted back up the family tree. Abigail Vogel Bontrager was my eight-greats-grandmother. The thought of all the stories between me and her took my breath away. I knew I'd never learn them all, but I would do anything to learn Abigail's.

I thought of the final words in her letter: *I have never been more sure of anything in my life, nor has Gorg. We hope you are feeling the same.* What were they so sure of? Whatever it was, I had a feeling it held the key to unlocking these secrets of the past.

Seven

Verna and I continued working through her boxes but found nothing else of note the rest of the day. I hated heading into the weekend with more boxes left to search, but my time was up. I didn't have a choice. Of course, Suzie wouldn't have minded my sticking around for the afternoon, unpaid, but I had orders to fill and lots of sewing to get done, so I really did need to go home.

At least my patience had its reward. When I returned the following Monday, Verna and I resumed our search, digging in eagerly. After about an hour, we came across the biggest find of all.

I knew the moment I saw it that it was something important, because the name "Abigail" on the front jumped out at me right away. Lifting it carefully, I realized that it was a pamphlet of some kind.

"What is this?" I held it up.

The cover, fragile to the touch, was made of a thick and yellowed coarse paper on which had been printed the words *A Reflection of My Experience Concerning the Indians of Long Ago*. Under that was the name *Abigail Vogel Bontrager*. Around the edges was a border design, with a single feather sketched into the top corner, as decoration.

"I've seen this type of thing before," Verna said, leaning forward to peer at it more closely. "I believe that's what's known as a 'chapbook.'" She went on to explain that chapbooks were small, crude publications made for the common people who wanted to read but couldn't afford bound books. "I believe they were still popular during Abigail's time, and probably for another hundred years after that."

At her words, my heart surged with excitement. I couldn't believe I was holding this piece of history in my hands.

I could scarcely breathe.

Verna didn't even touch it, probably for fear it might fall apart. Instead, she studied it for a long moment as I held it up. Then she told me to look inside.

"Be careful with it," she urged.

Hands trembling, I settled back into the couch, set the booklet on my lap, and opened the cover. The interior pages were of a thinner stock but also yellowed. The first page of the chapbook repeated the title and author from the front, with "D. Campbell, Philadelphia," and the year 1819 underneath.

"Who's D. Campbell?" I asked.

"A publisher or printer, I imagine."

I ran my finger across the date. "Wait. What year was Abigail born again?"

Verna couldn't quite remember, so I took a moment to pull out the page where I'd listed the family tree. "Here it is. She was born in 1743, so by 1819, she would have been…seventy-six. She wrote this chapbook when she was seventy-six years old!"

Verna was quiet for a long moment. "An old woman, looking back on her years. I can see that."

Something in her voice sounded wistful, and I was glad she'd had the chance to share at least some of her own stories with me these past few days. Perhaps that was part of what old age was for, to look back on one's life with the wisdom and perspective not available in youth.

"What should we do?" I asked, gently flipping through the first few pages. At first glance it seemed to be filled with mistakes, spelling and otherwise, at least from the perspective of a twenty-first-century reader.

But then I reminded myself that they wrote differently back then, and that these likely weren't mistakes at all but rather conventions that had changed over time.

"Why don't you read it aloud?" Verna said.

For some reason, the thought made me nervous. Taking a deep breath, I made myself more comfortable, and then I cleared my throat and began.

> *In our years together, my husband Gorg and I shared an uncon-fessed sin—one we would commit again and again if the situation arose. This is the story behind that sin.*

I stopped, eyes wide, and looked at Verna in alarm. Sin? What if the sin referred to here was the endorsement of violence against the Indians? My heart sank.

"Calm down, child," Verna said as if reading my mind. "We don't know where she's going with this yet."

I nodded, feeling just a little queasy. Why did the past have to be so messy sometimes?

Taking another deep breath, I started again, rereading the first paragraph out loud and then going on from there.

> *I was born in 1743 on my father's farm in what is now known as Manor Township, near the original land grant of William Penn, a man who boldly promised religious freedom. I was the youngest of five children who lived to adulthood, and the only girl.*

I looked up at Verna. "Manor Township? That's not far from here at all. Maybe three or four towns away?"

She nodded. "The boundaries may have differed somewhat back then, but you're right."

I continued.

> *There were no schools, but my beloved father taught all of us to read and write, to do sums and subtractions, and all that he knew about the world. Though German was his native tongue, he insisted that we use English, both the written and the spoken*

word, as much as possible. We were also taught to respect all
people, knowing they are all immortal beings created by God,
according to Scriptures.

I glanced again at Verna. "Well, that's encouraging. Maybe the sin she
refers to at the beginning is something else."

"See? You need to stop jumping to conclusions."

I smiled. "I know, but remember, she *is* writing this in retrospect at a
much older age."

Feeling a new wave of apprehension, I kept going.

> *Only a few miles from our home, also in Manor Township,*
> *was the region known as Conestoga Indian Town. William*
> *Penn had left the land there for the Conestoga Indians in his*
> *grant. Over the years, the property had dwindled down to a*
> *small portion of his original intention, though he had signed a*
> *treaty promising not to permit any "Act of Hostility or Violence,*
> *Wrong or Injury, to or against any of the Said Indians." Until*
> *the commencement of the French and Indian War, that treaty*
> *was honored by our people, and indeed all Pennsylvanians,*
> *who faithfully protected the gentle Conestogas from harm.*

So far, this chapbook was sounding just like the account of the same
period in one of the books Zed had loaned me. The next few paragraphs
talked about William Penn and his intentions for the region, as well as
how things progressed on that front once he'd passed away and his sons
took over. It became a little boring, but then the narrative took on a more
personal tone. I perked back up as I read it aloud.

> *My earliest recollections of Indian Town are the times I would*
> *go with my mother when she bought baskets there. The Indi-*
> *ans' homes were cabins, not wigwams, and they had gardens*
> *nearby, much as we did, though theirs had no fencing and*
> *seemed much less controlled somehow than ours. I remember*
> *seeing thick stalks of corn, vines heavy with plump pumpkins,*

*and many other varieties of squash growing in vivid splashes
of yellows and greens among the leaves.*

*One year in the spring, when I was still a child, I saw a
girl there, peeking around the corner of a cabin, who looked
to be about my same age. She had long black hair and wore
a cotton dress. I asked my mother if that girl was an Indian,
and she said yes, but I wasn't so sure. Her skin was paler than
that of the other Indians, who bore a dark countenance.*

*I remember that I waved at her and she smiled in return.
We never spoke or interacted in any other way, but over the
next few months I thought of her often. Near the end of August, when Mother said she was going back to Indian Town, I
made sure to go with her. Again we bought baskets. Again the
girl came around the side of the cabin to stare at us.*

*I waved. She smiled. I was normally quite shy and quiet,
but for some reason I took off running toward that girl. Startled, she stepped backward but did not flee. When I reached
her, I took her hand, squeezed it, and said hello. She squeezed
mine back and then surprised me by speaking in English,
pointing toward a field of flowers beyond the gardens and
asking if I wanted to come and play.*

I paused in my reading to look to Verna. "English? An Indian child?"
She shrugged. "I suppose with so many settlers around, the Indians
were bound to learn the language."

I cleared my throat and continued.

*With my mother's permission, I went with the girl and we
spent the following hour or two there together, getting along
quite well. We picked thick handfuls of helenium with their
vivid yellow and orange blossoms, and then we sat down in
the field and she showed me how to weave the stems into a
chain. Once our chains were long enough, we looped them
into circles and wore them as crowns and necklaces and
bracelets.*

*The next time we visited, the following spring, I ap-
proached the girl and spoke with her. Again, she seemed shy
at first but this time, as she warmed to me, she told me her
name. It was lovely and musical but so unusual that I wrote
it into the dirt with a stick, spelling it the way it sounded,
KAH-nen-kwas. She seemed so delighted by that, I rubbed
out the letters and tried again, this time using what I assumed to be the more correct spelling, Konenquas. She took
the stick from my hand and, underneath what I had written,
she did the best she could to scratch out the same letters. Taking the stick back, I wrote my name as well, and again she repeated it below.*

    Konenquas and Abigail.

    The Indian and the Amish girl.

    *We talked for a long while that day. She told me her
mother had died the winter before, following her father to the
afterlife, and I felt overcome with sadness. I asked who cared
for her now, but she simply gestured around her, indicating, I
supposed, the whole village. For some reason, that made me
feel even closer to her. Not only were the Conestogas Chris-
tians, but apparently they were as dedicated to community as
we Amish were.*

"How sad, but also how lovely," Verna murmured.
I kept going.

*The following spring, Mother was busy at home and kept put-
ting off a visit to Indian Town, so I finally went with my
older brother instead. That time I took along a shawl I had
made as a gift for Konenquas. She was very grateful for it.
With a broad smile, she ran into her cabin and came back
with a small pottery bowl for me.*

    *On the way home, my brother commented on our ex-
change and asked if I knew that my friend's father had been
a white man, a trapper who had married into the tribe and*

lived with them until his death several years before from cholera. I hadn't known, but it made sense, given Konenquas's paler color of skin. It also explained why she knew English better than some of the other Indians.

I talked my brother into going back to Indian Town a few weeks later, and that time I brought along my handwork. Konenquas and I sat together, me knitting and her weaving a basket, as we chatted. We talked about many things, including the Lord Jesus, of whom she already knew thanks to the Quakers. I taught her a Scripture verse too, one my father had compelled me to memorize the week before. I tried teaching her how to spell more words in the dirt, but we didn't get very far before my brother insisted that we go. The next time I visited, I brought along a copy of the entire alphabet, upper and lower case, which I had carefully written out on paper just for her.

Konenquas was clever, and over my coming visits she managed to learn not just the alphabet but quite a few written words as well. Back at home, we hadn't much ink or paper to spare, but I gathered for her what I could and brought it along on my visits. I also taught her more Bible verses, which she memorized with ease.

In the following years, I was able to visit Konenquas often. If my mother wasn't going to Indian Town, one of my brothers would give me a ride, or occasionally my father would take me and then spend that time helping the Indians with repairs to their cabins. Father was always generous with his carpentry skills.

Over the next few years, I came to think of my friend Konenquas with the same fondness and familiarity as I did my closest Amish friends. Our lives were so different and yet, in all ways that were important, quite the same. We loved the Lord and our families and our communities. As we reached our teens, we also both began to long for homes and families

of our own. When we were in our late teens, not long af-
ter Gorg Bontrager had begun to court me, I learned that
Konenquas also had her eye on a special young man, an In-
dian brave known for his hunting skills. She married sooner
than I, but we still felt the camaraderie of being young and
in love with men whom we adored and wanted to be with
for a lifetime.

I paused there, thinking about that for a moment. What an amazing friendship they had forged, despite their differences.

Glancing back down, I saw that there were only two pages left to the whole book, and that the next paragraphs moved away from the personal and back into a more factual recounting of historical events.

Verna needed a break before we got into that final section, so I set the chapbook aside, went into the kitchen, and put the water on. I stretched my neck and back until the kettle whistled, my mind a million miles away. We couldn't risk having beverages near the chapbook, so once our tea was ready, Verna and I sat in companionable silence at the table, both of us lost in thought as we sipped. After that, I cleaned and dried our cups and put them away, washed my hands, and then we returned to the living room and the last remaining part of our ancestor's tale.

As I began to read, my heart sank. I'd already known the facts of the massacre and the events leading up to it, of course, but reading them in context—by someone who lived through it—was still quite disturbing. The words were all about the rising tensions between settlers and Indians, not just in Pennsylvania but throughout the region. By Abigail's account, violent acts and misdeeds occurred on both sides—killings, kidnappings, and more—as slowly and steadily the settlers continued to advance west-ward, often taking for themselves lands along the way that had previously been granted to the Indians by treaties. The Conestogas remained peace-ful, but as other Indian tribes grew more resentful of the British, especially the Senecas, they mounted more and more attacks against the Colonists on the western frontier.

Ultimately, the French aligned with the Indians against the British, and the violence escalated as people were killed on both sides. The French and Indian War, as that time is now called, finally drew to a close in 1763, the year Abigail turned twenty. But even after that, suspicions between settlers and Indians remained high.

My voice slowed as I read the final words of the chapbook.

> *I worried so for Konenquas's safety, but there was nothing I could do—indeed, I was not even able to go and see her for almost a year. Though Father kept tabs on our Indian friends and brought them food from time to time, he had decided to call my own visits to Indian Town to a temporary halt, for safety reasons.*
>
> *By the end of the war, those around us, even some who were Plain, were frightened and suspicious of the Indians—all Indians, even the peaceful Conestogas. At one point, though the war was over, Father confided to Gorg and me that the Conestogas were afraid to go hunting or leave their village with their weapons, fearing that settlers would think they were on the attack.*
>
> *I was appalled. Yes, Indian tribes were bringing harm to settlers near and far, but the peace-loving Conestogas hadn't been involved in any conflicts with any settlers, as far as we knew. Besides, the land where they lived had been given to them in the treaty with William Penn. They had a legal right to be there. Yet that land was slowly being encroached upon and taken from them until they barely had enough game land from which to feed themselves.*
>
> *All along, Father insisted to any who would listen that the Conestogas were not involved in the conflict between the settlers and the Indians and that we could trust them completely.*
>
> *How very wrong he had been.*

To my shock, the story ended there.

Confused, I flipped back to see if I had missed something, but I hadn't. Those were the final words of the book, at the bottom of the page: *How very wrong he had been.* There was no explanation, nothing further to make sense of that astonishing statement.

"That's it," I said, dumbfounded.

"What? It can't be. What kind of an ending is that?"

Verna was as doubtful as I was, but when I flipped that last page over to prove there was nothing after it, I gasped.

As I held the chapbook open wide, I saw that there *had* been pages there, as many as we'd already read through—but those pages had been cut off and removed from the book, leaving just a tiny margin of paper along the center so as not to destroy the binding.

Someone had taken out the rest, someone who wanted to hide the truth of Abigail's story.

EIGHT

I held out hope that the missing pages of the chapbook were among the papers in the boxes, but they were not. After another week of sorting and purging, Verna and I hadn't found anything else of value, and we were almost finished. That Monday afternoon as I left Susie's, I took the chapbook and the letter with me to a store and had three photocopies made—one for Verna, one for Zed, and one to keep in my purse, where I'd have it handy for reference. That was my best bet for protecting the originals. That night I wrote to Zed and told him all about the letter and the chapbook, added his copies to the envelope, and stuck on a few extra stamps to cover the weight.

The next morning, I put the letter in the mailbox as I was leaving for Susie's house. Once there, I gave Verna her copy and tried to return the originals as well, but she insisted I hang on to them for safekeeping. I tucked them in my bag, promising to put them away in a drawer in my room once I was home.

After coffee, we returned to our search through the boxes, but we were nearly to the bottom of the last one. As we dug in, I could see that Verna was still feeling optimistic that we might find something, but I'd been growing far less hopeful. If the missing pages weren't here, or at least among the rest of the papers at Rod's farm, then we were out of luck.

I pulled my copy of the chapbook from my purse and studied it, a thought coming to me as I did. Turning to her, I asked if perhaps there might have been more copies back then than just this one.

"It was published, after all," I added. "Maybe one ended up in a local library, or a historical society."

Verna's brow furrowed. "I think it unlikely any copies would have survived except within the family. Libraries weren't common back then, and I doubt any museum collections would have been started."

That made sense, but I still felt frustrated. I stood and stretched as I wondered where else we could turn.

Verna hadn't had breakfast when I arrived, so I reheated the oatmeal left on the stove and started the kettle for a cup of tea.

As she settled into a chair at the kitchen table, she told me she hadn't slept well over the weekend.

"It's not normal for me. I usually sleep like a log."

"Are you feeling all right?"

"*Ya*," she said, but she didn't sound very convincing.

After I served her, I sat down across the table with my own cup of tea. "I'm so eager for those other boxes. Do you suppose Carl could go get them this week? Or should I ask my *daed* to do it?"

Verna took one small bite and then put her spoon back in her bowl. "No, Carl said he would get over there as soon as he could. Let's give him till Monday. If he hasn't gone by then, maybe you can ask your father instead."

I told myself to be patient. Even though Susie had volunteered her husband to get the boxes, I knew he was a busy guy. Besides, I had other things I should be doing anyway, namely more sewing and handwork for the shop.

Thinking of that, I remembered the two dresses I'd brought from home for Verna and hopped up from the table to get them, pulling them from my bag and returning to the kitchen. She had taken her bowl to the sink and was scraping what was left into the slop bucket. Even though this house was in town, the family kept a pig and some chickens in their shed out back.

"Here you go," I said, holding up the dresses. "These were Linda's when she was younger. I had a feeling they might fit you better than the ones you've been wearing."

"*Ach*." Verna smiled. "*Danke*."

I had already altered one of Verna's own dresses for her on Friday, but I thought it might help to have a few more. Linda had outgrown them by the time she was thirteen, but they looked to be a pretty good fit for our tiny great-aunt.

"Have you lost weight since you moved here?" I draped the dresses over a kitchen chair.

"Some. Susie's family doesn't eat the big meals I was used to on the farm, which is best. I'm not working like I used to, either."

I couldn't imagine she'd been doing that much before moving here.

The sound of the front door opening caught my attention, and then Susie's voice called out. "Izzy? Can you come up to the shop for a minute?"

"Sure," I called. "I'll be right there."

The door thunked closed and I got Verna settled on the couch, tucking the quilt in around her. The house felt draftier today than it did most mornings.

After telling her I'd be right back, I grabbed my cape and hurried to the shop.

When I entered, I spotted Susie standing behind the counter. "I have someone who wanted to meet you," she told me.

The only other person in the shop was a woman with curly brown hair piled high on her head. She wore a bright green coat with a pink scarf.

Susie stepped toward the woman. "This is Izzy Mueller," she said. Turning toward me, she said, "And this is Marcia Johnson."

The woman extended her hand. I took it, shaking it quickly.

"I was admiring your work," Marcia said. "You have a very distinct style."

My face grew warm at her praise.

Susie must have sensed my discomfort because she said, "Marcia is a costume designer."

"Oh?"

"Yes," the woman said, her tone vaguely aristocratic. "I make costumes for the Walnut."

I must have given her a blank stare because she added, "The Walnut Street Theatre, in Philly? Oldest theater in America?"

Although I was intrigued, all I could manage to say was, "Oh."

"I told Marcia you'd made some costumes too, although I couldn't remember the details," Susie said.

I nodded, my face growing even warmer. "They were for a film a friend made. It won an award and an endowment from the Pennsylvania Film Festival."

"Wonderful!" Marcia beamed. "I'm even more impressed. You must be so proud."

She meant it as a compliment, but I was mortified. Pride was not a desirable trait for an Amish woman. I froze in embarrassment—I hadn't meant to brag—but Marcia didn't seem to notice. Instead, she just had some questions about several of my pieces, including some unusual stitches I had used in one of my runners. We chatted for a while, and eventually she made her way over to the cash register, where Susie began ringing her up.

Trying to be helpful, as we talked I folded and bagged some of the larger items she was buying. To my astonishment, when we were all done, her total came to nearly a thousand dollars. She didn't even blink as she whipped out a credit card and handed it over. Once the sale was final, we both thanked her profusely. After she was gone, Susie turned and gave me a quick hug.

"I told you that having you around would mean a boost in sales!"

I smiled in return, my face growing warm. That smiled lingered as I left the shop and made my way back to the house.

When I got there, I stepped inside and called out to Verna as I hung my cape. She'd been resting on the couch, but when I came into the living room, she sat up straight and greeted me.

The final box was right where we'd left it, with just the last few inches to go. First came a letter and then more receipts—one from a general store; one from a Mr. Collins, who had sold hay to Verna's father; and one for a steer. Next was an old newspaper clipping about the end of the war in 1945.

"Oh, that was a glorious day," Verna said. "I remember it well. To have the war over, at last, was such a relief."

She was quiet for a long moment, and I asked if she was tired.

"A little. Maybe we should take another break. I'll doze again here on the couch and you can do your handwork. Susie was a little miffed at me yesterday that I didn't give you any time to do your embroidery."

"Oh, I worked at home yesterday afternoon. I got a lot done." I'd kept my promise to myself and my mother to stay focused. Besides the embroidery, I'd altered a suit jacket for an *Englisch* neighbor too.

Verna lifted her legs onto the couch and curled up for a nap. It seemed she was asleep in no time. I covered her with a second quilt and then retrieved my bag from by the door, settled down in the rocking chair, and got to work on my embroidery, thinking about Verna's other boxes and how soon we might get our hands on them.

After a while, my thoughts were interrupted by a sharp snore from Verna. I looked up as she turned to her other side and then quietly settled back to sleep.

She just seemed so tiny lying there, yet larger than life too, considering all she'd given to others—and to me. Not for the first time, I thought how glad I was to have taken this job. I had always liked her, but we had become much closer in the past week and a half. She had so many stories to tell, and it seemed that every letter, receipt, and document we ran across sent her off in a new direction. Some folks might have found our conversations tedious, but I had enjoyed listening to her as we sorted out the boxes together.

I worked on my embroidery for an hour and then decided to take a break to stretch my back. As Verna continued to sleep, I wandered around the room, finally coming to a stop at the last box, which we'd left open. I looked down at it. There were only a couple of newspaper articles at the bottom, with something curious poking out from beneath them. The clippings were both Lancaster County columns from the *Budget*, maybe even written by a scribe who was a friend of Verna's like some of the others we'd found. They didn't look that old.

I reached down and pulled the last item out and then studied it for a moment. I had a feeling it was a bookmark, but one made of cloth instead of paper, its words embroidered rather than printed. It looked really old, and feeling it between my fingers, I decided it was constructed of some sort of stiff linen, ivory colored, though it may have been white at some point. The words, "My help cometh from the Lord" had been stitched into the front in a beautiful script. The whole thing was lovely, except for a stain at the bottom that was perhaps water but maybe coffee or tea.

If I made some bookmarks like these, would they sell well in Susie's shop? I kept it out, eager to ask Susie what she thought. First, of course, I would show it to Verna when she awoke and find out if she'd ever seen it before or knew anything about it.

Eventually, I went back to my embroidery. I liked working alone, and yet it was comforting to have my great-aunt so close. I felt content for the first time in months—and it was no wonder. I'd made a new friend. I enjoyed spending time with her. I had time for my handwork—at least today. And I was intrigued by her boxes of documents.

Plus, it was good for me to see that Verna had a fulfilling life without a marriage and children, because the more I thought about it, the more I had to wonder if I might end up going down that same path. Until my feelings for Zed changed, I had never really longed for a husband or kids, at least not the way other girls my age did. I supposed that made sense, considering how much I liked order and calmness. I'd never done well with chaos. I was certain I wasn't made to be an Amish mother—at least not to a huge brood of children. Of course, Zed would make an excellent father. But he was Mennonite, which meant that the one man I did want to marry was not an option for me.

I sat back and sucked in a deep breath, confronting a hard truth I'd been ignoring for weeks. I was in love with a man who wasn't Amish.

I wanted to *stay* Amish—which meant I couldn't marry Zed. But if I couldn't marry him, then I didn't want to marry at all. Did that mean I was destined to be alone for the rest of my life?

If so, at least being around Verna had given me hope for a fulfilling existence outside of marriage, as she'd had. With that thought, I returned to the task at hand and soon I was calmed by the rhythm of my needle-work—stick, pull, stick, under, stick, over, pull.

Every once in a while Verna made a little noise in her sleep, but she didn't move an inch. She usually napped in the afternoon, not so early in the day, so after she'd been sleeping two hours, I decided to wake her up. There was a pot of soup for lunch, so first I went into the kitchen and put it on the stove.

Before it began to simmer, I returned to the living room and placed my hand on her shoulder. "*Aenti* Verna, it's almost time for lunch."

She didn't stir.

"*Aenti* Verna," I said again, growing a little alarmed. She was fine, right? Just a sound sleeper.

I shook her shoulder a little. She was still.

I touched her hand. It wasn't icy cold, but it wasn't warm, either. My stomach dropped. I watched for a breath. Nothing. I put my hand under Verna's nose. My heart dropped another notch.

Remember your training, remember your training, I told myself as I gripped her wrist. Felt for a pulse. Nothing. I tried to think of what the next step should be, but my mind was a blank.

Stepping back, I drew in a ragged breath and then turned toward the door, walking quickly. By the time I reached the front porch, I was running. By the time I got across the alley and rushed through the vines, fighting them off as if they were trying to grab me, I was sobbing. I burst through the back door to Susie's shop, unable to speak.

I managed to catch my breath and explain what happened, but Susie didn't seem alarmed at all. "*Ach,* she's a heavy sleeper. And she has poor circulation. You probably just overreacted."

"Would you check on her?" I took a deep breath as I dabbed at my tears.

"*Ya.* Watch the shop for me."

I readily agreed. Thankfully, it was empty. I stayed, waiting for Susie and stumbling around the shop like a sleepwalker.

Verna was fine. Just fine. She was a heavy sleeper, like Susie said. That's all this was.

Feeling as if I were moving in slow motion, I forced myself to calm down and focus on the items around me. I stepped toward a collection of faceless dolls that were for sale. Next to them was a rack of *kapps*. I wondered if *Englisch* people bought them. Not many Amish traded in Susie's shop.

I was examining a lace doily, still telling myself Verna was fine, when Susie returned to the shop and told me she was not.

"She's passed," Susie whispered, her face as pale as I'd ever seen it. She moved to the counter and reached for the phone before meeting my eyes. Given my history, she probably expected me to become hysterical.

Instead I just grew numb.

Susie made a call, though whether it was to a friend or relative or the mortuary, I wasn't sure. My head was pounding too loud to hear.

After she hung up, she closed up the shop and we both headed back to the house, ducking low under the grape vines as we went. All I could think was that Verna had been dead even when I touched her cooling hand. How could she be so alive and present this morning and then gone, just like that?

"In a way, it's a relief, I guess," Susie said as we reached the porch.

I froze.

At least she had the decency to blush a little at her own words. "I mean, not a relief that she's dead, just that she went in her sleep. You always wonder with old people if they'll get something painful and horrible and suffer through the end."

"But she wasn't even sick," I whispered.

Susie shrugged. "Apparently, something was wrong. She had lost a lot of weight recently." She opened the door. "I hope I don't sound callous. I'm just being realistic."

I didn't move.

"Come on in."

I shook my head. "I'll wait here," I said, not even sure who we were waiting for. She seemed to understand, because she reached out to give my hand a squeeze and then slipped inside without another word.

Standing there on the stoop, I thought of the other deaths in my life.

Phyllis, my favorite patient.

Freddy, Zed's father.

My grandfather, when I was just a kid.

His loving wife, my grandmother Nettie, six months after him.

I remembered again the morning *Mammi* Nettie passed. *Mamm* had seemed a little relieved, much the way Susie did now. Unlike Verna, my grandmother had suffered and my *mamm* had spent months and months caring for her in every possible way.

Maybe that's what Susie had been dreading. She was newly married, expecting a baby, and running her own shop. It would have been a hardship for her to care for Verna if she were too ill, and obviously I wouldn't have been much help if things had become really bad.

I shivered, even though the fall day had grown warmer.

A minute later Susie joined me on the porch, a bowl in her hands. "Why don't you eat some soup," she said, thrusting it toward me.

I shook my head, my stomach roiling. "*Ach*, I'm sorry. I forgot all about it. Did it burn?"

"No, I smelled it cooking and turned off the fire in time." Again, she pushed it toward me, but my hands remained at my sides.

"You eat it. But thanks anyway."

She brought the bowl closer to her chest and then took a bite, chewed, and swallowed. "I made this soup from one of Verna's recipes."

I shivered again.

Susie kept talking between bites. "She was always so good to me. When I was a girl, sometimes I'd go stay with her for weeks at a time in the summer."

I nodded, feeling a little envious that the history they had shared was so much more extensive than Verna's and my own.

"She taught me so much, more than my own *mamm* did. All about gardening and canning. Cooking. Sewing and crocheting and knitting. She's the one who taught me to really enjoy handwork, to see it as a time to be quiet and contemplative." Susie swallowed hard, adding, "She was really something."

She set the spoon in the bowl, her face full of grief.

"I don't understand how she could be perfectly fine one day and then be dead the next," I said. Or how she could be on the couch in the same room with me and just *die* like that. I shivered again.

"It's part of life, Izzy. You know that."

I did. Maybe not as clearly as Susie did—maybe because she'd been through death more times before than I had—but all Amish children grew up knowing that death, of both people and animals, was to be expected. Still I shivered again.

"Are you cold?" Susie asked. "We should go back inside."

I shook my head. "I really don't want to."

"You can go on home. Carl said he would call the mortuary and then head here himself. They'll probably both arrive soon."

"I'll wait." I couldn't leave Susie all alone.

"Do you want me to call your *daed*?"

I shook my head again. "I'm fine. I promise. Once they get here, I can drive myself home."

"If you say so." Bowl in hand, Susie opened the screen door and stepped back inside. Here she was in a family way, the one who had taken Verna in, and she was doing fine. Why was I a basket case once again?

I leaned against the porch wall by the door, feeling the cool bricks against my back.

Susie returned a minute later. "She looks so peaceful."

"Do you think she's in heaven?" I whispered. We weren't supposed to assume that's where everyone would go. That was up to God.

"She lived a more godly life than anyone I've ever known. Although maybe that's easier when one doesn't have a husband or kids." She chuckled as if she'd made a joke and then patted her stomach. We stood in silence for a moment until a black hearse turned down the alley. The people from the mortuary had made it here first.

A wave of nausea overtook me. I knew I wasn't cut out to be a caretaker. Why had I given it another try? I needed to concentrate on sewing and handwork, which I had no choice but to do exclusively now that this job was at an end.

Susie hurried down the steps as two men, both dressed in suits, climbed from the hearse. She spoke to them, and then they unloaded a gurney from the back. I stepped to the side of the porch as they passed by. They nodded at me, in unison, both solemnly.

I meant to follow them into the house, but I couldn't. I stayed frozen in place until they came back out. It wasn't until they were at the back of the hearse that my feet began to move, but by the time I reached the bottom step they had already slid Verna's body inside.

"*Danke,*" I whispered to her, knowing she wasn't there to hear. "For the companionship, even though it wasn't nearly long enough."

Susie talked with the older of the two men while I hurried back into the house and collected my things, including the history books of Zed's I'd intended to read to Verna.

When I came back out, Susie was still talking, so I went to hitch up the buggy. A few minutes later, I stepped around to the front of the house as the second man climbed into the hearse and they drove away.

"Can I help you with anything?" I called out to Susie.

She shook her head. "I'll make a few phone calls. The community will take it from here."

I hesitated, wishing her husband would hurry up and get home.

"You can go, Izzy," she urged. "I'm okay. Really."

I started to refuse but was saved by the clomping of a horse's hooves. Turning, I felt a rush of relief at the sight of Carl. Susie wouldn't be alone.

A few minutes later, as I turned my own buggy onto the highway, I thought of the boxes of papers that still waited to be searched over at Rod's farm. Somehow, the search seemed so much less important now that Verna wasn't a part of it. I began to cry again, great big tears that rolled off my chin.

Why hadn't God left me out of this one? There was no reason for me to get to know Verna so much better at the end of her life. I'd had my heart broken again, for nothing.

I planned to go home to my little room, open my Bible and journal, and never leave again.

NINE

It was God's will." *Mamm* stood under the clothesline with one of Stephen's shirts in her hand. Her face was dry, her expression matter-of-fact. I, however, had tears streaming down my cheeks as I clutched Zed's books, my handwork bag slung over my shoulder and my cape unfastened in the warm breeze of that mid-October day.

"But why did He have to involve me? Why didn't He have her die two weeks ago? Before she and I had a chance to get so close?"

Mamm gave me one of her looks as she pinned the shirt to the line. "Don't question God."

I hugged Zed's books even tighter.

"Honestly, Izzy," *Mamm* took another shirt from the basket. "Verna was my mother's sister. You've known her your whole life. What difference would two weeks have made?"

I couldn't explain to her how much closer Verna and I had grown during the time we'd shared together. I had never realized until then that she was interested in the same things I was—like handwork and history. I felt as though I'd lost so much more than just her. I'd lost all of her stories and everything that happened to her. She'd told me many tales as we went through the papers together, and it felt as if I had lived through it all with her. Her childhood on the farm. The Great Depression. The home front during World War II.

She had also been a fellow sleuth in the search for my connection to the past. Now I didn't know if I could bear to continue on with that search without her.

"Izzy?" *Mamm* actually had a look of sympathy on her face. "Remember that this too will pass."

I knew that. It didn't help to hear it.

The visitation and funeral were held two days later at the Westler farm, the home where Verna had lived until she moved in with Susie. I wasn't planning to go, but my parents insisted, using that tone of voice that left no thought of doing otherwise.

Somehow I managed to get through everything without completely falling apart, but only by forcing myself to go numb. The hardest moment for me was at the cemetery, when we first got there and I caught sight of the waiting hole in the ground. In that moment it struck me how *final* death was. Verna was now gone forever. Phyllis, forever. My grandmother Nettie had left me forever.

After the graveside service was complete, my family insisted we return to the farm for the post-funeral meal. I just wanted to go home and be alone, but *Mamm* wouldn't hear of it. She said that in this time of mourning it was important to be with family and community.

I swallowed back any further objections, deciding that though she might be able to make me go with them to the Westlers' place, she couldn't force me to interact much once we were there. When we arrived, I got out of the buggy and broke off from my family in search of Susie. I hated to be tacky, but I wanted to make sure she knew Verna intended for all the family papers to pass down to me.

Fortunately, I didn't even have to ask. She saw me coming and said the same thing herself—and that Rod knew as well. I promised that either my *daed* or I would take the boxes at her house off her hands within the next few weeks.

Once we finished talking, I glanced around to make sure no one was watching me, and then I slipped back out and walked over to where our buggy had been parked. I climbed inside.

Not one person seemed to notice. There in the scruffy velvet- and leather-lined quiet of the buggy's interior, I settled in all alone, pulled out my bag, and tried to start in on some embroidery. But then my tears began to fall, so I set my handwork aside and let them come. I cried hard, not just for Verna but for all of my losses—not just the deaths but Zed too, though he was a loss of a different sort. I must have cried for half an hour before finally winding down. Then, feeling utterly spent, I dug out some tissues, dried my face, and tried to return my focus to the needle and fabric in my lap.

Time passed, and eventually I was lost in the sewing rhythm that soothed me. I looked around occasionally, and as it turned out, my little hideaway was a pretty good vantage point for all of the goings-on. The meal had been served inside, but the October day had grown very warm, and soon people began to filter back out one by one. Children ran off to play in the big front yard. Teens clustered in giggling groups nearby. I saw some of the men move toward the barns and other adults just standing around and talking.

Several members of Zed's family were there, including his cousin Ada and her brood, and his grandmother Frannie, a tough old bird who had survived a stroke several years before. Frannie was walking with the help of a cane, her daughter Marta close at her side, and as the two of them made their way toward the line of parked cars up ahead, I couldn't help thinking that the old woman looked even less healthy than Verna had on the morning of the day she died. That thought again plunged me into sadness. I adored Frannie Lantz and couldn't bear the thought of her passing too.

Frannie and I had first come to know each other four years before, when I worked as a mother's helper for her granddaughter Ada. Ada had married Will Gundy, a widower with three young children, and in the beginning, as Ada got used to caring for a new husband, a thirteen-year-old daughter, and a pair of four-year-old twins, Will had insisted on bringing in a helper for her.

I had enjoyed that job, hectic as it was, but my favorite days at the Gundy household were when Frannie was added into the mix. She lived in the *daadi haus* at her daughter Klara's, but no one wanted her to be home alone, so whenever Klara had somewhere to go, she or her husband would bring Frannie over to stay with us at Ada's for the day.

Of course, I had been drawn to Frannie right away, as I always was to older folks. She wasn't much of a storyteller—it felt as though she held back, as if many of her memories were too painful to share—but she was always very kind to me and answered my questions as best she could. Most of all, it was just fun to watch her with her new step-great-grandchildren. She had a way with Christy and with the twins, Mel and Mat, that simply melted my heart.

Now I watched as she and Marta reached Marta's car, and my attention was so focused on them that I didn't see my own father approaching the buggy until he was at the window, a startled expression on his face.

"Izzy? What are you doing in there?"

I felt my face flush with heat, embarrassed that he'd caught me in hiding.

"I just needed some peace and quiet," I muttered, and I was relieved when he didn't press the matter any further.

He hitched up the horse, pulled us out from the line of buggies, and headed up the drive, coming to a stop where my mother and siblings were waiting to board. As they climbed in, my mother glanced at me in surprise but didn't say a word. I had a feeling she was putting two and two together and figuring out I had skipped the meal, but she was too embarrassed to fuss at me about it because she didn't want to admit she hadn't even noticed until that moment that I hadn't been there.

Soon we were on our way home, the rhythmic clomping of the horse easing everyone into quiet contemplation and soothing my own frayed nerves. It took a while to get there, but once our driveway was in sight, I felt myself exhaling deeply.

I knew I'd need to venture out to Susie's soon to deliver some finished goods, but otherwise my hope was not to leave home again for a very long time. I had no desire to find another job, at least not as a caregiver. I'd struck out twice in two months, both times dramatically. Why push my luck for a third?

A week later, I was sitting in my room doing my handwork when *Mamm* appeared in the doorway, her hands on her hips. "Anyone who isolates herself the way you have would be depressed," she said.

"I'm not depressed."

"Then why are you crying all the time?"

"I'm just feeling things rather strongly right now. That's all."

"Plan some outings or I'll plan some for you," *Mamm* said. "By tomorrow. But enough of this moping around. We buried Verna a week ago."

I didn't answer and she left. The rain had returned and beat against the small-paned windows. The cold had arrived too. I'd tried to ward it off with the quilt I'd wrapped up in, but my fingers were icy as I tried to manipulate my needle.

Plan some outings? I couldn't imagine anything I wanted to do less, even though I knew it was time to make a delivery to Susie's. I'd had some items ready to go for several days, in fact, but I had been putting that particular errand off in the hopes that my *daed* might take pity and run it for me. I knew Susie had to be getting impatient, as her Christmas rush would start before Thanksgiving, which was just a month away.

Putting a visit to her out of my mind for now, I continued to work, my thoughts looping, just like woven fabric, from Verna to Zed to Verna and back to Zed, until just before lunchtime when my father interrupted me. "Come see my shop. It's completely finished."

"How about after lunch?" I kept my head down.

"No, come now. You need the fresh air, girl."

He wasn't usually so direct, but I knew he was right. I put my things down and shed the quilt, following him to the mudroom, where I put on my cape and headed outside. Thomas had been playing on the front porch, and when he heard the back door slam, he hurried around, taking my hand.

When we neared the barn, Thomas let go of me and ran ahead of us to open up the side door to the shop as rain began to fall. When we stepped inside, I realized that not only was the shop finished, it was already in use. The scent of sawdust filled the air, and *Daed* had three tables halfway completed. In my contemplative state I'd missed that he'd finished getting the new place up and running, much less that he'd acquired orders. I was so glad. I knew the family finances weighed on both my parents.

He opened the door to the other half and stepped aside so I could go first. Another table, nearly finished, sat in the middle. He'd been staining it.

"Impressive," I said.

He said, humbly, "God's provided some work. That's good."

I met his eyes, embarrassed at my recent self-absorption. "I'm sorry I didn't get out here before now, *Daed*. I should've asked to see it instead of waiting for you to make me come out to take a look."

He started to say something in response, but then he held his tongue and simply smiled. "You're here now."

Outside a car turned into the driveway.

"I'll go see who it is," Thomas said, running out the door to the other room. A second later the outside door opened and slammed.

As we stepped into the workroom, Thomas returned. "It's Zed's *mamm*," he said, hovering in the doorway.

I frowned, not wanting to see anyone right now, especially Marta, who would only remind me of Zed and how much I missed him. But it was our way to be hospitable, so I squared my shoulders and followed my father and little brother out into the rain. Holding my hood out over my face, the icy water pelting my hand, Thomas and I waved her over as *Daed* called out, "Come into the house!"

Thomas ran ahead again, holding his straw hat atop his head with one hand, splashing through the puddles in his black rubber boots, the mud splattering up his pants and onto the back of his jacket.

Marta stepped to my side and we hurried along in silence with *Daed* walking behind us. My stomach began to churn as I speculated what would bring her here. Had something happened to Zed?

Once we were inside, my *mamm* beamed at Marta, her warm and welcoming expression reminding me that the two women shared a bond of a very unique sort. Marta was a midwife, and she had delivered all of my mother's children except for Thomas and Sadie. Some other midwife I didn't know had delivered my oldest sister, and Marta's niece, a nurse-midwife named Lexie, had been the one to deliver Thomas. I had been at school that day, much to my disappointment, but Sadie and Becky had both been home.

Though she always made an effort to be kind to me, Marta tended to come across rather abrupt and aloof, at least to me. I'd always been intimidated by her, but then again, I had a feeling there was a side to her I'd simply never seen. There had to be *some* reason that every one of her clients loved her so dearly. Zed did too. They had an easy relationship. I'd never heard him say anything negative about his mother at all.

Mamm took Marta's cape and hung it on the company peg, inviting her to stay for lunch as she did.

"I'd like that very much," Marta said. From her body language, I had the feeling she was here to talk to *Mamm*, not me.

Daed must have sensed it too, because he disappeared into the living room, probably to get some work done at his desk. *Mamm* sent Thomas to change his clothes. Without saying anything, I went back to my room, rewrapping my quilt around my core and taking up my embroidery, trying to imagine what Marta was doing here. It didn't seem to be an emergency. Surely she would have said right away if there had been some tragedy.

Fifteen minutes later, *Mamm* stood in the doorway to my room and told me to come set the table. She seemed, as she usually did these days, annoyed with me. I untangled myself, put down my work, and shuffled into the kitchen. After washing my hands, I set myself to the task.

Mamm stirred the pot on the stove, sending up the aroma of some kind of soup. My mouth watered. She was a wonderful cook, much better than I ever hoped to be. I grew distracted while cooking. It took too much time, keeping me away from my little room and work I enjoyed.

Mamm put the lid back on the pot and turned toward Marta. "Are you off to see a client this afternoon?"

"No," she said, tucking her hands into her apron pockets. Her gray hair was pulled back in a tidy bun under her rounded Mennonite *kapp*, and she wore a beige sweater over her blue print dress. "I'm taking the day off."

I counted out the plates from the cupboard and started toward the table.

"I'll do those," Marta said, reaching out her hands.

I transferred the stack to her and stepped back toward the cupboard.

As we all worked, the conversation between *Mamm* and Marta moved to the subject of our neighbor's son, Ben Yoder. He had grown up Amish but then went off to community college and then to Goshen, just like Zed, only he had majored in some sort of science and then gone on to medical school.

"He's still studying?" Mamm asked.

"He's finishing his residency—internal medicine. I think he only has another month or so."

"Oh," *Mamm* said.

I put the glasses on the table and returned to the cupboard. Ben's *mamm* and *daed* were in our district. I knew some Amish-raised people who had chosen not to join the church and gone on to further their education, but he was the only one I had ever heard of who had taken it this far and become a doctor. The Yoders seemed neither embarrassed by, nor impressed with, their son. Just matter of fact. One time I overheard his mother tell another woman, "It's what God intended for him." I didn't hear the other woman's question, but I could guess she wasn't minding her own business. Ben's mother's response was gracious, though, and, I believed, honest.

Still, I was sure it must have hurt his parents, on some level, for him not to join the church and become Amish himself. I knew it would hurt my parents if one of us didn't. I also knew the five of us who hadn't yet, likely would. Sometimes I forgot I hadn't already. I'd always wanted to please God. I had an essential relationship with Him, telling Him about my worries—over and over at times. I found comfort in the Scriptures—over and over too.

I put the last glass on and then counted out the bowls.

Marta asked about my siblings and how they were getting along, and *Mamm* gave a quick rundown as she sliced a loaf of freshly baked bread. She said that Melvin was courting a girl close to where he was working, that Becky didn't plan to teach next year, and that Sadie's youngest was finally sleeping through the night. Then, most likely because she didn't want to do all the talking, she asked about Ella, Marta's daughter who was married now and living in Indiana on an old family farm called the Home

Place. The property included a bakery and apparently Ella prepared her incredible treats daily and sold them to an eager clientele.

"Well, that's one of the reasons I'm here," Marta said. "Ella needs some extra help, a caregiver of sorts. And she and I both thought of Izzy."

I fumbled a bowl and it clattered onto a plate, rattling until I put my hand on top of it, settling it.

Mamm turned back to Marta, who was counting out spoons, knives, and forks. "Oh?"

Marta stepped back to the table. "Ella will need help for only a couple of weeks. My cousin Rosalee lives with Ella and Luke and works in the bakery, but yesterday she fell from a ladder and broke both her hip and fibula. Thankfully, the leg break isn't bad, but she will be in a walking cast for a few weeks. With Thanksgiving and Christmas coming up, Ella has more orders than she and Rosalee could handle as it was."

"I don't bake," I interjected. I used to like to when I was younger, but I didn't anymore. Over the years I'd burned more things than I could count.

Marta shook her head. "Ella can handle the bakery, but not if she's spending all of her time taking care of Rosalee. She needs a caregiver—"

"I don't do that anymore either," I blurted out.

"Izzy, stop." *Mamm* held her wooden spoon in midair.

I bowed my head and headed to the drawer for the napkins.

Marta looked at me with what seemed to be understanding. "Rosalee is in good health, Izzy, except for what just happened. But the breaks are so bad that she's going to be in a wheelchair with her leg straight out for a while."

I pondered that for a moment and then asked, "Isn't there a caregiver in their community who can do the work?"

Marta took a deep breath. "I'm sure there is, but there are some extenuating circumstances here."

"Oh?"

"Ella is expecting."

I couldn't help but smile at the news. Zed was going to be an uncle. I wondered if anyone had told him yet or if they just expected him to figure it out for himself once his sister began to show.

"Anyway, Ella remembers how good you were with her father, and she thinks you would fit in well in her household too."

"Fit in?"

Marta shrugged. "You're low-key, Izzy. Easy to be around. And that's exactly what she wants right now."

While I was flattered by the compliment, I wished I could feel as certain about this as Ella apparently did.

I met Marta's gaze and asked how old Rosalee was.

"Just over sixty," she replied.

Mamm looked at me. "See? That's not old at all. What do you think?"

I hated being put on the spot like that, so I mumbled, "I'm not sure," and then turned to busy myself with carefully folding each napkin and setting it into place at the table. As much as I didn't want to take on another caregiving role, there was one hugely important factor here. If I went to Indiana, I would be closer to Zed.

"How far is Ella's farm from Goshen College?" I asked Marta, my face flushing as soon as the words were out of my mouth.

She didn't react one way or the other. She simply said, "I'm not sure exactly, but Zed spends a lot of weekends at Ella's, so it can't be too far."

I nodded, my heart beginning to pound in my chest.

Was it possible? Was this God's doing? Was He making a way for us to be together?

"I know what I'm thinking." *Daed* stood in the doorway, interrupting my thoughts. "You should go. You need a change of scenery."

That's exactly what I was starting to think too. My desire to be with Zed outweighed my extreme trepidation at taking on yet another caretaking position.

"What about my work for Susie?"

"You can mail it." With a small smile, he added, "It'll get to her faster than it does now."

We all fell silent after that, and then Marta gave me a kind smile and said, "Just think on it, Izzy. You don't have to answer right this second."

I nodded, grateful she understood the need to process my thoughts. She seemed to understand that my parents and I would have to discuss it a bit more among ourselves as well, because after lunch she insisted on doing the dishes, saying, "The three of you go talk."

Thomas kept Marta company at the sink, chattering away, while my parents and I went down the hall, past the bathroom and bedroom, to my little sewing room, where we could speak privately.

"I really think you should do this," *Mamm* said in a soft voice as she closed the door and leaned against it. "Not just because their family needs your help, but because you need to get up and out again. You've been hiding here at home for far too long. It's time to go back into the world."

Regardless of what they were declaring, I knew it was my decision. They couldn't force me to go.

On the other hand, I realized, they weren't working with all of the facts. Bottom line, if they knew I was in love with my best friend, a Mennonite, would they still be urging me to go so strongly? They loved Zed, yes, but they also would recognize the conundrum here, that if he and I married, I would not be joining the Amish church. And that was huge.

For a moment I considered telling them the truth, but in the end I held back. I just couldn't bring myself to confess such a private matter of the heart to them when I'd barely gotten used to the idea myself. I felt bad about that, as though I were lying somehow. Then again, I was an adult now, and as an adult I was under no obligation to share the details of my thought life with my parents.

This decision would need to be mine alone because I was the only one with all the facts. I did love the idea of being so close—geographically—to Zed, and I could only hope my presence there would make us emotionally closer as well.

Unfortunately, there was the matter of living with Zed's sister, Ella, as she had always seemed so brash and pushy to me. Zed had mentioned several times in the past year or two how much she had softened since she'd moved to Indiana, converted to the Amish faith, and gotten married. I could only hope he was right. He also said her husband was a great guy, so there was that as well.

I didn't know anything about Rosalee, but the thought of caring for someone in relatively good health for a change was appealing to me. Of course, Verna had seemed in good health too, and look how that ended up. Then again, she was ninety-one, so statistically her chances of living much longer hadn't been great regardless.

At least Rosalee was younger—just a decade older than *Daed*. "Marta's sure nothing else is wrong with her?"

"That's what she said." *Mamm* crossed her arms over her sweater.

I chewed on my lower lip. "How will I get to Indiana?"

"The bus, I suppose," *Daed* said. "We can ask Marta what she has in mind."

My gaze shifted to the window and the rain pelting the glass. One more good reason to take the job was that it wouldn't hurt for me to get a break from *Mamm*. I knew she loved me, and I loved her, but our personalities were so different, and we were clashing more and more all the time.

"Izzy?" *Mamm*'s voice was pitched high. It was clear I was getting on her nerves even at that moment.

Even *Daed*'s voice held a hint of exasperation. "Are you still with us?"

I turned away from the window, slowly, and nodded.

"Then it's settled?" he asked.

"*Ya*, it's settled. I'll go to Indiana."

TEN

The long bus trip never happened, thanks to a family in our next district over who had hired a driver to take them to a wedding in Indiana. I was able to ride along with them, but by the time we arrived, I wished I *had* taken the bus, even though this way was faster and cheaper. People have the idea that Amish children are well behaved. Maybe they are compared to other American kids, but twelve hours in a van with seven children aged three to thirteen about drove me out the window. I pretended to sleep for the last three hours as an escape. We'd left at four a.m., so dozing, as best I could with the racket going on, wasn't a problem.

By the time the van reached our destination, my nerves were frayed. I may have saved some money, but I hoped I still had my sanity too.

The driver turned down the lane toward the Home Place, past the bakery that had a sign out front—Plain Treats. The words were carved and painted white.

As we continued up the driveway toward the house, through the dusk, I could make out woods to my left and an orchard to my right. Ahead was a huge house.

"What a nice farm," the driver said as he pulled to a stop.

It was.

I climbed out of the van, saying a farewell to each member of the family, and met the driver at the back of the van, where he retrieved my suitcase. I'd already paid him my share when he picked me up that morning, so I thanked him and started toward the front porch.

"Over here, Izzy!" Ella hurried down the steps from the house's back door, waving with one hand and wiping the other on her apron. Her brown eyes shone as a tall, dark-haired man appeared from around the back and joined her—her husband, Luke, I was sure. As I came closer, I saw a pile of lumber behind the house and realized he was still holding a saw in his hand.

Ella surged toward me, giving me a hug. Zed had never mentioned Ella's pregnancy, neither in person nor in his letters, so I had assumed it was new news. But from the feel of her belly against me, she was further along than a few months, more like six or seven. Of course, it was rude to ask or even bring it up, so I held my tongue and kept my eyes on her face as we pulled apart.

"This is Luke," she said, nodding toward him.

I'd heard he was handsome—but that was an understatement. Under his hat, black hair showed that matched his beard. His gray eyes smiled as he gave me a nod and took my bag from me. "Pleased to meet you."

I nodded in return, repeating the sentiment. Luke seemed to be just as nice as Zed had told me he was.

"We'll put you downstairs," Ella said. "We've moved Rosalee down too." She nodded toward the pile of lumber. "Luke is building a ramp for when she's ready to come outside."

The stairs were steep, which meant the ramp would need to have a switchback, or maybe two. Either way, it was a big job.

"Come on in," Ella said, grabbing my hand. "I'm so glad you're here." She seemed genuinely happy to have me.

As I climbed the steps and followed her into the kitchen, the smell of roasting chicken greeted me. I had forgotten what an incredible cook Ella was until that moment, and my stomach rumbled as I breathed in the scent. Luke disappeared down a hall with my bag, and she pulled me around a large table and through an archway into the living room. "Rosalee is in here. She's so glad you were available to come out."

Seated in a wheelchair facing the window was a woman with a quilt wrapped around her shoulders.

"Izzy's arrived," Ella said, stopping beside the chair and leaning over a little.

For a moment I feared Rosalee was much more frail than I'd been led to believe, but then she put her hands on the wheels of the chair and, as Ella stepped backward, maneuvered it around by herself.

Rosalee's skin was nearly as pale as her white hair and *kapp*, but she appeared healthy otherwise, except for her right leg sticking out straight on a horizontal leg rest. "Welcome," she said, her voice strong. She smiled then, a broad, friendly expression considering the trauma she'd recently endured.

We exchanged greetings, and she seemed nice enough. After that, Ella suggested I get settled in my room and then meet them back in the kitchen. "We'll eat in about ten minutes."

I headed in the direction she told me, down the hall to the last door on the right. Halfway there, I turned back to see that Rosalee was stubbornly propelling her wheelchair toward the kitchen, despite Ella's offer of help. The older woman was having a bit of struggle, but I was still glad to see it. I doubted I'd have to encourage her to take responsibility for her independence as I cared for her.

When I reached my room, I saw that Luke had put my suitcase on the floor by the single bed. On the nightstand was an oil lamp I was tempted to use but decided I still had enough natural light—barely—to unpack my things. I hung my dresses on the pegs lining the wall opposite the bed and then placed my other things in the drawers of the small bureau. It took me only a few minutes. I stood at the window and peered out into the woods, overcome with a deep sense of yearning, wondering how long it would be until Zed could break away from his studies and come to see me. Today was a Monday, probably a busy day for him, so I hadn't expected him to be here when I arrived. Still, I hoped he wouldn't have to wait until the weekend before he could come.

Then again, I wasn't even sure if he knew I was here. It had all happened so fast that there hadn't been time for me to write him about it. So unless he learned the news from Ella or his mother, he wouldn't have known. I considered asking Ella if she had said anything to him, but I didn't want to appear overeager, so I decided to hold my tongue and wait and see.

On the trip out, I'd studied the driver's map and calculated that Goshen College was only about twenty miles away from Nappanee and even closer, by a few miles, to the Home Place. That wasn't far at all, so I hoped to see him soon.

I raised the window a crack and made out the faint hum of Luke's saw and the fresh scent of the trees.

"Izzy?" Ella's footsteps followed her voice. "Do you need anything?"

"No, I'm fine. I'll be right there." I closed the window, made sure the matches were where I could find them when I came back to my room, and headed down the hall to the kitchen, hoping Rosalee's smile had been genuine and that she was as healthy, except for her broken leg and hip, as everyone claimed.

That night after supper, I was about to help Ella with the dishes when Rosalee asked me to sit back down, saying she wanted to discuss something with me.

"I was hoping you can help me with a project. It has to do with my old family recipes."

"Oh, I don't cook. I have a history of burning things. You should ask my *mamm*. Even she finally gave up on me."

Rosalee chuckled. "That's not what I need help with. I've been wanting to organize my collection for a while. I thought this would be a good time to do it, and Ella said you might be able to help."

I nodded. I'd much rather sort through recipes than cook from them.

She asked me to retrieve her recipe box, which was in the cupboard closest to the door. I did as she asked, noting the smooth, aged wood and rounded corners of the box as I carried it to her.

"Except for baking, I'm not too keen on cooking either," Rosalee confided. "But my mother was, and she and my father made this for me as a wedding gift. He built the box and she filled it with the family recipes."

"How lovely."

"The recipes are special and need to be preserved. The problem is that they have become so old and faded over years. My thinking is that we will copy them over onto fresh cards, recipe by recipe. I assume your handwriting is legible?"

"Um, yes. Of course."

"Good." She pulled blank cards from the back of the box and then asked me to get two pens from the desk in the living room.

When I returned and settled back down at the table, she handed me a stack of recipes and another stack of blank cards. It seemed simple enough. Settling comfortably in my chair, I got to work, starting with the first card on the pile, which was for chowchow, a cabbage relish.

Just like Verna, Rosalee soon began telling stories from the past as we worked, her memory jogged by the various recipes for familiar dishes from her childhood. She told me about her parents, how they had met in Michigan when her *daed* was visiting there, and then after they had married they moved into the Home Place.

"The home my mother grew up in was much smaller than this but crowded with lots of children. She mourned not being able to fill this place with kids."

"Oh?" I wrote as I listened.

"And then she was heartbroken when I didn't have any children either—nor remarry when my husband died."

"Why didn't you?" I looked up from the card.

"I never felt led to."

"*Ya*, I can understand that feeling."

Ella laughed, turning toward me as she dried the Dutch oven. "Izzy, you're all of eighteen."

"Nineteen." I smiled at Ella. "But I've never been boy crazy like you were."

Mortified, I clamped a hand over my mouth as soon as the words flew out. Thankfully, Ella just laughed. She didn't seem offended at all.

"Still," she said, "how could you not want a husband and children? Rosalee, you wanted that, right?"

"Sure," the older woman answered. "When I was young. But later I grew to accept that wasn't what God intended for me."

"See, Izzy?" Ella said. "You'll change your tune soon enough. Once you meet the right man…"

Her voice trailed off as she put the Dutch oven away, and I was glad her back was to me, because I could feel heat rise in my cheeks. Little did she know, I *had* met the right man—and he was her little brother!

"But you've had a good life, haven't you?" I asked Rosalee.

"I've been content, *ya*. But I'm not embarrassed to admit I've also been lonely. And isolated, even as I've lived in the middle of a close community." She pulled out another recipe.

I thought about that. If Zed and I didn't end up marrying, and if God's plan for me was to be single for life instead, at least I would never be isolated and lonely. I'd live with *Mamm* and *Daed* as long as I could. Then maybe whichever brother took over the farm would let me continue to live there, as Verna had done. As much as my siblings exhausted me, at least I had them.

"The truth is that I've been the happiest I've ever been since Ella moved in with me. Having her and Luke marry has been a double blessing, and then to have a baby soon in this old house, that's a triple blessing for sure. I'm amazed at God's goodness." Rosalee looked at me, her eyes bright. "Do you know how long it's been since a baby has been in this house?"

I shook my head.

"Sixty-two years. Since *I* was a baby." She poked at her chest with her index finger. "That's a long time."

I smiled, but the truth was, I'd never been crazy about infants. I'd thought Stephen and Thomas were both sweet—although not cute—when they were born, but I wasn't overjoyed with taking care of them the way Sadie and Becky and Tabitha and even Linda were. Thankfully, I'd be gone before Ella had her baby.

I continued to help Rosalee with the recipes, copying ten of them before she became too tired to continue. Ella had joined us at the table, working with a calculator and doing accounts.

"I'll show you the nighttime routine," she said, closing the book.

I swung Rosalee's wheelchair away from the table.

"You can push me down the hall," she said. "It's still a little hard for me to manage without bumping into the wall." We followed Ella.

Luke had already installed grab bars near the toilet and in the shower. The training I'd done in Lancaster had prepared me for taking care of Rosalee, including transferring her from the chair and helping her dress and undress. I hoped she had some handwork to do too, so I could focus on mine instead of copying recipes the whole time. I'd rather spend my days embroidering. Either way, I had enjoyed listening to Rosalee's stories, even if they didn't take place in Lancaster County and had nothing to do with my own ancestors or the period in history relevant to Zed's film.

An icy rain fell my second morning at the Home Place, but Luke was nearly finished making the ramp, so he continued to press on regardless. An hour or so after breakfast he was done, and when the rain finally stopped soon after that, he sprinkled salt over the slick boards and then told me to wheel Rosalee on out and give it a try. It was bitterly cold, so I bundled her up, put on my own cape and gloves, and carefully maneuvered her chair through the narrow doorway and into the mudroom. Then I turned it around and pulled it backward to get over the threshold of the back door and onto the ramp. Ella and Luke stood at the bottom, both smiling. Rosalee, grinning in return, clearly adored both of them.

As I took the first switchback along the ramp, Luke said to Rosalee, "In no time you'll be coming down this in the walker."

She nodded. "But right now I'm enjoying my ride."

Just as I reached the second switchback, a car started up the lane. I glanced up, squinting to see through the trees.

The car was red.

It was too far away to see if it was Zed's, but still my heart raced in anticipation. Could it possibly be him?

"Customer," Rosalee called out, but Ella seemed in no hurry to get over to the bakery. She wanted to see Rosalee safely down to the bottom of this ramp first. Swallowing hard, I tried to focus on my charge as we continued our slow roll downward.

But from the corner of my eye, I saw that the car didn't turn in by the bakery. It continued up the driveway instead. I chanced another quick look at the car, which was closer now, and felt a warm rush at the sight of its familiar dents and pings. It was, indeed, Zed's little old red Saab.

I wanted to call out, jump up and down, or cry with joy.

He'd come as soon as he possibly could! Perhaps he'd even skipped class to do so! That's what I felt inside, but on the outside I didn't dare give away the depth of my excitement to the others, especially Ella, who was no dummy and might put two and two together about my true feelings for her brother. Instead, as the car continued forward and then finally rolled to a stop, I focused on getting Rosalee safely down the ramp.

We made it, and then Ella turned back toward the car. "Oh, goodness. What's he doing here at this hour of the day?"

Luke turned around too, and we all—our little group at the end of the ramp—watched Zed turn off the car and climb out.

His eyes landed on me and a grin spread across his face. I couldn't help but smile in return.

"Hey, little brother," Ella called out to him. "Shouldn't you be in class right now?"

"I'm always in class. If I miss this once, I'll be okay."

"Why are you here?"

He shrugged, pocketing the keys and moving toward us. "I called Mom this morning. She said Rosalee had an accident—" His eyes landed on the older woman, and he spoke with genuine concern in his voice. "So sorry to hear that," he told her, bending forward to get a better look. "You have some serious stuff going on here with all of this." He gestured toward the cast and the wheelchair, where it held the leg aloft. "Are you okay?"

She nodded. "Thanks for your concern, but I'm fine now. It wasn't too fun at first, but the cast keeps it from being very painful anymore."

"That's good." He patted her on the arm and then stood straight again and looked me. We shared a broad smile.

"Mom said you arrived yesterday," he uttered, and it came out almost in a whisper. Then he turned to Ella. "Why didn't you tell me she was coming?"

She shrugged. "I don't know. You were studying for that big test—"

"It was yesterday afternoon. I could have come over last night."

"Well, you're here now, though you really shouldn't be."

He just laughed. "College is different than high school, Ella. Skipping class is no big deal as long as you don't do it too often."

We were all quiet for a moment, and then Rosalee turned to Luke and asked if he could push her back up the ramp. "It's getting a little chilly out here."

I felt my face flush. Shame on me. Of course she was getting chilled. "I'll do it," I said, again gripping the handles and tilting the chair back to pivot it around.

"No, no, no," Rosalee insisted. "Let Luke."

I glanced down at her, mortified. Was she afraid I wasn't strong enough to get the chair back up myself? I knew I was petite, but this was my job. I was up to it. I could handle all of Rosalee's needs just fine.

"This ramp is perfect," I said, trying not to sound hurt. "With all of these switchbacks, it's not too steep for me, not at all."

To my relief, she tilted her head back and gave me a smile. "It's not that," she said. "I know you can do it. I just want to give him the opportunity to enjoy this fine structure he built."

I wasn't quite sure if I bought what she was saying or not until she added, "Besides, you're bundled up well, and you could use some more fresh air. I thought you and Zed might enjoy taking a walk."

Smiling, I moved back from the chair and Luke took my place as Rosalee looked to Ella.

"Don't you agree these two *youngie* should go for a walk?" she prodded.

Ella turned to Zed and then glanced pointedly at her watch. "Sure, as long as they keep an eye on the time. Zed, you shouldn't skip all of your classes today."

"Not to worry," he replied easily, brushing his too-long bangs from his eyes. "My next one isn't for a few more hours.

With that, Luke began pushing Rosalee back up the ramp, and Ella gestured toward the bakery. "I'll be working," she told Zed. "Stop by before you go."

"Only if there's a sticky bun in it for me."

"How about a smack on the arm if you don't?"

"That works too."

Waving us off, she turned to head down the path.

Which left Zed and me standing there alone. How lovely it was to see his handsome face! I drank it in, relishing in the sight. Above us, Luke was already at the final switchback, and I could hear Rosalee talking about what a fine job he'd done and how handy this ramp would be even after she was better and back on her feet.

"Well, Izzy Bear?" Smiling, Zed thrust his hands in his pockets. "Wanna take a walk?"

I nodded. Usually I hated being out in the cold—but not today. Today, I wanted nothing more than time with Zed, alone. Goodness, I had missed him so badly.

"Ella's right, though," he added, "I only have a little while and then I need to get back to school. Let's stroll over to the pond. We can loop around and hit the bakery, and then I'll head out."

He asked me how my family was and I filled him in on *Daed*'s table making. That reminded him of the sets he'd helped build for the fall play, and he began telling me about the production. I half listened, mostly just thinking how happy I was to hear his voice. How happy I was to be with him. How happy I was I'd come to Indiana after all.

When we'd circled around to the orchard, he stepped off the driveway onto the mulch that Luke had most likely spread between the rows of apple trees. I followed.

"I know losing Verna was hard for you." Zed veered closer to me so that our shoulders brushed. A shiver zinged up my spine. "I'm so sorry."

I nodded. I knew he was. He'd said so in his last letter. Still, just being close to him and knowing he understood how I felt, I couldn't help but tear up. He put his arm around me and pulled me close but didn't say anything. That was one of the things I loved most about him. My emotions didn't scare him.

We came to a stop in the middle of the orchard and once I started talking, I couldn't stop, pouring out my heart about Verna's passing, her service, and *Mamm*'s frustration with me.

"Oh, Izzy." Zed pulled me closer and I put my head on his shoulder, wishing I could spend the rest of the day with him in the orchard, but he had class. Besides, I was cold and I was sure he was too.

"You need to go. We'd better head to the bakery."

He nodded.

As we walked back toward the driveway, I exhaled, determined to leave my sorrow among the scraggly branches of the apple trees. "So, how are your classes going?"

"Great. Especially my film class. I aced my test yesterday. And I'm pretty sure I'm going to be able to go to the coast spring term."

"The coast?"

"Yeah, L.A. Remember? We talked about this the night I had supper with your family before heading off to college."

"Oh, right."

"I'll be able to visit majors and mini majors while I'm there."

I had no idea what he meant, but it sounded like more movie talk to me.

"And I'll get some hands-on experience, more than what I can possibly get in either Pennsylvania or at Goshen."

I was relieved when we reached the bakery. He stopped talking and opened the door for me. Inside, an English woman was waiting at the counter as Ella filled her order. The only other customer was a man in a tweed suit, sitting at one of the tables and eating a sticky bun.

We got in line behind the woman, and then Zed surprised me by tapping her on the shoulder. She turned and a broad smile broke out on her face.

"Zed, how nice to see you!"

"Hello, Penny," he said, and then he gestured at me. "This is Izzy Mueller from back home."

"She's here to care for Rosalee," Ella added as she tied string around a pie box.

"Nice to meet you," the woman said, shaking my hand. She seemed to be around my *daed*'s age. She was short and a little plump, with dark hair that looked as if it were dyed. She wore a long down coat and jeans.

Ella moved to the front counter and set down the box. "I lived with Penny when I first moved out here to Nappanee."

"Ella's like my daughter," she said with a smile. "So if you're a friend of hers—and Zed's—you're a friend of mine. Let me know if you need anything, especially a ride somewhere. I specialize in those."

I couldn't imagine I would, but I thought it incredibly kind of her to offer and I thanked her. With a smile, Penny grabbed the box and then told all of us goodbye.

As the door fell shut behind her, Zed asked Ella if we could have some coffee to warm us up.

"Sure, and how about some sticky buns too? I have more than enough today."

"Hmm." Zed held out both hands, palms upward, and raised and lowered them as if he were weighing his options. "Sticky buns or a smack in the arm? So hard to choose."

Ella responded by making a fist and punching him right in the bicep. "There, now you can have both." She gave me a wink as she walked away and began to gather our orders.

Once we were served, Zed and I took our mugs and plates to a corner table and sat. I dug into the delicious confection while he gave me a rundown of all the movies he'd seen in his film criticism class thus far. Of course, I hadn't heard of any of them.

"Sounds like you're becoming quite the film buff," I said, pleased that I'd remembered the term.

His eyes narrowed, almost as if he were scoffing at me. "Uh, I prefer cineast."

"Oh," I said, surprised at his tone. My face flushed, but he didn't seem to notice. I wrapped my hands around my mug, as if I might be able to draw some comfort from it.

The English man finished his food, dumped his trash, and walked out, leaving Zed and me alone in the seating area.

Zed continued talking, rattling off several more titles, not from his class, but films he'd seen on his own. He pulled his phone from his coat pocket as he spoke, checked the time, and stopped in midsentence. "I have to go," he said, pushing back his chair. "I didn't realize how late it was. I can't miss my next class." He reached for his plate.

"I'll clear the table," I said.

"Thanks." He stood and turned toward the counter, calling out to Ella, who was filling the case with pastries. "Thanks, sis. Maybe I'll see you this weekend."

Maybe?

"Okay. Drive carefully," she called back.

He said a quick goodbye to me and dashed out the door. I sat for a moment, in shock, both at his abrupt departure and at how he'd acted. Sure, he had been his usual sweet self when he'd been listening to me, but what had come over him when he was talking about his classes? That person bragging about what he was learning and his plans for spring term wasn't the person I knew and loved.

"Are you okay?" Ella asked from the counter.

I nodded, but I wasn't. I was so confused. Had I been wrong to come to Indiana?

After stacking the two plates, I stood and headed toward the gray bucket on the stand along the wall, depositing everything there. "*Danke* for the coffee and snack," I said to her.

"Of course."

"I'm going back up to Rosalee." I returned to my chair for my cape and wiggled it over my shoulders, fastening it in the front.

"I'll be up by eleven or so," she said.

As I neared the door, a Plain woman with a little girl of about two came inside. Ella called out a hello and then said, "Izzy wait. This is Luke's *mamm* and sister, Cora and Annie. Their farm is next door."

After Cora greeted me, she gestured down at Annie and said, "She's a shy one. But only at first. She'll warm up to you in no time."

"Coming to the bakery is Annie's favorite thing to do," Ella said.

Annie nodded, her little *kapp* bumping against her *mamm*'s back.

"How long will you be staying?" Cora asked me as she slipped out of her cape and put it on the back of the closest chair.

"For a few weeks, until Rosalee is back on her feet."

"I hope you'll have a chance to meet Tom while you're here," Cora said, helping Annie out of her cape. "He's our oldest."

"And quite the catch," Ella murmured as an aside to me.

I smiled in return, not sure how to respond. If he was anything like Luke, I could imagine he would be a catch, but that made absolutely no difference to me. I wasn't interested. I loved Zed, no matter how rudely he had just behaved.

Annie ran forward and wrapped her arms around Ella's legs. I knew the girl didn't have any idea she would soon be an aunt. How fun for Ella's baby to have a playmate—and *aenti*—so close by.

I told Cora I looked forward to seeing her again soon and meeting the rest of her family. Then I left the bakery and went back up the path to the house. When I entered the kitchen, Rosalee greeted me from the table, where she was sitting and working on the recipes. I sat down to help her, deciding I would do my handwork after lunch while she rested.

"Zed is such a nice young man," she said, giving me a glance.

Still confused and not wanting to talk about him, I just nodded and changed the subject, telling her I'd met Cora and Annie in the bakery.

Rosalee smiled. "Wait until you meet Eddie. He's as cute as can be too. He looks like a tiny version of his big brother Luke."

"How about Tom?" I asked, trying to sound nonchalant. "Does he also look like Luke?"

Rosalee didn't answer for a long moment. Finally she shook her head and said, "Tom is as different from Luke as can be."

I wasn't sure of her meaning. Luke was tall, dark, and handsome. He was also sweet, kind, and dependable. If Tom wasn't anything like Luke, then perhaps he wasn't all that much of a catch after all.

ELEVEN

As the week wore on, Rosalee and I settled into a routine, and Ella's good nature persisted. I was sorely disappointed to learn that Zed had a big test to study for and couldn't come for the weekend, but I managed to muddle through without him. By that Monday, I couldn't believe I'd already been at the Home Place for a whole week.

Each day I assisted Rosalee with all of her personal needs, and we spent time copying her recipe collection as well. She was also working on crocheting an afghan for Ella's baby, so we usually devoted several hours each afternoon to handwork, and then I would continue working while she rested. Luke took a package to the post office for me and mailed it to Susie. I'd soon have another set of place mats to send. The good news was that I was getting as much work done in Indiana as I'd been getting done at home, even though Rosalee's sewing machine was a bit harder to use, powered by a foot pedal and not a generator. At least using hers wasn't as noisy.

Though I genuinely liked Rosalee, it turned out she wasn't the storyteller Verna had been. Perhaps it was because, as an only child, she didn't have as many people to talk about in her family as Verna did.

Eddie, Luke's nine-year-old brother, stopped by to visit most days. A few times he brought Annie with him when they were on their way to the bakery. But it wasn't until the end of my first full week at the Home Place that I met Tom. It was a bitterly cold day. The temperature had fallen to the low thirties, dipping into the twenties every night. There had been no precipitation and therefore no rain—just cold, cold air. I was hanging laundry on the line when an Amish man wandered out of the woods, and I knew immediately who he was even though Rosalee had been right. Tom was as different from his brother Luke as could be. He wasn't as handsome, for one thing, though he was much taller, with broader shoulders.

"You must be Izzy," he called out. "You're as pretty as my *mamm* said."

My face grew warm, even though the cold stung against it. His words were inappropriate, and I was trying to decide how to respond when he seemed to realize that himself.

"I'm sorry," he said. "Let's try that again." He came to a stop and gave me a broad smile. "I'm Tom. It's nice to meet you."

I forced a smile in return. "You too."

"How are they treating you around here?"

"*Gut.*" Bending down, I pulled a damp apron from the basket, and as I rose glanced at him again, once more comparing his looks with those of his brother. Somehow, where Luke's features were soft and kind, Tom's were sharper, his dark eyes and narrow lips sporting a vaguely sarcastic, teasing expression. Ella had told me Tom had courted several different girls but couldn't seem to settle on choosing a wife. Judging by his looks and magnetism, I imagined he'd broken quite a few hearts, though for some reason he didn't appeal to me.

"Will you be here long?" he asked and then winked, a dimple flashing in one cheek.

Turning away, I laid the apron across the line and speared it with a clothespin as I answered. "Just for another couple of weeks. I'll probably head home in time for Thanksgiving."

"That's a shame. What makes you want to hurry back to Lancaster County so soon?"

I shrugged.

"A beau?" he pressed.

I ducked my head as I told him that he was being inappropriate again, especially considering we'd just met.

Instead of looking properly chastised, he grinned.

"I'm sorry. I didn't mean to embarrass you," he said, but his apology did not seem earnest to me at all.

Before I could think of a response, Luke's voice boomed down from the barn loft, saving me from further embarrassment.

"Tom! Thanks for coming over. Be right down."

Tom looked over toward his brother and then turned back to me and tipped his hat. "I'm going to help Luke move an old axle. See you soon."

"*Ya*. See you around."

I finished up the rest of the laundry, but Tom never came back by. He did, however, come in with Luke for the midday meal, much to my surprise.

With more people around than just the two of us, Tom managed to tone down the charm. He was friendly rather than flirty, though a few of his gazes lingered a bit too long. The thing was, with two older sisters and two younger ones, I had seen guys like him before, and they held no attraction for me at all. The problem with them was that you just could never know if they were genuinely interested in you or they simply flirted from sheer habit.

When the meal was over and I was helping to clear the table, Tom's eyes met mine, and he gave me a discreet, sultry look I think was meant to make me swoon. Instead, I had to work hard not to laugh. He was handsome and charming, yes, but he was the kind of guy my mother called *glitschich*, or slippery. *Watch out for glitschich men, Izzy, because they think they can slide right into your life and then slide back out again just as smooth.*

I believed her and always took her advice. After all, *Mamm* should know. Before she married my *daed*, she'd had experience with a *glitschich* man herself, a guy named David who made her promises, gotten her pregnant, and then disappeared. My *daed* had married her soon after, knowing she was carrying another man's baby but willing to raise it as his own. That baby was my oldest sister Sadie, who once told me that our *daed* was her only *daed*, whether he was her biological father or not.

Tom didn't leave when the meal was over, but at least Ella kept the conversation going as she and I did the dishes, chattering on about a customer who had bought her entire batch of sticky buns that morning and then talking about Annie coming in with Cora.

"There's no way *Mamm* would have taken us for treats like that when we were little," Tom said. "And even if she'd wanted to, *Daed* would never have allowed it."

"Well," Rosalee said, "perhaps Annie has better parents than you did."

That stopped Tom for a moment, but then he began to laugh, as did I.

"I guess it's true what they say," Tom told us. "Parents tend to mellow with age."

The second week passed by quickly as I cared for Rosalee and focused on my handwork every afternoon while she rested.

On Friday morning the weather took a turn, growing colder, and at dinner Luke said a front was blowing in. "We'll have snow by tomorrow," he added. "And a huge drop in temperature, down into the teens."

Ella said if that were the case, she'd better get back out to the shop.

"Customers always stop by ahead of a storm."

"They'd better," Rosalee said. "If a storm blows in too early, it'll hurt profits."

I had already learned that Saturday was the busiest day of the week for them by far.

Once they left, I settled Rosalee into the living room in front of the fire, returned to the kitchen to wash the dishes, and then spent the next hour doing handwork. I tried to pry family stories from her, but it wasn't easy. The ones she came up with—about her ancestors who first immigrated to America from Switzerland—were ones I pretty much already knew because they had been featured in Zed's film about his wood carving great-great-great grandfather, Abraham Sommers.

Eventually we fell silent again and worked quietly until Rosalee said she needed to rest. I wasn't surprised. The home health physical therapist had come that morning and worn her out. Rosalee was using the walker more and more, but I followed to help transfer her to the bed.

Luke came through the back door as I returned to the living room. "Do you have anything to mail? I'm going into town to deposit Ella's receipts."

"Yes, but it can wait until Monday," I told him, explaining that I'd finished one of the runners and a set of place mats, but I wanted to get another set ready to go with them.

He shook his head. "I think this storm might be bad, Izzy. If you want your things to get there anytime soon, we should send them on their way now."

Luke was quiet and thoughtful enough that I couldn't help but take him seriously. The cold snap had continued for so long—going on six days—that whatever snow was coming with this storm would likely stick around a while. I packaged what I had and addressed the box to Susie, and then I retrieved money for postage from my room and gave it to him, thanking him as I did so.

"I'll keep feeding the woodstove," I added.

"*Gut.* I appreciate it. It takes a lot to heat this old house."

We shared a smile, and I couldn't help thinking, not for the first time, what a kind, even-tempered, and respectful man he was.

If only I could say the same about his brother Tom.

I spent the afternoon thinking about Zed, hoping he was planning to come for the weekend. So far, I'd been here in Indiana for eleven days and had only seen him that one time. He'd told Ella he'd be back soon, but to me it seemed as if it had been a long time. The more days that passed, the more the memory of his odd, snobbish behavior faded and the more I ached to see him.

Of course, if he was coming he needed to get here before the snow started or he likely wouldn't be able to come at all. I sure hoped it was the former. I couldn't imagine anything more wonderful than being snowed in here together.

At first I wondered if he even knew about the pending snowstorm, but then I realized he was surrounded by televisions and newspapers and other people all day long. Students and teachers had probably been talking about it nonstop.

On the other hand, if he was aware that the snow was coming, why hadn't he already made a point of getting here? Surely the window of opportunity for driving his car over from Goshen would be closing soon.

"Izzy, stop being so jumpy," Rosalee finally told me. "Every time a car turns into the bakery, I think you're going to leap right out of your skin."

She said it with a smile, and I had to wonder if she knew what was making me act this way. In response I stood and stretched, looking out the front window, glad to see that at least it wasn't snowing yet.

"Ella has had quite a rush on the bakery," I told her, glad to know that some of tomorrow's profits had come in today.

Rosalee was tired, so I helped her down for an afternoon nap and spent the next hour simply gazing out of the window, watching for that banged-up old red Saab to make its way up the driveway.

Ella came up to the house at four looking tired but pleased, saying she'd sold out, including the sticky buns she had prepared to bake tomorrow morning but had baked today instead, plus several extra pies.

"The *Englischers* said the prediction is for ice first and then snow," Ella said, filling the kettle with water.

"How long is it supposed to last?"

"I think they said it should snow all night and all day tomorrow and then finally taper off at some point tomorrow evening."

"Do they keep the roads plowed here the way they do back home?"

She nodded. "The main roads, yes, though it takes them a while to do the lane, which is a problem. Even once Luke clears the parking lot in front of the bakery, that doesn't do much good if nobody can get to it."

I wondered if he did the snow clearing with a shovel, or if their district permitted snowblowers.

"Anyway," Ella continued before I could ask, "can you do me a favor?" She took a package of stew meat from the refrigerator. "Run down to the root cellar and grab some potatoes and carrots."

Glad for the distraction, I flung my cape over my shoulders, picked up the flashlight from the shelf, and went outside into the falling dusk. Tiny shards of ice stung at my face as I made my way across the lawn.

I always loved the first snowstorm of the season, not so much to play in but to feel safe and cozy inside and curl up with a good book or a project. *Mamm* would make hot chocolate and *Daed* would build extra big fires both in the woodstove and the fireplace. The boys would trek in and out, back to their sledding and fort-building and ice-skating. I'd go skating a time or two each season myself, but it didn't appeal to me the way it did to my siblings.

I knew Luke's family had a pond, and I wondered if they ever used it for skating. Eddie was old enough, though little Annie was probably still too young. Zed was a good skater, but he'd grown so tall in the past year that I had to wonder if he'd still be as graceful as he used to be.

I pushed open the root cellar door and grabbed a burlap sack from beside the mountain of potatoes, shaking out the bag before I started to fill it, first with potatoes, then carrots, and then several onions. I turned and hurried out, hoping I didn't have any spiders hanging on me. It was completely dark as I headed back toward the house without even a hint of moonlight. The ice pelted my face and bare hands and danced at my feet as it hit the ground.

We'd just sat down to stew and biscuits when a knock fell against the back door. We barely heard it over the crackle of fire in the woodstove and the ice against the window. Luke stood and shuffled toward the door. My heart pounded, and I prayed it was Zed.

"*Ach,*" Rosalee said. "Who could that be out on a night like this?"

"Probably my stupid little brother," Ella replied with a roll of her eyes.

Sure enough, after a moment Zed came tromping into the kitchen behind Luke, his eyes shining, his cheeks bright red from the cold. I grinned, and it was all I could do not to jump up and throw myself into his arms.

"Cutting it kind of close with this weather, aren't you, college boy?" Ella asked him, her eyebrows angled in a stern expression.

He gave her a sheepish grin in return. "Not close enough, I'm afraid."

We all looked at him, wide eyed, as he described how he'd made it here fine, only to slide into the ditch right after he'd turned into the driveway, just a hundred feet or so from the house. Again, I wanted to hug him, this time out of concern, but I held myself in check.

"Maybe you should call a tow truck," Rosalee said.

Before Zed could answer, Ella shook her head. "Nah, sit down and eat supper first. Get warmed up. Your car's not going anywhere right now anyway."

Zed grinned and then hung up his coat while Ella set another place at the table across from me. Soon we all fell into easy conversation.

At one point, I couldn't help but compare this supper with Zed to dinner with Tom earlier in the week. I'd felt tense the entire time with Tom, afraid of what he might say next. But with Zed I hung on his every word, wanting to hear all the details of his adventures. A few times I caught myself smiling too broadly and reminded myself to tone it down.

It wasn't just with Zed that I felt comfortable. The longer I stayed at the Home Place, the more I enjoyed Ella, Luke, and Rosalee, and I couldn't help but imagine them as my in-laws. In fact, my relationship with Ella felt like a better fit than with my own sisters. I couldn't believe there was a time when I had found her abrasive and unlikeable.

As it turned out, Zed didn't have to call a tow truck. With the help of Tom and a team of draft horses, they pulled the car out and dragged it over to the first spot in the parking lot, where it would stay until the lane was plowed.

By the time I was readying Rosalee for bed, Zed was back in the house, talking and laughing with Ella in the kitchen. I wanted nothing more than to be with him and didn't even realize I was rushing Rosalee's bedtime routine until I transferred her into her bed too quickly, bumping her leg. She yelped.

"I'm so sorry!"

"*Ya*, I imagine you are. Next time don't be in such a hurry."

Zed's laughter rang out from the kitchen again, and my face flushed. I was sure Rosalee knew the reason for my recklessness.

I slowed down, carefully propping up her leg, fluffing her pillows, and tucking the blankets and quilt around her and adding an extra layer of covers against the cold. I refilled her water glass and asked if there was anything else she needed.

She smiled then. "Just for you to go have some fun. Sorry I snapped."

When I reached the kitchen, Luke, Ella, and Zed were sitting at the table with four decks of cards in the middle. "Dutch Blitz?" Zed asked.

I smiled, grateful to my siblings that I knew how to play, and play it well. Zed passed me the green deck, and he took the blue deck. I made stacks for my post, blitz, and wood piles, as did the others. Soon cards and laughter flew around the table, round after round. It was no surprise that Zed had the most blitzes, winning the first game. He was just so smart. We kept playing and although each of us won at least once, Zed was by far the most successful.

"Let's play again," he said, after he'd blitzed us for the tenth time.

"Are you kidding?" Ella groaned. "It's off to bed for us old folks."

She rose and began to clean up from the game, but I waved her away, insisting I would do it. Luke moved toward the woodstove to stoke it up for the night, but Zed did the same, telling him he would take care of that.

"The bed upstairs is made and ready when you are," Ella told Zed, and then she and her husband headed off to bed. I knew I should get to sleep too, so as they continued up the stairs, I went into the dark living room to check the fireplace and retrieve my handwork. Once we'd started the game in the kitchen, we'd let the fire in here die down, and now just the embers still glowed, smoldering orange and black lumps of wood.

Confident it would continue to smolder until it went out, I was adjusting the screen when Zed's voice interrupted me. "It's freezing in here."

"*Ya.* There was no reason to keep this fire going. It won't heat the house the way the stove does."

"Actually," he said as he grabbed some kindling from the box. "I have a ton of studying to do tonight. I'd rather work in here on the couch than in the kitchen."

I moved out of his way as he built up the fire, knowing I should go on to bed. Once he was finished, however, the tall crackling flames were so alluring that I couldn't help but step toward the heat, extending my hands.

Zed joined me, standing just inches away.

The fire sent shadows leaping around the room. I concentrated on the flickering flames, but soon my cheeks began to warm—and not just from the heat. Zed was watching me, I was sure.

I glanced up at him. His eyes were on me and the look on his face was one I hadn't seen before. There was both depth and tension in his gaze, mystery and perhaps even longing. He looked the way I felt.

Certainly, he'd never gazed at me that way before.

He nodded toward the couch. "We could talk for a little while."

"Just for a few minutes," I answered softly.

He sat on the couch, and though I would have given anything to curl up right next to him, I chose the opposite end instead, settling there and then turning toward him as we talked. Feeling suddenly awkward, I asked him to tell me more about the program in Los Angeles and his plans for his film. That led to a discussion about the costumes, and I shared with him the ideas I had had so far. The longer we were together, the more he seemed his old self, not the braggart he'd been the first time I saw him after I'd arrived. I was so relieved. Perhaps he'd just been trying to prove how much he had been learning at this new school.

Eventually, the topic of conversation shifted to Rosalee's recovery. "She's doing really well," I said. "By Thanksgiving, I'll be headed home for sure." I knew everyone assumed I'd be taking the bus, but I hoped to be able to ride home with Zed instead. Such a trip, unchaperoned, might be questionable to some, but I couldn't resist. Twelve hours to Lancaster County would give us so much time together, and he could relax and be even more himself.

Even if such a venture were frowned upon by the community, I knew my parents trusted us implicitly. Besides, if we left early and drove straight through, we wouldn't be spending the night anywhere on the road. That should make the drive proper enough, even if some wouldn't see it the same way. I considered proposing the idea to Zed now but then decided to hold my tongue, hoping he would come up with it on his own.

"Izzy?"

I jumped a little, realizing I'd been lost in my thoughts again.

"Are you about ready to nod off?"

Involuntarily, I yawned and then smiled.

"Go on to bed," he said. "You look exhausted."

"Are you sure?"

He gestured toward his backpack, which was by the door. "Absolutely. I'm going to study for a while and then turn in myself."

I picked up my handwork bag and stood, just as he rose too. Then we both took a step at the same time. Our shoulders bumped. I froze. Turning to see his face, I expected an apologetic smile, but instead his eyes were intense as they met mine. At first I thought he was going to kiss me, and my breath caught in my throat. Then, after a long moment, he gently chucked me on the arm, as if he were one of my brothers.

That didn't feel right, not at all. The notion of kissing Zed hadn't crossed my mind for several years, but that had changed. My feelings had changed.

I had changed.

More than anything, I wanted him to kiss me right now.

"See you in the morning," he said softly.

"*Ya,*" I answered. "See you then."

For the next hour I tossed and turned in my bed, thinking about him and how *Mamm* and *Daed* still thought we were just friends. I was getting more comfortable with the idea of us being more than that, but I realized I still couldn't share any of this with them. Not yet. Besides, if they knew how I really felt about Zed, they wouldn't let me ride home with him.

Still, it felt deceptive. What would they say if they knew I loved Zed? As much as they respected him and appreciated him, I knew they would be heartbroken at the thought of my not joining the church, and I'd feel horrible that I'd caused their pain. I took a deep breath, reminding myself of how I'd come to peace about that by putting the whole matter of our differing churches into God's hands and trusting Him to work things out according to His plan, not mine.

I couldn't help but think of Ella and how naturally she fit in the Amish world. God had wanted her with Luke, and He was the one who helped make it happen.

Perhaps, in time, God would make this happen with Zed and me as well.

TWELVE

The old house moaned with the falling temperature, and toward morning I woke cold and stiff. My first thought went to Rosalee, and I slid from my bed, wedging my feet into my slippers and wiggling into my robe. I tiptoed to the closet outside my door and grabbed another quilt from the stack on the shelf. Then I headed across the hall to Rosalee's room.

She appeared to still be sleeping, but as I spread the quilt over her, she opened her eyes. "How did you know I was cold?"

"I was, so I was sure you would be too," I said, sitting down on the edge of her bed and tucking the quilt more tightly against her legs.

She gave me a fond smile. "What time is it?"

"Five or so."

"What does it look like outside?"

I went to the window and pulled back the drapes. Yesterday's ice had turned to snow, and now it was falling thick and fast. The sun wouldn't be up for another few hours, but I could see pretty well regardless. The landscape had taken on that eerie, grayish-orange glow that can happen with snow sometimes, even in the middle of the night. Ella had been right—this was a big one. We'd received a good six inches already, and it was supposed to continue for almost the entire day.

I described what I was seeing to Rosalee and then suggested she try to get back to sleep.

"I've been awake for an hour. I'd rather just get up."

"Okay, but let me stoke the fire first."

By the time I reached the kitchen, I saw that Luke already had it going strong, so told him I would start the one in the fireplace. I went to the living room and quickly arranged the kindling and paper. I reached for the matches, but they weren't on the mantle. I turned toward the lamp, grabbed them, and then stepped back, startled. Zed was there on the couch, all sprawled out, his feet hanging over the far end, a text book resting on his chest. He had used his coat like a blanket but otherwise had no coverings at all. And the room was freezing cold.

I stood there and looked at him for a long moment. He was so adorable, all lanky and long, his dangling feet huge in their gray socks, his shaggy blond mane in dire need of a haircut. He seemed big and grown up, yet the expression on his sleeping face was as sweet and innocent as a child.

Oh, how I loved him.

I finally forced myself to turn away, praying that God would wake up Zed's heart to his true feelings for me soon. Very soon. Mennonite or not, there simply had to be a way for us to be together.

I headed back into the kitchen, where Luke was pouring water from the kettle into the French press.

"Zed's in the living room," I said with a smile. "Half frozen."

"We told him to sleep upstairs," he said, putting the kettle back on the stove.

"Could you see to him?" I asked, though that wasn't what I really wanted.

What I really wanted was to go back in there and slide in under that coat with Zed and wrap myself in his warmth and inhale the sandalwood scent of sleep from his skin. Better someone else go in my stead and get him out of there for me.

I hovered in the kitchen and listened as Luke did as I asked. A brief, low mumble of their voices ensued, followed by some shuffling and then a soft clomping up the stairs. It was so early yet, Zed would probably climb into the guest bed up there and sleep another five or six hours before starting his day.

I returned to the living room and started the fire. Once the blaze took, I moved back down the hall to Rosalee.

An hour later, she and I were both dressed and in the kitchen, sharing breakfast with Ella and Luke. Even though the sun had yet to rise, Ella made a comment about Zed sleeping the day away.

"He was up late studying," I explained in his defense.

"*Ach*, the life of a college student," Rosalee commented. "I'd hate it. Studying all night and sleeping all day sounds like misery to me."

It didn't to me, but I didn't say anything. I couldn't help but yawn, though.

After breakfast, as the first light of morning finally began to appear, Luke and Ella headed off through the falling snow to the bakery. They didn't expect any business, but they wanted to make sure the pipes hadn't frozen during the night. I did the dishes, and then Rosalee and I settled into the living room, wrapped in quilts, and watched through the broad front windows as the day continued to dawn. We both had handwork to do, but our projects sat idle in our laps for a long while, each of us content to gaze at the snow- and ice-covered fairyland that was coming to life outside.

As the morning wore on, I fed wood into both the woodstove and the fireplace, doing my best to keep the old house cozy. Because Rosalee couldn't move around, it would be easy for her to become chilled. That wouldn't be good for her pain level or for her healing.

Zed finally appeared around ten, his hair disheveled and his clothes wrinkled. As he stepped into the room, his eyes went to the window and his face broke out in a broad smile. "It's so pretty," he said, without even telling us good morning first.

Rosalee sighed. "Like a painting."

"Remember how much fun we had that time we went ice-skating on the Gundys' runoff pond?" Zed asked, looking at me.

I nodded. A few years ago, not long after Zed's cousin Ada had married Will Gundy, she had invited us to come skating at his family's farm.

Zed and I had brought along all four of my younger siblings, and between us and them and various extended family members of the Gundys, soon there were a good two dozen people out there on the ice, laughing and gliding and slipping and falling.

Before that, I had never seen Zed skate before, and I remember being surprised at how good he was at it, how graceful and steady—and fast. I knew he was naturally athletic, but the skating had been even more impressive than his abilities on a basketball court. When I complimented him on it later, he'd just waved off the praise and said it came from years of wintertime pickup hockey games with kids in his neighborhood.

"I wish we could go skating today," he said. "But my skates are back in Pennsylvania."

"Mine too."

"Ella and Luke have skates that would probably fit," Rosalee volunteered. "They're in the mudroom."

"Is the ice thick enough on the pond yet?" I asked her.

"With the cold snap we had, I would guess so. Yesterday, Luke told Eddie it was frozen enough for him and Annie to skate on the shallows—with supervision. I imagine it's that much more solid today. But Luke could check again."

I hardly thought Luke needed another thing to add to his to-do list. "We can do it," I said. "Zed knows what to look for."

"Let's go for it." Grinning, Zed clapped his hands together.

I was about to run off to my room to put on more layers when I remembered my charge.

"Actually," I said, working to keep the disappointment from my voice as I stayed in place, "I'm taking care of Rosalee right now. Maybe later."

"Oh, I'll be fine," she countered. "You go ahead and go."

I hesitated, not wanting to be negligent in my duties.

She gestured toward her leg. "I only have one regret in life, and that's not having more adventures while I could. Go have an adventure, Izzy. No worries about me."

"If you're sure," I said. "I won't stay out for long."

"Stay out as long as you want." Rosalee pointed to the kitchen and smiled. "First get Zed something to eat, though."

He offered to make himself some oatmeal. He knew how much I disliked cooking.

"There's leftover ham slices too," I told him. "On the bottom shelf of the fridge."

"Cool. Thanks." He headed off for the kitchen.

Before I went to get changed, I took a moment to make sure Rosalee had everything she might need at hand—extra blanket, crochet bag, glass of water.

"You're all set then?" I asked, hands on my hips as I glanced around.

She didn't reply, so I looked at her face and saw that her eyes were twinkling.

"He's so smitten with you," she whispered.

"I wish," I blurted out before thinking, and then I felt my face flush with heat. "I mean—"

"Ah. The feeling's mutual. I knew it."

Heart pounding, I glanced toward the kitchen and then moved forward to perch myself on the arm of the couch as we continued to whisper.

"Please don't say anything to anyone," I implored her. "I'm sure whatever you saw is because he and I have been the best of friends for so long."

"Not *just* friends."

I swallowed hard. "For years, yes, just friends. But then…" I couldn't believe I was telling her this. "But then one day, two or three months ago, just before he left for school, I realized that I…that for me, it was more."

There. I had said it aloud, to another person. I guessed that made it official.

"You're in love with him," she said, as matter-of-factly as if she had announced the sky was blue or the beans were ready.

I hesitated and then gave her a nod and a shy smile. "So far, though, it's all very one-sided, I'm afraid. He doesn't realize my feelings have changed. And he still thinks of me like a sister."

She chuckled. "He doesn't look at you like a sister."

I felt a flush of embarrassment, even as my heart raced with joy.

"It's true, Izzy. You're a beautiful young woman—and even more lovely on the inside. He's well aware of that, I assure you."

I met her gaze. Could it be true? Was Zed falling in love with me at last?

"You ready yet, Iz?" His voice boomed in from the kitchen. "Be sure to put on lots of layers. And don't forget a hat and some gloves."

Rosalee and I shared a secret smile, and then I held a finger to my lips and she nodded sagely in return. It wasn't until I had dashed off to my room to pile on the clothes that it struck me to wonder at the woman's enthusiasm for what she'd discovered. Rosalee knew Zed was Mennonite and I Amish. She was Amish as well, and as such, she should have been discouraging the relationship, not encouraging it—much less enabling it.

Once I was dressed and ready to go, I met back up with Zed at the fireplace. His arms were loaded with skates and coats.

"Better try these on," he said, handing me the smaller pair of skates. I sat on the edge of the couch and did just that, glad to see they were only slightly too large. I took them back off, confident that if I laced them up extra tight, they would do just fine.

I pulled on the heavy coat he held for me, and then I poked at the fire as he sat down to try on the other pair of skates. He seemed to be having the opposite problem—they were a tad too small—but he assured me he could make do.

"Is there a broom?" Zed asked Rosalee as he worked to pull the skates back off.

"Yes, take the push broom from the back porch. And grab the whistle too, in case anyone gets in trouble. It's on the hook near the door."

"Thanks."

He stood, skates in hand, but I continued poking the fire.

I glanced at Rosalee. "I won't stay out long," I assured her.

"Go," she urged, sensing my reluctance. "Have fun. I'll be fine." Then, with a mischievous glint in her eye, she added, "You two *friends* take as long as you need."

It was cold outside but so beautiful, the snow falling gracefully now, the tiny flakes landing on my eyelashes as we walked. Everything was just so quiet—that unique, hushed silence of snow—as though the whole world had gone to sleep under one big fluffy white blanket. Zed and I walked side by side behind the barn, skirting the woods to the pasture.

As we neared the pond, I spotted a lone figure sitting on a log and lacing up a boot.

"Eddie? Is that you?" I called out. He looked up, saw us, and waved. As we drew closer, I asked, "Who's here with you?"

He beamed. "My *mamm* is on her way with Annie. Can you believe all this snow? And it's only going to get deeper!"

Zed gave the boy a high five as a hello, and then he stepped out onto the ice in his shoes and began clearing a section with the broom. I sat down beside Eddie and put on my skates.

Zed continued to sweep snow from the ice until my boots were laced up tight, and then we traded places. Of all of my siblings, I was the least athletic, and I felt wobbly as I made my way toward him. My older sisters and all my brothers used to tease me about my lack of grace. The truth was, I almost always preferred to be inside as compared to out.

Once I had the broom in my hand, I used it for support as I swept, listening to the conversation while Zed sat on the log to put on his skates and he and Eddie talked about school.

"Ella's still helping me with my reading," Eddie said. "We started the book about the wardrobe."

"And the lion and the witch?" Zed asked.

"*Ya*, that one."

"That was one of my favorite books growing up. Still is."

"*Ya*, I know. Ella told me."

Once Zed was ready, he invited Eddie out onto the ice with us.

The boy stood and looked back in the direction of their house. "I'd better wait for my *mamm*."

"Good thinking, buddy," Zed replied.

He got back on the ice, wincing at the feel of the tight boots, and then with a few quick strides he was gliding smoothly over to where I stood.

"I'm glad it isn't snowing any harder than this," he said, taking the broom from my hands. "Otherwise, our sweeping would be kind of pointless."

I looked around at the area we had managed to clear thus far and then watched as he expanded it more rapidly now that he had on some skates. He really was graceful on the ice. It was a pleasure just to stand there for a few minutes and watch him.

"Okay," he said finally, glancing around and then giving me a satisfied nod. "I think we'll be fine as long as we stay in this area. The water's shallow here, which means the ice should be good and solid."

We glanced over toward Eddie, who was waiting impatiently at the shore for his *mamm* to show up. Before we could say a word, we heard a loud whooping sound come from the woods—and then Tom emerged instead.

He strode quickly across the field, his thick winter coat a splash of black against the white landscape. As he marched closer, I saw that he was twirling two long, dark sticks above his head.

"Anyone for a game of hockey?" he called out loudly.

Zed's eyes lit up, but I groaned.

"Where's everyone else?" Eddie asked his oldest brother, not sounding all that pleased either.

"Annie fell asleep—*Mamm* thinks she's coming down with something. So she sent me out instead."

Eddie slumped back down on the log. "I wanted to skate with Annie."

Tom reached his brother and came to a stop, propping the sticks against a tree. "Too bad," he said. "You have me instead." Tom unwound the skates he'd slung over his shoulders and then sat on the log and began putting them on. "How's the ice?" he called out to us.

"Firm," Zed replied. "Feels good."

"Great. Should do for a game of hockey."

"I don't like hockey," Eddie said, sulking.

"That's 'cause you don't know how to play." Tom pulled a puck from his pocket and threw it up in the air, snatching it quickly. "No sweat. I'll show you."

The child looked so disappointed that I decided to intervene. "Hey, Tom, if you and Zed are going to play hockey, then I'll need Eddie to help me skate around. Do you mind?"

Eddie's face lit up as Tom agreed.

"How 'bout you, Zed?" Tom called. "Need me to teach you how to play hockey?"

"That's okay," Zed replied easily. "I think I might remember the basics."

"Suit yourself."

Zed handed me the broom, and I flashed him a warning look as he did. "Go easy on him," I whispered.

He just winked in return.

"You guys can play here," I said more loudly, meaning the large area Zed and I had managed to clear. "Eddie and I will use the broom and go around that way if you two think it's safe."

Zed looked toward the place I indicated, along the curve of the shore, and nodded. "That part should be fine, but only go out as far as that clump of tall weeds. Don't go past there."

"Okay."

"And if you hear a crack, scram."

We smiled at each other, but I knew he was only half kidding.

Bracing myself with the broom, I managed to skate back over to Eddie. Grinning, he made his way onto the ice and then took my hand. I showed him the part of the pond that would be ours, and then we took turns sweeping off the snow to create a path as we made our way forward.

Behind us Tom hit the ice and then the two guys launched into their game. My back was to them, and I couldn't turn to see without chancing a fall, so I merely listened instead to the good-natured teasing, the swish of blades on ice, the thwack of sticks hitting the puck. Eddie and I made slow progress along the curve of the shore, but after a while I realized that the lighthearted words of the game behind us had ceased, leaving only the sounds of play: sticks clacking and puck skidding, punctuated by grunts and gripes. For some reason, I began to feel uneasy, as though there was more going on than just a game. Was there animosity between Zed and Tom? It almost sounded like it, though that was odd, considering that they were friends and also related by marriage through their respective siblings.

I kept going, but after a while it struck me that with all of those clacks and whacks and clicks and grunts, they sounded not unlike two bucks in rutting season, banging antlers together in a frenzy.

When Eddie and I reached the outer limit of our area and I could finally turn to watch, I was startled by the intensity of what I was seeing. Sure enough, this was no casual hockey game like the one Zed had played back home with Will and Ada and the kids. This was far more intense, like a battle between rival teams. Both men seemed to hit that puck with all of their might, and when the play drew them together, they rammed shoulders and jabbed sticks with a vengeance, as though every point scored were a matter of life and death.

Were they showing off for me? Trying to earn my attention and affection?

If so, then too bad for them because I refused to play along.

"Come on, guys," I called out, just as the black puck skittered loose and shot across the pond. "Take it down a notch, would you? If that puck comes flying over here, Eddie or I could lose some teeth!"

Either they didn't hear me or they chose to ignore me because nothing changed. Both men lunged toward the errant puck, pushing each other out of the way to get there first. Once they had it, the frenzy started all over again, and they were zigzagging across the ice like two ninnies.

Clicking my tongue in disgust, I took Eddie's hand and started back the way we had come.

"You're a bender!" Zed cried as he raced Tom to the puck.

"My ankles are straighter than yours," Tom replied with a growl. "You'd better keep your head up, man."

They were both skating hard, moving closer together. Then as they drew even, Tom suddenly lunged to the right and bodychecked Zed, sending him flying.

"Yes!" Tom cried, skating off across the unswept ice in pursuit of the black disc as Zed landed on the ice in a heap and kept sliding.

I was fed up with them both, but I couldn't help but pause and watch to make sure Zed wasn't hurt. All arms and legs, he finally came to a stop at a snowdrift, and then he just laid there a minute, catching his breath.

I was about to call out to ask if he was okay when I heard a distinct *crrrraaaack*.

Stunned, I twisted my head toward the sound and watched as Tom quickly came to a halt, much further out on the ice.

The crack wasn't loud—but we all heard it. Tom stood frozen in place.

"Get off!" Zed yelled. I thought he was talking to Tom, but then he added, "Izzy! Go! You and Eddie, get off the ice!"

I turned my attention back to him just as he was getting to his feet. Then, to my horror, he started skating again—directly toward Tom.

"Zed, no!" I called, but he ignored me.

He slid to a stop about ten feet from Tom, held out an arm, and said, "Slow and easy, man. You can do it."

"It's not that bad," Tom replied.

Another *crrrraaaack,* louder this time, and closer too. Eyes wide, Tom scampered backward, trying to put some distance between him and the sound. Zed did the same, but then came the sound of another crack.

Eddie and I watched in horror as the ice split in two, shooting out a dark, jagged wet line, halfway between us and them.

THIRTEEN

"D on't move!" Zed yelled.

"Oh, please," Tom scoffed as he pushed off and skated forward again.

But he only made it a short ways before we heard another giant *crrrack*. Then the ice disappeared from beneath his feet, and he was in the water.

Eddie and I both gasped. I had horrors of Tom slipping into the blackness and never finding his way out again. But to my relief, his head didn't even go all the way under. Instead, his arms flailed wildly as he bobbed there at the surface amid smaller chunks of ice.

I had no idea how much time he had before hypothermia would set in, but I knew it couldn't be more than a few minutes.

What were we going to do?

I looked around, thinking Zed might be able to pull him out with one of the hockey sticks. But then I realized Tom's stick was in the water, beneath him, likely gone for good, and Zed's was lying too far out on thin ice to retrieve. We still had the broom, and I decided to skate out to help. Then I remembered Eddie, whose eyes were wide with terror. What was I thinking? Job one was to get this little boy safely to land.

"Come on," I said giving his arm a tug as I pushed off with the broom and we began skating quickly toward the bank. As we went, I prayed for Tom—and Zed. After all, he was pretty close to the edge of the gaping, icy hole himself.

When we reached the bank, I made Eddie scramble onto the snow-packed ground and ordered him to stay there. Then I turned, push broom still in hand, and made my way out toward the two men. As I went, I saw Zed carefully lowering himself to his hands and knees on the ice, proba-bly to better distribute his weight. Tom, meanwhile, was grabbing at the rim of the hole and attempting to pull himself out, but each time the ice he was holding would break off in a chunk and plunge him in again.

Halfway there, I skidded to a stop and called out to Zed. He looked my way, his face taking on an expression of half fear, half anger.

"Izzy, no! Don't come any closer."

"I'm not. I'm going to slide the broom to you. You can use it to help pull Tom out."

"All right, but be careful."

Kneeling, I laid the broom on the ice, turning it so that the bristles were face up, and gripped them in my hands. Then I looked at Zed, took aim, and pushed forward with all my might.

The broom turned and skittered sideways across the surface, even fur-ther than I thought it would. It finally came to a stop about ten feet short of Zed, and he started crawling toward it. As he did, I could hear him yell-ing out instructions over his shoulder.

"Come on, Tom," he cried, "I know you're cold and want to get out of there, but what you're doing isn't going to work."

"Got any better ideas?" Tom snarled as he once again fell back into the icy circle.

"Yes, I do. Are you listening?"

To my surprise, Tom stopped flailing around and did just that.

"Okay," Zed said, reaching for the broom with his fingertips and pull-ing it toward him. "The trick is to *swim* yourself out. Like, start swimming in the water, and *keep* swimming even when you reach the ice. Keep kick-ing, and your body will continue moving forward until you've managed to beach yourself there at the edge, kind of like a seal. Then, once you're out, try to scoot forward, still on your belly, very carefully, until you can reach the broom."

Zed moved as close to Tom as he dared and extended the handle as far as he could.

Without a word, Tom did as Zed had instructed. He backed up from the icy side and then, arms forward, he laid horizontal in the freezing water and started kicking. To my amazement, it worked! When he reached the ice, still kicking like crazy, his hands and arms and shoulders simply kept going, sliding up onto the surface. Wiggling his hips and grabbing at the ice with his fingertips, he managed to keep squirming forward until half of his body was out of the water. Then he grabbed the broom and held on as Zed pulled.

I sucked in a breath as I watched. I knew that Tom's wet hands had to be nearly frozen by now, but somehow he managed to hang on as Zed dragged his sopping wet form to safety, farther from the icy breach.

Finally, the two men were shoulder to shoulder, crawling together in my direction. Zed gave me a wave that said "stay where you are," and then he pushed the broom back toward me to free up his hands.

Once they had crawled another ten feet or so, they finally stood and began to skate. Zed scooped up the broom from where it had come to a stop then continued on to me. Tom kept going toward shore.

Only then did I realize Eddie was cheering loudly from the bank, and I glanced his way to see him jumping up and down, clapping with glee. I shared his joy but shuddered to think how differently this could have ended.

Tom never said a word, so as Zed tucked an arm in mine and began to propel us in that direction as well, I asked him if he thought Tom was okay.

"Are you kidding?" Zed whispered. "The poor guy is about to die."

My eyes widened. "What?"

"Yeah, of *embarrassment*." Zed chuckled softly at his own joke, but I didn't think it was funny.

"He really could have died, you know. You could have too."

Growing sober, Zed nodded. "I know, I'm sorry. But it's all over now. Tom will be fine as long as he gets out of those wet clothes and into something warm right away."

When we reached the bank and climbed out, I saw that Tom's fingers were trembling and his lips were blue. Still, he wouldn't look at either of us or accept any help from his little brother as he worked to undo the laces on his skates.

"Better move fast, man," Zed told him.

"That's the plan," Tom snapped in reply, teeth clenched.

Somehow he managed to get one skate untied enough to pull it off. As he started in on the other, he finally glanced our way.

"I'm glad you're okay," I told him earnestly. "I was so worried."

"Oh, yeah?" he said, returning his attention to the laces. "Must not have worried all that much."

I blinked, feeling hurt. I tried to come up with a response but was speechless.

"Why would you say that to her?" Zed demanded.

Tom got off the second skate and then slid his feet into dry boots before standing up and meeting my gaze.

"Because that might have been the kind of situation where it would have helped to blow the whistle."

With that, he grabbed his wet skates from the ground and took off toward home.

Eyes wide, Eddie turned to me, watching to see how I would react.

All I could do was look down at my chest, where the shiny silver whistle hung from my neck. I had completely forgotten about it.

My face flushed with heat, I looked at Zed, the only person on earth who would not judge me when I did something this scatterbrained.

"Figures," I said, reaching for the whistle, putting it to my lips, and giving a soft blow.

"You'll probably remember next time," Eddie said, his voice full of encouragement.

The three of us couldn't help but laugh.

Zed and I saw Eddie safely to the path that would lead him home and then we made our way back to Ella's house. We got there just as she was setting out the midday meal. She could tell something was up, so after Luke led us in silent prayer, we explained to both of them what had happened.

Ella was horrified, but Luke seemed to find the entire incident rather humorous. When he chuckled out loud, she flashed him a stern look and said, "Stop that. Your brother could've been killed—or at least seriously wounded."

"The only thing wounded on that boy is his pride," he replied, stifling another chuckle.

After we ate, Zed offered to run next door and check on Tom, just to make sure he really was okay. He seemed genuinely concerned. For some reason, that pleased me very much.

"You won't gloat?" I asked as he pulled on his coat.

He slipped on a hat and then tucked his hands in his pockets. "I promise I won't."

While he was gone, I cleaned the kitchen, Luke returned to his work out in the barn, and Ella went down to the bakery. It was closed due to the snow, but she wanted to go through her inventory and put together a list of needed supplies in case the delivery truck was able to get through. No plows had yet to make it up the lane, but we hoped one would soon.

I settled Rosalee down for a nap, and by the time I came back out, Zed had returned from next door and was just sitting down at the kitchen table near the heat of the woodstove. I grabbed my handwork bag and joined him there.

"That was fast," I said, wondering if I had taken longer in Rosalee's room than I realized.

"Yeah, I ran into Tom's mother and little sister halfway there. They were coming to the bakery to see if Ella was getting many customers with all the snow and ice. Little Annie was pretty disappointed when I told them it was closed."

"She *loves* that bakery."

"She loves Ella's sticky buns. Then again, so do I."

We shared a smile.

"So how's Tom?"

"He's fine. His mom said when they left he was wearing his warmest pajamas, wrapped in a couple of blankets, and sitting by the fire sipping hot cocoa."

I tried not to laugh as I pictured it. Poor Tom. He would probably be even more embarrassed if he knew his mother was passing on information like that.

I pulled out the runner I had been embroidering and repositioned the hoop. I wanted to fuss at Zed for his behavior today on the ice with that stupid hockey game, but I didn't have the heart considering that he'd practically saved Tom's life afterward. I decided it was a draw and let it go.

He unzipped his backpack and started unloading books and papers onto the table. He held up one of them for me to see, and I read the title, *The French and Indian Wars*.

"Is that for a class?"

"Nah, I found it in the library. There's a page in here about the Conestoga Indian Massacre." He opened the book and flipped through the pages. "And a painting that shows them advancing on the Workhouse in Lancaster."

"Oh, goodness," I said, setting aside my handwork and taking the book from him to get a better look. "I thought the massacre happened at Indian Town."

"It did. I'm talking about part two of the massacre, remember? They killed everyone in Indian Town, but then they learned there were other Conestoga being hidden at the Lancaster Workhouse, so they went there a few days later and killed all of them too."

"Oh, right," I said, studying the painting. In it, the Paxton Boys wore black hats and long coats. Some were shown wearing long pants, but a few had on knickers. They were surrounded by the buildings of downtown Lancaster, and in the second story window of one of those buildings were three Indian men, shirtless and all wearing feathers in their braided hair.

"Do you have a pencil?" I asked Zed. "And some paper?"

He rummaged in his backpack and produced both for me. The paper was a little raggedy but unlined. I began sketching costumes for the Paxton Boys first because those were the most obvious in the painting.

After a few minutes I held up what I had for Zed.

"That's great!"

"Any idea yet how many Paxton Boys you're going to put in the film? I mean, I know you can't do two hundred and fifty."

He chuckled. "Camera tricks, my dear. If you know what you're doing, you can make ten people look like a hundred."

"Do you think it's going to be hard to come up with a cast?"

"Are you kidding? There are a ton of aspiring actors and actresses on campus. So many would love a spot in a movie that I'll probably end up holding auditions to narrow it down."

I thought about that, and I wondered if perhaps I had bitten off more than I could chew. I totally wanted to do the costumes. It was just that I might need to start sooner than expected or else bring in someone to help me.

"Where will we find the hats for everyone?" I asked.

"We probably can buy some of them online."

I hadn't thought of that. Putting down the pencil, I asked, "Now that you say it, couldn't you find *all* of the costumes that way?"

He shook his head. "Not believable ones. I want this to be as historically accurate as possible. As does Ms. Wabbim, I feel sure."

Smiling, I picked up the pencil and started again with a fresh piece of paper. I wasn't having any trouble envisioning the settlers, but the costumes for the Indians were going to be a different matter. From what I'd read so far, the Conestoga Indians had adopted many of the settlers' ways, including their dress. That's why, as my eyes returned to the picture in the book, I just knew the men would not have been bare chested like this—especially in December—much less with feathers in their hair. I had to wonder if this particular artist had taken a lot of poetic license.

I asked Zed what he thought, and he agreed. He suggested the Indians probably wore shirts, though they may have been made of buckskin. I guessed the women would have worn buckskin dresses or perhaps ones made of cotton, as Abigail's description of Konenquas indicated, or muslin or wool. I wondered where I could research this further—using something more accurate than this one artist's rendition. I wasn't sure, so for now, I just scribbled a note on the corner of one of my sketches, reminding myself to follow up.

I continued drawing as Zed lost himself in the book. Every once in a while he shared something he read, including several paragraphs about the extreme environment of fear the Indian Wars had caused among the settlers. "They had been murdered in their sleep or while working in their fields. Of course, the Conestoga weren't involved in any of that, but people like the Paxton Boys couldn't seem to differentiate between the separate Indian groups."

"Hadn't those who were murdered settled illegally on land set aside for the Indians?" I was sure I'd read that. Not that it justified the killings, but the Indians had had reason to feel threatened before striking back.

Zed nodded. "It's a really complicated story to tell. Good and bad on both sides."

"Doesn't complicated make it even more interesting? If you can condense it down to the essential elements, I mean."

He started to respond but broke into a smile instead.

"What?" I asked as I took in the sight of his dancing eyes.

"Nothing." He looked away and brushed his bangs from his forehead. "I was just thinking, for someone who never goes to the movies, you sure do have good instincts."

I ducked my head shyly and then couldn't help but look back up at him again.

"Hey," I said softly, "I learned from the best, didn't I?"

Our eyes held for a long moment, way longer than usual. Finally, he broke our gaze, returning his attention to the book in front of him.

Feeling happy somewhere deep inside, I went back to my sketching, though it was all I could do not to doodle out the words, *I LOVE YOU, ZED BAYER!* in flowery script surrounded by hearts.

For the next two hours, I made sketches and then lists of what I would need as he continued with his reading. Of course, until I had a cast list, I wouldn't have an exact idea of my fabric needs and other notions, such as thread and trimmings. I knew I would need muslin, cotton, and wool for sure. And buckskin, if Zed was right. I didn't know what that would be like to sew, but I was willing to give it a try. Fortunately, my machine at home could accommodate heavy-duty needles if I put it on the right setting.

Once I heard the ring of Rosalee's bedside bell and knew she had woken from her nap, I put down the pencil, aware that I'd never had such an enjoyable afternoon. Zed glanced up at me as I stood. I smiled at him and he grinned in return.

"This has been a lot of fun," he said, but then he blushed. "Does that sound silly? I mean, we've just been sitting here…"

"No. I know exactly what you mean. I was thinking that too."

In fact, I thought as I went to help Rosalee, I wished that every day could be like this. Getting snowed in together had made this weekend even cozier, because until the lane outside got plowed, nobody was going anywhere.

A few hours later, to my great disappointment, we were just finishing up dinner when we finally heard the sound of the snowplow scraping its way up the lane.

"Oh, thank goodness," Ella said as she stood to clear the table. "It's about time."

I stood too, grabbing the nearly empty bowl of mashed potatoes and the gravy boat. I was happy for her sake, but otherwise I didn't share her enthusiasm with being connected to the outside world again. A cleared lane meant Zed would be able to leave.

And the last thing I ever wanted Zed to do was leave.

Fourteen

At least Zed came back the very next weekend. He didn't arrive until late Saturday afternoon, and he said he wouldn't be spending the night, but I was determined to make the most of the time we did have. First, he and I took a nice long walk through the woods to the road, where we watched the sunset over the still snowy fields. Then we came back and ate a delicious dinner of shepherd's pie, creamed corn, and sour milk biscuits with the rest of the family. Finally, once the table was cleared and the dishes done, I checked in with Rosalee, who had wheeled her chair near the fireplace, and asked if she needed anything.

"Nope, and after the long nap I had this afternoon, I won't be ready for bed anytime soon. Why don't you get a board game out to enjoy with the others?" She pointed to a cupboard along the far wall of the living room.

I chose Scrabble, a set that looked as if it had been around for several decades, and headed back into the kitchen. "Want to play?" I asked Zed, holding up the box and giving it a shake.

He glanced at his backpack and then said, "Oh, why not? I can do homework anytime."

I turned toward the sink, where Ella was rinsing out the dishcloth. "Ella?" I asked. "You guys want to join in?"

"I will, but Luke's busy fixing that busted pipe on the trough."

Ella, Zed, and I sat at the table and focused on setting up the game. We launched right in and were soon neck and neck on the scoresheet. As we played, I thought of how glad I was that Ella had changed so much in the past few years and that I'd had this chance to get to know her better. I could easily imagine her as my sister-in-law, just as I could easily imagine my life with Zed, the two of us side by side in front of a fire, him reading or on his computer, me doing handwork, sharing an occasional comment or idea between us. Or perhaps a kiss. I sighed, overcome with joy. We were so compatible as a couple.

Why couldn't he see that?

"Izzy?"

Both Zed and Ella smiled at me. "Your turn," he said.

"Oh, sorry," I replied as my face flushed with heat.

I turned my attention to the game, my eyes going from the board to my tiles and back again. Then I nearly squealed in delight as I spotted a way to maximize my points. Grabbing all but one of my tiles, I spelled out the word *BLAZER*, stretching it from a triple letter score under the *B* to a double word score under the *E*.

Zed groaned as Ella said, "Well, if I can't win, I'm rooting for her."

Ella and I totaled up my score together, but the sound of our voices didn't drown out a faint buzz coming from Zed's pocket. He glanced at Ella, looking properly embarrassed for having a cell in her Amish kitchen. He pulled out the phone and looked at the screen.

"Forty-six points! Take that!" I crowed—just as he pushed the button and answered it.

"Hello?"

Ignoring him, Ella hooted and gave me a high five. I grabbed the pencil and paper from Zed's place to write down my total.

He stepped away from the table toward the hall, putting a finger in his free ear as he said, "Sorry, that's Ella and Izzy." And then, "Oh, gosh, no. Izzy's just a friend. I've told you about her before. Remember? My old buddy from back home?"

I froze, the pencil still in my hand. Again I could feel heat flushing my face. At least I was saved from having to meet Ella's eyes when the back door suddenly swung open and Luke stepped inside, his coat and work boots on.

"I need some help," he said. "Where's Zed?"

"On the phone," Ella answered. "Can I do it?"

"*Ya.* I just need someone to hold the pipe while I screw on the gasket."

"Be right back," she said to me.

I stared at the board as Zed's words went through my head.

Izzy's just a friend. My old buddy from back home.

The very thought made my stomach churn.

As his phone conversation continued, I tried to hear what he was saying but could only pick up a few words here and there.

"No way...so much better than I do...seriously?...of course...what time?...nothing important...if you want...I can be there in..."

His voice faded back out, so I wasn't sure, but it sounded to me as if he was making plans to head out of here and meet up with someone else. Feeling nauseated, I stood and went to the living room, away from Zed entirely, deciding to check on Rosalee.

The afghan, yarn, and her hook were all in her lap, but she was staring into the fire.

"Are you doing all right?" I asked.

She assured me she was.

"I think I'll go out and see if I can help Luke and Ella then."

She nodded.

It was entirely an excuse, but I needed to do something to clear my head—not to mention get as far away from Zed Bayer at that moment as possible. I hurried to the mudroom, slipped on my boots, and grabbed my cape, swinging it over my shoulders and then fastening it. After pulling my black bonnet and gloves from the shelf, I stepped out into the snowy night.

I guessed Ella and Luke were at the trough, so I headed that way, determined to be useful, but before I reached the barn, Tom stepped out of the woods, startling me. In the eerie light of the winter landscape, he called out, "Izzy, is that you?"

"Yes."

He increased his steps to a jog as he came toward me. "I was just coming to see if you wanted to go for a stroll."

I turned and looked toward the house, knowing if I went with Tom now, Zed would be…what? Angry? Irritated? Hurt?

Good.

"Where to?" I asked a bit too forcefully as I turned back toward Tom.

"Wherever," he replied, and I tried to calm myself as we set out.

We started off fast but then slowed it down as we detoured into the orchard, finally coming to a stop under the snow-covered branches, looking up at the few stars peeking from behind the clouds. Then we continued on down the driveway, past the bakery and toward the lane. We didn't talk much as we went, and I was relieved to see that Tom didn't try to take my hand or even stand too close to me as we walked.

As we crossed the empty parking lot he paused, as though there was something he wanted to say. But my mind was still fuming over Zed, and I didn't even realize he was talking to me until he said my name.

"Izzy?"

I shook my head, trying to focus. "I'm sorry, what?"

"I was just apologizing for my behavior last Saturday. At the pond. I acted like a jerk. I'm sure in all the excitement that you just forgot about the whistle. I had no call to bite your head off."

His apology had taken me by surprise. I wouldn't have guessed he had it in him, but I thanked him just the same and told him not to worry about it. "I'm glad everything turned out okay."

"You and me both," he replied with an easy laugh, and then we began walking again.

The packed snow along each side of the lane was still nearly four feet high where the plow had pushed it, and it formed a dim sort of tunnel down the center. If I'd come here with Zed, before the phone call, I would have thought it terribly private and romantic. Now it was just a reminder of the wide gap between us, the utter cluelessness of the man in the house on the phone, the man making plans to go see someone else instead of continuing to hang out here with his "old buddy" Izzy.

Unbelievable.

Ahead and off to the side was an especially large mound of snow. Tom stepped up to the bank there and began scooping his hand into it. Behind us, I could hear the sound of a car inching up the lane.

I knew before I turned to look that it would be Zed. Sure enough, I watched and waited as his twin headlights came closer, illuminating us there in the night. When it reached us, the old Saab came to a stop, and then Zed rolled down the window and leaned slightly out. "There you are. What gives, Izzy? I was looking for you to say goodbye."

I didn't answer.

The defrost fan in his car was at full speed. He leaned out further. "I'm really sorry, but I need to get back sooner than I'd expected."

"You...*need*...to get back?" I managed to say.

Even though he had the decency to blush, all I could do was stare at him, the panic and anger that had been building for the past fifteen minutes bubbling up toward the surface. Beyond that, had he not even noticed that I was out here in the dark *with Tom*?

Or had he noticed and just didn't care?

"It's a long story," Zed said.

I was trying to think of a good reply, something along the lines of him being the *master* of storytelling, when suddenly I felt a tug at my neck and something icy cold strike my back and then slide down along my bare skin.

Tom burst into laughter even as I arched, jumping around and squealing as I tried to get at it. Somehow, he had managed to pull the collar of my cape and dress back far enough to drop in a snowball. After blazing an icy path down my spine, it settled at my waist, and I tried my best to dislodge it, swatting at my lower back with one hand, pulling my dress away from my legs with the other.

I pranced and swatted until finally I got most of the snow out of my dress and onto to the ground. Finally, I spun back around toward the car—just in time to see Zed speeding off, his window rolled up tight.

"I think someone's jealous," Tom said, stepping closer as we both watched Zed's red taillights bump down the lane.

Though I knew I shouldn't feel that way, a part of me could only hope he was right. If Zed was jealous, then surely that meant he thought of me as more than just a friend.

I glanced at Tom, my eyes narrowing at the glee on his face. He was no better. After all, I felt sure he'd put the snowball in there in the first place specifically to make Zed jealous.

But instead of revealing how annoyed I was, I sweetly said, "I need to get back."

Tom's voice gave away his disappointment. "So soon?"

"Rosalee's alone now that Zed left." I took off at a march, and Tom hurried to keep up with me.

When I reached the back door, I said a quick good night and slipped inside, regretting that I'd wanted to use Tom to make Zed jealous.

Later that night I helped Rosalee get to bed, taking my time and giving her an extra dose of tender loving care. Then I sat on the couch in front of the dying fire, alone, and tried to sort out my thoughts. I felt embarrassed by how I'd been thinking of Zed up until tonight, as if our coming together as a couple was only going to be a matter of time. Now, I was forced to face facts, as it was clear that any chance of us having a future together was remote.

Sitting there in the shadows, I tried to picture a life with Tom similar to the one I'd imagined with Zed, but I couldn't. Tom was okay, and he was Amish, but I knew he wasn't the one for me.

Zed *was*, but apparently I was the only one who would ever know.

The next morning was a church Sunday, and even though it would make for some extra trouble, it was obvious Rosalee wanted to go. She dropped hints at breakfast until finally Luke teased her, saying, "Guess I'd better see if that wheelchair of yours collapses enough to fit in the buggy. Otherwise, you'll be wheeling yourself all the way down the highway on your own."

Chuckling, Ella assured Rosalee that they would make it work one way or the other. Sure enough, with a little maneuvering, we were able to fit the four of us plus the chair, and off we went. Though I was a little hesitant about being around such a big group of people I didn't know, I ended up feeling really glad we'd made the effort. The congregation was warm and friendly, and the Spirit of the Lord filled the room.

Everyone was so nice, and they made a huge fuss over Rosalee, who thrived under all of the attention. Watching her, I realized she'd probably been a little stir-crazy with no freedom to come and go and only the three of us for company day after day.

Ella sat with Cora and Annie up toward the front, but I sat on the very last bench on the women's side with Rosalee's wheelchair beside me. As often happened when I was upset, I had a hard time concentrating on the sermon. I felt bad about that, but there wasn't much I could do to control it. Mostly, I just kept replaying the evening before, over and over in my mind. Zed's phone conversation. My walk with Tom. Zed stopping to tell me goodbye. Zed speeding off.

Where had he been going last night? Who was there waiting for him? And where was he this morning? My head pounded with unanswered questions.

"We must surrender to God, no matter how dark the tunnel we find ourselves in," the preacher was saying, his voice kind and gentle. That got my attention as I remembered the dim tunnel of snow down the lane. "God will see us through our suffering, but we must trust Him completely, knowing He is good and His will is what is best for us."

I thought about that for a moment, reminding myself that I had to trust Him completely, no matter the outcome. As the preacher continued, a deep ache slowly took root as I was forced to admit that it very well could be God's will that I *not* marry Zed.

My mind worked on that thought for a long while, until the preacher of the second sermon spoke along the same theme and made mention of the difficult roads the apostles and martyrs had traveled for the sake of their faith. Listening to him, I knew I had no right to complain. My living life without the man I loved paled in comparison to the sacrifices and sufferings they had endured.

That afternoon, while Rosalee napped after her big outing, I sat down on the couch with my handwork. But soon I happened to notice a manila file on the writing desk that hadn't been there yesterday. My curiosity got the best of me, and I took a closer look. It was for me! Fixed to the top was a yellow sticky note with my name, in Zed's handwriting.

I picked up the folder and returned to the couch, wondering if he had pulled the file from his backpack after he ended his phone call last night, wanting to give it to me. I pictured him searching the house and then leaving it on the desk.

I opened the file. Inside was a photocopied article—it looked as if it came from a scholarly magazine—with another sticky note on it that read: *Thought you'd like to see this. Not sure which version of the story is the true one, but it's something to consider as we're plotting out the film.*

I couldn't help but feel pleased he wanted to include me in the process and even felt a little guilty for running off with Tom. The title of the article was "Evaluating Subjective Histories." The subheading read, "Oral accounts are a valuable resource for historians but need to be presented in context and not as fact."

I wasn't sure why Zed wanted me to read the article. We weren't working with any oral accounts except for the little Verna had been told. I kept reading.

The author began with the statement that oral histories could not be discounted, especially in cultures with strong storytelling traditions. *For example, in the case of the Conestoga Indian massacre...*

I gasped. Oh, my goodness. What had Zed found?

I read as fast as I could. The author cited an oral history that had been passed down through generations of a Native American family that had an ancestor who claimed to have escaped the massacre as a boy.

That differs from the written record, the author stated, *which claimed all the Conestoga had been murdered. The account also differs on one other important detail.*

I practically held my breath as I read.

Instead of being massacred at the Workhouse in Lancaster as the written record states, according to the oral tradition the Indians were worshipping in a church when the Paxton Boys attacked them on December 27, murdering them as they recited the Lord's Prayer.

I gasped again, this time in pain. *There's no way to know which account is accurate,* the author of the article summarized. *But this account does corroborate the written record that the Conestoga Indians had been Christianized.*

The author continued to evaluate the value of oral histories but I stopped reading. Feeling sick to my stomach, I closed the file.

I couldn't help but be a little embarrassed by my panic the night before about my own problems. A deep sense of shame overtook me at the thought of Abigail or Gorg or Bernard supporting the persecution of the Conestoga, anywhere—let alone a church. A renewed desire to finish tracking down the truth, knowing Verna would have wanted me to, overtook me. As soon as I returned home, I would go over to Rod Westler's and ask for the remaining boxes. I would go through them piece by piece, even if it hurt to be doing so without Verna.

For now, instead of reading more, I sat on the couch and rested, praying too, until I was interrupted by a knock on the back door. I hurried down the hall to the kitchen, not wanting Rosalee to wake before she was ready.

Tom stood on the back stoop, a smile on his face as I swung open the door. "Want to go for another walk?"

"No, thank you," I answered and then covered my mouth as I yawned.

"Tired?" he asked.

I nodded. "And resting."

I hoped he would get the hint that I wasn't interested in him, but he seemed undeterred as he said, "Next time, then," and flashed me a broad wink before turning to walk away.

The cold hung on for several more days. On Wednesday Luke hired a driver and went with Rosalee to the doctor, who removed the cast and put her in a walking boot. I should have done the wash while they were gone, but the north wind blew extra strong that afternoon and I opted to stay by the woodstove and do handwork instead. By Thursday I couldn't put off doing the laundry. After running it through the gas-powered wringer washer in the basement, I hung the clothes piece by piece, standing on the snow-packed lawn.

As I worked outside, Rosalee was busy with the physical therapist inside, a visit that was probably going quite well. She'd had an excellent week, progressing from the wheelchair to a walker with almost no trouble at all. Within a few more days, she would be on her own and my services would no longer be required. I wasn't sure how I felt about that. While I had missed my parents somewhat, I wasn't exactly eager to go, as leaving Indiana meant leaving Zed behind.

When I was only half finished with hanging the wash, Tom stopped by again. I turned toward him, shading my eyes from the morning sun.

"I have something for you," he said, trying to sound mysterious.

"Oh?" I wondered what it could be, hoping it wasn't anything special or romantic. Was he never going to take the hint and realize I wasn't interested in him that way?

Tom held out two fists side by side. "Choose one," he said.

Wishing I could just ignore him, I tapped his right hand. He opened both up, revealing a small snowman pincushion. "So you'll remember our walk in the snow," he said. "And so you'll forgive me for the snowball down your back. I was only kidding around."

"*Danke,*" I answered, taking it from him. I had to admit it was a sweet gesture.

"Seems like I keep having to apologize to you for my behavior," he said with a shrug. I didn't know how to respond to that, so I simply studied the pin cushion more closely for a moment. Then I slipped it under my cape, finding the pocket of my apron. He leaned against the metal post that supported the clothesline and launched into conversation, not even offering to help. I was polite and nothing more—yet he just kept talking. Soon, he was telling me all sorts of personal things.

"We're refinancing one of the loans on our dairy. *Daed* and I went into town first thing this morning. We have a better rate now."

I didn't answer, though my mind was racing as he continued.

"We'll be able to pay it off sooner, not to mention the lower payments will mean we can afford to go ahead and build another house on the property."

As he kept going on about his plans for the future, it finally struck me what was happening. This was no casual conversation.

Tom Kline was declaring his intention to court me.

"Anyway," he said before I could stop him, "I was hoping I could talk you into staying longer. I think you and I really have something special, Izzy, and, well, you know…"

I froze, my mind reeling. I had to tell him I wasn't interested, but as I tried to figure out how, anger began to rise in my throat. This was absurd. Was he really that arrogant, that self-assured? Was he so used to women falling at his feet that he expected me jump at this chance? I had given him zero encouragement since the day we met.

I felt like telling him exactly what I thought of him and his presumptuous ways, but I held my tongue, knowing it wouldn't do to create problems with Luke's brother. Instead, I was trying to form a kinder reply when he suddenly winked at me and said, "I'll take that as a yes."

Then, without another word, he turned and headed toward the woods, whistling as he went. For a moment, I thought about calling after him, but what would I say?

You're out of your mind?

You hold about as much attraction for me as a slop bucket?

You are blind and clueless and so full of yourself that you don't even realize how ridiculous this is?

Of course I didn't say any of that, sure it would come out all wrong. Better to calm down first and take the time to come up with the right words later.

FIFTEEN

Dessert that night was a blueberry pie that Ella had brought up with her at the end of the day. As I dished out ice cream to go with it, she told me she had a message for me.

"Zed called the bakery earlier and asked me to pass on an invitation for you to visit Goshen tomorrow to see a documentary that's being shown on campus."

I stiffened, dripping ice cream from the scoop onto the table.

"Ordinarily I wouldn't encourage such a thing," she added as I reached for a towel to wipe it up. "But he said the film is about the history of the Amish. As far as movies go, I suppose, this one doesn't sound too bad, at least for a girl still on her *rumspringa*."

I was astounded—and apprehensive—but also deeply pleased. Even if we were just to be friends, I longed to spend as much time with Zed as I possibly could. I was leaving early next week, and considering that today was already Thursday, we were nearly out of time. The thought of getting tomorrow with him filled me with joy.

"What did you tell him?" I asked, passing out the plates of pie à la mode to the others at the table like playing cards.

"That you would go unless he heard otherwise."

"Thanks, Ella," I said, wondering what the school would be like and hoping that once we got there I wouldn't stick out like a sore thumb and make him sorry he'd brought me.

That night a warm wind blew through, and the snow began to melt. I awoke the next morning to a constant drip falling from the eaves, and by the time Zed picked me up at one, slush covered the lawn and field.

We immediately headed back to his school.

"Too bad we can't make a whole evening of things," he said as we zipped past a large dairy farm. "I have to work."

"Oh? Where?" This was the first I'd heard of him having a job.

"In the library. It's only a few hours a week, but as luck would have it, this week I pulled Friday night and Saturday morning."

"Tonight and tomorrow," I echoed.

"Figures, huh? Otherwise, you could have stuck around after the film and maybe even met my roommate. As it is, I'll have to bring you home as soon as it's over. Sorry."

"That's okay. I understand."

We rode along in silence after that, passing more farms, then a cemetery, and then a lake that Zed explained was actually a pond. Its surface was covered with large slabs of ice, though I felt sure they were starting to melt on this unseasonably warm day. As we neared Goshen, we bumped over the railroad tracks, creating an odd squeal somewhere under the hood. I looked at Zed in alarm, but he just shrugged and told me that sound had been coming and going for days.

Eventually we reached our destination, and he slowed and pulled into a parking space along the street.

"Is this it?" I asked, craning my neck to see the campus to our right.

He nodded proudly, and then, after he turned off the car, he surprised me by reaching out and taking my hand. "I've wanted to show you this place since the first day I came here."

Our eyes met, and my pulse surged. He looked so excited and happy. Zed gave my hand a squeeze and then climbed from the car. I climbed out as well, the heat from his hand still warming my skin.

"We'll walk onto campus," he said, sounding like a tour guide. After locking up the car, we started down a sidewalk and then passed under an archway with a wrought iron sign that read "Goshen College."

Right away I could see that the place was beautiful. Trees lined the sidewalks, and between large brick buildings acres of open space spread across the campus. We walked along, side by side, with Zed pointing out various structures as we went. The dining hall. The administration building. I took it all in, after a while deciding that the century-old trees and the light posts with glass globes reminded me of the Narnia stories.

I'd been so curious to see Zed's school that it was a thrill to be here in person at last. I had also been curious to see the students as well. Were they Plain? Fancy? A mix of both? One woman with brightly dyed red hair passed us, and then a young man zipped by on a bike. Off to our right, a group of girls in matching purple-and-white long-sleeved T-shirts approached. This was the warmest it had been all week, but I was still surprised when I saw they wore no coats—and were all in shorts. It wasn't until I spotted their mesh bags filled with balls and other pieces of equipment that I realized they must be members of some kind of sports team.

We turned onto a brick pathway that led us to what Zed explained was the student store and center. He held the door for me, and after I stepped through, he scurried to my side to lead the way. A group of girls, their hair long and loose, sat on couches arranged like a horseshoe just inside. They wore jeans, jackets, and boots, all very modern and fancy, but then over by a bulletin board stood two women in traditional Mennonite dresses, *kapps*, and black shoes. Despite the fact that this was a Mennonite school, they didn't seem to be the norm.

One of the girls on the couches—she had blond hair and big blue eyes—called out a hello to Zed. He waved and said hello back but didn't stop to introduce me.

"Who is that?" I whispered as we headed toward the bookstore.

"Shelly."

Shelly, I repeated in my mind, wondering if she was the girl who had called and taken him away from me the weekend before.

The bookstore seemed to carry everything but books. There were snacks and drinks and coffee cups and hats and T-shirts and sweatshirts.

Finally, over to one side, I spotted the bookshelves, which were divided into sections labeled Philosophy, History, Literature, and more.

I wanted to take a closer look, but as I started over, I noticed that Shelly was staring at me through the big glass window that separated the bookstore and the sitting area. She was still there on the couch, but her eyes followed my every move.

Zed didn't seem to notice, so I tried to ignore her as I scanned the various titles. *Essays on Morality. The Pacifist Revolution. The Scarlet Letter.* I'd read that last one, but nothing else looked familiar.

"Come on," he said, tugging on my cape. "Let's go see the rest of the campus. The film will be shown in the library, so we'll save that for last."

Shelly continued to watch us all the way to the door, and I was glad when we were outside and out of sight. We headed down a narrow sidewalk, and as we walked past one building, I could hear the sound of a piano, its notes going up and then back down again. As we kept walking, that sound was replaced with the mournful tune of a violin. I decided it must be a building where students learned about music.

The next stop was the lobby of Zed's dorm, a large area that was cozy and inviting—and completely empty.

"Do people spend time here?" I asked.

"When we have meetings. Study groups. Get-togethers."

I wondered if we would get to see his room, but he didn't offer, so I didn't ask. Perhaps it wasn't allowed.

He glanced at his cell phone and said we should get going to the library because the film would be starting in ten minutes.

"*Ach*, I hope we can get a good seat."

Zed laughed as he opened the door for us to step back outside. "I don't think that will be a problem."

"No? Won't everyone come?"

"You mean all the students?"

"*Ya.*"

"On the whole campus?"

I nodded.

"Probably not," he said, sweetly. "There are lots of other things to do. And they wouldn't all fit in the room anyway."

When we reached the library, I followed him past shelves and shelves of books, far more than the library back home. "You get to work here?" I asked.

He nodded.

I had been impressed with the bookstore, but it paled in comparison to the library. Here students sat at tables at the ends of the rows, some in groups of two and three, others alone. One girl sat knitting, a book propped up before her on the desk. I smiled at her, but she remained focused on both projects.

When we reached the end of the aisle, we turned into a hallway with a row of doors. Zed opened the last one and we stepped inside.

To my surprise, almost no one was in there, just five students, plus a man at the front of the room, wearing a tie.

I was hoping to slip in unnoticed, but as soon as he saw us his face lit up.

"Welcome," he said warmly, coming toward us, his hand extended.

Zed introduced the man as his History in Film professor, Dr. Stutzman, and then me as his friend Izzy Mueller from back home.

"Lancaster County, then?" the professor asked.

"*Ya*. I'm here in Indiana for a few weeks, staying with Zed's sister."

"Well, Izzy, I'm pleased to have you join us today."

"*Danke*."

He turned to go, paused, and turned back. "There's a Q and A after the film," he said to me, "so I hope you'll stick around and field any inquiries that are beyond my expertise."

I had no idea what he meant, but I nodded and smiled just the same. Once Zed and I were sitting down, I asked in a whisper what I had just agreed to, and he explained that because the film was about the Amish, the professor was hoping I might answer any questions afterward he might not be able to.

"Oh," I whispered, but Zed didn't respond. He was looking over at a small group of students who were just filing into the room.

I glanced their way and was disappointed to see that that Shelly person was one of them. She gave Zed a wave—a really friendly wave—but then as soon as he waved back and turned his attention elsewhere, she focused her gaze on me. Her eyes narrowed, and she shot such an angry scowl my way that I practically jumped. Had I done something wrong? Or was she just jealous that the most handsome man on campus was with me and not her?

She and her friends sat in the rear, a few rows behind us, so I turned toward the front and tried to ignore her. I wished they had been here first so we could have sat behind them instead. I could feel her gaze burning a hole in my back.

A few more students trickled in, some of whom were friends of Zed. He introduced a dark-haired young woman with a beautiful complexion to me, adding that she was from Belize.

Soon it was time to start, and Dr. Stutzman quieted everyone down with his welcome. He gave a brief introduction to the film, explaining that it had been made about eight years ago by a group of seniors in his Digital Media Production class.

When he was finished speaking, he walked over to a table and pressed a few buttons on a computer, someone else got the lights, and the film began.

I drew in a deep breath at the brightness on the screen, startled by the intensity of the images, not to mention the size.

Music began to play and then a beautiful landscape of rolling hills filled the screen. That faded into a close-up of a valley with a stream running through it.

A voice began to narrate, telling the story of the beginnings of the Anabaptists in Switzerland in the early part of the 1500s. The facts were familiar to me, of course, but I enjoyed hearing them just the same.

Soon the subject moved to the persecution of the early Anabaptists and how thousands were tortured and killed. One gruesome image after another began to appear on the screen, and I could hear several people in the audience gasp. But I recognized every one of the drawings as having come from the Martyrs Mirror, a book that was a standard in every Amish home I knew.

Looking at the screen, I remembered the sermon on Sunday about God seeing us through our suffering. The thought was comforting.

Actual video was used, probably taken in modern-day Switzerland,

and also illustrations and photos. The film continued through the history of our people as they practiced nonresistance and then dispersed throughout Europe, seeking asylum. The narrator explained the differences between the Mennonites, named after the early Anabaptist leader Menno Simons, which came first, and the other group that evolved from that, the Amish, named after Jacob Amman. The film continued, covering the next forty or so years until the Amish began immigrating to northern America.

"Thus a new chapter began in their quest for freedom," the narrator said, winding down for the conclusion. "Leaving the old world behind, the Plain people found a country where religious tolerance existed."

That cut to a video of what was supposed to be early Anabaptist immigrants walking off a ship and into the new world. They seemed weary but relieved, as if they had finally reached the place where they belonged.

The camera panned up to the blue sky, and over that was a quote:

"No people can be truly happy...if abridged of the Freedom of their
Conscience as to their Religious Profession and Worship."
William Penn
Pennsylvania Charter of Liberties, 1701

That faded out into black and then the credits began to roll. Once they were done and the music and video had stopped, someone turned on the lights and Dr. Stutzman asked if anyone had any questions.

Zed raised his hand. "What kind of cameras were used?"

The professor thought for a moment. "Primarily a Panasonic HD, from what I recall. Probably the DVC pro P2."

Zed nodded as if he understood what the man was saying. "And the shots of Switzerland? Were those made specifically for this documentary?"

The teacher smiled. "Well, I'd like to say our budget allowed for filming jaunts to Zurich, but I'm afraid that's not the case. All the international scenes came from stock video footage."

"How about the ending, at the ship?" another student asked. "That wasn't stock, was it?"

"No. We filmed that up near Chicago at a tall ships festival, using students from the drama department."

"No offense," someone else said, "but that particular ship wasn't historically accurate for the time period."

The professor held up both hands, as if in surrender, and smiled. "You got me there. We did the best we could with what we had."

"Who made the costumes?" I asked. The question flew from my mouth before I could stop it.

"That was a joint effort between the art department and a theater special projects seminar."

I nodded but was embarrassed when no one else followed that up with another question.

"How about something less technical?" the professor urged, his expression good natured as his eyes scanned the audience. "Something about the Amish, perhaps?"

"Yeah, why don't they go home?" a female voice said from the back, just loudly enough for me to hear.

"Excuse me?" Dr. Stutzman asked, placing a hand at his ear. "What was that?"

"Nothing," the voice said, much louder this time, and then the whole group of girls burst into giggles.

I glanced at Zed and saw that the tips of his ears were burning bright red. Looking straight ahead, he raised his hand and rattled off something quickly, just to diffuse the moment. "I find it ironic that the persecuted Anabaptists found safety in America, only to witness the persecution of the Native Americans who lived around them."

"Nonresistant groups offered assistance to the Native Americans," Dr. Stutzman replied. "Look at William Penn."

"What about his sons?" Zed countered.

I remembered what I'd read thus far about that time period, how the land set aside for the Indians had dwindled significantly under the management of Penn's heirs.

"And how about the Plain people who didn't protect the peace-loving Native Americans during the Indian Wars?"

"You're right. I don't want to generalize, but that failing has been recognized," the professor said. "In fact, a couple of years ago a group of Mennonites, Quakers, and Presbyterians in Lancaster County apologized to

Native Americans, including a descendant of one of the Conestoga Indian chiefs, for stealing Indian land and breaking official treaties."

"Really? I hadn't heard about that." Zed took out his phone and opened up an app. No longer was he trying to draw attention away from smarmy comments but was instead fully engrossed in the conversation. "I'll have to look into it more. Thanks."

"You're welcome." Things were quiet for a moment, and then the professor added, "So on that happy note..." He held out his arms and smiled at the audience. "Class dismissed."

On the way back to the Home Place, Zed seemed agitated but quiet. I was so embarrassed by what had happened that I didn't even know what to say. Finally, to fill the awkward silence, I began gushing about how much I enjoyed the film.

"Give me a break, Iz," he finally said, startling me with the vehemence of his words. "Why do people bother to make a film if they're not going to at least *try* to get it right?"

I wasn't sure how to respond. "What do you mean?"

"Please! The ship? The costumes? The twenty-first-century skyscrapers you could see off in the distance if you really looked?"

I blinked, realizing he wasn't all worked up about Shelly's comment. He was just irritated at the movie.

"I realize it was a student project, and the teacher said there wasn't much of a budget, but you know what? I had *zero* budget for *Carving of a Legacy*, and look what we managed to accomplish with that."

I nodded. He was right. In Zed's case, where there was a will, there was a way. Then again, he was a genius and a perfectionist when it came to his films.

"I'm sorry," he said. "I don't mean to get all riled up. I just have this thing about....mediocrity. Settling. What were Dr. Stutzman's words? 'We did the best we could with what we had'? Good grief, if we all felt that way, then all we'd be producing is a bunch of junk."

"Isn't that his right, though?" I pressed. "Just as it's your right to be so picky when it comes to your own movies?"

He brushed his bangs from his forehead and exhaled slowly. "Maybe.

But the problem is that one bad film, one poorly produced piece of schlock like that, can make us all look bad."

I didn't reply, unsure of what to say. Mostly, I was just embarrassed at my inexperience, that I didn't even know it *was* schlock.

Turning my head toward the window, I watched fields of corn stubble poking through the slush and leftover snow flash by as the afternoon light waned.

"Izzy, I..." His voice softened and broke off. I looked back at him, but he kept his gaze on the road, his arm muscles visibly tensing beneath the fabric of his sleeves. "I know I shouldn't be this worked up. It's not just the stupid movie. It's..." His voice trailed off for a moment. "It's what Shelly said. I feel really bad about that. I have no idea what got into her, but I promise you, I'm going to have a word with her later."

"Please don't. Please. That'll only make it worse." Not to mention, that would mean the two of them spending more time together, time hashing out whatever had led her to say such a mean thing in the first place.

Since leaving the film, I had been trying to forget her words—to forgive her for them, even—but the memory still hovered at the back of my mind like an angry hornet.

"It's okay—"

"It's not okay," Zed said, cutting me off. He lifted his hand from the steering wheel, as if to place it over my own, but then he seemed to think better of it and clutched the wheel again. I pretended not to notice.

"Well, I don't want you to do anything about it, Zed, but I do appreciate your saying that."

We drove in silence for a while. I willed him to lift his hand again, to reach over and pull mine close, but that didn't happen. I decided to change the subject.

"It's a shame you have to work tonight. Maybe you can come over after work tomorrow?"

"Doubt it. I have a lot of studying I need to do."

"Oh."

"Sorry." Zed took his eyes off the road for a moment and smiled at me, apparently trying to soften his response.

"I understand," I answered, keeping my voice light. "It's just that I'll be heading home next week, and I hoped to see you as much as possible before I go."

"Home? Already?" He gripped the steering wheel harder than before.

"*Ya*. Rosalee is right on schedule with her rehab. The physical therapist wants her using the walker as much as possible. At first I thought it was too soon, but she's been doing great. Ella told me just this morning that I'd be free to go in a few days, and because Thanksgiving is next Thursday, they were thinking I could take the bus Tuesday, which will get me home on Wednesday in time to help *Mamm* with the cooking and cleaning."

"That's right." Zed ran his free hand through his hair. "Thanksgiving's next week. Man. Time flies."

"*Ya*." I laughed.

He smiled, a little sheepishly.

"You're coming home too, aren't you?" I asked. He looked confused, so I added, "Real home. Lancaster County, I mean."

"Oh."

"Because I was thinking, if you are, maybe I won't have to ride the bus." I shifted toward him. So much for waiting on him to come up with the idea. "I could ride with you instead. It would make the trip easier for both of us."

He rested an arm on the door handle. "The thing is, I don't think I can afford the gas."

"Oh," I said. "Well…I can split it with you. Or even put what my bus ticket would have cost toward the trip."

He shook his head. "It's not just that. My car keeps making that weird sound. I don't know what I'll do if it gives out before I can save up enough to get it fixed or buy another one."

I sank back against the seat. I'd so looked forward to all that time with him in the car, not to mention having him around town for several days back home.

"Sorry," he said again, his voice sympathetic.

"At least I'll see you at Christmas. Right?"

"Definitely. I'll be finished with finals by the middle of December. I'll get home then no matter what, though I may have to leave my car at Ella's and catch a ride with another student."

I imagined him being with someone else for twelve hours—Shelly, for example. She probably owned a car, a really nice one that didn't make funny noises. My stomach lurched. I didn't want to know if she had a car or what kind. Nor did I want to know if she actually had designs on Zed, as I suspected. Why torment myself?

As he slowed to make the turn onto the lane, I felt even more uncertain about our future. At least we would always be friends. Then again, if he ended up marrying someone like Shelly, someone who would want to keep us away from each other, then at most I'd be part of his past. The thought made me angry.

The truth was, I didn't want to be a fond memory or even a good friend. I wanted to be his wife, but with the way things were going, all I'd ever be was his old Amish buddy from back home. I shuddered at the thought.

"Cold?" Zed asked as he took the curve by the bakery.

I shook my head, swallowing back my tears.

As he came to a stop at the house, he said, "I don't have time to come in. I hope I'll see you before you leave, but if not, have a great trip."

I nodded, cringing at the thought of him bumping me on the shoulder with his fist as he'd done before.

He didn't, thank goodness. I couldn't have taken it right now, the ultimate buddy move.

"Don't look so sad, Iz. We'll see each other in December."

"*Ya. Danke*, for everything."

He grinned and I tried to smile back, fumbling for the door handle and then finally finding it.

"Bye," we both said at the same time, although his sounded like his mind was already on the next thing, and mine sounded like a bird dying.

As soon as I got out of the car and closed the door, he backed it around and drove away. I watched until he took the curve by the bakery again, and then I trudged on up to the house, wishing it didn't hurt so bad to love someone who obviously didn't love me back.

SIXTEEN

Saturday morning Rosalee maneuvered around the house using the walker. After our noon meal, as she and I settled in the living room, she said, "I do believe that by the time Ella's baby arrives, I'll be able to do the cooking and dishes. Maybe even work in the bakery some." That was a couple of months away. Three months was a good amount of time for her recovery, so she *was* right on schedule.

We'd both started on our handwork and were busily working away when Ella called out my name, a measure of alarm in her voice.

Rosalee and I exchanged a concerned glance, and then I jumped up to hurry to the kitchen. "Are you all right?" Saturdays were Ella's busiest day of the week, and I knew she wouldn't have left the bakery at this hour without good reason.

She stood in the mudroom, hanging up her cape. "It's my grandmother, Frannie," she said. "Mom called and said that *Mammi* is in the hospital. She's had another stroke."

"Oh, no!"

We heard Rosalee's concerned voice from the living room, asking, "Ella? Izzy? Is everything all right?"

Ella and I went to join her.

"It's Ella's grandmother," I said to Rosalee. "Frannie Lantz. She's had a stroke."

"Oh, poor Frannie." Rosalee sank back against the couch. "How bad is it?"

"Mom said she can still talk, but her left side is weak and nearly unusable." Ella glanced at me. "She asked for you."

"For me?" My heart fell.

"Yeah. Mom wants to make sure you're going home next week as planned. They would like for you to be *Mammi*'s caregiver once she gets out of the hospital. You could start the Monday after Thanksgiving."

I swallowed hard.

"What about your aunt Klara?" I asked. "Can't she take care of Frannie?"

"When *Mammi* had the stroke, she fell and Klara hurt her back trying to help her. Her doctor said she can't lift a thing for the next month."

"Oh," was all I could manage to say.

"Thank goodness your recovery is going so well," Ella said to Rosalee.

The older woman nodded as she reached for me. "I know you'll be a blessing to Frannie too," she said, squeezing my hand.

I felt horrible about it, but taking care of a dying Frannie Lantz was the last thing on earth I wanted to do. My face must have indicated my feelings, considering what Ella asked next.

"What's the problem, Izzy?"

I pulled my hand away from Rosalee. "Let me think about it," I said, feeling clammy all over. I didn't want to be with Frannie when she died, but I couldn't say that to Ella. She wouldn't understand.

"I should probably talk to my parents…"

"Sure," Ella said. "Use the phone in the bakery anytime you want."

But it wasn't my parents I needed to talk with. Not at all. It was Zed. He was the one who helped me see things clearly.

"Let me know your decision as soon as possible so I can call Mom." Ella headed toward the kitchen and I followed. I assumed she needed to get back to the bakery, but instead she told me she was running to the store and asked if I needed anything.

"The store?" I was startled by the abrupt change. Wasn't she upset? If it were *my* grandmother who had just had a stroke, shopping would be last thing I would be doing. Then again, Ella was a far more practical person than I.

"My supply shipment doesn't come until Tuesday, but I'm nearly out of cinnamon and cornstarch. Luke's going to watch the bakery while Penny takes me." She retrieved her cape and pulled it on, but I could tell she didn't really want to go.

"I could go for you," I said, seeing an opportunity.

"Would you?"

"That way I can pick up some snacks for the trip home," I said, feeling a little guilty about the plan that was developing in my head. I thought Penny would be game to help me. It wouldn't hurt to ask.

A half hour later, Penny and I headed down the lane, away from the bakery.

"Any chance we could go to the grocery store in Goshen instead of the one in Nappanee?" I asked.

She glanced at me. "Why?"

My face grew warm and I couldn't manage to say the spiel I'd prepared. We reached the main road, and she came to a complete stop. "Would this have anything to do with a certain young man?"

I nodded.

"Well, in that case…" She turned her blinker on to the right instead of the left and pulled out. "I'm happy to accommodate you. I always enjoy visiting grocery stores—and colleges."

"Thank you," I whispered.

"No problem." As she drove, Penny chatted away, avoiding the subject of me and Zed and focusing on Ella and Luke and the bakery instead.

We stopped at the store first, and I quickly found Ella's cinnamon and cornstarch, and then I chose a couple of oranges and a box of crackers for myself for the trip home. I knew there was some leftover meat from last night's roast back at the Home Place, so I decided I would use that to make a sandwich in the morning, and take a couple of their apples too.

I couldn't tell Penny how to get to Goshen College, so she looked it up in her GPS and followed the instructions it gave to her out loud. By the time we arrived, it was 2:30 in the afternoon. I had no idea where to look for Zed. As she turned on to the campus, I was overcome with anxiety. I didn't know which room was his, and even if I did, I couldn't go down his hall. How would I find him? I'd have to ask someone. And what if he wasn't there?

I didn't know where else to look except the library. What if he'd gone out with friends or something? Could he be off in some gym, playing a pickup game of basketball?

Not wanting Penny to witness my dilemma, I suggested she wait in her car in the parking lot. I climbed out quickly, straightened my *kapp* as I walked, and headed for the front door of Zed's dorm.

The bright afternoon sunshine bounced off the metal trim of the building. A window slammed shut on the second floor. A horn honked in the distance.

Please let me find him, I prayed silently.

I stopped a few feet from the door as movement caught my eye, off in the distance to my left. I looked over, startled to see Zed standing there. He was with Shelly, and they were gazing toward what looked like a dormant garden. They seemed to be deeply engrossed in conversation, and when he slightly turned, I realized why. He was holding his arms out in front of them, his fingers forming a square, framing for her the scene before them. I could imagine it in his film, maybe as a plot of land behind the Indian cabins.

The sound of *No!* welled up from deep within me, so powerful and visceral I thought it had exploded out—but then I realized I hadn't made a sound. I tried to breathe. That was *our* pose, what he was doing the moment I realized I loved him.

I finally managed to draw in a breath of air. It wasn't as if they were doing anything wrong. I hadn't caught them kissing. Or even holding hands. And yet, to me, this seemed far more intimate.

They stood so close. He listened intently to what she said. She leaned toward him.

Then she placed her hand on his arm. Could she feel his muscles? His heat? Did he smell as good as he did that day he showed me the tumble-down cabins? Like sandalwood?

Shelly smiled up at him. Was she falling in love with him at that very moment, just as I had?

Worse, was that what he wanted?

I needed to leave, right then, but just as I was about to turn and go, Zed looked my way.

"Izzy? What are you doing here?"

I forced myself to wave.

He started jogging toward me. Shelly sauntered after him. I put one foot in front of the other, meeting him, trying my best to focus on why I'd come, determined to mask my dismay at what I'd just witnessed.

I started to explain about his grandmother, but he stopped me, saying he already knew. His mom had called earlier to tell him.

Shelly stopped beside him, not saying a word. I kept talking, passing on all the information Ella had given me.

"So you're going to take care of *Mammi*?" Zed asked me.

"I'm not sure," I said, still wanting to have his advice on the matter but unwilling to ask for it in front of Shelly.

"My car's doing better. I should go home too. We can ride together." He turned toward his dorm. "I just need to check my work schedule first."

Walking backward, he said, "Stay here. I'll be right back."

I expected Shelly to follow him—or at least leave—but she didn't. She just stood there, and then once he was inside the building and the door had swung to a close, she turned and stepped closer to me.

"I know what you really want," she said, her voice quiet. "But you had your chance. It's my turn now."

My earlier devastation came flooding back. She was beautiful. She was determined. Besides, I'd seen them framing the shot. I'd witnessed what they had together.

"I have to go," I mumbled. "Tell Zed never mind. I'll take the bus home instead."

Once I was in the car, God bless her, Penny didn't ask me a single question about what had just happened. She did try a little uncomfortable small talk at first, but I was so unresponsive that she finally gave up and drove in silence.

The car was quiet, but the noise in my head was louder than a threshing machine. I couldn't believe Shelly would be that blunt. I would never dream of acting so arrogantly.

But she was beautiful. And clearly an active part of Zed's world.

What had made me think I could keep his interest when I was an uneducated, Plainly garbed Amish girl from back home? I could never compete with fancy makeup, modern clothes, and sexy hair. What value did natural beauty have when compared to a glitzy package? Shelly was like a bolt of fine silk, while I was a dusty old roll of burlap.

When we reached the bakery, I thanked Penny sincerely, gathered my bag, and told her goodbye, hoping she wouldn't follow me in. She didn't.

I slipped into the bakery and moved to the back room, putting Ella's things on the counter. Then I headed back out the front door as all the while Ella waited on an *Englisch* customer who seemed to be buying her out of her pies.

I headed up to the house. When I entered, it was blessedly quiet. I put my things away and then found Rosalee dozing in the living room by a dwindling fire.

After stoking it, I sank down on the stool and gazed at the flames as my mind went back to Zed. And Shelly.

"Oh, you're back." Rosalee raised her head.

"*Ya*," I answered softly.

"Something's wrong."

My eyes stung with tears.

"Izzy." Tenderness filled her voice. "Are you all right?"

I took a deep breath and blinked. "I saw Zed, that's all." I didn't want to give her details. Thankfully, she didn't ask.

She offered me comfort, though, saying, "Don't worry. If it's meant to be, it'll all work out."

Her words surprised me. "Are you encouraging a relationship?"

She hesitated, though from the slight smile on her face, it seemed as if that was exactly what she was doing.

"But why?" I pressed. "What about our different churches?"

Rosalee's eyes warmed even more. "A few years ago I wouldn't have felt this way, but that was prior to Luke and Ella. Since then, I've realized God can work miracles in an obedient heart if the man and woman involved love the Lord and are determined to seek His will in the matter and not their own."

That was quite the speech for Rosalee. I thanked her. It was what I thought too—or at least *had* thought, back when Zed and I still had a chance.

"Now," she said, grasping the handles of her walker. "I'm going to take myself down the hall to the bathroom." She stood. "I can't tell you what a joy it is to be independent again."

I could only imagine.

When Ella came back up to the house, I told her I thought I'd go ahead and leave on Monday instead of Tuesday so I'd have another day to help my *mamm* get ready for Thanksgiving. "If you don't mind," I added. Of course, the main reason I was leaving a day early was simply to get as far away from Zed as possible—or at least from the pain of having to see him in his new world.

"No problem. We can get you to the bus station then." Ella leaned against the kitchen counter, seeming tired. "Zed called, by the way. He said you'd stopped by the college earlier but then just disappeared. What's going on?"

"Nothing," I answered, my heart sinking. "Penny took me there after we went to the store. I went to say goodbye, but it was just too hard, so I left. And he was tied up with things anyway."

Ella nodded toward the back door. "I told him I'd have you call him back."

That was the last thing I wanted to do.

"Go on," she prodded. "Then I could use some help with supper."

Reluctantly I did as she said and went to use the bakery phone. I was hoping the call would go into Zed's voicemail, but it didn't. He answered almost immediately.

"Ella?"

"Izzy."

"Izzy! What happened? I came out and Shelly said you'd left in a hurry."

"I decided to take the bus after all," I mumbled. "It's just easier that way, and Ella's all set to get me to the station."

"That's fine, but why did you leave like that? You didn't even say goodbye."

As I tried to come up with an explanation that would suffice, Zed's voice softened. "It's *Mammi*, isn't it? You're so worried that what happened with Verna is going to happen again, aren't you?"

That was true, but it certainly wasn't why I left...

"I hope you'll dig deep and take the job anyway," he continued, oblivious. "I would give anything to see her cared for in her final days as lovingly as you cared for my father." I could hear his breath through the phone. "Izzy, you have a gift, and God wants you to use it."

His words touched me, truly, and my hurt began to melt away.

"Listen," he said. "You think about it. I need to get going for now. Shelly's here to help me study for a big exam we have on Monday, but I'll check back with you tomorrow if I can."

"Oh," I muttered, the weight of my earlier sadness falling on me anew.

"I guess I won't try to get home for Thanksgiving myself," he added. "With the car problems and all..." I didn't hear the rest of what he had to say. Just the final farewell, which I managed to mimic back to him as I hung up the phone.

Somehow I made it through helping Ella with supper and cleaning up, and then assisting Rosalee, although very little, with her bedtime routine. I went to my room immediately afterward. I tried to pray, telling God I'd rather be a piece of burlap woven by Him than the finest silk cut by the world, but I wasn't sure I believed it, at least not in that moment.

The next morning was the Sabbath, but because it was a no-church day, we relaxed, something both Ella and Luke sorely needed. Rosalee, however, was feeling antsy, so finally Luke offered to drive her to the home of a good friend of hers in the next district over so they could visit.

Her face lit up. "*Danke*," she said. "This cabin fever is really getting to me."

Once they left, Ella gave me the bus schedule and my final paycheck for the care of Rosalee. Then she asked me if I'd made a decision about caring for her grandmother.

I exhaled, slowly.

"I don't mean to be pushy, Izzy, but you're so great at caregiving, not just with Rosalee, but with my father too. I remember how wonderful you were with him." She sounded just like Zed. "I don't know what Mom would have done without you. Honestly, it was a tremendous comfort to all of us."

I decided it wouldn't hurt to open up to Ella as we sat at the table, having a cup of tea. Summoning my nerve, I told her about my fear of death, of how I'd reacted after my patient in the care center passed away—and then that I'd done the same thing when Verna died. "Zed and I decided that it's all related to my grandmother dying when I was a little girl," I said. "Her death took me by complete surprise, and I think I've been reacting to that ever since. It's almost getting to be like a phobia."

Ella headed to the stove with her mug. "Sure sounds like a phobia to me. Though I have to wonder about the cause…" She paused, refilling her mug with hot water before she continued. "Have you reacted this way ever since your grandmother's death?"

I thought about that for a moment. "I don't think so. I lost a great-uncle about five years ago, and while that was sad, I didn't come unhinged." I looked at her. "Even when your father died, I didn't fall apart. There was something about his final days that had been so peaceful, you know? So healing to everyone."

Ella nodded. "My mom's forgiveness for all he'd done made that a time of reconciliation rather than just grief."

I nodded. "It was after that, I guess. With Phyllis at the senior home. She was there one day, and then she was gone the next. It was shocking."

"I can imagine," Ella said, turning toward me and resting her back against the counter as she sipped her tea.

"That whole day I just kept thinking that life is so random, so unpredictable." My face colored, as I knew such words were practically blasphemous. "I know God is in control, and that nothing happens outside of His will. But her death reminded me that—" I clapped my hands together as I barked out, "*Crash!*"

"Crash?"

"Like, *boom*, like, *wham*, like anything can happen, out of the blue, at any moment—and then someone dear is simply lost to you forever."

Ella peered at me over her mug.

"Interesting choice of words, *crash*," she said. "Brings to mind...Zed's accident."

My eyes widened. Zed's accident had been one of the great traumas of my life. It had happened more than three years ago when I was caring for Freddy in his last days and Zed and I were first growing close. I was in the cottage with Freddy, waiting for Zed to get home on the bus. Then I heard tires screeching outside, followed by a thick, sickening thud, the sound of the impact.

Somehow, I knew in that moment it was Zed. Leaving Freddy alone, I dashed out of the house and to the road. Sure enough, there he was, sprawled out on the pavement, the car stopped, the distraught driver climbing from his seat.

I reached Zed first, fearing the worst, and pulled his head onto my lap—an action that I later learned could have been as fatal to someone with a head and neck injury as the impact itself. I thanked the Lord every day that it hadn't been.

Sitting here now, it was as though I were reliving that moment. I gripped the edge of the table with both hands, remembering. In the hospital, I'd acted brave for Zed's sake, even though I'd been so afraid.

Do not fear, was what Jesus had said over and over.

But I did fear. I feared like I had never feared before. I feared I would lose the kindest, sweetest, smartest, funniest friend I'd ever had. I feared that this young man who was so full of *life* would die.

"Do not be afraid," I whispered. *But how?*

"Izzy?" Ella was back in her chair, leaning forward, her hands flat on the table in front of her.

"You're right," I said, stunned. "I don't know why I didn't think of this before. Phyllis's death was so random, just like Zed's accident was so random." I looked at her, my eyes wide. "I know I'm a worrier by nature, but this has to be when things took a turn for me. I see it now. This isn't just a phobia of death. It's a lack of faith, of trust."

"A spiritual issue."

"Yes, that more than anything else. But whose faith doesn't waver when something terrible that like just happens out of the blue?"

Ella took a deep breath, thought for a moment, and then met my eyes. "Honestly? I think you may have forgotten that our Father is in charge, and that nothing is 'out of the blue' in His eyes. To God, nothing is random." She went on to recite a verse from the Psalms, though in a different translation than the one I knew. "'Your eyes saw my unformed body; all the days ordained for me were written in your book before one of them came to be.'"

I took it in, knowing that verse would become my comfort from now on.

"God may not have caused Zed's accident," Ella continued. "But He definitely knew it was going to happen long before it did."

I closed my eyes and inhaled deeply, letting that truth soak into my very core. Of course. God knew. God was in control. God was never taken by surprise. Already I felt better, just having come to that understanding. Opening my eyes, I gave her a smile.

"So will you take the job?" she asked. "With *Mammi*?"

I nodded, still apprehensive but not nearly as much as before. "I will."

Ella's face lit up. "I'm going to go call Mom right now."

I sat at the table, thinking through my discovery—thanks to Ella—and feeling as if a million pounds had been lifted from my shoulders. I prayed to God for forgiveness, and for restoration to my hurting, sinful soul.

SEVENTEEN

When Ella returned, we started preparing dinner, a new baked chicken dish using fancy ingredients, such as rice wine vinegar, soy sauce, crushed tomatoes, shallots, and basil. Ella came up with the most amazing recipes.

As she positioned the chicken to cut it into pieces, she said, "I was thinking that maybe I should fill you in with some...uh...lesser known details about our family. Just so you know what the dynamics are. You will be there in the thick of things, after all."

I was pretty sure Zed had already told me every one of his family's secrets, but I wanted to hear what she had to say, so I didn't tell her that.

"I'm sure you already know most of this from Zed, but just in case he left anything out..." Her voice trailed off for a moment, and then she said, "Would you chop the shallots?"

"Of course." She had brought in two big ones from the root cellar. I scooped them up and carried them to the cutting board.

"Anyway," she continued, "with *Mammi* doing so poorly, my mom has sent word to various family members to come home—while they still can, if you know what I mean."

I nodded. In other words, *before Frannie dies*. I swallowed hard.

"We don't know yet who is and who isn't going to show up, but if everyone does, things might get a little…weird around there, at least at first."

Weird? "Who might be coming?" I asked as I retrieved a knife from the drawer.

"I'm sure Lexie will fly in, both to see *Mammi* and also to help out my mother with her practice to free up her time a little."

"She did that when your father was dying too. I remember."

"Oh, that's right. So you already know her."

"Kind of. We didn't spend much time together, but she seemed nice, and really smart and competent. I know your mom depended on her." I began to peel the shallots and then asked, "Who else?"

Ella gave me a glance, her expression unreadable. "My aunt Giselle from Switzerland. I'll believe it when I see it, but Mom seems to think she might actually come."

I pulled the last of the brown skin off the first shallot.

"If Giselle does come, it'll be the first time in, like, almost thirty years." She paused as she did the math. "Yeah, twenty-eight years. Giselle left home twenty-eight years ago and hasn't been back since."

"Wow," I whispered. The thought saddened me. "Poor Frannie. I'm sure she has missed her. Is Giselle the oldest of her children?"

Ella shook her head. "She's the middle child. Aunt Klara is the oldest, and my mom's the youngest."

Knife in hand, I sliced the shallot in half lengthwise, revealing the translucent whitish pink onion inside.

"Lexie says the story of our family sounds worse than a country music song." Ella told me with a laugh. "And she's right. It does."

I smiled, careful to keep my eyes on the small vegetable in front of me as I held it steady with one hand and began to chop it into narrow slices with the other.

Ella launched into her story, beginning more than forty years ago when Frannie lived here in Indiana with her husband, Malachi, and their three daughters, Klara, Giselle, and Marta. Ella said theirs was not a happy home, that Malachi was a terrible husband and father who abused his family both verbally and physically.

"Things were different back then," she added. "People kept stuff like that secret. The church tended to look the other way. The victims were made to feel as though it was somehow their fault."

I nodded, thinking of a situation of abuse a few years ago in my district back home, one that had been dealt with swiftly and thoroughly.

"Anyway, even as a child Giselle displayed incredible artistic ability, which she'd inherited from her mother and grandmother."

I paused and looked over at her. "Really? Is Frannie artistic?"

Ella nodded, and I smiled, realizing that must be one of the things that drew me to the old woman in the first place, our kindred creative spirits.

"The problem was that Malachi refused to allow art of any kind to be created in his home. That was a rule Giselle frequently disobeyed, so she was often the target of his abuse."

I paused, stunned at the very thought. I knew that making art could lead to various sins, such as pride or lust or the creation of graven images, but there were so many other ways that art could lead to good and godly joy, especially when reflecting the magnificence of God's creation. As long as one understood that and used their gifts appropriately, how could they be denied that right? For me, being forbidden to create would be like being forbidden to breathe.

I dabbed at my eyes with my sleeve, though I wasn't sure if I was crying from the onions or from Ella's story. Cupping my hand, I slid the chopped pieces of the first shallot out of the way and started in with the next as she continued. Ella explained that in the early '70s, when Giselle was about ten years old, Malachi was killed in a farming accident, dragged by his team when he failed to hitch it up properly. I felt bad to hear that but also relieved. At least the suffering he had caused for others had come to an end.

Ella stood straight for a moment, stretching her back. "After that, *Mammi* had to figure out some way to support herself and her girls, so a few months after he died, she moved them all to Lancaster County to live on her brother's farm and work for him as a housekeeper."

I was aware of this part of the tale, how Frannie's brother was a widower by then, living on a farm that belonged to his late wife's family. Once he died, Frannie and the girls stayed on, renting the place for a few years before eventually buying it. That was the farm where she lived still, only nowadays she stayed in the *daadi haus* and her daughter Klara and her husband lived in the main house.

"Once the girls were older," Ella continued, "Klara joined the church and married Alexander Rupp, but Giselle followed a different path. During her time of *rumpsringa*, she got caught up in an affair with her boss, an *Englischer* named Burke Bauer, who had a wife and a kid of his own. Eventually, Giselle ended up getting pregnant by him."

I knew this part of the story too, but I listened as Ella went on to explain, saying that Giselle had managed to keep the affair a secret until she was obviously showing, and even after that she refused to reveal the identity of the father. The one person who knew the truth about that was Alexander, and only because he had once spotted Giselle and Burke together, after hours, in Burke's office. Alexander had kept that knowledge to himself, thinking Giselle's affair was between her and God, but eventually, as she neared the end of her pregnancy and still refused to divulge the father's identity, he felt compelled to share it with Frannie.

Unfortunately, Giselle was so angry and defensive that when they confronted her about it, she went on the attack, denying that Burke was the father and making terrible insinuations about Alexander himself instead, even implying that *he* was the father. He denied it, of course, but though Frannie believed him, his own wife did not. Poor Klara, who had been raised by a cruel and evil man, had assumed the worst about her husband as well. It was all a big mess, and life on the farm was like living in a pressure cooker.

By the time the baby was born, Giselle hated both Alexander and Klara so much that in a final, horrific moment of spite, she named the child Alexandra. Of course, that act caused no end of grief for poor Alexander, who now not only had to defend himself and his conduct to his wife but also the church. Fortunately, he had involved the bishop from the beginning, so he was never formally accused or forced to confess a sin he did not commit.

"The story goes on from there," Ella continued, waving her spoon in the air, "and the details aren't important, but basically Giselle and Burke ran away together, and they stayed gone for nearly a whole year. By the time they broke up and she came back home again, she was pregnant once more. Can you imagine? She was still so young then, in her early twenties, I think, and now she was faced with being a single mother of a toddler *and* an infant."

I shook my head, unable to fathom such a thing.

"To make matters worse, once the baby was born, Giselle ended up with severe postpartum depression. One day, just a few months later, when she was supposed to be watching little Alexandra—or Lexie, for short—Giselle fell asleep, and the child wandered outside and down to the creek. She fell in and would have drowned if not for my mother, who thought she saw something and went to check and ended up rescuing the child."

I shuddered at the thought.

"The incident shocked everyone, but Giselle most of all. That night, she packed a bag and ran away, leaving both kids behind along with a note, asking Klara and Alexander to raise them as their own."

I pulled the baking pan from the oven and scooped all of the chopped shallots into it, coating them in melted butter. Ella showed me how to add in the chicken pieces as well, so as I dipped them into the butter then flipped them over in the pan for baking, she took out a bowl and began mixing up the other ingredients that would be poured over all of it.

"Klara was happy to take the infant but not the toddler," Ella continued. "She still had suspicions about Alexander being Lexie's father, so she refused to keep her—or let *Mammi* keep her, either. Through a friend, they arranged for a private adoption instead, by an older, childless Mennonite couple who lived out in Oregon. That couple, the Jaegers, adopted and raised Lexie, starting when she was about two years old."

I washed my hands at the sink. "And the infant that Klara and Alexander adopted, that was Ada, right? But she didn't even know she was adopted until a few years ago?"

Ella nodded as she measured out the soy sauce. "It wasn't until Lexie came to Lancaster County, trying to find her own birth parents, that Ada's story came out too. It was a big mess at first, but in the end, Lexie's husband, James, pulled us all together and somehow convinced *Mammi* and Klara and Mom to admit what happened. It wasn't easy at the time, but it ended up being a huge blessing for the whole family. Since then there's been a lot of healing."

She grew quiet after that, stirring together the ingredients and then pouring them in with the buttered chicken and shallots.

"Tell me again how Zed's story fits in with Giselle's. I know they're connected somehow too, more than just being aunt and nephew, I mean."

Ella glanced at me and smiled. "Country song, verse two," she quipped. "Okay, let's see if I can make this simple. Burke Bauer, the man who had the affair with Giselle and ended up fathering Lexie and Ada, already had a son named Freddy with his wife. Freddy was about the same age as my mother, and the two of them ended up sort of bonding amid all the Giselle drama back then. Eventually, they married and had me, which makes Burke Bauer my grandfather."

"But your last name was Bayer, not Bauer."

Ella nodded, sliding the pan into the oven and then tackling the messy countertop. "Freddy chose to anglicize it, mostly as a dig at his own father. He changed Bauer to Bayer before I was even born."

My eyes widened as the puzzle pieces clicked into place. We were talking about Freddy Bayer, the patient I cared for in his dying days. "Okay, now I get it," I said, and I knew where she was going next.

As she continued to clean, she told me how Freddy eventually ended up doing the same thing his father had done years before, not just having an affair with a young Amish woman, but also getting her pregnant.

"While he was still married to Marta?"

"*Ya.* My mom found out about what had happened, and though it was hard to forgive my father for what he'd done, she was willing to try. Mom of course held no ill will against the baby—or really even all that much against the mother. In fact, she offered to adopt the child once he was born so she and Freddy could raise him together. Lydia was young and unmarried, so she agreed to let that happen."

I finished the story for her, relieved at last to have all of these facts sorted out in my mind more clearly. "And when that baby was born, they took him home to live with his birth father and his adoptive mother. And that baby was Zed."

She nodded. "Except that our father took off soon after, leaving Mom to raise me and Zed all by herself."

I took a deep breath, thinking about the women in this family and all that they had endured...

Frannie, who had suffered abuse by her husband, but after he died she went on to make a life for herself and her three daughters.

Marta, who had lovingly taken in and raised the very child who was the product of her husband's infidelity.

Giselle, who had given up both her babies for adoption and then fled to Switzerland, where she made a life for herself—a successful one by the world's standards. I couldn't judge by God's. Zed had told me she was a fabric artist, that she combined weaving and appliqué and made a living from her work.

Even Klara, who had adopted her sister's baby and raised her with love and care into a fine young woman.

In a way, I felt intimidated by these women and their strength, but I respected them too. They stayed on my mind all evening, even later, after Luke and Rosalee returned and we all consumed Ella's amazing dinner. Afterward, we sat by the fire, enjoying our final night together. Sadness overcame me at my imminent departure, but that sadness was tinged with anticipation.

I would just need to trust God that my time with Frannie would be a blessing to her—and to all the women of the Lantz family.

The next morning Ella had the coffee started and oatmeal bubbling on the stove by the time I made it out to the kitchen. I quickly set the table.

"Zed left a message for you on the machine. I heard it when I went down to the bakery to put the sticky buns in the oven."

I didn't think I knew anyone who worked as hard as Ella Kline, except maybe my *mamm*.

She turned down the burner. "He said have a good Thanksgiving and he'll see you at Christmas."

My face grew warm, even though the fire in the woodstove had barely heated the kitchen yet.

"He sounded conflicted," Ella said and then turned around, facing me, the expression on her face one of disapproval. "I guess I'm a little slow to catch on, but I think I have the picture now.

I blushed, looking away.

"This thing between you two…it's more than a friendship, isn't it?"

"Ella…" We'd gotten along so well. I didn't want it all to unravel right before I left. Still, I couldn't lie to her.

"It's…one-sided. My side. He's oblivious, as always."

"I'm not so sure about that." She was pursing her lips, her forehead wrinkled into a scowl.

"What do you disapprove of? That he's Mennonite and I'm not?"

She stirred the oatmeal on the stove. "Mostly, it's the timing. Izzy, he's still a boy. You both have a lot of growing to do. Marriage isn't for children."

I couldn't help being hurt. I didn't respond.

"No offense," she said. "I had a lot of growing up to do—by myself—before I was ready to get serious with Luke. Now it's Zed's turn to grow. Think of a newborn pony and how clumsy and trembly and out of proportion it is. Zed's still a young pony, personality-wise. He just has to get through these early stages, and then he'll mature into a fine racehorse." She stirred the oatmeal one more time and flashed me a smile as she turned the burner off. "Correction. He's too off in his own world to be a racehorse. More like a fine, dependable buggy horse, one that is always there for you and takes you where you want to go."

I couldn't help but smile, feeling a little better as I did. Maybe she was right. Perhaps I should focus more on growing up myself.

After breakfast I returned to my room to pack up the last of my things. Luke and I would need to leave for the bus station soon, and though I'd wanted to tell Eddie, Annie, and Cora goodbye, I didn't have the time to go over there. I'd also needed to speak with Tom and finally set him straight. I didn't want to, but I could hear my *daed*'s voice inside my head, telling me to do the right thing. It wasn't fair to lead Tom on or make him think there was any possibility for a future relationship. Glancing at my watch, I decided I would just have to write to them—and to him—instead.

Once I was packed, I attended to Rosalee one last time, but she really didn't need my help. She was well on her way to recovery, and I was very glad for that.

Ella had to go down to open up the bakery, though she told me to come say goodbye as we were leaving. Luke went to hitch the horse to the buggy.

I retrieved my bag from my room and set it down in the kitchen, and then with a heavy heart I ventured to the living room. Rosalee stood, leaning on her walker as I gave her a hug.

She thanked me for everything I'd done, and I thanked her too for more than I could say.

Tears stung my eyes. "I hate goodbyes," I muttered as we pulled apart.

"No surprise there." She chuckled. "Izzy, they're part of life. You'd never get to say hello if it weren't for saying goodbye."

We shared one more hug and then I left, grabbing my bag in the kitchen and my cape from the mudroom. I flung it over my shoulders and then hurried down the ramp to head for the bakery. As I did, I was surprised to see Cora and Annie step out of the woods.

"Luke said you were leaving today," Cora said. "We came over to tell you goodbye."

Tears stung my eyes again. "*Danke*," I said. "Please tell Eddie goodbye too. I'm sorry I didn't have time to come over."

"I'm here!" I heard Eddie's voice a second before I saw him. "I'm going to cut through the fields to get to school. *Mamm* said I could."

Cora smiled. "Just today. So he could tell you farewell."

Eddie, followed by Annie, ran toward me and I gave them both a hug.

"Now run along, Eddie," Cora said as I let the children go. She lifted Annie into her arms as her youngest son took off toward the orchard. The school was on the other side of Rosalee's north field.

I continued on toward the bakery and Cora walked along with me. A crow flew overhead and Annie pointed at it and then said, "Caw, caw."

I smiled at her and then watched as the crow landed in an elm tree.

Cora glanced toward the path through the woods to their house. "Tom's coming over to say goodbye too if he can get here in time. He's hoping you might be able to return soon, once Ella's *grossmammi* is better."

I hesitated, wishing I could tell Cora the truth and trust her to relay it to her son for me, but it wouldn't be fair to reject a suitor via his mother.

He needed to hear it straight from me. "If he doesn't make it, tell him I'll write."

"I will."

Annie wiggled and obviously wanted down. "Ella's going to miss you," Cora said and then to her daughter, added, "And Rosalee too. We'll come back and pay them both a visit after we finish our chores."

After one last hug, Cora and Annie veered off toward the woods, and I continued on to the front of the bakery.

Just as I reached for the doorknob, however, I heard a man calling my name from behind. I stiffened, recognizing Tom.

"So you're really going," he called out.

I nodded, stepping toward him.

"But you'll be back, right? And we can pick up where we left off?" He stopped in front of me, a little too close for my comfort.

I shook my head. "I'm so sorry, Tom, but I'm afraid my interest doesn't match yours." Trying to adopt a lighter tone, I added, "Although I have been flattered by your attention."

Pain flashed across his features, but then he straightened his back and shrugged his shoulders in indifference.

"Whatever. You'll be missing me soon enough. See you around, Iz." He gave a halfhearted bow, almost sarcastic in its execution. Then he turned on his heel and walked back the way he had come. I almost felt sorry for him. I hoped he would find someone soon. As for myself, I wondered, and not for first time, if I could ever love anyone but Zed.

I highly doubted it.

The front portion of the bakery was empty. I put my bag down and moved to the counter, letting Ella know I was there.

She appeared from the back, drying her hands on her apron. "Aw, Izzy. How can I thank you? I don't know what we would have done without you."

"I think you would have managed."

I thanked her not just for her wisdom and the good example she'd set for me, but also for our conversation the day before. "I feel a trillion times better about caring for Frannie now," I told her. The truth really could set a person free. I marveled that just realizing one missing piece of what was going on inside my head could bring such healing. My fears hadn't gone away, but somehow they seemed much more manageable now.

She came around from the counter and hugged me, her belly brushing against my side. "Take care. And thank you again for helping out with *Mammi*."

I nodded, unable to speak. She walked me to the front door of the bakery, where I retrieved my bag before stepping out into the cold behind her. Luke had brought the buggy up. She went to his side, and he looked down toward her as I climbed up to the bench, turning away from their tender gaze.

I settled onto the seat and then took one last look around. As we headed off, my eyes took in the house, the garden, the barn, and even the woods dividing the land. I'd be thankful my entire life for the time I'd spent at the Home Place and for all that I'd learned here.

Even if some of the lessons were harder and more painful than others.

EIGHTEEN

I settled into a seat in the middle of the bus, next to the window, knowing the drive from Nappanee to Lancaster was going to take about eighteen hours, far more than my trip out in the van, thanks to various stops and detours along the way.

At least I had a double seat to myself. As I positioned my bags overhead and settled in for the long trip, my mind drifted back to the encounter with Shelly at Goshen.

She had acted in an incredibly aggressive manner, which had been hurtful, yes, but also confusing. I knew Zed well enough to know he preferred far more demure women. How could he possibly be attracted to her? Was there a chance he just hadn't seen that side of her yet? The thought made me feel better. I could only assume that if she was determined enough to speak to me that way, she would no doubt show her true colors to Zed eventually too, and then that would be the end of that.

Maybe there was still hope.

Wishing it wasn't all so painful, I turned my attention to the passing scenery as the bus drove out of town, noting the acres of corn stubble decomposing in the fields. I told myself that maybe this was just a season for Zed, a time when he needed to explore his options. See what the world had to offer. Realize that what he really wanted had been there next to him the whole time.

Such a process was probably necessary, but that didn't make it hurt any less. For me, it would have been easier simply to look away for a while, so I didn't have to observe from the sidelines while he played the field. The idea was tempting, but I knew I couldn't do that. If I wanted any hope of a future with Zed, I needed to do the very opposite—in fact, I needed to stay close and insert myself into his world as much as possible. To that end, I was grateful for the research and costuming of the film. At least that gave me a reason to interact with him frequently, and perhaps, at some point he would realize his true feelings for me too.

Opening my handwork bag, I pulled out the book he had left me, deciding to use my time to do more research. As the bus rolled down the highway, I read quickly but then slowed for a quote by William Penn. After I read it one time, I read it again.

They that love beyond the world cannot be separated by it.
Death cannot kill what never dies.
Nor can spirits ever be divided, that love and live in the same divine
principle, the root and record of their friendship.
If absence be not death, neither is theirs.
Death is but crossing the world, as friends do the seas;
they live in one another still.
William Penn
Some Fruits of Solitude / More Fruits of Solitude

His words comforted me deeply, especially the line *Death is but crossing the world, as friends do the seas; they live in one another still.* It made me think of my ancestors who first emigrated from the Palatinate region of Germany, through England. They must have known this to be true when they crossed the Atlantic to America, leaving loved ones behind that they had to know they would never see again in this lifetime.

I couldn't help but wonder whom Bernard and his wife left behind. I thought of their daughter, Abigail, and the rest of her mysterious story. Whatever took place, it was no doubt very painful. When it came to Indians and settlers, there was much pain on both sides for many years.

In the side pocket of my bag, I'd tucked the papers with the family tree Verna and I had created from her Bible. I knew that Indian conflicts continued in this country for a long time, and as I studied the list closely I pondered how many generations passed before most of the Indian conflicts finally came to an end.

I returned to the history book to check the timeline in the back, skimming down to Custer's Last Stand, which I supposed marked the end of the worst of it. That hadn't happened until June of 1876—113 years after the Conestoga Indian Massacre.

I dug in my bag and pulled out the family tree list I'd made with Verna, from the chart in her Bible. Looking at it, I counted down through the generations and saw that by 1876, Abigail was long dead and her great-great-granddaughter, Odette, would have been thirty-five. Wow, I thought, five generations of ancestors—no six, counting Odette's children—had lived through a time of serious Indian conflict. That was even more than I had expected. Folding up the paper, I decided that regardless of what Abigail and Gorg and Bernard did or did not do in their time, the whole thing was heartbreaking for everyone on both sides, settlers and Native Americans. I couldn't believe these matters had been handled for so long with acts of violence, greed, and more, causing such pain and loss.

I put away the family tree and the book and pulled out my photocopy of the chapbook written by Abigail instead. As the bus continued to rumble down the road, I read it through again. Then I put it away and took out my handwork, all the details and unanswered questions of Abigail's story swirling around in my mind as I embroidered. Afternoon turned into night, but I couldn't sleep. Cushioning my head against the window, my mind was a jumble of imaginings from the past. The ship that brought Bernard and his wife to this country. Abigail as a child, gazing at the curious little Indian girl. Abigail's continuing relationship with Konenquas, even into adulthood. The rest of the story we might never know.

The one thing I did know was that her story, as recorded in the chapbook, surely ended with the massacre of the Conestogas, Konenquas included. The thought made me ill.

I managed to fall asleep eventually, though I didn't dream. I awoke at dawn, thinking of Zed and feeling overwhelmed with sadness again—an emotion I couldn't seem to shake all day, no matter how hard I tried. By the time I reached Lancaster that afternoon, I felt raw with grief.

My father had hired a driver and met me at the station. On the way home I asked *Daed* if he could get the remaining boxes from Rod's house, the ones Verna told me should be mine. He said he would, but not until Monday. I'd hoped to have the boxes to look through over the weekend, but it was too far for me to go alone with the horse and buggy, and I knew I couldn't rush my father. I settled back against the bench seat of the van. It was just as well. It would have been rude to show up at the Westler place right before Thanksgiving anyway.

I resigned myself to waiting and then asked about Frannie.

"Last I heard, she's still in the hospital but stable. They're thinking she'll probably be sent home early next week, so you should plan to start on Monday or Tuesday."

Even in my nearly exhausted state, I found myself feeling ready to care for her. I could hardly believe that somehow, with Ella's help, I had managed to go from not wanting the job at all to almost looking forward to it. My thoughts fell back to Zed's letter from earlier this fall, the one where he encouraged me to push myself. I would.

Daed and I shared a comfortable silence the rest of the way home, but once we got there, I braced myself for the usual chaos. To my surprise, however, there was none. As he carried in my bag for me, he explained that *Mamm* and Thomas were out running errands, and Linda had gone to pick up Stephen from school. Once he headed off to the barn, I was alone in the empty house.

Enjoying the quiet, I took a long hot shower, washing away the grime of my trip. Once I was finished and dressed in a fresh, clean set of clothes, I went straight to my little sewing room and worked. My plan was to do as much machine sewing as I could for the next few days so that I could bring as many unfinished pieces as possible to Frannie's, where I would complete them—whether with embroidery or crocheting or some other kind of needlework—by hand.

Of course, when Linda got back, she bombarded me with questions about my trip. Then she bemoaned the fact that I was off to care for Frannie Lantz the next week. "You're so lucky."

"But you've been working too, right?"

Linda made a face. "*Ya*, but you get to be around grown-ups. I'm tired of changing diapers and wiping noses."

I shook my head. She wouldn't last a day as a caregiver.

Linda added, "It's not just that. *Everyone* wants your help."

"Including me." *Mamm* stood in the doorway. "Welcome home, Izzy. Now both of you, come into the kitchen and put away the groceries. We have a lot to do to get ready for Thanksgiving."

I put my embroidery down and followed Linda, wishing—and not for the first time—that my mother was a more affectionate, demonstrative person. Hadn't she missed me? Wasn't she glad to see me?

Perhaps being at Frannie Lantz's little *daadi haus* wouldn't be so bad after all. I'd missed my family while I was gone, but now that I was back with them, I was already remembering the reality of day-to-day life around here. All work and no play—and not nearly enough love. At least not enough affection.

I went into the kitchen as directed, but before I jumped in to help, I took it upon myself to give *Mamm* a hug. She seemed startled at first, but then, to my surprise, she wrapped me tightly in her arms and held on for a long moment.

"I missed you, child," she whispered, bringing tears to my eyes.

Her words kept me warm the rest of the day.

I spent all of Wednesday helping *Mamm* clean and cook. The day after that was Thanksgiving, which started with devotions as a family. We fasted until our noon meal of turkey, mashed potatoes and gravy, stuffing, fresh bread, green beans, cranberry salad, pickled beets, cookies, and pies.

All of my siblings, the spouses of the older four, and my nieces and nephews came, so we had a full table. Afterward, Tabitha, Linda, and I cleaned up. Then, as everyone else sat around in the main room visiting, I retreated to my little room to catch up my journal. Every once in a while the laughter of my family pulled me out of my thoughts, but mostly I kept focused on writing down my experiences at the Home Place.

After about forty-five minutes, *Daed* came to the door of my room. "Aren't you going to join us?"

"I'm content in here."

"But we're all together."

"*Ya*," I answered. "I'm just in here."

"Izzy, I want all my offspring in one room. I'm so thankful for the full quiver God has given me. Please."

Reluctantly I followed him. I listened to my family laugh and joke for the next hour, enjoying them to a certain extent but not joining in. It wasn't that I didn't want to be an active part of this family. It's just that my mind kept wandering away to other things, as it always did.

The next day Marta stopped by, and I officially accepted the job as Frannie's caregiver. She asked me to start the following Tuesday and said I could stay in the *daadi haus* with Frannie.

"We'll have to take it day by day, but depending on how she does, we'll try to give you a few days off to come home at some point in two or three weeks."

I assured her I looked forward to caring for her mother.

On Sunday, as I packed, I made sure to include the photocopies of the letter from Abigail to Bernard, and Abigail's chapbook. I couldn't fathom where to go from here, but I simply had to find the rest of the story. Surely somewhere out there were the answers I needed.

I thought of my *mamm*. I had already shown her the letter and the chapbook—both of which she'd found only vaguely interesting—but now it struck me to ask her if she had any ideas on how to proceed. After all, these were her ancestors too.

I took the two documents downstairs with me and went in search of her. The scent of corn bread baking found me before I found her. She stood at the stove with a wooden spoon in her hand, heating up hamburger soup to go with the corn bread for our supper. Holding the documents up so she could see them, I asked if she knew of any other old family records or papers from her mother's side that might be somewhere other than with the papers Verna had. "The chapbook was professionally printed. It seems as though another copy would be somewhere—an intact one."

"I've never seen or heard of one." *Mamm* stirred the soup as she spoke. "When my grandparents died, the bulk of that kind of stuff went to Verna.

From what I can recall, there were at least several boxes' worth, a big jumbled mess of things that should have been thrown away." She put the spoon into a mug on the counter. "My grandmother was a bit of a pack rat. Then again, so was Verna."

There was no reason for me to comment on what people chose to save or not—that wasn't the issue. In my opinion, it was far better to save too much than too little, but my *mamm* probably would have disagreed.

"*Ya.* Those are the boxes Verna and I went through, and there was a lot of junk in them. But in and among the junk was some important stuff too. I just wondered if there was any chance that part of the collection got divided out and went to your mother."

Mamm shrugged. "I have no idea, Izzy. I didn't pay much attention to that sort of thing." She thought for a moment. "Actually, I did end up with a few special papers that were my mother's, but I haven't looked at them in years. I think they are mostly just recipes and mementos and stuff she kept in a drawer in the old desk."

My heart beat a little faster. "Could I see those papers?"

"Sure. They are still there in the right bottom drawer, in a manila envelope." She opened the oven door and pricked the corn bread with a fork. As she stood, she added, "Now that I think about it, there were some documents in there too. You're welcome to take a look if you want."

I hurried into the living room and knelt beside the large pedestal desk. It was definitely an antique and well worn. The top was stained with ink, and the sides were marred. I knew *Mamm* hoped *Daed* would refinish it when he had some extra time. Scuffed up or not, I had always loved the desk, and as a child I used to sit at it and write and think, having no interest in what was inside. Now there was nothing I wanted more than to examine the contents of that bottom drawer.

I opened it and found the packet. Holding it to my chest, I retreated back to my room. After opening the envelope, I spread the contents across my bed, sorting the items slowly into piles. Sure enough, I found recipes, but also some official-looking documents, including marriage certificates, death certificates, birth certificates, and then a bundle of papers tied with a string.

I carefully sorted through the small stack, realizing these papers were all church related. There were a few death notices and a couple of letters about membership, but not for anyone I knew. Then again, I decided to compare the names to the family tree, just to be sure.

After that, I came across a document that made me do a double take. I didn't recognize the names of the people involved, but what struck me was how odd it was to see something like this in writing. In the Amish church, any sin could be forgiven if the sinner was willing to confess and repent, but the process was always a verbal one, not something anyone would ever write down. Yet this looked to be just that: a confession and statement of repentance, signed by the sinner and his presiding bishop. Continuing on through the pile, I found several more of these, including one for a man who had conducted a dishonest business dealing and another for a woman who had stolen her neighbor's cow. Then I came to another, and it stole my breath away. It was the church document Verna had told me about, the excommunication declaration and subsequent signed confession of Bernard, Gorg, and Abigail.

The ink had faded and the handwriting was hard to decipher, but I lit my lamp and held the brittle page underneath it.

The document was dated 11 April 1765, and the message was brief:

> We, the undersigned, do willingly declare that we betrayed, both in word and deed, the Conestoga Indians, a tribe known to be peaceful, God-fearing, brothers and sisters in Christ.
>
> We now confess these sins to God and His church, requesting to be reinstated to the fellowship and the faith.

At the bottom, it had been signed by four people: Bernard, George, Abigail, and somebody named Ingemar Joblenz, who I assumed was the bishop involved.

With the document still in my hand, I sank down on the edge of my bed. It wasn't as if I'd found the rest of the chapbook, but at least now I knew that whatever happened to harden Abigail's and the others' hearts against the Conestogas hadn't defined their entire lives. According to this, they had confessed and reconciled with the church in the end.

Late Monday afternoon, as I double-checked the bag I'd packed to take to Frannie's, the sound of a buggy turning into our drive sent me dashing to the window. It was *Daed*! I'd been waiting all afternoon for him to come back from Rod's.

I ran down the stairs and through the kitchen, grabbing my cape, banging open the back door, and tearing toward the barn.

He had pulled the buggy to a stop.

"Did you get the boxes?" I called out.

"Whoa," *Daed* said, climbing down to the ground. "How about a hello first?"

I ducked my head, acknowledging my bad manners.

He nodded toward the back of the buggy. "Rod wasn't sure where everything might be, but he did manage to locate one box of papers and he promised to root around for the rest."

"*Danke*," I said, both thrilled to get one box but disappointed to not have everything in my possession. With a new baby, Rod and Ruth Ann probably didn't have much time to go poking around in the attic or basement. As soon as I had a day off, I would hire a driver if I had to and offer to do the poking around myself.

I hurried to the back, tugging on the wooden box until I could get both of my hands on it.

"I'll carry it in," *Daed* said, coming toward me.

It was heavy but not impossibly so. "I have it," I said, lifting the box in my arms.

I took it straight to my room, knowing I only had about twenty minutes before supper—just long enough for a quick perusal. I went through it all, skimming the papers for the missing pages of the chapbook or another, intact copy.

Sadly, I found neither. Of course, other things of importance could be in here, so I decided to take the box to Frannie's with me and use my downtime there to sort through it more slowly. But overall, I was deeply disappointed. I simply *had* to find those pages and learn the rest of the story.

The next morning, I told *Mamm* goodbye and then *Daed* drove me to Klara and Alexander Rupp's farm, where Frannie lived.

On the way over, he asked about the box he'd brought the day before, if it had done any good and what, exactly, I'd been hoping to find. I reminded him of the chapbook and explained I was on a quest to recover the missing pages.

I sighed, gazing at a covered bridge up ahead. "I just don't understand why anyone would cut up something like that."

He didn't comment right away, but a few minutes later, once we'd crossed over the creek, he ventured some guesses.

"There might have been shame—for someone in the family—in helping the Indians or in harming them. Perhaps there was fear. There were certainly Plain people who were terrified by the Indians and who didn't protect them the way they should have."

"But why destroy just half the book? If that was the case, why not just get rid of it completely?"

He shrugged. "Maybe someone didn't want a particular person in the family to know the story but still wanted the early history of the family known someday."

"Maybe so," I said, wondering if I would ever find out.

Nineteen

When we reached the Rupps' farm, *Daed* offered to carry my stuff into the *daadi haus* for me, so we said our goodbyes in the driveway. As he loaded up and began walking toward the back of the property, I moved to the door of the main house and knocked on the door.

I expected things to be a little confusing at Klara's, but I wasn't prepared for the turmoil going on inside. Alexander let me in, saying as he did, "Izzy, *ach*, I'm ever so thankful you're here." He wore his work coat and gloves and looked as if he was heading out to the field. "They're in the kitchen. Go on in."

"*Danke*."

"Izzy's here!" he called out.

As soon as I stepped inside, he slipped out. I peeled off my cape, hung it on a peg to the right of the door, and headed through the living room to the kitchen.

Pots and pans were stacked on the stove and counters. Marta stood at the sink, tackling a mountain of dirty dishes. She wore a lavender print dress, and her rounded *kapp* sat back on her head a little too far, as if it had been knocked askew and she'd not had a chance to set it right again. She turned toward me and said a quick hello, swiping at the beads of sweat on her forehead with the back of her hand, even though the house was cool.

"Is everything okay?" I asked.

Klara, who was as thin as her sister Marta was plump, leaned against the counter with one hand and clutched the small of her back with the other. She greeted me too and then said, "We're running a little behind. We had quite the day yesterday. Ada was over with little Abraham, but he got sick. She was afraid it was the flu, so she left in a hurry, hoping not to expose all of us."

"And then I got called away for a birth," Marta added.

"And then our neighbor needed Alexander's help with a pipe that burst, and he didn't get back until late. Needless to say, I couldn't keep up with what needed to be done."

"Wow. How's Abe?"

Marta sighed. "I thought he just had too many cookies, but Ada said he threw up last night and was running a fever this morning, so I guess I was wrong."

Poor Abe. I hoped the illness would run its course quickly and that no one else would come down with the same thing.

I looked to the two women and asked where to jump in. "Should I take over with the dishes?"

"No, why don't you handle the linens," Klara said. "We had a hospital bed and table delivered yesterday, and Alexander adapted it to work with a battery. It's out in the *daadi haus*, right in the living room. The sheets should be out there as well. Once you've made up the bed, come back to help Marta."

Marta glanced at me over her shoulder and added, "Thank you for coming to us like this, Izzy. There's no one else we'd rather have." She glanced at Klara and then back at me, adding, "I know it's a sacrifice for you."

I shrugged, thankful she hadn't said "effort" or "stretch." I considered reassuring her I was better in that regard since talking with Ella, but it was too complicated to go into right then.

"It won't be easy," Klara said, "but at least Ada should be able to spell you some. And as soon as my back is better, I'll help. In the meantime, I'll keep up with the organization of *Mamm*'s care—orchestrating meds, that sort of thing. We'll all work together to get her better."

It turned out the sheets weren't in the *daadi haus*; they were still on the line. Ada had washed them the day before, but after she'd left in a hurry no one else had remembered to retrieve them. Thankful it hadn't rained, I collected the sheets and the full load of towels that were out there too and hauled them all into the main house so Klara could tell me where everything went.

Once I'd dumped my load on the kitchen table, Marta helped me fold while Klara sat in a chair, icing her back.

"I know you folks are relieved Frannie's finally coming home," I said as I reached for a pillowcase.

The two sisters glanced at each other, and I was reminded that Frannie's being sent home from the hospital was probably more of a hospice-type decision than an indication of any improvement. I asked about her prognosis and then braced myself for the answer.

"It was a hemorrhagic stroke, which is the worst," Marta said.

Klara nodded. "She had one a few years ago."

I knew that from Zed.

Marta continued. "Klara was with her this time and was able to get help for her immediately. So at least the damage isn't as bad as it could have been, meaning she could have easily died. She can still talk, and her mind is mostly clear, but she's very weak, much more so on her left side. She wants to come home. She thinks her time is close."

"She wants to be with family," Klara added, "so we've contacted the ones who live out of town, and it looks as though most of them are going to try to get here."

"Really?" I asked, wondering if that included Zed. His Christmas break wouldn't start for another ten days, and though I would love to have him here sooner, I hated the thought of him missing school, especially at the end of the semester.

"First to arrive will be our niece Lexie," Marta said as she folded a towel. "She lives in Oregon, but she's coming out as soon as she can. Once she gets here, my patient load will lighten enough that I can jump in more with *Mamm*."

I nodded. Zed was crazy about Lexie. He would be thrilled to learn she was coming.

"Is her husband coming too?"

"James? Not at first," Klara said. "Maybe later, if need be."

I assumed "if need be" probably meant if and when Frannie died. "Who else?" I asked, suddenly grateful Ella had brought me up to speed on all of the family dynamics.

"Zed, once school gets out on the thirteenth. If Ella is able to get away from the bakery by then, she will travel with him. Luke would most likely come as well."

Both women were quiet for a moment, and then Marta added in a soft voice, "Giselle. Our sister from Switzerland. She might come."

Klara made a face.

Marta turned to her and spoke defensively. "It would be good for *Mamm*. You know how much she longs to see her."

Klara shrugged, trying to act nonchalant but not really pulling it off. "Personally, I think it would be too much for *Mamm* right now. For everyone, really."

Marta's eyes filled with tears, something I'd never seen before. "I don't think that should be a factor in anyone's decision. We don't have much time left. If Giselle is ever going to come, she should come now."

My hand practically trembled as I placed the folded pillowcase on the table, unnerved by Marta's tears and the tension in the room. No one said a word for a long moment. I searched for something to say that would set the sisters on a different course. "Where will everyone sleep?"

"Klara and I have been talking about that," Marta said. "Giselle may want to stay in a hotel, but Lexie—and James, if he comes—can stay at Ada's. Zed, Ella, and Luke will stay with me."

I turned to Klara. "I'm surprised Frannie hasn't insisted everyone just stay here so they'll all be around her as much as possible. Certainly, this big old house has enough bedrooms." Even as I said it, I realized it may have come out sounding presumptuous, but neither one seemed to take offense.

Marta answered for her sister, a towel tucked under her chin as she folded it in thirds. "That was the original plan, but with Klara's back out,

I'd rather not burden her with any extra cooking and cleaning if we don't have to. Of course, anyone who really wants to stay here would no doubt be welcome to, I'm sure."

She glanced at Klara, who paused a long moment and then replied, "*Ya*, anyone except Giselle."

The medical van carrying Frannie arrived just after lunch. We were ready for her, the sheets tucked into the corners, her favorite quilt spread across the bed, and her house scrubbed clean. We managed to get her inside and all set up, and then she fell into a deep sleep almost immediately.

There was still more to do in the main house, and Alexander needed to get back outside, so once Frannie was asleep, Klara and Marta left her in my care and returned to their other duties. After so much noise and commotion, the *daadi haus* felt blissfully silent, the only sound the steady if somewhat raspy breathing coming from the bed.

Glancing around the tiny living room, which was nearly eclipsed by the large hospital bed, I decided the best place for me to sit when I was with her was on a small padded chair to her right, between the bed and the wall. The room was cramped but not uncomfortably so, with a recliner shoved in on the other side of the room next to a settee. As in the main house, the *daadi haus* had an open floor plan, so from where I sat I could see the whole kitchen, as well as the hall that led to the bathroom and two bedrooms.

Later, I would dig out my handwork and pass the time that way, but for now I simply watched Frannie sleep.

Without her *kapp*, I could see how thin her hair was. Her face looked peaceful, her eyelids nearly translucent, and her skin amazingly unwrinkled considering her eighty-four years. I thought of my own *Mammi* and how I used to sit by her side for hours at a time when I was little, right up until the evening before she died.

As I had told Ella when she and I talked about it, I was heartbroken after *Mamm* explained that my grandmother had died during the night. I hadn't expected it. I'd thought she'd go on staying in bed, with me visiting her and holding her water glass and listening to her stories, until I was grown. Why hadn't anyone prepared me? Instead, it was one of those times when my *mamm* and sisters said I was being *too* sensitive and *over-reacting* and *not* being able to accept God's will. That wasn't it. I just felt the loss, deeply.

Thinking of that time now, I was nearly on the verge of tears. But then I heard footsteps outside and managed to pull myself together just as the door was opening.

"Getting settled?" Marta asked, coming into the room and stepping toward her mother.

I simply nodded.

She rested her hand on the silver bars at the foot of the bed. "*Mamm*'s meds are in the kitchen, and the next dose is at three. If Klara doesn't bring her pills out here to you, be sure to go in and get them. She's resting her back now, and she may fall asleep."

"Of course. No problem."

"You'll see that I brought easy-to-swallow things for *Mamm* to eat, like soup and yogurt. She should be able to take that kind of food without too much trouble."

"Thank goodness she can still swallow."

"I know. I'm afraid her mobility will be limited, though."

I nodded. I expected that. I could handle the physical care just fine. It was the emotional part that concerned me.

"And, of course, there are groceries in the fridge for you." Her eyes looked tired. "Though you're welcome to have some of the soup too if you would prefer that."

"*Danke*," I said, thinking of all the times I'd fed Freddy soup when he was ill. Marta and I had made a pretty good team back then, and I felt sure we would find our rhythm again this time as well. "Which bedroom should I use while I'm here?"

She gestured toward the hallway. "There are only two. Use the guest room at the end of the hall."

"Okay."

"If you have any work for Susie, I'd be happy to deliver it. I drive by there nearly every day."

"Wonderful. I'll give some to you tomorrow." I'd finished the last runner while on the bus ride home from Indiana, but I still needed to press it.

Marta glanced at her watch. "I'm heading out for now. Do you have everything you need?"

I assured her we were all set and would be fine. She didn't seem too confident about that, but I didn't take it personally. She was worried about her *mamm*, that was all.

We'd been so busy since I arrived that I hadn't had the chance to unpack, so after she left I decided to start with that. *Daed* had left my stuff—my handwork bag, a small suitcase, and the box from Rod's—piled in a corner of the living room. I carted it to the back bedroom in two trips and then hung up my clothes and used a drawer in the bureau for everything else.

As I slid the empty suitcase under the bed, I wondered how long I would be here. It was hard to tell. The way everyone talked, Frannie could be dying any minute—or she could hang on for weeks. I hoped it ended up being the latter, of course, especially for poor Zed, who loved his grandmother so much. If she could hold on at least until his Christmas break, he could spend time with her.

Back in the living room, I saw that Frannie was still asleep but doing fine. I was feeling too antsy to sit and do handwork, but I wasn't in the mood to go through the box of papers, either. I had noticed an iron and ironing board in the linen closet earlier, so I decided to use the time to press the runner for Susie.

While the iron heated on the stove, I set up the board and arranged the runner on it. I enjoyed ironing and found something about it quite peaceful—except on those rare occasions when I became distracted and burned a finger. I laid the handle aside, on the counter, and after a few minutes reattached it to the hot iron. I pushed it over the fabric quickly, pressing the wrinkles out of a good-sized section before it cooled. Then I placed the iron back on the stove, detached the handle, waited another three minutes, and repeated the process. Occasionally as I worked, I glanced over at Frannie, who continued to sleep.

Once I finished the runner, I readied it for transport along with everything else I'd made since the last batch of items I sent to Susie. I left the iron in the kitchen to let it completely cool. Then, after putting the ironing board away, I looked at the time, noting that Frannie would need her medication soon. Klara hadn't come yet, so I headed to the house.

Sure enough, she was sound asleep in the living room, softly snoring on the couch. With a smile I walked into the kitchen and reached for the container that held Frannie's meds, which we'd decided to keep on the shelf nearest the sink. It was one of those plastic boxes divided up by days and times. I scooped the pills from the correct square into my hand and then carried them back to the *daadi haus*.

I hated waking Frannie when she was resting so well, but knew I needed to. I remembered from my training how important it was for stroke patients to get their blood thinners at the correct times.

In the kitchen I filled a glass with water and plucked a straw out of the box by the sink, and then I returned to her side.

"Frannie," I said, leaning close to her. "It's time for your pills."

She stirred a little.

I repeated myself.

She opened her eyes.

"Where am I?"

"You're at home, in your very own *daadi haus*."

Her gaze wandered the room for a long moment before coming to rest on my face. She smiled. "You're still here."

"*Ya*, I'm staying with you. As your caregiver."

She seemed pleased by that even though I'd already told her earlier. I raised the bed with the control, and when she was high enough I told her to open her mouth. I slipped in the first of the pills and then positioned the straw. She swallowed and sputtered but then took another sip and swallowed fine. It was a blessing the stroke hadn't hindered her ability to eat and drink. Otherwise she probably would have needed someone more skilled than I was, someone who could handle a feeding tube.

When she'd finished taking all of the pills, I put the glass on the table and asked if she would like something to eat.

"Goodness, no," she replied, seeming concerned. "Is it time for supper? Or breakfast?"

I shook my head and gave her a reassuring smile. "It's a little after three in the afternoon. I just thought I'd offer."

"I see," she whispered, closing her eyes.

I was about to ask if she needed another sip of water when I realized she had already fallen back to sleep.

The rest of the afternoon passed quietly, punctuated only by a quick visit from Alexander and several from Klara. Frannie dozed off and on, and though Klara expressed concern that her mother hadn't been sleeping this much in the hospital, I assured her it was likely the transfer from there to here that had worn her out so.

"I bet she'll be better by tomorrow," I said.

And I was right. The next morning I was up and dressed and at my post by the time Frannie awoke, and I could tell right away that her mind was a bit clearer than it had been the day before. She also spoke with a stronger voice, and her eyes seemed more alert.

I got her to eat a little yogurt for breakfast, administered her morning meds, and then helped clean her up for the day.

Though she dozed off and on throughout the morning, she fell into a deep sleep after lunch. I wasn't in the mood to do handwork, so I decided to use the afternoon to do a thorough job of sorting through the box my *daed* had brought to me from Rod's.

I carted it into the living room, placing it on the floor by the settee, and began to go through it more slowly than before. The task reminded me of Verna, and I noticed that for the first time since she died, the familiar pang of loss was tempered by a warm, happy fondness of her memory. I wondered if that was how the process was meant to work, that slowly the pain faded while the warmth of happy times grew and eventually eclipsed it.

Late that afternoon, Frannie woke again, still fairly lucid. I had papers from the box in piles around me on the floor and as I quickly put them away, she asked what I'd been doing.

"Researching some of my ancestors." I didn't go into detail about the chapbook or the other things I'd found, but I did say, "Zed is doing a new film, and I'm gathering information to help him with the script."

Frannie smiled a little and said, "I still haven't seen his first film, but I've really wanted to. It's about my own great-grandfather, Abraham Sommers, you know."

I did know. Abraham Sommers was the name of the wood-carver from Switzerland featured in the film.

"Zed promised to bring over his computer and show it to me, but we never got around to it. And I got permission from the bishop and everything." She paused in thought. "Will this next movie also be about Abraham Sommers?"

"No. Zed wants to focus on an ancestor again, but this time he's going with the ones who settled in Lancaster County in the 1700s."

Frannie blinked, her forehead wrinkling. "I don't know what he's talking about. My family immigrated to Indiana, not Pennsylvania. And that wasn't even until the 1870s."

Puzzled, I said, "But Zed believes his nine-greats-grandfather lived here. A Hubert Lantz?"

"Oh, I see. He's talking about my late husband's family line. He's right. Malachi descended from a group of Amish settlers who came here in the 1700s. They were originally from Germany. I think their ship was called *The Virtuous Grace*." She smiled, seemingly pleased with her memory. "The whole Lantz clan ended up moving on to Indiana a century later, so I tend to forget they lived in this area for a while first."

I smiled back. Those were indeed the ancestors Zed was trying to get information on. A few years ago, he and I had worked together on a genealogy project, and we'd learned that we'd both had ancestors on the same ship, for the same sailing. Looking into it further, we found out that the two families even ended up in the same general region and were in the same church district.

At the time I had wondered if such close proximity between the two families had led to any marriages down the line, because, if so, that would mean Zed and I were related. But then I learned that his family ended up leaving the region to resettle further west. When I pointed out that probably meant we weren't related after all, Zed reminded me that Marta was not his birth mother, so biologically, at least, such a connection wouldn't matter anyway. At the time, I was a little disappointed, but now that I was in love with him and not just his "buddy," that was a very good thing to know.

"It's nice of you to help him," Frannie said. "You helped with the last film too, didn't you?"

"*Ya,* I made the costumes. And I'll be making the costumes for this one too. I'll need to research the period, though."

"Look through the shelves in my bedroom. I have quite a few history books, some of which might have drawings that show the period dress." She went on to tell me about her daughter Giselle's work with fabrics and weavings. "She's sent me quite a few books over the years on fabrics and textiles too that might also be helpful. Feel free to help yourself."

"*Danke,*" I said, as pleased as could be. "I will."

Later on she had a little bit of an appetite and ate almost a whole bowl of soup for supper. After that I readied her for bed and she was soon back to sleep again. To the sound of her gentle snoring, I took the lamp down the hall with me and stepped into her room. A beautiful old quilt covered her bed. I'd guessed it to be sixty years or older, perhaps her wedding quilt. Beside her bed was an old Bible.

The bookcase was along the far wall, next to the small window. I put the lamp on the floor and knelt beside it. The light cast an eerie shadow upward over the books. I had to squint to read the titles. *Martyrs Mirror, The Ausbund* hymnal, and a prayer book caught my attention. Then *The Rise of Protestantism in Switzerland.*

The next book that caught my eye was *Stoff und Kunst,* which was German for fabric—or maybe material—and art. I slipped it from the shelf and held it down by the lamp. On the cover was a weaving of a mountain scene. I scanned through the first few pages. It was in German, and there were lots of photographs, all in color. First the photos were mostly of weavings, but as I continued through the book, I saw wall hangings made from fabric, including appliqué, as well.

Near the end of the book was a picture of a wall hanging that depicted the profile of a girl in an Amish bonnet. I peered closer. Behind her was a waterfall. A shiver rushed up my spine at the sight of a Plain girl in the beautiful piece of art. The caption ended in two words that took me by surprise: *Giselle Lantz.* Zed had said she was an established artist, but I had no idea her works had been published in any books.

Seeing this, I truly hoped Giselle decided to come to Lancaster County to be with her *mamm.* Despite the family drama such a visit might create,

I wanted to meet her more than ever. She and I weren't related, but we definitely shared a common interest.

I took one last book from the shelf, *Native Americans in Colonial America*, and then carried it and the German one back to the room I was sleeping in. I put them on the nightstand. After I readied myself for bed, I slipped under the quilts and left the lamp burning as I opened the book about the Native Americans. A painting on the first page was titled "Penn's 1701 Treaty with the Indians at Conestoga Town" by Edward Hicks. It showed barely clothed Indians with feathers in their hair and white men wearing brown, tan, and red coats; black, broad rim hats; knickers; and stockings. At first I thought there was one woman in the painting, sitting down in a dress, but as I studied the image more closely, I realized it was a man with some kind of fabric spread across his lap.

Except for him, their clothing was typical for that period, as far as I knew. Examining their English dress, I felt sure I could emulate the styles, though it wouldn't be easy to find the right fabrics. These were rough and knobby and carried the imperfections of having been woven by hand on a loom.

As for the Indians, that would be harder. Even if I could find real buckskin to use, I would never make costumes so scanty. Thinking about that, I decided I would need to keep looking for more drawings until I found at least one that showed how the natives dressed in colder weather.

On the bottom of the painting were the words *Penn's Treaty with the Indians, made without an Oath, and never broken. The foundation of Religious and Civil Liberty, in the U.S. of America.*

I closed the book and put it on the nightstand, sick at heart at the thought of how that treaty was eventually broken—possibly even by my very own ancestors. More than that, for some reason those ancestors had turned against the tribe they had supported and loved for so many years before.

Closing my eyes, I prayed that God would somehow help me find the reasons behind that astounding betrayal.

TWENTY

Frannie slept most of the next day.

Marta stopped by in the late morning, and before she left I gave her my items for Susie. Then I started on Christmas gifts for my *mamm* and sisters—handmade cloth bags for shopping days.

I managed to get a little bit of soup into Frannie around noon, but she fell right back to sleep and I continued with my work.

As I did, I found myself thinking about the costume designs for Zed's film. Back then Plain people wouldn't have dressed too much differently than the average country person, except maybe drabber with no ornamentation. Certainly, their dress would have been quite different from society people in the city. How fun it would have been to research it all so as to make every stitch historically accurate. Of course, without the rougher-hewn fabrics of that period, which had likely been handmade on looms, nothing I would make could ever be exactly correct.

I continued with my embroidery, keeping a watch on Frannie as I did, and after a few more days, we had fallen into somewhat of a routine. I had expected to see the Gundys in the first day or two that I was there, but according to Marta, Abe's stomach bug had moved on to other family members, so they were staying away. As it turned out, it wasn't until the following Wednesday—eight days after I'd started working with Frannie—that Ada and the twins were finally well enough to come over. They stopped by after school, the two girls, Mel and Mat, wearing matching blue dresses, aprons, and *kapps*. Ada had left little Abe back at home with his big sister Christy, much to Frannie's disappointment. "Bring him the next time you come," she said to Ada. "And Christy too. It's been a long time since I've seen them."

"It was right before your stroke, *Mammi*. Just two and a half weeks ago."

Frannie just shook her head and then lay back on the pillow.

Seven-year-old Mel gazed up at me with her big brown eyes, as if to say, "She doesn't even remember?"

Taking her hand and pulling her aside, I gave her a reassuring smile and whispered, "You know how it is when you don't feel well. Your days can get all jumbled."

Her twin sister, the bolder of the two, opened her mouth to say something in response, but Ada cut her off and instructed them both to head into the main house to see their *grossmammi* Klara. They went happily, and in the quiet their exit left behind, Frannie drifted off to sleep almost immediately.

Turning to me, Ada asked if there was anything I needed. I told her I was fine, and that things had been going very well.

"Are you sure you're all right caring for *Mammi* all by yourself, Izzy? I can come and help while the girls are in school."

She was being kind, but I knew that with a baby, the twins, Christy, and her husband, Will, Ada already had her hands full at home.

"Really, I'm okay for now. I think it'll be obvious when more help is needed. So far, though, it's been very doable for one person."

"But aren't you going stir-crazy?"

I motioned toward the kitchen and led the way. I didn't like to speak in front of a patient, even if they were asleep. It seemed disrespectful, and besides, we didn't know Frannie was asleep for sure. Perhaps she was just too exhausted to keep her eyes open.

"I mean," Ada whispered, leaning against the counter. "Don't you need to be around other people? Get out? Talk to someone?"

I shook my head. "No, I enjoy being alone."

Ada gave me a rueful smile, and it struck me that as an only child, she had probably grown up living a solitary life. Now she was part of a large, chaotic household—and that seemed to suit her much better.

We were still in the kitchen when we heard the front door crash open.

"*Mamm! Mamm!*" a little voice cried out.

Mat stood in the doorway, breathing hard.

"Hush!" Ada scolded. "You'll wake up *Mammi*—"

Mat's eyes were full of tears. "Something's wrong with *Mammi* Klara!"

We tore out of the *daadi haus* just as Alexander came running from the barn with Mel behind him.

"*Mammi* Klara fell," Mat said, running ahead of us to the back door of the main house. "Like *hours* ago. And she can't get up. She's crying because her back hurts so bad."

We made our way into the house, through the kitchen, and into the living room. Klara was on the floor beside the couch. The afghan covered her in a haphazard way, as if she'd fallen with it still wrapped around her.

"*Mamm!*" Ada cried, kneeling at her mother's side. "Are you okay?"

Sure enough, just as Mat had said, Klara was crying, big, wet tears that rolled down the sides of her face and into her ears.

"It's so stupid," she wailed. "You'd think a grown woman could get herself up off the floor."

"How long have you been here?"

"Too long. I don't know," Klara said, accepting the tissue Ada handed her and dabbing at her face. "A few hours. I woke up and forgot that the afghan was around my legs. I managed to trip and couldn't catch my balance because of my back."

Oh, no. I knew checking on Klara wasn't my responsibility, but still I felt bad to think I'd been so close but totally unaware of what she was going through.

Alexander came around to her. "Klara," he said. His voice was tender, but she just looked embarrassed.

"Please, get me off this cold, hard floor and back on the couch. Then give me a muscle relaxer."

"But what if the fall injured you somehow?" I couldn't help but say. "Worse than you already were, I mean."

Klara just shook her head. "The only thing I injured in the fall was my knee—and even that's just a bruise, I'm sure. I banged it on the floor when I landed."

Alexander helped her roll onto her stomach and then raise herself up on all fours. She was obviously in a lot of pain, but with his help she stood and moved back to the couch. She wasn't able to sit, though, so I stepped out of the way as he helped her sort of lean downward, sideways, until she was lying horizontal again. As she sank into the cushions, Ada slipped a pillow under her knees.

I picked up the afghan that had fallen to the floor and spread it over Klara as Alexander adjusted her head on the pillow. Then he knelt by her side and they spoke quietly to each other.

"She needs to see a doctor," I whispered to Ada. I was surprised when she merely shrugged.

"I'll call Marta and get her to stop by, but I don't think we'll need to do more than that. *Mamm* has seen doctors for this before. It's a herniated disc that flares up sometimes. There's not much they can do unless it gets really, really bad, but she's not to that point yet."

We both looked at Klara, who was still speaking softly with Alexander.

Ada turned and moved toward the kitchen. She came back a moment later with an ice pack from the freezer.

"You know the routine," she said to Klara, in the same voice she sometimes used with the twins or little Abe. "Ice and rest and ibuprofin and gentle stretching. No stress, no lifting, no bending..." Her voice trailed off as she helped slide the ice pack under the middle of Klara's back.

"She's right," Alexander said. "And no tree climbing or cattle herding, either," he added, a twinkle in his eye.

Ada stood up straight, hands on her hips. "*Ya*. No marathons, no hopscotch, and absolutely no break dancing."

I doubted Klara even knew what break dancing was, but she chuckled just the same. So did Ada and her father, though the girls didn't crack a smile. Instead, they just stood there, off to the side, holding hands, looking at their grandmother with wide eyes and trembling lips.

Klara wasn't exactly the warm and fuzzy type, so I was surprised when she opened her arms to the two children. Instantly, they rushed forward and then stopped to carefully settle themselves into her embrace.

"I'm really okay," she told them, patting their backs. "Please don't worry."

Ada reached out and patted Mat's back as well. "*Mammi* Klara's a tough old bird, don't you know that?"

When they didn't respond, Klara looked around, slightly embarrassed, and said, "Want to see what I did to my stockings?"

At that, they both pulled back, nodding, so at Klara's request Ada gently moved the afghan aside and then slid her mother's skirt up just above her knee, revealing a giant tear in her black stockings. Where the skin was exposed, there was a welt, red and swollen and angry looking, with tinges of purple already showing around the edges.

"You need ice for that too," I said. I went to the kitchen and retrieved another pack from the freezer.

When I returned, I paused there in the doorway, taking in the sweet family scene. Despite Klara's pain, I could feel the warmth of this moment, especially when she and Ada finally got the girls to giggle somehow.

I handed the ice pack to Ada, who put it in place on her mother's leg. Then I gave a nod to Alexander and slipped out of the room, glad to know all was well.

My happy glow ended when I entered the *daadi haus*, however, and noticed immediately that Frannie's breathing had changed. It was much more labored than before, and her complexion had grown paler too. I checked her pulse and respiration. Both had increased.

"Frannie." I put my hand on her shoulder. "How are you feeling?"

She stirred a little.

I raised the bed, thinking that perhaps a sitting position would help.

She opened her eyes.

"Are you all right?"

She nodded. "Just tired."

"Do you feel short of breath? Light-headed?"

She started to shake her head but then stopped. "I think I'm all right. Maybe a little dizzy."

"Okay, let me talk to Ada and see what we can do."

"Ada? Is she here? I haven't seen her in so long."

"*Ya*," I answered as I tucked her blanket in closer.

"She's my granddaughter. A lovely girl."

I didn't reply except to say that I'd be gone for just a minute. I hurried to the door and then out into the chilly afternoon, my hand pressed atop my *kapp* to keep it down in the wind. As I neared the back door, it swung open, and Ada stepped out, wrapped in her cape.

"Oh, Izzy, you scared me. I was just going to the barn to give Aunt Marta a call. I'm sure my *mamm* is fine, but it wouldn't hurt to get her checked out, just to be safe."

I nodded, shivering. Gusts blew against me, whipping my dress against my legs. "Tell her I need her out in the *daadi haus* too. And to bring her stethoscope."

Ada's eyes widened.

Trying to keep my voice calm, I added, "It's okay. I just want her to listen to Frannie's lungs."

"I don't think it's pneumonia," Marta said. "But there's definitely something going on." She handed the earpieces of the stethoscope to me. "Listen."

I did.

"Do you hear the rattle?"

I nodded. "Sounds like extra fluid in there." I took the earpieces out.

"Right. It could be pulmonary edema. Her heart could be failing."

I knew what that was.

"Do you have pain in your chest wall?" Marta asked her mother.

Frannie shook her head.

Marta turned to me. "No cough? Or mucus?"

I shook my head.

"I have a mother in labor, so it might be a while before I can get back here." She handed me the stethoscope. "I have a second one. Why don't you hang onto this one so you can keep tabs on her?"

"*Danke*," I said, motioning toward the door. "I'll walk you out."

I grabbed my cape at the door and followed Marta onto the porch.

"What should I do if she gets worse? I assume she'll need to go back to the hospital."

Marta surprised me by shaking her head no. "They won't do anything there but keep her comfortable. We can do that much better here."

"But if she's ill—"

"Izzy," Marta said, looking me in the eye. "My *mamm* has an advanced directive. It's about palliative care at this point. If something happens, let Alexander know—and call me, of course—but otherwise just keep her comfortable."

I nodded. I'd thought I was ready for this, but maybe I wasn't.

"Don't look so sad," Marta said. "Remember, she is weak and ready to go. She doesn't want to be saved only to suffer more. Death is as much a part of life as birth. It can be just as beautiful a transition."

I'd never seen a birth so I wasn't sure exactly what Marta meant, but I had seen a death—and there wasn't anything beautiful about it at all.

Not long after she left, a soft knock fell on the door. "Come in," I called out. The door opened slowly, and Alexander stepped inside, his hat in one hand.

"You have a letter," he said, extending an envelope toward me.

I stepped over and took it from him. "*Danke*," I said, knowing already from the handwriting that it was from Zed.

"How's *Mamm*?"

"Hanging in there," I said. "How's Klara?"

"Ornery," he replied, but by the smile in his eyes, I could tell he wasn't complaining.

Once he headed back out to work, I opened the envelope as I returned to my chair at the side of the bed and sat down. This was the first letter I'd received from Zed since I'd left Indiana, and my heart was in my throat as I began to read.

> Hey, Izzy Bear,
>
> Hope turkey day was good for you. I forgot what a difference it makes when Ella is the one cooking the big

> feast. I think I ate enough dressing and mashed pota-
> toes to feed a small country.
>
> Been thinking on the film some more. So far Abigail's
> story is way more interesting than NGGH's. If we can
> figure out the rest of what happened with her and her
> family, we may end up wanting to focus more on her in-
> stead of him. So keep digging!

I felt a surge of irritation at his words. Of course I would keep digging, movie or not. They were *my* ancestors. I had to know what happened to turn them against the Indians and then what convinced them to repent of that a year later. I kept reading.

> If I do base the movie on Abigail, I'll most likely give
> the part to my friend Shelly—yeah, that Shelly. Sorry, I
> know she wasn't exactly kind to you, but she's just such
> an amazing actress, I hate not to take advantage of that.

I stopped. Blinked. Read that line again. Then I stood and crumpled the paper into a ball and flung it across the room.

How *dare* he? Shelly? To play *my* ancestor?

He could forget it, that was for sure. I didn't want to see my own family featured in some stupid documentary if she was involved—much less if she was the star!

My heart pounding, I began to pace around the tiny room. As I did, I was thankful Frannie was asleep and that no one else was around to see.

The nerve. The absolute nerve.

I paced some more, willing my heart to stop pounding, my eyes returning again and again to the balled-up wad of paper on the floor. Finally, I retrieved it and returned to my chair, smoothing it open again onto my lap. I couldn't help it. I had to know what other wonderful bits of news he had chosen to share. Like maybe he'd gotten her name tattooed to his chest or put a down payment on a honeymoon for them.

I started reading again.

> Anyway, we can talk about all of this when I get home,
> which will probably be on the 13th or 14th. I found a

ride as far as Pittsburgh, but that's not close enough. Ella wants me to drive my car so she can come along and see Mammi. It's not a bad idea. At least we could split the gas that way, which would help me afford it. But I just don't know if Ol' Red will make it all the way there and back or not. I guess we'll decide in the next few days. Maybe you can check with my mom and ask what the final plan is.

Can't wait to see you. Lots to talk about, as always. Mom says you're doing a great job there with Mammi. Thanks again for doing it, and hang in there. Reinforcements will be arriving with the cavalry!

Zed

I refolded the wrinkled letter and placed it back in the envelope and then into my apron pocket for safekeeping, thinking how hard it was to stay mad at someone who was otherwise so adorable.

As I sat staring at Frannie but thinking about Zed, Marta returned from checking on Klara.

"She's sore, but I think she's going to be fine. More ice and rest should do it." Marta came to a stop at the end of the bed.

I told her I had just received a letter from Zed, but at the time he'd written, he wasn't positive if he'd be driving or not. "Do you know if a final decision has been made?"

Marta smiled broadly, something I hadn't seen her do often. "Yes. They'll be here Sunday. Ella's coming too."

"You think his car will make it?"

Marta chuckled. "Now it will. Luke offered to cover the cost of getting it checked out by a mechanic and fixed if necessary."

"I bet Zed appreciated that."

"I'm sure he did, but Luke didn't do it for him. He just didn't want his pregnant wife to end up stranded in the middle of Ohio."

Clearly, Marta adored her son-in-law. "As it turned out, all Zed needed was a new belt." Marta seemed as if she was trying to hide her amusement. "It was an easy fix and the car is fine."

The thought of Zed coming home both thrilled me and made me

nervous. I knew he had to be back at school by the second week of January. That would give us three weeks. Just twenty-one days for him to open his eyes and see that he loved me.

"I can't believe how things are coming together for everyone," Marta continued. "Lexie's flight gets in on Saturday morning, and even Giselle is talking about getting here Saturday night."

"Really? She is coming, all the way from Switzerland? Frannie will be thrilled."

Marta nodded and then put a finger to her lips. "Not a word yet, though. To be honest, my sister can be a bit…uh…flaky. We'll tell *Mamm* only if and when Giselle has actually reserved a flight and bought herself a ticket."

TWENTY-ONE

By the next morning, Frannie seemed to have rallied somewhat. Her color was better, and I could no longer hear the rattle in her lungs when I listened with the stethoscope.

She also seemed less confused than she had the day before, not to mention more talkative. She wanted to know about everyone's comings and goings, so as we waited for the water for her Cream of Wheat to boil, I caught her up as best I could. I explained Lexie would be flying in on Saturday from Oregon, and Zed and Ella would get here the day after that.

"Ella? Really? Do you think she'll be okay to travel?"

I nodded. "She still has eight weeks to go, so Marta said she would be fine."

Frannie closed her eyes, a smile illuminating her features.

"James can't get off of work until the following week, so he's planning to fly out on the twenty-first."

"Oh, how lovely," she said, her eyes opening again. "That means he'll be here for Christmas."

I nodded, smiling at the thought. I'd never met James, but I had heard wonderful things about him from both Zed and Ella.

"How about Luke?" she asked.

"I think he's hoping to come around the same time. I know it's not easy to leave a farm, but his brother lives right next door and can take over while he's gone. He really wants to come. And I know he would never want to spend Christmas away from Ella's side."

"He's a good man."

I nodded.

"And Giselle?" she asked finally, her eyes full of hope.

I couldn't out-and-out lie to her, so I hesitated and then said, simply, "As far as I know, she hasn't yet bought a ticket." But then, feeling guilty for not telling her the whole truth, that Giselle really was planning to come, I jumped up and went to the stove to attend to her cereal.

"We *must* convince her to come," Frannie said from her bed as I stirred the grains into the pot of bubbling water. "I'll pay for the plane ticket myself, if need be."

I still couldn't look Frannie in the eye, so once the Cream of Wheat was cooking, I wet a clean dishcloth and wiped down the counter and table.

"This sounds really important to you," I said, noncommittally.

"It is. It truly is. It's hard to explain why, exactly. It's not that there's anything I want to say to her. If that's all it was, I suppose I could do that over the phone. It's just that I want to see her. More than that I want to hold her. And I want her to know how much I love her."

Tears filled my eyes at the thought, especially when she added, "I haven't seen my daughter's face, in person, for twenty-eight years."

"Oh, my," I managed to say, blinking my tears away as I moved to the sink and rinsed out the cloth. "You're right. I think it would be good if she came too."

After I'd finished feeding Frannie and getting her ready for the day, Marta stopped by, clearly upset. I stepped to the end of the bed so she could sit in the chair.

"You'll never believe what Klara did!" she said, speaking both to me and to her mother.

Frannie's eyes widened. "What?"

"She called Giselle and told her to think twice about coming. That she didn't think it was what was best for you."

Frannie sat up in the bed, the first time I'd seen her do so voluntarily for days. "No! That's not true! I *want* Giselle to come—desperately so."

Marta patted her mother's arm till she lay back down. "Klara knows that."

"But Giselle doesn't. Call her and I'll tell her," Frannie begged. "On your little phone. Right now. Right here."

"I will." Marta pulled her cell phone from her pocket, dialed, and held it to her ear. It seemed like it rang for a long time but finally she said, "*Gut-n-Owed!*"

It was evening there.

Marta began speaking English after her greeting. I was surprised, but then I realized that Giselle may have forgotten much of her Pennsylvania Dutch without anyone over there to speak it with. And Marta wouldn't know the modern Swiss German that Giselle likely spoke now.

"*Mamm* wants to talk with you," Marta said into the phone and then paused. "No, I'm serious. She really does. I'm going to put you on speaker."

Marta stepped closer to Frannie as I stepped away from the bed, feeling as if I were intruding but too riveted to the scene to go far.

Holding the phone in the air close to her mother, Marta said, "Okay, *Mamm*, go ahead and talk."

Frannie's eyes widened. I suspected she didn't speak on a phone very often. She said, softly, "Giselle, are you there?"

"*Ya*," the voice answered. "I'm here." Her voice wasn't soft at all, not like I imagined it would be. "But I can barely hear you."

Frannie squared her shoulders. "I'll speak louder then." She did, a little. "I want you to come home, Giselle. I need to see you. Don't worry about what Klara says. She's hesitant, is all."

Giselle laughed but didn't say anything. Embarrassed, I retreated to the kitchen, listening as they continued.

"Your sister will be fine once you're here."

"She didn't sound fine on the phone."

"*Ach*, she's troubled sometimes, but it would do us all good for you to come over. It would do *me* good. I have money set aside for your airfare."

"Don't worry about that, *Mamm*. I'm okay as far as finances."

"Well, then. We can talk about that when you come. Just make your arrangements soon."

"All right. I'll think about it."

"*Danke*," Frannie said with an exhale. I turned to see her leaning back against her pillow. "Let Marta know what you decide. And don't listen to Klara anymore."

"Yes, I hear you."

"*Gut*." She closed her eyes. "*Tschüs*."

I couldn't help smiling at the sweet, informal goodbye.

"*Tschüs*," Giselle replied.

The call was over, just like that, leaving Frannie exhausted. I had a feeling she would fall right to sleep.

I returned to the dishes I had been washing, and after a moment, Marta joined me in the kitchen. I finished drying the pan and put it in the drawer under the stove.

"I hope that wasn't too stressful for her," she said, glancing over her shoulder at her mother.

I shook my head. "I think it would have been more stressful if you hadn't tried to convince Giselle to come."

"Well, it's done. Call me if she gets out of sorts."

I promised her I would.

She left and Frannie napped for a while, but as soon as she awoke she asked, "Is Giselle coming?"

"I don't know," I answered, patting her arm. "I hope so."

She looked so distressed that I sat down beside her bed, trying to distract her by telling her about my current historical research. I just meant to touch on it briefly, but she was so quiet that I kept babbling on until I had talked about all sorts of things, including my own ancestors' apparent support of the Paxton Boys.

Frannie seemed pained, though I doubted the actions of my ancestors were what was bothering her. "These things happen," she said with a sigh. "We raise them to walk a certain path, but sometimes they detour away…"

Her voice trailed off as she closed her eyes. Somehow, I had a feeling the path she was talking about was Giselle's.

Later, after Frannie woke up, she seemed much more alert.

"Maybe I dreamed this," she said as I raised the head of the bed and smoothed the covers around her, "but did you say something earlier about the Paxton Boys? And the Conestoga Indian Massacre?"

"*Ya*. I'm researching my ancestors and looking for information."

"That's right. Well, I just remembered something. I might be able to help you."

I sat up straight. "Oh?"

"I know for a fact that among my husband's family papers is a small pile of pamphlets about the massacre. Several of them were even written by his ancestor, the nine-greats-grandfather Zed told you about."

I gasped. "Zed showed me one of those. But are you saying you have additional pamphlets about the massacre, written by other people?"

Frannie nodded.

I hated the thought of it, but I knew there was a chance my ancestors had written some as well, though taking the opposite stand, of course.

"Where are they? Do you have them?"

She thought for a moment. "I think I do. They would be in the attic in a cardboard box labeled 'Malachi's Mementos,' or something like that."

"Would you mind if I looked for it?" I asked, trying not to sound as excited as I felt.

"Of course not. Take the flashlight with you."

She gestured toward the cupboard by the front door. When I looked inside, I saw that it was a big, black, club-like type that didn't fit in my apron pocket.

"Oh, and get the step stool from the kitchen to pull on the rope. You should be able to reach it that way."

I followed her directions, taking the stool to the hallway. I easily grabbed the rope and pulled on it, unlatching the stairs from the ceiling with a loud, rusty *boing*. I continued to pull as I stepped down, moving the stool with my other hand and clutching the flashlight at the same time. Once the stairs were secure, I turned on the light, shone it upwards, and started ascending. We had a similar set in our house, although on the second floor. I always felt as if I were walking up toward heaven until I reached the attic. Then it was either really cold or really hot and obviously not anywhere I'd want to spend much time.

Frannie's attic welcomed me with an icy wall of cold air. I shivered, wishing I had thought to put on my cape. I shone my light around as I reached the top and saw that there wasn't an actual floor—just boards positioned across the rafters. Rows of boxes, mostly cardboard of all different sizes, were stacked on top of the boards along each side. Taking them all in, I could only hope that the one I wanted wasn't too far back—and that it wouldn't be too heavy for me.

I stepped onto the wide center board and inched forward along it as I shone the light at the boxes. The wind had picked up outside, and a branch that had been scraping against the siding was louder up here. I hoped Frannie wouldn't get chilled from the trapdoor being open.

I tried to move quickly, playing the flashlight along the sides of the boxes. Only one had Malachi's name on it that I could see, but instead of mementos, the label said, "Malachi—Miscellaneous."

Downstairs, I could hear voices, and I realized someone had come into the *daadi haus*. Thinking this was better than nothing, I grabbed that one box—grateful it was lighter than I'd expected—and headed for the stairs.

It wasn't as easy getting down as it had been going up, but somehow I managed to juggle the box and the flashlight without breaking my neck. When I reached the bottom, I lifted the stairs back into the ceiling, holding onto the rope to stop the whole thing from snapping up too quickly. Once it had eased its way upward, I let go and the steps clicked into place.

Feeling as if I'd been shirking my duties, I hurried to the living room, where I found Marta talking with Frannie. She looked at me questioningly, so I simply gestured toward the box with my head and said, "Doing research for Zed's next film."

"That's all I need to know," she replied with a laugh, holding out one hand to stop me from elaborating. We smiled at each other, two veterans of our beloved Zed's creative energies.

I showed Frannie the box, turning it so she could read the label.

"That's the one. Malachi Miscellaneous. Sorry about that. Open it up."

I did, and after rustling through a couple of worn maps, some old agriculture department brochures, and an ancient manual to a threshing machine, I came across two rubber-banded packets of pamphlets. They were old and yellowed, and there looked to be about ten in total of varying sizes. The rubber band holding them together popped the moment I tried to remove it, but the pamphlets themselves seemed intact enough to be handled—with care. This I did, flipping through them, my heart pounding as I searched their covers for the name Vogel. Would one of these pamphlets contain the information I'd been seeking?

Sadly, there did not seem to be a Vogel among them, though I still wanted to take a closer look. I decided to set them aside for now and do that later, when I was alone. I started to put the pamphlets back in the box, but then I noticed a zippered bag of fabric in the bottom. Placing the yellowed booklets on the table, I turned my attention to the bag, pulled it out, and set it on the edge of the bed.

"Unzip it," Frannie said.

Marta stepped closer.

The zipper caught in a few places, but I worked it back and forth until I got it all the way around and could pull open the flap. There was a blanket on top or, more accurately, a coverlet, a woven bedspread that had to be an antique. Next was another woven piece of fabric, much smaller, that looked like velvet. I took it out, unfolding it carefully.

"Oh, my," Frannie said. "Isn't that fancy?"

"You found this with *Daed*'s stuff?" Marta asked. "What on earth would he have been doing with this?"

Frannie didn't seem too concerned. "I don't know. These must be some of Judith's leftovers."

"Judith?" I asked.

"Judith Lantz, my mother-in-law, God rest her soul. She was a seamstress, a very talented one. She specialized in fabric repair. Vintage and antique fabric repair in particular."

"What do you mean?" I asked, intrigued.

"She took in work from the local antique shops and a museum or two. Whenever they would obtain a fabric item in need of repair—an antique pillow or seat cushion or quilt or toy—they would usually look to her. Not only did she do excellent mending work, but she had a huge collection of fabric to pull from, some dating back a hundred years or more. With the right cloth, she could usually piece things back together in such a way that you'd never even know the items had been damaged."

"Wow." I was quiet for a moment as I gazed at the fabric, wondering if this was all that was left of her collection. "How far back do you think these pieces date? This coverlet has to be at least a hundred years old. Is that possible?"

Frannie shrugged. "Sure. Everyone in the community knew to give their old material and fabric goods to Judith rather than throw them away. She had a storage area in their old house, so there was plenty of room. For her, the biggest issue was keeping it all organized so that she could find what she needed when she needed it."

"I can imagine."

Marta reached out and ran a finger across the velvet. "I wonder why *Daed* kept these particular pieces, the coverlet and a scrap of velvet. Do you think they were important in some way?"

Frannie leaned back against the pillow, looking tired. "They could have been, though I can't imagine why. I know his siblings got rid of most all of that once their mother died. He probably just grabbed these things to keep as mementos."

Marta shifted her attention to the coverlet. "If this is as old as Izzy thinks, I wonder if it could be valuable."

"Probably so." I picked it up and studied it. The weave was looser than what modern machines did, though the stitches along the seams were impeccable. "You should get it appraised, just in case."

"Giselle might know what they're worth," Frannie said. "Keep it out for when she comes."

Marta and I shared a glanced, and I knew we were both thinking the same thing. *If she comes.*

I placed the velvet on top of the coverlet and then slid them both into the plastic bag. "If it turns out that it's not valuable, I know Zed would love to borrow it. This would make an amazing prop for his next film."

"You don't think it would fall apart the minute he tried to use it?" Marta asked.

"It might." I zipped the bag shut. "Even so, I could still use it as an example to replicate. And it would be helpful when choosing the costuming fabrics too. I'd like to find ones that emulate this weave."

Just the thought of it got all of my creative juices flowing, but Frannie was starting to fade, so I left her with Marta and carried everything to my room. Later, I would return the box to the attic, minus the fabric and the pamphlets, which I couldn't wait to read through. I also couldn't wait to show all of this to Zed.

The brief interaction had worn Frannie out, but she slept fitfully after Marta left. I kept busy, checking on her, preparing her dinner, and then readying her for bed. It wasn't until I went to bed myself that I could finally take a closer look at the pamphlets.

I started by laying them all out on the bed and again checking the names of the authors. Right away, I spotted the one by NGGH I'd already seen plus two more I hadn't. To my disappointment, there didn't seem to be anything written by any of my ancestors. Still, these items were useful for our research, so I started back at the top of the pile and began skimming through them anyway.

Two were especially well written and caught my attention. The first was against the massacre, and I, of course, agreed with it wholeheartedly. The second was pro massacre. There was nothing I could condone about the argument, but I did find the logic of the writer fascinating as well as disturbing. Of course, there was no mention of the many treaties broken with the Indians, the land taken, and the slaughter of Indians of all ages by settlers, not to mention the European diseases that wiped out so many of the Native Americans. There were, however, many accounts of Indians murdering settlers and of kidnappings too.

Although I would never endorse violence against any human being, I could see how the events that happened led to fear, which led to panic, which resulted in the massacre. And that was just it—this particular tribe was a remarkably easy target because they were peace loving and had already been decimated by disease.

Later, knowing it was the only choice I had, I took it all to prayer and thanked God that I was given a heritage of nonviolence. It was the only way to stop the vicious cycle because violence always begets violence.

The next morning after breakfast, as I watched Frannie nap, I decided to work on the cloth bags I'd been making as Christmas presents for the women in my family. I realized I ought to make something for the women in this family as well—Frannie, her daughters, and granddaughters—some item that would be both lovely and useful. I was mulling over what I might create when I remembered the bookmark I'd found right before Verna died. I went down the hall to my room and dug it from my purse. I read the embroidered words again, "My help cometh from the Lord." I knew it was from the Psalms. I would show it to Frannie when she woke up and ask her if she had ever seen anything like it.

Perhaps I could make bookmarks with the verse embroidered on it for the Lantz women. That was something they could use.

I returned to the living room, sat by Frannie, and resumed my sewing. The time passed quietly until Marta, looking as if she'd slept in her clothes, burst through the front door. "She's coming," she croaked in a voice hoarse with emotion. "Giselle is coming home."

Frannie stirred but didn't wake up.

Marta clutched the metal bar at the end of the bed and for a minute I thought she might collapse. I stood, my sewing falling to the floor. I hurried to her side, putting my arm around her.

She was shaking.

"Are you all right?" I asked.

She shook her head and then whispered, "I'm glad *Mamm* is asleep. I don't know what's wrong with me."

I didn't respond. I'd never seen Marta like this. I never would have guessed she was capable of so much emotion.

She took a deep breath.

"I'll get you some water," I said, not knowing what else to do.

"*Danke*," she whispered, leaning against the railing.

When I returned, she downed the entire glass. "Maybe I'm a little dehydrated. I don't know. I fell asleep on the sofa, and then Giselle's call woke me. I came straight here."

"When is she arriving?"

"Tomorrow," Marta answered and then exhaled, slowly. "By tomorrow night, we'll all be together. For the first time in almost thirty years." She looked at her mother, her eyes filled with a myriad of emotions.

Frannie began to stir, and Marta skirted around the edge of the bed to her side, while I took the glass back into the kitchen.

"*Mamm*, I have some news."

"I hope it's good," Frannie said.

"It is. You'll be so pleased."

I stepped back into the living room as Marta said, "Giselle is coming. Tomorrow."

Frannie grabbed Marta's hand. "Are you sure?"

"She called. Just half an hour ago. I came straight here. She promised she's coming. She bought the ticket online as we spoke."

Frannie's whole body relaxed, and then she smiled. She looked as beautiful as an angel.

"*Kumm esse*," she whispered, which was a funny thing to say. It was what mothers said when inviting everyone to the table.

But Marta must have understood what her mother meant because she just nodded and said, "*Ya. Kumm esse* indeed."

TWENTY-TWO

After Frannie drifted off to sleep, I made Marta some tea and we sat talking at the kitchen table. She couldn't stop talking about Giselle coming home and was relaying the specifics of her itinerary. "She'll leave Zurich at twelve thirty p.m. tomorrow and will arrive in Philadelphia tomorrow afternoon around a quarter of four."

"How will she get from the airport to here?"

"I'll go pick her up. Barring any traffic, we should be back around six or seven tomorrow evening."

"And she's staying in a hotel?"

Marta shook her head. "No. Believe it or not, she said no hotel. If she's coming all this way to see *Mamm*, then she wants to stay with *Mamm*. Klara won't be happy about her being so close, but *Mamm* will be thrilled."

"Should I move into the main house so Giselle can have my room?"

"No, you stay where you are. Giselle can just use *Mamm*'s room."

I stood to carry my cup to the sink. "Will you be picking up Lexie also?"

"No, she'll rent a car and drive here herself. Her flight gets in at nine thirty in the morning, so she'll be here around noon, which is good. That will give her time to get settled and maybe rest a bit from the redeye before she meets Giselle for the first time that evening."

I thought about Giselle being Lexie's birth mother, and that Lexie and Giselle had never met in person before—or, at least, they hadn't seen each other since Lexie was just a toddler. Giselle was Ada's birth mom too, but they had met when Ada went to Switzerland a few years ago.

Footsteps sounded on the porch and then a rapid knock startled us. I thought it might be Klara, but she wouldn't knock. Alexander might, but not so loudly.

Confused, I walked to the door to see who it might be. Standing there was my own mother. My hand flew to my throat.

"Is everything okay?" I whispered, sure just as things were looking better for Frannie's family that something horrible had happened to mine.

"You worry too much, Izzy," *Mamm* said as she stepped inside and slipped off her black bonnet. "I just stopped by to say hello and deliver some soup and bread for Frannie—and for you too."

I closed the door behind her as she gave Marta a quick hello. I led her to the kitchen, asking how things were going with everyone.

"Fine," she said, placing the basket on the counter. She handed me the soup and directed me to put it in the fridge, as if I didn't know to do that. She took out the bread, put it on the counter, and then looped her hand through the basket again.

"Will you be coming home next weekend as planned?" she asked.

"As far as I know. But we'll have to play it by ear as it gets closer." I didn't add that it depended on how Frannie was doing by then.

We heard a shaky voice from behind us. "Is that you, Peggy?" The commotion had wakened Frannie.

"*Ya*, how are you?" *Mamm* asked, stepping to the end of the bed.

"*Gut*. So much better there are no words."

"Well," *Mamm* said, chuckling. "It sounds as if my Izzy is some caregiver."

Frannie smiled. "She is, of course, but there's more."

"Oh?" *Mamm* stepped closer but as she did the sound of footsteps fell again on the porch. I hoped it would be Alexander. It wasn't. Klara shuffled in, holding her back as straight as possible.

"Oh, my," she said as she stepped inside. Looking at her mother, she added, "You're having quite the gathering. I take it you're having a good day."

"*Ya*," Frannie responded. "The best."

"She was just about to tell me her good news," my *mamm* said.

"Oh?" Klara looked from Frannie to Marta to me and then finally to my mother, who, in a moment of uncharacteristic uncertainty, said, "Weren't you, Frannie?"

"*Ya*, I was."

Again there was a pause.

Finally Klara said, "And?"

Marta took a step toward Klara. "Giselle is coming. She already bought her ticket."

Klara froze.

My *mamm* must have felt the tension because she said, "I'd best go so I'm home before dark."

Seemingly relieved by the interruption, Marta thanked her and so did Frannie. I walked her to the door. "Leave me a message," she said.

I nodded and told her goodbye.

Once I'd closed the door, I made a point of heading to the kitchen, out of everyone's way, but the room was silent until finally Klara spoke.

"When is she coming?"

"Tomorrow night," Marta said.

"And when is Lexie arriving?"

"Tomorrow morning."

"Well, at least that gives you a chance to talk to Lexie ahead of time and let her know her biological mother will be here too." She stepped away from the bed. "I guess I'll go leave that same message for Ada now."

I felt a pang of concern for Klara as I watched her leave. She walked slowly toward the door and left without saying goodbye. She seemed frail and much older.

Marta, still at her mother's side, reached out and took Frannie's hand.

Later, once everyone was gone, Frannie awoke from a nap and I fed her a bowl of soup. Then, as I ate one too, I showed her the embroidered bookmark. She held it tenderly in her hands. The blue thread had nearly faded, making the words hard to read. She traced them with her fingers as I said, "My help cometh from the Lord."

"Ah," she said. "Psalm 121:2. My mother quoted that verse at times, I think as a reminder to me. But it was a favorite of my grandmother's also." Obviously it had been a favored verse of someone else's too.

I told her I planned to make bookmarks like this for her daughters and granddaughters.

"That's a *wunderbar* idea," she said. "*Danke.*"

I sat back down with one of her nightgowns to mend. There was a small tear in a shoulder seam. As I stitched the worn fabric, she stared at her hands.

"A penny for your thoughts," I finally said.

She raised her thin eyebrows and said, "I was just thinking about Klara. We all came to terms with the truth in the family a few years ago. I thought healing had taken place then—and I think it did. But she's still unsettled."

I didn't respond, hoping my silence would encourage her to say more.

She sighed. "Guess it's just our nature, *ya?*"

"Maybe once she sees Giselle in person she can put it all to rest."

Frannie didn't answer. Instead, she closed her eyes and soon drifted off to sleep.

I finished the nightgown and then cut out the bookmarks from fabric I'd brought along. I also had some interfacing with me that I would use between the two pieces of linen, but first I would do the embroidery.

At nine o'clock, Frannie stirred and awoke enough for me to get her ready for bed. She assured me she wouldn't have any trouble getting back to sleep. She was right. By ten o'clock she was snoring gently.

I took the lamp with me down the hall to my room and dressed for bed myself. As I climbed in under the sheets, I picked up *Native Americans in Colonial America* from the nightstand. I knew I shouldn't read about something so troubling at bedtime lest I have nightmares, but I needed to push the events of the day out of my mind, and I knew a little research could help with that. I still wanted to learn more details about the massacre itself, so I flipped through the book to where I'd stopped before.

I skimmed several pages, trying to focus on the facts and not the gory details. The account said that twenty Conestoga were left living at Indian Town at the time of the massacre, but only a handful were there the morning in mid-December when the attack took place. The rest were off working.

Following the massacre, the remaining Conestoga were moved to Lancaster Workhouse for their protection, but the killers came back two weeks later and completed their mission by murdering those Indians as well. Of course, that was the official version. Remembering the article Zed had left for me at Ella's house, I knew the Indians may not have been hiding in the Workhouse but rather praying in a church when it happened. Either way, what had been done to them was unconscionable.

I skimmed to the end of the chapter, where a Christian Shawnee chief was quoted as saying, "The white man prays with words while the Indian prays in his heart."

Closing the book, I couldn't help but agree with him to an extent. Lying there, I thought about all the suffering the Native Americans had endured at the hands of the settlers, and for some reason it made me want to cry. I knew violence had been on both sides, but tonight my heart was with the Indians.

A branch scraped against the siding, startling me. I twisted down the wick in the lamp until it went out, and then I scooted down so the quilt was up to my nose.

That's when the tears finally began to come.

As they did, I tried to figure out what was making me so sad. It wasn't just the story of the massacre.

It was the thought of Frannie dying, I supposed. It was the thought of Zed showing up and not loving me the same way I loved him. And Lexie coming out from Oregon. And maybe even Giselle arriving. Wiping my eyes, I decided that most of all it was the drama of the Lantz family.

I wasn't sure if I could handle it or not.

The next morning, as Frannie napped and I was finishing up the breakfast dishes, I heard a knock on the front door. When I answered it, I was surprised to find my *daed* standing there, holding a box.

I gasped. "Is that what I think it is?"

He smiled. "I imagine so. I went out to Rod's again. He said he finally had a chance to take a good look around for Verna's papers and was able to track down everything."

Grinning, I glanced toward the driveway and my father's buggy. "So there's more?"

"*Ya*, but not with me. All that was left besides this box was a big wooden trunk too heavy to move." *Daed* must have seen the disappointment on my face because he quickly added, "Rod told me to let you know you're welcome to come out and look through it anytime you want. And for now at least you have this."

He was right. With a grateful smile I took the box from his arms and thanked him for his efforts. He simply nodded and said he had to be on his way. He had a table to deliver.

The moment he was gone, I checked on the still-sleeping Frannie and then carried the box straight back to my room. Placing it on the foot of my bed, I took a deep breath, opened the lid, and began to dig in. The contents didn't seem promising at first, but eventually I struck gold. Within the first fifteen minutes I found three more copies of the chapbook!

Ecstatic, I flipped through the first one only to find that it had been cut at the same place as the one Verna and I had found. I grabbed the second. It had also been cut. So had the third, although not quite as close to the margin. I could make out a few letters, but no words, along the edge. Incredible. Someone really had intentionally removed the rest of the story, just as Verna and I had thought, but not just in that one copy. They had done it in all of them.

For a moment frustration nearly overwhelmed me, but that feeling soon turned to determination. I had to learn the whole truth of this situation, no matter what.

I couldn't fathom what horrible thing could have happened to Abigail and Gorg to turn them into Paxton Boys' sympathizers and almost be excommunicated. Especially not after Abigail had so dearly loved Konenquas. My imagination soared, but nothing I came up with made sense.

A short time after noon, as I sat beside Frannie's bed working on a bookmark for Klara, a knock startled me.

Frannie stirred a little but didn't wake. I put my work on the edge of her bed and hurried to the door, expecting a member of my family again.

Instead, I swung the door open and found Lexie Jaeger Nolan, Frannie's granddaughter. She hadn't changed at all and was still as beautiful as ever. Today her blond hair was pulled back in a ponytail. Her brown eyes smiled. "Izzy," she said, giving me a hug.

She came inside and stepped to the foot of the bed as I closed the door behind her.

Her eyes immediately fell on the sleeping Frannie. Lexie asked, "How is she?"

"Tired this morning. She has good days and bad. Some when she's super alert. Others where she wants to sleep."

"Is she eating?"

"*Ya*, but just soup and porridge. A couple of spoonfuls of yogurt. But not much." I grabbed my embroidery off the bed. "You should wake her. She'll be so happy to see you."

I moved away from the bed so Lexie could take my place. She took her coat off and set it on the chair and then leaned down closer to Frannie. "*Mammi*," she said. "It's me. Lexie."

Frannie stirred a little, opened one eye and then closed it.

"*Mammi*," Lexie said again.

The older woman turned her head toward us. This time she opened both eyes. "Giselle?"

"No, Lexie."

"Oh, you're here." Frannie reached for her granddaughter. "I'm so glad you came."

Lexie patted her grandmother's hand and asked how she was.

"So happy we're all going to be together."

"*Ya*," Lexie said, although her voice sounded hesitant.

Frannie's voice cracked. "You'll get to meet Giselle. At last."

"*Ya*," Lexie said again, this time hitting the right inflection. "Aunt Marta just told me."

I stepped to the end of the bed, pretty sure I had a front row seat to a story better than any *Englisch* movie as I imagined Giselle and Lexie—birth mother and daughter—together at last.

Footsteps fell on the porch again, and this time when the door opened, in came Klara.

"Lexie. I thought it might be you," she said without even a hello first.

The younger woman rose and stepped toward her aunt, giving her a hug.

Klara spoke quietly. "Are you as apprehensive about all of this as I am?"

"I'm not sure," Lexie said, her voice barely a whisper. "I only just found out a few minutes ago from Aunt Marta."

Klara nodded and they were both quiet for a moment.

"How is Ada?" Lexie asked, and I remembered that the two sisters, separated as small children by adoption, had become the best of friends once they were reunited as adults.

Klara smiled. "So excited about seeing you. She's going to come by with the kids after a while."

"Yay!" Lexie replied, a grin lighting up her pretty face. Then she looked at her watch and added, "At some point I should take a nap. I'm exhausted from the flight. Do you mind if I crash on your couch later?"

"If crash means sleep, then by all means, feel free. Better yet, why don't you use one of the empty bedrooms upstairs?"

Lexie thanked her and then Klara said to come on over when she was ready. "I'm going to go ice my back."

After she left, Lexie offered to spell me. "You could go for a walk," she said. "Or have some time in your room."

That's when I realized I hadn't had much space to myself, but I hadn't missed it either. Sitting with Frannie was so peaceful that I hadn't needed my usual quota of quiet.

Nevertheless, I took Lexie up on her offer, grabbing a pen and paper and then stopping in the entryway to slip on my boots and cape. I'd been thinking about Abigail's chapbook and the minute possibility that a copy might have ended up in a local library or museum or historical society somehow. When I'd mentioned that to Verna, back when we first discovered the chapbook, she'd told me it wasn't likely. But now, with nowhere else to look, I decided to give it a shot anyway, just in case.

I stepped onto the pathway, taking in the vast pewter sky that looked as if it might send down a snowstorm at any time. I headed straight to the barn, to the bench where Alexander and Klara kept their phone. Thankfully, a phone book was next to it and I opened it, looking for places to contact and then making a list of local historical societies and museums. I didn't want to take time to call now, and I was never all that comfortable using a phone anyway, so I decided I would give the list to Zed once he got home and let him follow up on it.

As I left, some movement caught my eye, and I turned and spotted Alexander at the far outside corner of the barn, praying. I hurried on, not wanting him to see me. I veered off to the left, breathing in the cold air as I reached the trail along the creek. It was too muddy and the water was too high to walk beside it, so finally I came to a stop, exhaling slowly, the vapor from my breath swirling in front of my face.

I enjoyed the quiet for a long moment, thinking about the sight of Alexander on his knees before God. I knew he had forgiven Giselle for all she had done to him and Klara back then, which just went to show what a good man he was. No doubt, today's prayer was for his wife, for her anxiety over the return of the sister who had wrought such havoc in their home so long ago.

On the other hand, I thought, if not for Giselle and all that she'd done back then, Klara and Alexander would never have had the opportunity to raise Ada. Perhaps as he prayed for his wife to have peace in this coming situation, he might also be adding in just a little thanks too for the blessing of the wonderful daughter she had become to them both.

The sound of a buggy coming down the lane urged me back to the *daadi haus*. Ada and her children had arrived, and I didn't want to miss them greeting Lexie for anything.

Alexander caught up with me by the time I reached the buggy in front of the main house, and he took the reins from Ada. I helped little Abe down. His hat fell off as he landed on the ground, revealing his dark curly hair. I patted him on the head and then swung Mel and Mat down too.

Christy climbed out of the buggy last. At seventeen, she was truly beautiful with her strawberry blond hair and brown eyes, framed by thick, dark lashes. She moved toward me gracefully with a cheery hello, and then she took Abe's little hand as we headed to the *daadi haus*, with Mel and Mat right behind.

"Remember," Ada said to the smaller children. "Inside voices. *Mammi* is very ill. We need to be extra considerate. After we've visited a while, you can help your grandfather with the chores."

Abe nodded his head and the girls spoke in agreement behind us. Before we reached the porch, Lexie bounded out of the little house.

"I thought I heard voices out here!"

Ada rushed into her sister's arms. Christy and Abe were next in line, and Lexie *oohed* and *aahed* over them both. Mel and Mat hung back a little until Lexie said, "Come on, you two." The twins obeyed and she enveloped them in her arms.

When she finally pulled away, she said, "Let's go. *Mammi* is anxious to see all of you."

I followed, pulling the door shut behind me. As they chatted, I headed to the kitchen to put on the kettle, thinking hot chocolate might be a good idea for the children. And I could make tea for Christy, Ada, and Lexie.

Soon, overhearing the conversation, I was drawn back into the living room.

Frannie was asking Ada, "How do you think Giselle will do here?"

Lexie put her arm around Ada, pulling her close.

Ada's back was to me, but I could hear her words. "I think she'll feel unsettled and with good reason, but I hope that after a few days she'll adjust. *Mamm* too."

"*Ya*," Frannie said. "I hope so."

The kettle began to whistle, and I asked Ada if it would be all right if the children had hot chocolate. She said it would and I busied myself making it for them, putting the three mugs on Frannie's little kitchen table. I helped Abe onto a chair. Mel and Mat stood stirring their hot chocolate and then taking little sips. I added more milk to Abe's.

Then I started the kettle for tea.

"Do you think we can go over to *Mammi* Klara's now?" Mel whispered.

"Not until your mother says so," I replied.

When the girls finished their hot chocolate, they carried their mugs to the sink. Then they came back to help their baby brother. Ada looked over and told them, "You can go find *Mammi* Klara. Tell her I'll be in soon."

TWENTY-THREE

The afternoon grew quiet once Ada and the kids left and Lexie went to the main house for a nap. I couldn't help but wonder if it was the calm before the storm as I sat by Frannie's side. Around four Lexie returned to the *daadi haus*. It felt as if we were both holding our breath, waiting for Giselle to arrive. As the time drew closer, Lexie seemed to grow more and more nervous, something I hadn't expected of her. She was always so confident and assured. The truth was, I couldn't imagine what it must be like for her, the anticipation of meeting her birth mother, face-to-face, for the first time.

Would they look anything alike? Act anything alike? Be anything alike?

Lexie sat for a few minutes by Frannie's side, watching her sleep, but then she popped back up and checked her phone. A few minutes later she was up and getting a glass of water.

I tried to help distract her by chatting a little, about how Ella was doing and what the Home Place was like. Then about Frannie's stroke. And finally about the mild weather in Oregon.

Around five, Lexie called Marta "just to touch base."

She listened for a moment and then said, "So you've left the airport?"

She listened again and then said, "All right. See you in an hour or two." She turned to me as she hung up and explained. "Giselle is with her but traffic on the Blue Route is bumper to bumper. They'll be here as soon as they can, and they'll pick up pizza."

She slipped her phone back into her pocket. "I'll go tell Aunt Klara. And let Ada know to come back over around seven."

I felt sympathetic toward Lexie, but I knew there was nothing I could do except prepare for the imminent crowd of people. I cleared off the counters to make room for a buffet and then rummaged through Frannie's cupboards and found a stack of paper plates and enough paper cups for everyone. Then I pulled a handful of napkins from the drawer and put them on the counter too. Marta had brought fresh veggies the day before—carrots, celery, cucumbers, and broccoli—just for me, but I cut those up to share with everyone and then heated some soup for Frannie, even though she was sleeping. Then I sat back down and waited.

When Lexie returned I gave her my chair and went into the kitchen, deciding to scrub the cupboard doors to keep busy. But soon after she retreated to Frannie's room, probably to count off the minutes in private.

At seven fifteen footsteps were heard on the porch. I froze, anticipating the moment I'd waited for, even though I had no right to witness it and no actual connection to it. I was just relieved Lexie would get to meet her birth mother without the whole family gathered around. Even Frannie, though here, was asleep.

The door swung open and Marta walked in, carrying three large, flat boxes. I stepped forward and took the pizzas from her.

"This is Giselle," Marta said. "Giselle, Izzy."

A woman appeared in the doorway. Thin and short, she looked nothing like either Marta or Klara, and not just because her uncovered hair was red with gold highlights and spiked. She wore skinny jeans and boots, a long leather coat, and the most beautiful scarf I'd ever seen. It was orange and fuchsia and scarlet and looked as if it had been hand knit by a child, but perfectly so.

There was something intelligent about her that reminded me of both Ada and Lexie, but she didn't necessarily look like them, either.

"I'm pleased to meet you," I managed to say, nodding my head over the pizza boxes.

"Likewise," Giselle answered, but I could see her eyes moving from me to her mother across the room. If she hadn't seen the woman in twenty-eight years, she was probably quite shocked at how old Frannie looked now. Giselle managed to hide her reaction well, but I could tell the sight had thrown her.

Before we could wake the sleeping woman, the door to the bedroom swung open and Lexie came walking out, talking on the phone as she did. When she reached the living room, she looked up and then froze, her eyes locked on Giselle.

"I have to go," she managed to murmur into the phone, and then she turned it off and slid it in her pocket.

Looking far more confident than she was probably feeling on the inside, she stepped toward the startled redhead. They stood there for a long moment, Lexie towering over her more diminutive mother.

Then the two of them did an uncomfortable sort of dance, each starting to shake hands, then not, and then finally meeting in an awkward embrace.

When they pulled apart, Lexie said, "I'm so pleased to finally meet you."

I swallowed hard to keep the lump from rising in my throat. Marta dabbed at her eyes.

Before they could say or do anything else, the door opened again and in came Klara, followed by Alexander. Again I practically held my breath as Klara simply said, "Hello, Giselle."

She hugged her sister quickly and then stepped aside. Alexander extended his hand, saying he was pleased to see her.

"Likewise," was her reply.

It was all so stiff and awkward that I was glad at the moment Frannie began to stir. The entire group shifted toward her. I put the pizzas on the kitchen counter and then hurried to the raise Frannie's bed so she could see Giselle. As I did, her eyes opened and then quickly filled with tears.

"She's here," Frannie whispered.

"*Ya*," I said, releasing the button once the bed was high enough.

Then I stepped away from the bed, making room for the daughter who had finally come home.

Frannie reached for Giselle's hand and held on to it. Neither said anything, but Giselle leaned forward, burying her head against Frannie's neck. Marta and Lexie stood at the end of the bed, hands on the railing, watching the two. Klara and Alexander stood behind them. I retreated to the kitchen, overcome with emotion. My *mamm* and I had our share of problems, and she didn't understand me, but I couldn't imagine going twenty-eight years without seeing her.

As Ada, Will, and the children entered the *daadi haus*, I grabbed one of the napkins off the counter and wiped my eyes.

Giselle pulled herself away from her mother, turned to look toward the door, and darted across the room to her youngest daughter, taking her in her arms and hugging Abe at the same time.

Ada introduced the twins, Mel and Mat, and then Giselle hugged Christy warmly—they had obviously bonded when the girl had traveled to Switzerland with Ada. Then she wrapped her arms around Will. He'd been there too, and it was evident Giselle felt safe with him.

Cramming so many people into the little house felt a bit ridiculous, considering Klara's big home was just a few feet away. But that's what we did as Ada and her crew hung up their coats and came inside.

I suggested we all eat before the pizza grew cold. Alexander led us in a silent prayer and then Christy put a piece of cheese pizza on a plate for Abe, followed by the twins helping themselves, as I dished up soup for Frannie.

"I'm too excited to eat," she said when I sat down beside her with the bowl. "I just want to watch everyone." I gave her water to drink and put the soup on the table, hoping she would change her mind.

"If only Ella and Zed were here," she said.

"They'll be here tomorrow." Marta stepped closer. "Which means we'll be even more crowded. I think we should move your bed into Klara's living room."

"Oh, but I like it here," Frannie responded.

"It's so small, though." Marta gestured to the kids crowded around the table and then to Giselle sitting in Frannie's recliner and Lexie on the floor.

Klara, who stood at the end of the bed, stiffened but then said, "Can we do it tomorrow morning? I don't think I'm up to it tonight."

"Of course," Marta answered.

Frannie didn't reply. I asked again if she wanted her soup. She assured me she did not.

I took the bowl into the kitchen and poured it back into the pot to keep it warm. I started to take a piece of pizza for myself but realized I wasn't hungry. The twins laughed loudly about something. Abe kicked the table leg. Christy ordered him to stop.

As Klara, in the living room with Giselle, Lexie, Will, and Alexander, described her back injury, I slipped from the kitchen and down the hall to my room, leaving the door cracked open in case anyone called for me. As much as I appreciated being allowed to witness this reunion, I knew this family needed their space.

After so much drama, so did I.

Finally, everyone left and I readied Frannie for bed. Exhausted, she fell asleep immediately. That left Giselle and me awake in the *daadi haus*. I hoped to show her the fabric we found, but when I started to mention it, she cut me off.

"It's straight to bed for me," she said. "I've never been so tired in my life."

As I watched her go, I had to wonder, between her and Lexie, what it was about flying that made people so tired. The plane did all the work, yet the two of them had acted exhausted, as though they had flown here on the power of their own flapping arms.

I was feeling pretty tired myself, so I got ready for bed too. As I did, my mind kept going to Giselle, and I couldn't help but think what an odd woman she was. Hot and cold, sweet one minute and curt the next, treating each person in a completely different way, some nice, some mean, some in between. She was like no one I had ever met before.

No doubt, she had "issues," as Zed would say, perhaps the lingering results of having had an abusive father. Just the thought broke my heart—and made me even more determined to be a friend to her, no matter which of her many ways she treated me in return.

I awoke the next morning, thrilled that I would soon be seeing Zed. He and Ella would arrive, God willing, by nightfall.

Despite the Shelly-related incident, I'd missed him desperately and couldn't wait to see him. I took extra care getting ready that morning, even though it would be hours and hours before he arrived.

I made extra oatmeal for breakfast, thinking Giselle might want some, but she kept sleeping. Frannie slept most of the morning too and into the early afternoon. She awoke around two, and I had just managed to get a small bit of soup down her when Will arrived with Alexander to move the hospital bed into the main house.

We transferred Frannie to her recliner and then Will and Alexander wheeled the bed toward the door. I couldn't believe Giselle could sleep through the commotion, but there wasn't a peep from her room. I knew her body was adjusting to a new time zone, but was she going to sleep all day?

Once Will and Alexander made it out the door, I managed to get Frannie dressed in her robe and then slid her slippers on her feet. Next, I grabbed her favorite quilt, maneuvered her to a standing position, and then wrapped it around her as if she were a baby before lowering her back into the chair.

When Alexander returned, he asked if I would go make up the bed because Klara couldn't handle it, thanks to her back. Frannie seemed relieved that it wasn't yet time to leave her little home.

I passed Will on the walkway as he was coming back to the *daadi haus*.

As I made the bed, Klara told me that Will had brought over a whole meal from his grandmother, Alice, to serve as a welcome home supper later for Ella and Zed.

"Looks like lasagna," she added, "so I put it in the fridge for now."

"Sounds yummy," I said as I pulled the clean sheets taut over the mattress and then folded the corners.

"Lexie and Ada will drive over tonight after we eat," she added, "and bring dessert. Will's going to stay home with the kids and get them to bed."

Listening to her talk, I decided it sounded much like last night, another pulled-together party at the Rupps'.

Then I had to smile again when I recognized my own reaction. At home, with my own family, I usually dreaded such things. But here, among these people, I was eager for all of us to be together again, even though we'd just done the pizza thing with Giselle the night before. That had to say a lot not just about what nice and interesting folks these people were, but also how well I fit in with them. Daring to dream, I decided that perhaps someday they would be not just my friends but my in-laws.

In the living room, I spread a soft cotton blanket on the hospital bed, followed by a quilt, and then I told Klara we'd be right in with her mother.

At the *daadi haus*, I opened the door and said, "All set."

Will asked Frannie if she was ready to go.

"I suppose," she sighed, and I realized that this could well be the last time she would ever cross the threshold of her beloved little home.

The thought brought a tear to my eye, especially when I saw Will take off his stocking cap and gently put it on Frannie's head. Then the two men made a chair with their hands, lifted her up, and carried her out the front door. I dried my eyes as I followed behind.

We settled her into the bed, and then Alexander built up the fire as Will returned to the *daadi haus* for the battery and Klara and I fussed with the covers. Soon Will was back, the bed was fully wired for power, and Frannie was all set.

Finally, around four, Giselle came through the back door of the main house. "Goodness," she said. "I'm feeling so much better." Without saying hello to Klara or to me, she sat down beside hospital bed, taking her mother's hand in hers.

Frannie opened her eyes at her daughter's touch and for the next hour, although she wasn't very talkative, she stayed awake.

By five o'clock I had managed to coax Frannie into taking a meager supper of no more than half a cup of chicken noodle soup, after which she had fallen asleep, Giselle by her side. Now, Giselle was just watching her mother as she dozed. Klara was up in her room with the door closed, and I assumed she'd been resting her back and had fallen asleep as well.

Checking the time, I went into Klara's kitchen to finish getting the food ready for Zed and Ella's arrival. The meal Alice had sent included a big lasagna, which I'd been heating for the past half hour, a salad, and a fresh loaf of bread.

I set the table for seven—Klara, Alexander, Giselle, Marta, Zed, Ella, and me—though I also set a stack of nine smaller plates to the side, knowing Ada and Lexie would be joining us later and bringing dessert when they came.

When I finally heard the front door swing open, it was all I could do not to race across the living room and fling myself into Zed's arms.

Then I realized that it wasn't Zed and Ella who had arrived. It was their mother.

"Zed called," Marta said, taking off her cape. "They've been delayed by car trouble."

My heart sank as I watched her move into the room.

"They made it all the way to Carlisle before it happened, so if worse comes to worst, Zed can leave the car in a shop there and either Lexie or I can drive over and get them. In the meantime, there's no need to hold dinner. They could be several hours."

I took in a deep breath and blew it out slowly. At least they were close. By car, Carlisle couldn't be more than an hour and a half away.

Giselle stood. "In that case, I'm going out to *Mamm's* little house and scramble myself some eggs. Maybe take a little nap after that."

"Won't you eat with us?" Marta asked.

Giselle shook her head, moving toward the kitchen. "My body clock is all messed up. No offense to Alice, but as far as my stomach knows, it's time for breakfast, not supper."

Marta and I smiled at each other as Giselle continued out the back door. Neither one of us could know what jet lag felt like, so we would have to take her word for it.

"Should I wake you up once they get here?" I asked.

"No, that's okay," she replied as she headed for the door, "I'll check back later." With that, she left.

I removed Giselle's place setting from the table as Marta headed upstairs to wake her sister. Ten minutes later, Marta, Klara, Alexander, and I were sitting down to eat while Frannie continued to sleep. Halfway through the meal, footsteps fell on the back porch followed by voices. Could that be who I thought it was, already?

Then the door opened, revealing Ella, who looked as if she'd doubled in size in the last three weeks. Zed followed her, flicking his bangs from his eyes, a shy smile on his face, something about him seeming both vulnerable and tender to me.

I'd been anxious about seeing him, but now my heart pounded at his appearance. Reaching up, I smoothed my hair under my *kapp* and drank in the sight of his handsome face.

"You got the car fixed!" Marta pushed back her chair and hurried toward her children. She gave Ella a big hug, a look of pure joy on her face.

Once they had pulled apart, Ella said, "*Ya.*" She poked Zed with her elbow. "After the nice man who stopped to help us figure out what was wrong."

Zed's face reddened.

"Tell 'em, little bro."

He hung his head. "I ran out of gas."

Ella laughed. "And he's supposed to be the smart one in the family!"

"Well," Marta said, hugging her son. "That can happen to—" she paused. "To the best of us." I was pretty sure it had never happened to her.

Zed laughed. "It's okay. I know I can be a little absentminded."

"Absentminded?" Ella hooted. "How many times did I ask if we didn't need to stop for gas and you kept saying, 'We're fine'? I think *denial* is your problem."

Zed shrugged. "My gauge is a little off." Finally, he looked around, but instead of giving me a smile, he avoided my eyes entirely and said to his mother, "Where's Giselle?"

"She's out in the *daadi haus*."

"She'll be back," I added in a cheery, too-loud voice, assuming he just hadn't noticed me.

That still didn't make him look, though Ella gave me a broad smile and said, "Hey, Izzy."

"Hello," I answered as I rose and moved around the table.

I gave Ella a long hug, realizing I had missed her.

"How are you?" she asked.

"*Gut.*"

"Me too," she replied, affection in her voice.

Unable to help myself, I turned and gave Zed a hug as well. He had just taken off his coat, and he felt solid and warm and strong. I inhaled deeply, looking into his eyes as we pulled apart, disappointed to see that he would not return my gaze.

What was going on?

Klara and Alexander had followed me from the table and now they greeted their niece and nephew too. Alexander had already finished eating, so after that he excused himself to go outside to finish up his chores.

"Are you hungry?" Marta asked her children as she gestured toward the two waiting places at the table.

"Famished," Zed said, taking a seat, scooping up a huge serving of lasagna, and plopping it on his plate.

Ella was about to sit down too when she spotted Frannie across the room in her bed.

"When did you move *Mammi* in there?" Ella whispered, startled.

"This morning," Marta answered. "Now that everyone's home, it's easier for all of us this way."

"How is she?"

"Not so *gut*," Marta answered. "She sleeps, mostly, although she was alert for a while yesterday."

They both moved into the living room, and, to be polite, I followed, although I noticed Klara sitting back down at the table to resume her meal. The three of us stepped toward the side of the bed as Marta said, "She's been looking forward to you two coming."

I nodded in agreement. I knew Frannie hadn't seen Zed since August and Ella in nearly a year.

Finally, Zed got up to join us, wiping his mouth with a napkin as he stepped to the other side of his grandmother's bed. He stroked her hand, and then his eyes fell on her peaceful face.

Suddenly feeling that I was intruding on a family moment, I slipped away, back to the table and my supper. By the time Marta, Zed, and Ella also returned to the kitchen, both Klara and I had finished our food. Klara said she needed to rest her back some more, so she excused herself, grabbed an ice pack from the freezer, and headed upstairs. I knew her back really did hurt, but I suspected that her primary motive in that moment was simply to be out of there by the time Giselle returned. From what I had seen, the two women simply avoided each other as much as possible.

Once everyone was done, I cleared the table and then started on the dishes as the others drifted back into the living room and over to the hospital bed. Zed was still acting so strange—almost cold—toward me, and my mind raced to figure out why as I scrubbed each plate clean.

I was on the last one when the back door opened and Giselle stepped inside.

"They're here?" she asked me, but before I could reply, Marta was on her feet, calling out to her sister.

"Giselle, the kids have arrived!" Her voice sounded so enthusiastic, and I realized I had never seen her as animated as she'd been this evening.

"Come on," I heard Marta say to her kids. "Come meet your Aunt Giselle."

Giselle crossed to the living room, where they all met on the other side of the couch. Drying my hands, I couldn't help but stand there and watch.

Ella hugged Giselle first, saying, "We've looked forward to this for so long."

Giselle, I was pleased to see, patted her niece's back warmly before releasing her.

Zed extended his hand next, which Giselle took, but then she jerked his arm forward, to bring him in for a quick hug. They both laughed.

When they pulled apart, she told him, "I've been so excited to meet you in person, Zed. I feel as though I know you from all the emails we've exchanged. It's as if I've watched you grow up."

Beaming, he simply said, "I've been eager to meet you too."

As they were all still standing there, the front door swung open, and Lexie and Ada came inside, each one carrying a pink box.

With a cry of enthusiasm, they greeted Zed and Ella as well.

"I had a feeling that heap of rusted metal out there was yours," Lexie teased as she gave her cousin Zed a hug.

"Ha-ha," he replied, but he didn't seem offended. "At least it gets me where I need to go."

"Unless you forget one little thing," Ella responded, coming over for hugs as well. "Future reference, Zed? It's spelled G-A-S, and it comes from a hose at those places called 'gas stations.'"

As the teasing and laughter continued, I stepped forward to relieve both women of their boxes. I carried them into the kitchen, set them on the counter, and opened them up. Inside one was a lemon pie and in the other, cherry.

"We *bought* them," Ada confessed as she joined me there. "I've never bought a pie in my entire life."

"Hey, Ella," Lexie said as she joined us, "too bad they won't be as good as yours."

"You can say that again," Ella responded, full of sass and with one hand on her hip.

Soon everyone was back in the kitchen, laughing and talking and eating dessert. Alexander returned from his chores and joined in, assuming his usual place at the head of the table.

That left Klara as the only one missing from this fun family gathering—besides Frannie, who was still in her bed in the next room, peacefully dozing away. Glancing over at her, I wished she would wake up at least long enough to see her family members gathered together like this. It would make her so happy.

As we ate, the conversation turned to Switzerland, and Ada began pumping Giselle for information on all the people she had met over there on her trip several years before. Giselle seemed to grow quite chatty as she responded to Ada's questions. She talked about the current state of Amielbach, which I knew was the beautiful old home and property where Abraham Sommers once lived and worked as an artist and wood-carver. Thanks to Zed's film, I almost felt as though I had visited there myself. The building had been passed down the family line all the way to Frannie, but according to Zed, she had sold it years ago and then used the proceeds to buy this farm.

Giselle said the current owners of Amielbach were having a great success in running it as a boutique hotel, and that her artwork sold well in the gift shop. "Daniel and Morgan's tour business is doing great too."

I knew that Daniel and Morgan were friends of Ada's—and obviously of Giselle's as well.

"In fact," Giselle said, "they're in California visiting Morgan's mother, and after Christmas they'll travel to Indiana. I told them to come here if they have a chance."

"Oh, that would be great!" Ada clapped her hands together.

Giselle leaned back a little. "Don't get your hopes up too much. I know they're going home by the end of the month. They have tours booked in early January."

"What kind of people go on their tours?" I asked.

"Church groups, mostly senior citizens, and usually from the US. But they've also had college groups and international groups. It's very profitable. They give history tours, specifically Anabaptist history tours."

"Oh!" I gushed, unable to help myself. I was so fascinated by Anabaptist history—indeed, by all history—that such a tour sounded like a dream come true to me. "Do they ever address historical Amish clothing styles?"

"They do," Giselle answered. "They had me put together a display about textiles from the seventeen hundreds for their new lighted case near the hotel's registration desk. It really catches people's eye and, in fact, has been so popular that now they want me to help them create a line of cloth dolls for the gift shop, ones that show exactly what the early Anabaptists would have worn."

"Really?" Zed pushed his empty plate to the center of the table. "You've studied early Anabaptist clothing?" He sounded so enthusiastic that for a moment something twisted deep in my gut.

"Not yet. Well, except for last night, looking through some of the books I've sent *Mamm* over the years. I'm thinking I'll do the research and create the designs for the dolls myself but hire out the actual handwork."

"Good thinking to use your talents where they're most effective and delegate the rest," he said. "I learned that lesson from my last Foley artist, who had a real knack for sound."

"Exactly. Any talented seamstress can carry out a good design."

"And everyone knows *you* can produce good design," Zed replied.

He was practically falling all over himself with Giselle, like a slobbery puppy with its new owner. Surely he wasn't considering dumping my costume work in favor of having Giselle do it, was he? I couldn't fathom such a thing.

Then again, at least that would help explain why he'd been acting so weird toward me tonight. Maybe he had decided he didn't want me to do the costumes for his film, but he didn't know how to tell me. If that wasn't it, I wondered, what else could it be?

Was he embarrassed about running out of gas?

Afraid to tell me he and Shelly were dating?

Worried I might want too much of his time while he was home?

Or something else?

Whatever the reason, he didn't seem to be himself at all—at least not toward me. I couldn't help but think of what Ella had said, that he had a lot of growing up to do. If so, I decided, maybe he was just pouting—for who knew what reason.

Taking a deep breath, I told myself to stop speculating and let things take their course. Zed had almost a month before he had to be back at school.

Surely he would relax and open up to me by then.

Twenty-Four

After dinner, Lexie drove Ada home and Giselle headed out to the *daadi haus* at the same time Alexander went up to bed. Marta, Ella, and Zed moved toward Frannie, which left me alone in the kitchen. I was about to start in on the dishes when I heard Marta direct Zed to help me.

I glanced over to see her and Ella settling in on each side of Frannie's bed. Zed stood halfway between them and me, hesitating, looking not unlike a deer in headlights. Then he began to move in my direction, but he wouldn't meet my gaze, and it was obvious he didn't want to be anywhere near me.

Once we were side by side at the sink, me washing and him rinsing, I tried to make quiet conversation.

"How was your trip?" I asked, my own voice sounding strained to my ears.

He shrugged, taking a plate from my hand and swishing it in the rinse water. "We hit some snow around the Pennsylvania state line, but the plows had gone through before us, so it wasn't too bad."

He fell silent, so after a moment, I tried again.

"How were your finals?"

"Fine."

I took a deep breath. I could barely stand small talk with anyone, but especially not with Zed Bayer, so I stopped trying and we finished the dishes in silence.

After we were done, however, I told him I had something to show him. "I'll be right back." I went out into the cold to the *daadi haus*, grabbed the flashlight, and headed down to my room, retrieving the pamphlets that had belonged to Malachi. I also grabbed the list of phone numbers for places that might have a copy of Abigail's chapbook in their collection. Now that Zed was on break and had a little time, I had a feeling he wouldn't mind helping out with this part of the search.

I returned the flashlight to the cupboard in the entryway and hurried back to the main house, directing Zed to sit at the table. I gave him the list first, explaining what I needed. He agreed to make the calls for me and then folded up the paper and tucked it into his pocket.

Once he was seated, I took the chair across from him and spread the pamphlets out in the space between us.

"What is this?"

I beamed. "Frannie suggested I look in her attic, and these were in a box of things that belonged to your grandfather."

Zed was thrilled. As he looked everything over, bit by bit, and talked about them, he slowly began to relax. Seeing my chance and unable to stand the suspense any longer, I worked up the nerve to ask if he still wanted me to do the costumes.

"Of course. Why wouldn't I?" he replied, his attention on the papers.

He seemed sincere, and I was relieved. But if that wasn't what was bothering him, what was? Clearly, there was still *something* strange going on between us.

If only he would open up and tell me what it was.

The next morning I found Giselle standing at the kitchen window of the *daadi haus*, a cup of coffee in her hand.

She startled when I greeted her.

"Sorry," I said. "How'd you sleep?"

"So-so."

I reached for a mug and poured my own cup of coffee. She'd brewed it extra strong.

Still at the window, Giselle seemed melancholy, and I wished there was something I could do to cheer her up.

That's when I remembered the fabric I'd found in Frannie's attic.

"I have something for you," I told her as I left my cup on the counter and headed back to my room. "Your mother wanted you to have it. I found it up in her attic a few days ago."

I returned with the plastic bag, unzipping it as I walked. When I reached the table, I lifted the two pieces of fabric out.

"One is a coverlet," I said. "And the other is a remnant. Velvet." I placed the fabric on the table.

Both items seemed to catch her eye right away, as I knew they would.

"Your *mamm* and Marta and I were wondering what you could tell us about them from a textile standpoint. And we wanted to know if you think they could be worth anything as antiques. They seem awfully old."

Giselle put her cup on the counter and said she'd be right back. She returned after a few minutes, looking frustrated.

"What's wrong?"

"I was hoping I might have left a pair of cotton gloves in my purse or in one of the pockets of my suitcase, but I didn't. I don't want to handle these without them."

"How about rubber gloves? Would that do?"

She shook her head. "They need to be cotton. Preferably white cotton. And spotlessly clean."

I thought for a moment and then suggested she try the cupboard by the door. "You'll see a basket in there of winter gloves, but I think I noticed at least one pair of glove liners in there too. They might be cotton."

"Good idea." She left for the entryway. After a moment she came back with the ones I'd been talking about.

"These will work," she said, sliding the white cotton glove liners over her hands.

She sat down in a chair and began to examine the coverlet and then the remnant, handling them carefully. As she did, she grew silent, so I remained quiet as well, watching as she took stock of the items inch by inch.

I was more interested in the coverlet, but she kept going back to the velvet, running one gloved finger across the nap and holding it this way and that in the light.

"This piece looks so familiar," she said, her voice trailing off as she continued to gaze at it.

Intrigued, I asked her what she could tell me about it.

"Well, it's made of silk and combines an uncut looped pile and a tufted cut pile. That's why it's so luminous."

I had no idea what she was talking about, but I still found it fascinating. "How old do you think it is?"

"Old. Maybe as much as two hundred years. I know this sort of thing was popular in Italy in the late eighteenth century."

"What kind of dye is it?"

"Plant based."

"But it's so vibrant."

"They did amazing things back then, considering what they had to work with." She placed the fabric back in the plastic bag and then took off her gloves. "How would an Amish family end up with such a fancy piece of fabric from so long ago?"

"We don't have any idea," I answered, zipping the bag. "It was in a box of your father's things."

Giselle froze, and for a long moment she just sat there staring down at the bag of fabric, her skin drawn and pale, her eyes a myriad of emotion. I didn't know what to do, but the look on her face frightened me. Was she okay? Did she need something?

Finally, I jumped up and got her a glass of water, but when I tried to hand it to her, she suddenly snapped to attention and began waving me off. "Not around the fabric," she cried, even though both pieces were securely back inside their protective holder.

Suddenly, she stood and grabbed the plastic bag with both hands. "I don't know what makes me angrier," she hissed, clutching the bag to her chest. I thought she was mad at me until she added, "The fact that he took it away, or the fact that he lied about keeping it."

With that, she turned on her heel and marched off to the bedroom, closing the door soundly behind her.

Two hours later, I was still puzzling over what Giselle had said and done in the kitchen of the *daadi haus*. I had no idea what that entire interaction had been about, but I had to assume it was yet another thread in the complicated tapestry that had been her relationship with her abusive father. I wanted to help but wasn't sure how I could, except maybe to say a prayer for her—and offer a listening ear if she ever wanted to talk.

Giselle finally joined me and Frannie in the main house around ten, and she came in acting as if none of it had ever happened. Taking my cue from her, I tried to do the same. Soon, I was busy on the couch with my handwork, and she was settled into place at her mother's side. As the morning wore on, I noticed that she seemed content just to be with Frannie, chatting whenever the woman was awake and sitting quietly, her mind somewhere far away, when she slept.

Zed popped in just before noon to let us know he would be working at Will's Christmas tree farm all week. "My hours will fluctuate each day, but I'll come over whenever I can."

I smiled at his words, glad to know, at last, that he actually wanted to spend some time with me, but when I looked at him, I realized he'd been speaking primarily to Giselle.

He pulled his phone from his pocket and glanced at it. "In fact, I'm working the rest of the day. I need to get going. I was hoping maybe we could go on a research jaunt in the morning."

Now he was looking at me, so I said, "We?"

"Yeah. You and me."

That was a relief.

"Why? What's up? Did you make those phone calls already?" My pulse surged. "Did you find someone who has a copy of the chapbook?"

He shook his head. "No. I called all the numbers on your list first thing this morning, but none of them panned out."

My heart sank. "So where is it you want to go?"

"I was thinking Rod's farm. To look through the trunk. Isn't that what you've been dying to do?"

I nodded, my excitement growing again.

"Can I come?" Giselle asked.

Zed and I both looked over at her.

"Absolutely," he said. "If you don't mind riding in my excuse for a car."

She shrugged. "I could use the fresh air," she said, but I had a feeling what she really needed was a little space and some time away from the intensity of the situation here.

"Iz?" Zed asked. "Do you think you can get away from here for an hour or two tomorrow?"

"Sure. As long as Klara can manage things. I'll ask her." I didn't think it would be a problem. Frannie was sleeping so much now that it wouldn't be as if Klara would need to lift her or anything.

In the afternoon, after I'd managed to feed Frannie some custard, I settled on the couch. Giselle had gone, yawning, out to the *daadi haus*, probably to sleep, so I pulled the book that featured her work from my bag.

A while later the back door opened, and I assumed it was Alexander coming in from the field.

"What are you reading?" It was Giselle. She'd snuck up on me, not on purpose I'm sure, in her stocking feet.

Embarrassed, I held up the book. "I like your piece in here." Immediately my face grew warm.

"Oh, that. I used to send books to my mother now and then."

"*Ya*, she has a nice collection."

"I understand you do handwork."

I nodded.

"What are you doing now?"

I pulled one of the bookmarks I'd been embroidering from my bag and handed it to her. Then I pulled out the original card, stored in a plastic bag, that I got the idea from, sure she'd be interested in it.

"This is quite the find," Giselle said, holding it in her hand. "Women used to make these long before the mass greeting card industry started."

"Really? This is a greeting card? I thought it was a bookmark."

Gisele shook her head. "Where did it come from?"

As she sat down on the other side of the couch. I told her all about

Verna's boxes and going through them and how I'd been able to hear so many of her wonderful old stories.

"Fascinating," Giselle said, but then she stifled a yawn. "Though personally, I'm much more interested in fabric than old people's stories." Giselle handed the card back to me. "So you're doing the costumes for Zed's next film, huh?"

I must have given her a surprised look.

"He told me. We email back and forth."

I'd gathered it from when they had greeted each other. I just hadn't known they chatted about me.

"He asks me questions. That sort of thing," she said.

I couldn't help but ask, "What kind of questions?"

"Oh, historical things about Switzerland. Or European viewpoints." She laughed a little. "Whatever."

I put the card back in my sewing bag.

"He's mentioned you many times," she added.

Now my face burned.

"All good, of course. He says you're very smart, very gifted. You helped with the costumes for his last project too, right?"

I nodded.

"He said you're one of the reasons the film won at the festival."

"Zed is being too generous."

Giselle shifted toward me, and for a moment I thought she was settling in for some girl talk. She just seemed to grow so animated, her eyes so sparkly, that I expected her to come out with some question about me and Zed and our relationship. Instead, she said, in a breathless voice, "Tell me about the costumes you have in mind."

I smiled. Clearly, this was a woman after my own heart.

For the next hour, until Frannie woke, Giselle and I discussed fashions, costuming, and fabrics. I was thrilled to have someone so knowledgeable to talk with, someone who knew even more about this stuff than I did. It was rare to find another person this much into sewing, and it made me feel, well, *normal* for a change, as though I weren't the oddball in the room.

Instead, for now at least, she and I could be oddballs together.

The next morning, after Frannie had fallen back asleep, Klara sat at her side as Giselle and I left with Zed for our expedition to Rod's farm. Giselle slipped into the back seat before I reached the car and refused to move up front. Zed smiled, indicating it was fine.

When we arrived at the old Westler place, Rod met us in the driveway, and I introduced both Zed and Giselle to him.

She stepped forward and shook Rod's hand. "I'm Frannie Lantz's daughter."

"Oh," Rod said. And then as if it had just registered who Giselle really was, he said, "Oh!" again, but this time more loudly.

I suddenly saw her from Rod's point of view. The skinny jeans. The spiked hair. The leather coat. The medallion around her neck.

He smiled. "I remember you from when I was a little boy."

Giselle laughed. "I haven't changed a bit, have I?"

Rod chuckled and tugged on his thick, dark beard. "Neither have I."

She laughed as he motioned for us to follow him. "The trunk is in the shop."

A couple of chickens darted in front of us as we followed him, and then as he slid open the door to the barn, a lanky cat ran in.

I squinted in the dim light. We walked around a stack of hay bales and through a door. The cement floor was swept clean. A bird flew up in the rafters, startling us.

Rod pointed to the corner of his shop. The trunk was old and warped, looking as if it had gone through a flood. I hoped the contents hadn't.

"Like I told your *daed*, Izzy, that's the last of Verna's old papers, though I think everything in there is mostly junk. He said you would want to go through it anyway."

"He was right."

Smiling, Rod brought out several paper bags from under his workbench. "Very well. You can use these for anything you want to take with you, and while you're at it, go ahead and bag up the rest for the burn barrel."

I thanked him, grateful he hadn't already destroyed the contents.

"I'll be in the barn. Holler if you need anything."

I opened the trunk and tried to prop up the lid, but it fell back down. I opened it a second time and Giselle stepped to the side to hold it. A moldy smell greeted me, which didn't bode well. A mix of things—newspapers, magazines, and papers—halfway filled the inside.

"How about if we each grab a handful," I suggested. "It will go faster that way."

Zed stepped close to reach in, and as he moved aside I grabbed stacks for Giselle and myself. She closed the lid and then we all sat down on the cement floor and started going through the material, making one pile for newspapers and one for magazines.

I came across several water-stained receipts and what looked like tax records from 1959. Fearing the contents were just another collection of junk, I worked faster, sorting through several moldy magazines and more receipts.

"Look at this," Giselle said, holding up a yellowed piece of paper. "Oh, my goodness. It's dated 1 August, 1764."

I held out my hand, making give-me motions with my fingers.

Zed laughed. "Technically, it does belong to Izzy."

Giselle handed it to me. "It's too faint for my old eyes to read, anyway."

The bottom of the page was water stained but the rest was fine, except that the ink had faded considerably.

I held it close to my face, cleared my throat, and then read:

> *Dear Papa,*
>
> *I received your news about Mother's grave illness with a heavy heart. She has rallied so many times before, but I fear as you do that she is surely at death's door this time. Gorg and I have assessed the maturity of the growing fruit here in North Carolina and have determined that returning to our home with you is what is best for our family.*
>
> *As the journey could take two or three weeks, please pray she will hold on until we get there.*
>
> > *Your loving daughter,*
> > *Abigail*

"Wow!" Zed scooted to my side, reading over my shoulder. "Looks like

Abigail and Gorg must have returned to Lancaster County that summer, about six months after they left."

"What does she mean about the fruit?" Giselle asked.

I explained that they had been staying down there on an apple orchard with a family friend. Looking down, I read the letter again, to myself this time. The situation sounded sad, of course, but otherwise there was nothing unique or unusual about this letter, such as no mention of "recent unrest" as there had been in the first one.

I looked at Zed, my lips pursed. "What if we've been wrong, and their trip to North Carolina had nothing to do with the massacre at all? What if she and Gorg really did go down there just to learn some new kind of growing techniques and the dates are simply a coincidence? Maybe when she said 'period of unrest,' she was talking about something as simple as a blight."

"Or an infestation of some kind of bugs in the orchard," Zed agreed.

"Or problems hiring enough apple pickers," Giselle offered.

Zed and I looked at each other, stumped. As exciting as this new find was, it was starting to feel that every answer we ran across only brought up more questions.

I folded the letter and slipped it under my cape into the pocket of my apron. We went through the rest of the trunk, but there was nothing else worth keeping. Once we got to the bottom, we crammed all of the contents—except for the letter in my pocket—into the paper bags and carried them with us into the main part of the barn to find Rod.

We told him about the letter, and though he seemed enthused for our sake, he didn't even ask to see it.

"Where do you want the stuff to be burned?" Zed asked.

"The barrel is behind the shed. Thanks so much."

Once we were on our way again, we tried to decide what our next step would be. We were out of time for today, but Zed said he was free in the morning if we wanted to follow up with any of this elsewhere. I told him it depended on how Frannie was doing—and if Klara would be willing to spell me again.

"If it works out," he said, "tomorrow we should go by the Mennonite

Information Center. We could see if by some wild chance they have a complete copy of the chapbook."

"Weren't they on that list of numbers I gave you to try?" I asked him. "I thought you said nothing panned out."

"When I called, the woman I needed to talk to wasn't in. The guy on the phone suggested I come in some other time and pursue the matter in person."

"Oh. Okay. I guess it's worth a shot."

"Wanna come too, Giselle?" Zed asked, glancing in the rearview mirror.

"Nah. When it comes to research, I'm more into textiles than to people."

"There's a fabric museum in town we could go to," Zed offered. "We'll probably have time to do both."

"Oh, great! In that case, I'm definitely in."

Later that afternoon, as Frannie slept, I took out my notebook and pen and began writing out a list of characters I knew for sure would be in Zed's film. I already had some designs in mind, but soon I would need to start collecting swatches of fabric as well. With Giselle here, there would never be a better time for that.

I brought it up when she came in to sit with Frannie for a while. In response, she shocked me by saying, "Actually, I've been thinking it would be really cool to weave the fabric for the costumes. That's why I wanted to do some research, to see what I'd need to know to pull it off."

I gaped at her. "From scratch?"

She grinned. "That's how weaving usually works, yes."

"But...but we would need so much."

"That's what looms are for."

"I don't know a thing about—"

"Not you, silly. Me."

I shook my head. "Are you serious? That sounds like a lot of work."

"But it would be authentic. Can you imagine the close-ups, Izzy? And how fun it would be for you and me to experience all of this the way an eighteenth-century seamstress would?"

I thought about that for a moment, intimidated by the scope of the project but thrilled by the enthusiasm that shone on her face.

"These people would have woven their own fabrics?"

Giselle nodded. "Some did. Some purchased it from a weaver. Either way, once they had the fabric, they would have sewn it by hand."

That I knew, of course, but then I realized what she was implying. Not only was she offering to weave all the fabric, she was suggesting I use that fabric—and sew all of the costumes *by hand*!

"We might be talking about an awful lot of costumes here. Authentic or not, I don't know if you or I are up to that."

She shrugged. "Right now it's just food for thought. Have you made any sketches yet?"

I nodded, flipping through the notebook as she came and sat on the couch at my side. I showed her what I had—britches and a shirt, patterned off the painting in Frannie's book. A woman's cape dress, with a long skirt. An Indian's leather leggings and vest.

"These are really good," she said. "I'm impressed."

Barely whispering, I answered, "*Danke.*" From the time I was little, I had enjoyed sketching clothing, but this was the first time I'd ever shown my drawings to anyone besides Zed.

Later, Giselle went out to the *daadi haus* and returned with a large piece of paper and a section of fabric. "I found some muslin in with *Mamm*'s sewing supplies. Pattern paper too."

"What are you going to do with all that?"

"What do you think? I want to make a prototype for one of the costumes you designed, maybe the shirt, for an *Englisch* man."

I was shocked and thrilled. Here was a world-renowned fabric artist about to execute one of my designs. Incredible. I didn't know what God was doing in my life with all of this, but I couldn't help but be thankful for it every step of the way.

Wednesday morning, the information center was just opening as we arrived. I'd been one other time with Zed and had enjoyed both the displays and the bookstore.

This time I'd brought along the chapbook, zipped in a gallon-sized bag, and Zed handed it the woman at the counter. She read the title through the plastic as we asked if she'd ever see anything like it.

"Sure. It's a chapbook. These were popular back in the seventeenth and eighteenth centuries and contained things like poems, ballads, and religious tracts. The word 'chapbook' comes from—"

"Actually," Zed said, cutting her off, "what I meant was, have you ever seen this one? Specifically. We're hoping to find a duplicate copy."

"Oh." The woman handed it back. "No, but let me check our database." She stepped to the computer and typed in a few things, and then she leaned over to the chapbook and reread the cover before shifting her attention back to the computer. Finally, she shook her head. "Nothing. You could try the Lancaster Historical Society. They might have a copy."

"We can go there after the textile museum," I told Zed.

"Did you say the textile museum?" the woman asked. "I'm sorry, that closed down."

"Oh." Zed looked at Giselle, who was crestfallen. "Sorry."

It was just as well, because as soon as we got back out to the car, Zed got a call from Will, who asked if he could come in to work early. He dropped us off at the house, suggesting we give it a shot again tomorrow, this time at the Lancaster Historical Society.

Back at Frannie's, I was glad to see she was awake and more alert than she'd been in a few days. At least that was how it seemed at first. Once we relieved Klara and took our places by Frannie's side, she lasted only another fifteen minutes or so before falling back to sleep.

She dozed off and on for the whole afternoon, and I was touched to see that Giselle never left her side. I, on the other hand, was feeling unusually antsy, so I ended up taking a long break to do the wash, leaving Frannie in Giselle's care as I tackled a load with the wringer washer and then hung it all out on the line. When I returned to the house, Frannie was awake and Giselle was telling her all about Switzerland.

"The cottage is down the hill from the big house, closer to the creek," she said in a voice that was soft and almost musical. "Across the creek is a cave where the Anabaptists used to worship. I've been in there, and so has Ada."

Frannie seemed pleased by that and closed her eyes.

"In the distance are the Bernese Alps, and around Amielbach the hills are green with trees, mostly pine. In the winter, snow blankets the ground like a white coverlet and the creek freezes. When I first moved to Switzerland, I used to slide down that creek with the neighbors."

Frannie smiled, her eyelids fluttering a little. "Tell me about the people," she whispered.

Giselle started with Herr Lauten, the man who bought Amielbach from Frannie decades ago. "He's grown frail over the last year. His son, Oskar, runs the kitchen. Daniel and Morgan are in charge of the gift shop and the tours." She listed a few others, employees of the hotel, and then said, "That's about it. We're a small but happy group."

Frannie smiled again, seeming pleased that Giselle had a community of people she could count on.

Klara wandered in and out of the living room as Giselle spoke, but I couldn't tell if she was listening or not.

Later, when Frannie awoke again, Giselle offered to read to her.

"*Ya,*" she answered. "Psalm 23. There should be a Bible on the right side of the fireplace."

I looked up to see Giselle's frown as she followed her mother's directions, wiggling behind the hospital bed to the bookcase. I got up and stoked the fire. It was another cold, damp mid-December day.

The Bible was big and heavy. Giselle managed to balance it on her lap and started reading.

"'The Lord is my shepherd; I shall not want. He maketh me lie down in green pastures: he leadeth me beside still waters...'" She didn't get to the third verse before Frannie was asleep.

I picked up my handwork and settled down on the couch again, while Giselle stayed at her mother's side, staring out the window.

I could tell she was lost in her thoughts, not just at that moment but for the rest of the evening. She was more withdrawn and distracted than usual, as though she was eager to be alone, and yet once we called it a night and went out to the *daddi haus,* she acted as if that was the last thing she wanted. As I changed into my nightclothes, I could hear her puttering around noisily, first in her own room and then in the kitchen, which was quite unlike her. Something told me not to go on to bed but instead to seek her out.

I found her sitting on the floor in front of the sink, the cabinet open, just staring inside.

"Giselle? What's wrong? Is there a leak under the sink?"

Startled, she turned to look at me. "No. But there is a vase."

She reached inside and pulled out a simple glass vase, one that had probably been used by Frannie countless times over the years. Standing, she closed the cabinet and carried the vase over to the table as she continued.

"When I was a little girl, my grandmother used to say that no matter where you go or who you're with, chances are if you need a vase, you just have to look under a kitchen sink." She flashed me a kind of "go figure" look, and then sat, still holding the vase. "I don't know why that stuck with me, but it did. Sometimes even now, when I'm in someone else's home, I'll take a peek. More often than not, I find that my grandmother was right."

What an odd statement. I wasn't sure how to respond, so I didn't. Instead, I just gave her a reassuring smile and offered to heat up some milk.

"Thanks. That would be nice."

As I went to the refrigerator, I could see that her mind was wandering away again. Lost in thought, she just sat there at the table, staring off into space as I worked in silence getting out the milk, pouring some in a pan, and setting it on the stove. I took out the honey, two mugs, and a spoon. As I stood and watched for the liquid in the pan to heat, she began to speak.

"*Mammi* Judith, my father's mother, was such a fascinating woman. She was the one who first taught me about fabrics, about sewing and mending and textiles. She had a room in her house filled from one end to the other with cloth goods—and not just bolts and remnants, but all kinds of vintage pieces to pull from too. Cast-off damask tablecloths. Old silk handkerchiefs. Used chintz seat cushions. She had one whole drawer just for rickrack and fringe. Can you imagine such a thing, a Plain woman, with all those embellishments? That drove her bishop crazy, but what could he do? It was her job."

I didn't want to speak aloud for fear Giselle would stop talking and pull back into her shell, so I just smiled and shook my head as she went on.

"I was only six or seven when she died, but I remember her so well. After her funeral, I asked my father if I could have her entire collection. Even then, I think I knew I was meant for a life that would involve cloth goods and creativity. Just like her."

A bubble popped on the milk's surface, so I removed the pan from the heat, gave the milk a stir, and poured it into the two cups.

"He was such a mean man, you know. Instead of explaining anything, he just said, 'Sure, Giselle, you can have every single item that's left' and then he brought me straight over to her house. Despite my grief over her death, I had never been so thrilled, and I can remember racing up the steps, through the front door, and down the hall toward the fabric storage room. Then I came around the corner and just froze."

Swallowing hard, I stirred honey into our cups as I waited for her to continue.

"The room was completely empty. Turns out, one of his sisters and her husband had gone in there three days before—the very day Judith died—and thrown everything out. They'd done it at the request of the bishop, who had been struggling with her and her fancy fabrics for years. Like I said, he'd tolerated it when she was alive, but once she was gone, he declared that was to be the end of that."

"Oh, Giselle," I whispered, picking up our cups and carrying them over to the table. I set one in front of her, and she put the vase aside and took up the cup as I lowered myself onto the chair across from her.

"Anyway, that day at her house, all I could do was stare in shock at the stripped-out room. Once my father caught up to me and saw the look on my face, he just laughed. Out loud. Can you imagine? Here I am all of six years old, my heart utterly broken, and my *daed* thinks it's funny."

"I'm so sorry," I said, swallowing back the lump in my throat. I couldn't imagine anyone behaving that way to a child, but especially not the child's father.

"At first I refused to believe what I was seeing. I insisted on pulling open every drawer, every cabinet, but to no avail. Finally, between a big chest of drawers and a wall, I spotted the one item they had missed. It was a remnant of velvet, made of silk, and so luminous that it practically glowed. I wouldn't have her magical roomful of fabrics and trims, but at least I had that one piece to remember her by."

I set down my cup and closed my eyes, so very sad for her. No wonder she had reacted the way she did when that remnant turned up again all these years later.

"My father didn't seem to care that I had found something and wanted to keep it for myself. I took the remnant home and put it away. But for weeks, whenever I would miss *Mammi* Judith, I would take it back out and hold it to my face and just inhale. It smelled of that room, of threads and lace and sewing machine grease and the work of my grandmother's hands. I should have known he couldn't let me have that. Once he realized how important it was to me, he took it away. He grabbed it out of my hands and said I was sinning in my adoration, that I was turning it into an idol."

She took a sip of her milk and then set her cup back down.

"I was devastated, of course, but my hope was that he would give it back to me once he calmed down. A few days later, he seemed to be in one of his rare good moods, so I summoned up the nerve to ask him about it over the breakfast table. I thought he would tell me sure, I could have it back. Instead he said, 'Too late. I burned it with yesterday's trash.'"

Later, as I tossed and turned in my bed, trying to get to sleep, Giselle's sad story kept rolling around in my mind. We had talked for another hour, connecting on a level that probably neither of us was used to. I had asked more about her *daed*, about what she thought had made him the way he was, especially if his own mother had been such a kind and loving woman. Giselle wasn't sure, though she said she'd always suspected it had something to do with his father's tragic death and the ways his life had fallen apart in the wake of that.

Apparently, when Malachi was only ten years old, he had witnessed his *daed* get caught up in a threshing machine and crushed to death. Not only did he suffer the trauma of seeing that, but soon after he and his mother and siblings were forced to move out of their home and into much smaller quarters elsewhere. And though the Amish community helped to support them financially, this had been during the Great Depression, when everyone—even the Amish—was feeling the loss of income caused by reduced sales.

Thus, from the time he was about eleven years old, Malachi had had no choice but to work practically around the clock to help support his family. According to Giselle, between witnessing his father's accident and being forced afterward to spend years in grueling labor, he had grown up to become a bitter man. Until his death in his forties—ironically, in a farming accident himself—Malachi had spent much of his adult life lashing out at others, trying to relieve his misery by causing pain to those around him.

I thought her explanation made sense, and I found myself feeling sorry for the man—or at least for the boy he had been before his life underwent such a dramatic change.

Giselle went on to reveal to me the story behind the coverlet as well. She said it was Klara who had come through with that information. That afternoon while I'd been out back doing laundry, Giselle had talked to Frannie at length about both the velvet and the coverlet, trying to figure out why Malachi had hung onto them. Klara had come down for some ice, overheard Giselle and Frannie talking, and joined in, asking them to describe little blanket. Once they did, she volunteered what she knew, that it had been her father's when he was just a boy. He had kept it tucked away and so Frannie had never noticed it, but Klara did because she had run across it once in the bottom of a trunk, when she was just a teen, and had taken it out and laundered it, meaning to use it on her bed. When her father saw what she'd done, he'd been livid, insisting that she fold it up and put it back where she found it, hissing that it hadn't been used as a bedspread since he was a child—and that it never would again.

Just as the velvet was a memento of his beloved mother, we decided the coverlet had more than likely been a memento as well—one of his life prior to the day his father died and his happy boyhood world changed forever.

The next morning, Klara agreed again to sit with Frannie so Giselle and I could go with Zed to the historical society. I would have thought she was just being gracious, except I had a feeling that mostly what she wanted was to keep Gisele out of the house as much as possible.

When we got there, we followed Zed straight to the library, where he logged into a computer.

He seemed to know what he was doing, and it wasn't long until he said, "There's no chapbook credited to an Abigail Bontrager in the collection."

My heart sank, though I didn't know why I should be surprised. Verna had warned me from the very beginning that the only copies likely to have survived were ones kept in the family.

Next he tried Konenquas's name. She showed up in several articles, listed as one of the Conestoga killed by the Paxton Boys. But that was it.

Then Zed searched the family history log for Vogel, which was Abigail's maiden name, and Bontrager, which was her married name, just to see if anything popped up that we didn't already have. Nothing new, just that Bernard and Veronika Vogel had come over on the *Virtuous Grace* and settled in Manor Township.

"What about the census records?" I knew they were a good source of information.

"Yeah, I already looked for those online, but the furthest back I could find was 1790."

"They weren't in there?"

"No, the records are spotty, and I couldn't find either the Vogels or the Bontragers. Actually, let me ask…"

His voice trailed off as he stepped to the help desk and spoke to the librarian. After a moment, I followed along so I could hear.

"Some of those have been reconstructed through tax records," the man was saying. "Let me log you on again through a database we have access to. I think you'll find what you need."

With a few clicks, he pulled up what looked like photographed documents and said, "Here you go."

Zed took over as the man walked away, and after less than a minute, he managed to find a Vogel in the 1709 census. He clicked on the image to enlarge it.

"I see it. Bernard Vogel. That's him." My eyes skimmed the listing until Zed scrolled down a bit.

He pointed. "Look, here's Bontrager too. Gorg and Abigail. Looks like by 1790, they had one, two, three…six children."

I explained to Zed that I had already learned that from the chart in Verna's Bible. "I descended from their eldest child, a daughter named Helen."

"Oh, yeah. There she is. Helen." He studied the listing for a moment. "Wait a minute. This shows her as being born in May 1764."

"So?"

"That means Abigail would have been pregnant with her at the time of the massacre." He counted the months backward, doing the math. "About four months pregnant, to be exact. I don't know if that's significant, but she and her husband traveled all the way to North Carolina less than a month later. Does that seem odd to you, that a woman five months pregnant would leave her home to go with her husband several states away?"

"Not necessarily. Women had babies on the Oregon Trail, didn't they? Back then, people did what they had to, you know?"

With a shrug he moved on, but the thought stayed in my mind. I doubted the pregnancy would have stopped them from going, but what if it was more than that? What if, I wondered, the pregnancy was part of the reason they left in the first place? I posed that thought to Zed.

"What do you mean?"

"I don't know. Like maybe Gorg couldn't bear the thought of his wife and future firstborn child living around here with all that mess going on. She was friends with an Indian woman, after all. Good friends. Who's to say they didn't threaten her because of that friendship?"

"They? You mean the Paxton Boys?"

"*Ya.* Maybe Gorg was afraid with all the mob mentality happening, that once the Paxton Boys finished killing the Indians, they were going to come after people like Abigail next, friends of the Indians. Do you know if the Paxton Boys attacked any settlers who were pro-Indian? Or just the Indians themselves?"

He shook his head. "Just the Indians themselves."

I thought about that for a moment.

"Besides," he said, "don't forget that within a year of the massacre, Gorg and Abigail became *supporters* of the Paxton Boys. I can't imagine they would do that if they'd ever felt threatened by them."

I had a feeling he was right.

We were interrupted by the librarian, who brought us a printout of the passenger list for the *Virtuous Grace*. I had seen it before, of course, but I'd never had a copy of my own, and when the man handed it to me, I felt a strange thrill. It was such a link to my past, a memento of my very own ancestors—and Zed's.

Together, we searched for their names, Hubert Lantz and Bernard Vogel, and then I held the list close and smiled as Zed patted my back.

"Feel free to print out copies of the census too," the librarian said. "You can pay before you leave." He nodded toward the list in my hand. "But that one's on the house."

Clearly seeing an Amish girl so happy had touched him.

When Zed dropped us off, we found Ella sitting with Frannie. She was telling her about the Home Place and the bakery, about Luke, about Rosalee. Frannie seemed to drift in and out as she listened.

"And when the baby comes," Ella said, "We'll—"

Frannie's eyes flew open. "Ella, are you with child?"

"*Ya*. You didn't notice?"

Frannie shook her head slowly, her features radiating pure joy as she took in Ella's ample figure. "No, I suppose I did not. But I can see it now. I'm so glad you told me."

The women hugged. As Ella pulled back, Frannie began to cough— and then she couldn't seem to stop.

"Izzy!" Ella called out.

"I'm here." I hung my cape on a peg. "Raise her bed."

Ella stared at the buttons as I crossed the room, Giselle right behind me. Frannie began to make choking sounds. I rushed to the bed, reaching around Ella to grab the control. I pressed the "up" button with one hand and placed the other on Frannie's shoulder as I did to keep her stable.

She stopped coughing. I picked up the glass of water and placed the straw in her mouth. She took a drink and swallowed.

"Is she all right?" Ella asked. She looked terrified and guilty, as if it had been all her fault.

"*Ya*," I answered. I hoped so. I put the glass down. I retrieved the stethoscope from where I'd been keeping it on the bookcase and listened to Frannie's lungs again. The rattle was back. I decided to call Marta. I wanted a second opinion.

She came right away. After checking her mother's lungs, she called Lexie and asked her to stop by too, as soon as she could. Lexie was a licensed nurse-midwife with more medical training than Marta.

Klara, Ella, and Giselle all gathered around when Lexie arrived an hour later. She listened to Frannie's lungs with her stethoscope, looking at Marta as she did and nodding. When she was done she said, "We need to keep her as comfortable as possible. Keeping the bed raised will help. If she seems to be in pain, contact her doctor about meds."

"Is it pneumonia?" I asked.

Lexie bit her lip. "I'm not sure. If it's not, it's very close."

Klara pulled the covers back up to her mother's chin. "Shouldn't we take her to the doctor?"

Marta shook her head. "Remember she has the advanced directive. This is what she wants."

Klara frowned.

"It's hard, I know," Marta said. "But she doesn't want us to prolong her suffering."

Klara sat back down in the chair by Frannie's side.

"However," Marta said, stepping to the end of the bed. "I did ask a doctor to come by. Do you remember Ben Yoder?"

Klara nodded, and Marta turned to Lexie, explaining. "He just finished his residency. He grew up Plain."

Lexie smiled.

"I just want to make sure we're not missing anything." Marta gripped the metal bar at the foot of the hospital bed and added, "I'm just glad all of you made it home in time." Her eyes fell on Frannie. "Because she's definitely taken a turn for the worse."

Ben arrived around ten the next morning to check on Frannie. I was in the kitchen when he arrived, and I dried my hands on a towel as I headed back to the living room.

The young doctor wore khaki pants and a light blue shirt under a dark coat. "I can only consult with you," he said to Marta. "Considering she's not my patient."

Marta nodded. "That's all I want."

Ben stepped to the side of the bed, the one Klara wasn't sitting at, and spoke quietly to Frannie. He rubbed his hands together, warming them, as he did. I couldn't hear what he said, but she opened her eyes. He pulled a stethoscope from the pocket of his coat, slipped it around his neck, and listened to her chest.

Then he asked her a question.

She nodded.

He said something else to her and she shook her head.

I marveled at his bedside manner, wondering if he planned to set up a practice catering to the Amish. He asked Frannie a few more questions and then repositioned her bed, moved her head slightly, and then bowed his head. Obviously he was praying for her.

She turned toward him, I was certain with tears in her eyes. He bent down and said something more to her.

I swiped at my own eyes. Ben Yoder had a gift. I could see that God had led him into medicine.

He told Frannie goodbye and then stepped toward the door. Marta followed and motioned for me to too. He stopped in the entryway and then smiled when he saw me. "Izzy, what are you doing here?"

"She's *Mamm*'s caregiver," Marta answered.

I nodded.

"Well, you're doing a good job." Then he spoke to both Marta and me. "Frannie could have a week or so left. Or less. She says she's not in too much pain, but if it increases, call her doctor. Otherwise, she's well cared for, that I can see. All of you are making the process as easy for her as can be expected."

"*Danke*," Marta whispered.

"It's up to God's timing," he said. It was evident Ben hadn't turned his back on his faith. I wouldn't even say he'd turned his back on his family or the Amish church. It seemed God had simply called him to serve in a different way.

After Ben left, I told Marta I didn't need to go home for the weekend.

I was finally supposed to be taking my two days off, starting tomorrow, but now I couldn't bear to leave.

"No, you need a break. There are plenty of people here now to cover for you."

Disappointed, I asked her, "Will you let me know if Frannie takes a turn for the worse?" A few months ago, I was terrified to be with someone who was dying. Now I was afraid of being away when it happened to Frannie.

Marta assured me she would leave a message on my *daed*'s phone if there was any change. "Why wouldn't I? You're family."

Her words rang warmly in my ears. I *was* family with these people. In a way, I was a better fit here than in my own home.

That night on the way to the *daadi haus*, Giselle trailed behind me. I stopped on the pathway and waited for her. The clouds had broken up and a crescent moon hung above the pine trees towering over the house. "How are you doing?" I asked.

She sighed. "So-so." As she spoke she stumbled on an uneven rock on the pathway, catching herself before she fell. I quickly stepped to her side, taking her arm.

"Thank you. I guess I'm more exhausted than I thought."

Once we stepped into the pitch black *daadi haus*, I fumbled for the flashlight on the shelf in the entry but knocked it to the floor. It took me a few moments to locate it, and when I turned it on nothing happened. I hit it on the end and the light flickered.

The house seemed absolutely void. It had sat empty all week, except for me and Giselle. Without Frannie, it felt as if the life had been sucked out of it.

"I'll light the lamp," I said, making my way to the kitchen.

Giselle's voice was weary. "Don't you get tired of all this?"

"Of what?" I shone the flickering light onto the countertop and located the box of matches.

"Supposedly this is the simple life, but nothing about it is." She sighed. "Flipping a light switch. Now that's simple."

I lit the lamp, but the house still felt dark. "It's not so bad." The truth was, I'd never lived where I could flip a light switch. This was all I knew.

A short while later, as I crawled into my bed and extinguished my lamp, I thought of what it meant to be Amish, all the way back to my ancestors, Abigail and Gorg. I shuddered to think about what my life would have looked like if they *had* been excommunicated back then, if they hadn't repented and passed their Amish heritage all the way down to me.

It gave me a new appreciation for Zed's film, *Carving a Legacy.* True, Abraham Sommers didn't turn back to the Lord until later in life, but his revelation of truth and steps toward reconciliation had left a foundation of faith for his family.

I remembered that Frannie had wanted to see the film, and then I nearly sat up in bed when the idea struck me. Zed needed to show it to her! To the whole family, actually. Together. What could be better, for all of them, than Zed's beautiful reminder of where they had come from.

TWENTY-FIVE

Zed was the one charged with bringing me home for the weekend, and he showed up the next morning right on schedule. Giselle and I were both still out in the *daadi haus* when he knocked on the door.

Unable to contain my enthusiasm, as soon as he came in I blurted out that he should show his film to Frannie and the rest of the family.

His eyes lit up. "That's a great idea. I have my computer in the car. We could show it right now."

"Perfect. You took out that picture of my face, right?"

"Ah," he said, looking embarrassed. "No. I forgot. I'm sorry."

My shoulders slumped. We would have to wait.

Giselle stepped out of the kitchen. "Oooh, I want to see the film too. Why don't we make an event out of it, just like going to the movies? We can all gather around *Mamm*'s bed to watch it together."

"I'll be gone all weekend," I said.

"It can wait. You'll be back on Monday, right?"

I nodded, fearing Frannie might not last that long. I didn't want to be the one to say it, though, so I held my tongue. Surely she could hold on until then.

"Monday it is," Zed said. "But it'll have to be in the evening. I'm working all day."

As I gathered my things, I could hear Giselle and Zed talking easily, like old friends. It wasn't long before they were on the topic of the costumes for his next film. It sounded as though Giselle had told him her plan for weaving the fabric for all of the costumes, and he was thrilled.

On the way to my house, he swung by Susie's shop so I could drop off my latest batch of work. I showed her the bookmarks I'd been making, and she agreed they would sell well. "Like wildfire," she said.

By the looks of her belly, she'd be having a Christmas baby soon, with either Marta or Lexie at her delivery. I embraced her warmly before Zed and I left to continue on to my parents' house.

Because he had to get to work, he wasn't able to come in when he dropped me off. I thanked him, told him goodbye, said I would see him on Monday, and then I grabbed my bag, swinging it slightly as I started up the back steps to the house. I'd only been gone for two weeks this time, but it felt like forever.

Mamm was in the kitchen when I walked in, making beef stroganoff, which happened to be one of my favorite dishes.

"Where is everyone?" I asked.

"Skating. Tabitha and Linda took the boys. You should go on down."

"I have some work to do."

"Why don't you work in here? After dinner you can help me make snowball cookies. I thought I'd give them out to the neighbors this year. And I'll make an extra plate for you to take back to Klara's."

We chatted as she cooked and I embroidered, sitting on the step stool against the wall, close to the woodstove. I told her about how Frannie was doing and about Lexie, Giselle, Ella, and Zed arriving. I left out telling her about my trip with Zed and Giselle into Lancaster, though.

I told her about Ben Yoder coming by and how well suited he seemed to being a doctor, trying not to be obvious as I gauged her reaction. How she felt about Ben not joining the church, I thought, might give me an indication to how she would feel about me if I chose to do the same.

"I can see why his parents let him *be*," I added casually. "It's good they didn't stand in his way."

Mamm smiled a little but didn't respond. Instead, she changed the subject, telling me what Tabitha and Linda had made the boys for Christmas—hot chocolate mix—and said that all of my siblings would come for Christmas Day. "They're doing Christmas Eve with their in-laws this year."

"How's *Daed*'s business?"

"*Gut.* He delivered several more tables to be given as gifts." She motioned to the desk in the living room. It was covered with papers. "He's having a hard time keeping up with everything. We're going to figure out how I can help."

I was relieved to hear that.

"I have a stack of mending. It's in your room. I told Tabitha to do it, but she hasn't."

"I'll work on it later," I said. "No problem."

There was a commotion at the back door and then in the mudroom. A moment later Stephen and Thomas came inside in their stocking feet, their cheeks rosy and chapped, their hair dark with sweat and their eyes bright.

"We had so much fun," Stephen said, sliding on the linoleum toward *Mamm* and wrapping his arms around her waist. Thomas followed and did the same. The two of them nearly knocked her down. She laughed and shooed them away. "Go break the ice in the trough," she said.

"We just took our boots off." Stephen started toward the living room.

"Now!" *Mamm* commanded. "Get it done before your *daed* gets home."

Stephen hung his head a little and started toward the back door as Tabitha and Linda came in, telling me a quick hello. "Set the table, girls," *Mamm* said.

My sisters chattered away as Tabitha grabbed plates and Linda counted out the silverware. *Mamm* opened two jars of green beans and dumped them in a big pan.

A few minutes later *Daed* walked in the back door. He saw me right away. He crossed the kitchen in one big step and swept me up in a hug.

"So how is Frannie?"

I teared up as I told him the rattle in her lungs was back. "She was doing so well," I said. "Ben Yoder thinks she has a week or so left."

"Maybe she was just waiting for everyone to get home."

"But her family still needs her. Especially Giselle. For just a little while longer."

"*Ach*, Izzy. If people held on as long as they were needed, no one would ever go."

After dinner I retreated to my sewing room and started on the mending while Tabitha and Linda helped *Mamm* with the dishes and then cookies. I tried to pray for Frannie and her family, but the boys playing a game of checkers in the living room, rather loudly, distracted me. *It's good to be home,* I told myself.

But I wasn't all that convincing.

The next day was a non-preaching Sunday, and Zed showed up to invite me to go on another scouting expedition with him. I happily agreed, so glad it was the Sabbath.

We visited several places—a park with a woodsy area, the banks of a creek that had been untouched by development, and the sloping hill of a pasture with an oak tree at the bottom. He felt all of the locations held promise for shooting his film. Afterward, he invited me to lunch, so we went to a nearby deli in Mountville.

As we waited for our food, I finally worked up the courage to ask the question I'd wanted to for a while, ever since I'd received his bombshell of a letter.

"Are you sure you want Shelly to play Abigail in the movie?"

Zed rolled his eyes and said, "Yeah. It's a shame she's such a good actress. She's a real pain as a person."

Shocked, my head jerked back. A pain as a person? What did he mean?

"Didn't you pick up on that when you were there? She'll do anything to get in front of the camera. Anything."

We were interrupted when the waitress showed up with Zed's sandwich and my soup and salad special. After a silent prayer, he picked up his pastrami on rye and continued.

"She thought I was going to cast *you* in the part of Abigail. She assumed that was why I took you to the film on campus, so you could get an idea of how it all worked."

I poked at my salad with my fork, processing his words. "Oh, goodness,"

I said, thinking of what Shelly had said to me a few days after that, when I returned to Goshen with Penny. She told me to "give up and go home," that I didn't know what I was up against. What were her exact words? *I know what you really want, but you had your chance. It's my turn now.*

Sitting here with Zed, almost a month later, I finally understood. When she said that, she hadn't been protecting a relationship with him—she'd been protecting her role in his film.

"So you're not dating her," I managed to say without breaking out into a grin. I took a bite of lettuce to cover up my expression.

"Dating her? No way! She has a boyfriend—and I wouldn't trade places with him for a million dollars."

"She's very pretty, though."

"Yeah." He thought for a moment. "But only on the outside." He took a bite of his sandwich, chewed quickly, and swallowed. "Like that remark she made that day at the film screening. That's what I mean about her being ruthless. She'll do anything to eliminate competition for a role. She's a talented actress and really smart, so she makes a good study partner sometimes, but otherwise I can't stand her."

I took a bite of my cheesy broccoli soup. The creamy warmth comforted me but not nearly as much as Zed's explanation of Shelly. I'd never felt such relief. Now the only thing standing between me and Zed was—Zed.

After lunch we stopped at one more location. It was a dirt road in a township in the far western part of the county, close to the river. "Wanna guess what scene this is for?" he asked.

I didn't know what he meant, but I looked around to try to figure it out. The area was pretty, but the muddy ruts had frozen. If it weren't so cold, we would have surely become stuck, just as they would have in their buggies more than two hundred years ago.

"Oh!" I cried, turning back to him. "The Great Wagon Road! Is this it?"

"No, sorry. The real Great Wagon Road is now Interstate 81."

"You're kidding."

"Nope. But this could make a nice stand-in, don't you think?"

Stepping in closer, Zed held up his hands, framed the shot, and then motioned for me to take a look. I did. "If we end up going with Abigail's story, don't you think it would be perfect for the scene where she and Gorg and the baby first leave for North Carolina?" I could feel his breath against my face, we were that close.

"Izzy?"

"*Ya*," I answered, aware that he was no longer looking up the road. He was staring down at me. I turned toward to him, and as I did he said, "Aw, Iz…"

Then, to my astonishment, he leaned forward and kissed me. His lips were warm on mine as his cold hands moved toward my face, framing it instead of the road. I leaned into him, kissing him back, amazed at how natural it felt to be together this way. I'd yearned for this moment for so long. So long.

When he finally pulled away, he dropped his hands and said, "Aw, man."

I studied his gaze. "What?"

"I shouldn't…Ella told me…" His voice trailed off.

I blinked, mortified. Had Ella told him how I felt about him?

"Yes?"

"Ella warned me not to start something with you unless I was fully committed."

"What did she say?"

He shrugged, his cheeks turning red. "She gave me a real talking to, practically all the way from Indiana to here. She warned me not to enter into a romance with you unless I mean to take it all the way to church membership and marriage."

That explained a lot. "Is that why you were acting so weird when you first got here?"

"Yeah, I was confused. Ella doesn't mince words, you know. She's also really perceptive. It's not surprising she picked up on my feelings for you."

My knees grew weak as I spoke. "And…what are your feelings for me?"

His eyes glistened. Perhaps it was the cold. Perhaps not.

"I love you, Izzy. I want to spend the rest of my life with you."

My heart pounded at the words I'd longed to hear.

"I know it may seem weird, us being friends and all, but I started realizing it a while back, and I just haven't known what to do about it."

I smiled. "I know what to do about it."

This time I raised up on my tiptoes and kissed him, our lips meeting sweetly once again.

When we pulled apart the second time, I looked deep into his eyes and said, "You know I love you too, right?"

His eyes widened as I continued. "I think I always have, but I didn't realize it until the day before you went away to school. In August."

He shook his head, his face slowly breaking into a huge grin. "I had no idea. I can't believe it took me so long to catch up."

We both chuckled as he reached for my hands and entwined his fingers with mine.

"Ella was right, though. This is no small thing. We're talking about two different churches."

I nodded. "But your mom left the Amish church for the Mennonites, and she's fine."

"Yeah, and Ella left the Mennonite church for the Amish, and she's fine."

We were quiet for a moment.

"So whatever we end up doing, we'll be…fine. Right?" I asked.

He shrugged, as if to say he didn't know.

I didn't know either. In fact, I was stumped as far as what to do next, but I certainly knew how I felt. I loved Zed Bayer with all of my heart.

And now I knew he loved me too.

TWENTY-SIX

That night I broached the topic of my feelings for Zed with my parents. I'd asked them to join me at the kitchen table while my younger siblings played Scrabble in the living room.

"What are you saying?" *Daed* pushed back his chair.

My face grew warm. "Zed and I care about each other. I'm considering the possibility of joining the Mennonite church—"

Daed leaned forward toward me.

"—rather than the Amish."

"Izzy," he groaned.

I glanced toward *Mamm*. To my surprise, she seemed more curious than angry. But *Daed*'s expression was all pain as he said, "I don't know how to respond."

"You don't need to," I answered. "I just wanted you to know."

Daed couldn't leave it alone, though. "Did you ask him to join our church?"

"No."

"Did he ask you to join his?"

"No. All we've done so far is to put it in God's hands—"

At that *Daed* stood, saying, "What were we thinking to let you spend so much time with that boy? *Of course* this was bound to happen." He marched away from the table to the mudroom, grabbing his work coat and then heading out into the night.

Tears filled my eyes. In all my life I had never seen him react so strongly.

"I know you both want me to join the church more than anything," I said to *Mamm* after the back door had banged shut.

"No, not exactly. What I want most is for you to walk with the Lord. It's up to you to decide how to do that."

I looked at her, astounded. "Like Ben Yoder…"

She nodded. "Like Ben Yoder. Should he not have become a doctor?"

I shook my head.

"Don't misunderstand, Izzy. I wouldn't have this conversation with any of your brothers or sisters. Only you. You're the only one this might work for. You're the only one who has been reading Scripture and praying in that room of yours all these years. Yes, you're intense and you worry, but I know you're connected to God. You're the one who wouldn't get caught up in the ways of the world. You're the one who could stay true to your faith without necessarily staying true to your church."

I shook my head, trying to comprehend her words. "You wouldn't be… disappointed in me?"

She narrowed her eyes. "Of course not. I love you. And I will always love you, no matter what you decide. And you will always be welcome here, as will your husband."

"What about *Daed*?"

"He'll come around."

I didn't think so, but I couldn't bear to have conflict between us without at least trying to resolve it. I grabbed my cape and headed out the back door. A light shone in the window of his shop at far end of the barn. A minute later I pushed open the door. He stood with his back to me, his hands flat on an oak table.

"*Daed*, I'm sorry."

He turned around, slowly. "I shouldn't have left like that."

"I understand. This isn't easy."

He took a deep breath and then asked, "What did your mother say?"

I told him, ending with, "She said the most important thing was that I follow the Lord."

He ran his hand through his gray hair and then said, "She's right." He shook his head, looked out the window, and then back at me. "How you follow the Lord is your decision, Izzy, including whether to join the church or not. Will I be disappointed if you don't? *Ya.*" He paused, exhaling slowly. "But I will love you no matter what you decide. Not everyone is cut out for this life."

Tears filled my eyes.

"And not everyone must stay. But everyone born into an Amish family must decide what they will do." He stepped across the divide between us and wrapped his arms around me. "There was a time when I would have been ashamed to have you go, but not anymore."

I was sure I'd never heard my *daed* say so much. I leaned my head against his chest.

He continued. "Izzy, you are kind and humble and a model Amish woman." His voice teased a little as he said, "Except for being so easily overwhelmed and not wanting a large family." He tightened his hold on me. "I guess what I'm saying is...what I've already said. Your future is between you and God."

"*Danke,*" I whispered.

As he let me go he asked, "So what do you plan to do?"

"I don't know." I had no idea what was best for Zed and me. At this point I honestly couldn't imagine either option.

I left my *daed* in his shop and to his own thoughts as I hurried back through the cold to the house and then down the hall to my little room for some solitude and prayer.

Until that moment, much of my reluctance about leaving the Amish church had to do with not wanting to disappoint my parents. But now that I had their blessing regardless, at least to some extent, I still felt hesitant about what to do.

I finally understood it wasn't about pleasing my parents—it was about pleasing God. I listened for that small voice inside of me as I closed my eyes against my own thoughts and asked Him what I should do.

Wait.

As clear as day, I knew that's what He wanted, for me to wait. And so I would.

Zed was at work Monday morning, so Lexie picked me up from home and took me back to Frannie's. On the way she told me the family was excited about watching Zed's movie.

"He's showing it tonight. And the most excited one of all is *Mammi*."

I couldn't have been more thrilled.

When we got there, I was dying to see Frannie, but I needed to put my stuff away first. So as Lexie headed for the front door, I grabbed my bag and went straight to the *daadi haus*. By the time I was inside, my hands were icy cold even though I had gloves on.

I put my bag in the room I'd been sleeping in, relieved to find out that at least everything in there was as I'd left it, even the books I'd borrowed from Frannie's room. The bed had been perfectly made. Ella was so industrious, I had a feeling she had probably come out here and changed the sheets while I was gone. I exhaled slowly, admitting to myself that I was relieved to be back. I felt at ease with Zed's family in a way I didn't with my own. I hated to admit it, but it was true. Part of the reason was shared interests. Part of it was similar personalities—the Lantz women, except for Klara, seemed to be more contemplative than the women in my family. More like me. It wasn't that I didn't love my family. I just didn't feel understood by them.

I headed back to the main house, eager to take a turn caring for Frannie and spend time with her family. But as I crossed the porch, it struck me how very much had changed in my own life since leaving here on Saturday morning, just two days ago.

Zed had told me he loved me. And my parents had freed me to make my own decision about the Amish church.

As I pushed open the back door, I said a prayer of thanks to God for such tremendous blessings.

That evening Giselle sat with Frannie in the living room as I straightened up in preparation for our big movie night. Klara was in her room, where she'd been since supper, and Alexander was off somewhere outside, doing his end-of-day chores with the help of James and Luke, both of whom had arrived over the weekend while I was gone.

Zed wouldn't get off work until eight, but he had instructed the whole family to be assembled and ready by the time he got here. Around seven, I heard voices on the porch and realized they had begun to arrive.

I opened the door to see that Lexie was here, and that she'd brought Alice Gundy, Will's grandmother, with her. I was glad Alice had come to visit, as I knew she and Frannie had been best friends for years.

What I had forgotten, until I saw the enthusiastic way she and Giselle greeted each other, was that they were friends as well. Alice had gone to Switzerland on the same trip as Ada, Christy, and Will several years before. Of course she would want to see this movie, as Abraham Sommers had been a central focus of their time there in Switzerland.

After saying their hellos, Alice settled into a chair near Frannie's bed and Giselle asked Lexie if she could run her up to the nearest convenience store, saying, "There's something I need to pick up for tonight."

Soon the two of them were off, leaving Frannie and Alice alone but for me.

Looking their way as I moved to the sink, I decided Alice seemed extra thin. I knew she wasn't helping Ada much with the children anymore. Thankfully, Christy was done with school and had been able to take her place.

The two old women began to chat, and as they did, I watched Alice reach for Frannie's hand and hold it gently in hers. I retreated to the kitchen to do the dishes, marveling at the longevity of their friendship and how close they seemed still.

I wondered why I had no special girlfriends like that. Even my siblings and I just barely connected. My sister Tabitha and I were only two years apart, but we weren't close at all. She'd always been a take-charge person compared to me, and I'd never liked her telling me what to do. My youngest sister, Linda, didn't seem to mind, and she and Tabitha were good friends. My older sisters, Sadie and Becky, were best friends too. That had always left me as the odd one out.

As different as I was from my *mamm* in other ways, I knew that in this way we were much alike. She'd never had many close women friends either that I knew of. Her sisters were nearly twenty years older than she was, not to mention they lived several counties over. Every once in a while, *Mamm* would hire a driver and go see them, but other than that, they weren't close. I went with her once. Neither of my aunts seemed happy to have us visit and they both complained a lot.

I plunged a bowl into the soapy water and swished it with the scrubber. *Mamm* didn't have a best friend in our district, not the way Alice and Frannie had. And neither did I.

A lump began to rise in my throat until I realized that was wrong, I did have a best friend. *Zed.* He'd been my best friend for the last four years. He'd been the one I shared my thoughts and feelings with. He'd been the one who cared most about how I was doing.

Of course, I'd had friends through school and church. Girls I would eat lunch with. Girls I'd share books with. Girls I stayed on the fringes with.

But perhaps having Zed as a best friend had kept me from befriending other young women in the last few years—or at least from further developing those friendships from my childhood.

I thought through the other women my age in our district. Most were sweet and would make fine friends—but I felt so different from them. Our faith and lifestyle connected us, but that seemed to be all.

I felt more of a connection with some of the women in this family than I had with anyone else in years. First Ella, then Frannie—and now I was even starting to feel close to Giselle. She wasn't very touchy-feely, yet in many ways she was a kindred spirit.

I finished the dishes, glancing out the kitchen window now and then, eager for more family members to arrive. Lexie and Giselle returned from the store, and as Giselle unpacked the bag, I couldn't help but smile. She had gone out for popcorn kernels and some fresh butter. Just the sight of it made me tear up, in a good way, thinking of Verna and her trip to *Ben Hur.*

"It's not a movie without the popcorn," Giselle told us, and then she began to root through the cabinets for the right-sized pot to cook it in.

Marta arrived soon after, looking tired from her day but pleased to be there. Ella came with her, and soon the kitchen was filled with the happy feminine chatter and laughter—mine included. I felt more at home here, in that moment, than I ever had at my house.

Zed, Will, and Ada showed up at eight fifteen, at which point Klara came down and Alexander, James, and Luke returned from outside. Luke greeted me warmly, and then he introduced me to Lexie's husband, James.

"I've heard so many great things about you," James told me, shaking my hand. Not surprisingly, he was quite handsome, with curly golden hair and green eyes.

"You too," I replied, glancing toward Lexie, who gazed lovingly at him from across the room.

As he turned and moved toward her, I looked around at the assembled family members. Earlier, I'd been a little concerned that some of them might be hesitant about watching a film, even one like this, but apparently they had all cleared it with their various bishops. As I was still technically on *rumspringa*, I didn't need permission, which meant we were free to watch it and enjoy.

Zed set up everything, but before calling anyone to attention, he took advantage of the general chaos to pull me aside, saying he needed to talk to me about something. It was too cold to go out, so we waited until Giselle and Ada were carrying bowls of popcorn into the living room and then we moved into the nook off the living room, by Alexander's desk. I couldn't imagine what he needed to say, but as soon as I looked into his eyes I realized it was something important.

"I've been thinking, Izzy Bear."

"*Ya?*" Smiling, I inhaled deeply, breathing in the scent of pine that lingered on his clothes and skin from his work among the Christmas trees.

"About the whole Mennonite–Amish thing."

I nodded, suddenly afraid he was going to ask if I had told anyone about the new developments in our relationship. He probably would have been surprised but pleased to learn that I had, indeed, discussed the situation at length with my parents. But I wasn't ready to tell him that yet. It's not that I didn't want him to know; it was just that I needed to think about it some more first. I wanted to process things and gather my thoughts—especially given that sense I'd had afterward, that quiet urging to *wait*.

Zed placed a hand on my arm and gave it a squeeze. "I'm going to become Amish."

My eyes widened and I couldn't help but take a step back as I whispered, "*What?*"

He nodded. "Last night, while you were at home, I came over here and talked to Alexander. He said I can farm with him."

I was speechless for a good thirty seconds. Finally I blurted out, "Did you talk to your *mamm* about this?"

His eyes narrowed. "No, not yet. I wanted to work out some of the details first. So far, the only person I've spoken with is Alexander."

My mind raced. This was wrong, all wrong.

"Izzy?"

"You can't farm!" I cried.

"Why not?"

I lowered my voice, my heart pounding. "You weren't made for farming."

He seemed taken aback. "I do okay on Will's Christmas tree farm. I can learn the rest."

"Zed." My mind raced as I looked him in the eyes. "You can't join the church for me. For God, maybe, but not for me."

"What does it matter?" He took a deep breath and attempted to give me a reassuring smile, but I could tell it wasn't a peaceful one. "My relationship with God will be the same no matter which of the two churches I go to, but it will make all the difference as far as my relationship with you. So I'll do it."

"But what about school? And filmmaking? And all the research projects you want to do? What about Los Angeles? And the endowment? And the movie about the Conestoga?"

"That's just it. If I become Amish, I won't have a need for any of that, ever. That's what I realized last night, that I shouldn't waste any more of my time—or my tuition money—if that's the step I'll be taking in the end anyway."

Before I could even think of how to respond, our conversation was cut short by Giselle, calling out from the living room.

"Come on, guys. What's the holdup? Let's get this show on the road."

Zed and I shared one final, lingering glance and then he squeezed my arm again and whispered, "We can talk more later."

He turned and moved toward the crowd gathered for the viewing of the film. I followed slowly, my heart racing, my mind a jumbled mess.

Zed was willing to join the Amish church for the sake of our relationship?

I should have been pleased. I should have been thrilled. Instead, all I could think was, *Why does this feel so wrong?*

TWENTY-SEVEN

I raised the head of the bed, bringing Frannie to a near sitting position and then pulled the hospital-bed table across her midsection. Zed positioned his laptop on the table so she could see the screen and then called out to the others, "Gather around."

They did, crowding the bed on both sides, Mel and Mat in front of Ada, and Will behind her holding Abe. Christy stood beside Ella. I stayed up by Frannie's head with a perfect view of everyone and the screen.

"Everybody ready?" Zed called out, and then he turned down all of the lamps.

Standing there in the dark, watching the glow of the computer, I felt a thrill of anticipation. Zed had made the movie we were about to watch. My Zed.

He leaned in to hit the button that would start it going, and then he stepped back, making room for the rest of us to see. Instantly, the black screen came to life with a beautiful photograph of a wooden bench and then the title, *Carving a Legacy*. As music swelled and the picture faded to an image of a small Swiss village, I realized I was holding my breath and had to let it out.

The movie focused on Abraham Sommers, their ancestor who had been a wood-carver back in the 1800s and lived in Switzerland. It was all about his journey to faith, as well as his appreciation of place. Nowhere were those things depicted more beautifully than in the three boxes he'd carved that had been passed down through generations in the family. Zed had film footage of all three boxes—the one of the family bakery in Fruti-gen, Switzerland, that was now in Ada's possession; the one of the estate Amielbach in Switzerland that had inspired Lexie to search for her birth family and belonged to her; and the one of the Home Place in Indiana that was given to Ella by Frannie. Zed told the story of the family by describing the significance of each box.

As the film played, Ada commented that the bakery, which she had seen on her trip to Europe, still looked much the same as in the carving.

"I hope I can visit Amielbach someday," Marta said, in a voice so wist-ful that I had a feeling she might just make that happen eventually.

"Shhh." Zed was clearly annoyed.

"Oh, that would thrill me so, to think of you going to Switzerland and spending time with Giselle," said Frannie.

The sisters, who stood beside each other, locked eyes and smiled.

Zed crossed his arms. "Don't you people know you're not supposed to talk while you're watching a film?"

Klara said, "I can't imagine traveling all the way to Switzerland. It's so far from home."

Zed threw up his hands.

Lexie smiled and Ella shook her head, seemingly in disapproval at her brother's antics, but no one else responded. At least the kids were being quiet, even little Abe.

Next the film focused on still shots of landscapes in Switzerland. Then a current photo of Amielbach faded onto the screen as a voice told how Abraham had wandered away from the flock.

"In the end," the voice-over said, "Abraham confessed his sins and rec-onciled to God, continuing the faith of his childhood. That legacy of reconciliation has been passed on through the generations of his descen-dants, along with the beautiful carved wooden boxes. It lives on in his family today."

Klara sniffled. Surprised, I looked around the bed. Lexie wiped away a tear. Then Marta. Ada pulled a Kleenex from her pocket and blew her nose.

I glanced down at Frannie, afraid she may have faded out again, and though she wasn't crying like the others, she was alert and glued to the screen.

The last image was of the hands of the carver, or at least the actor who was representing him, putting his tools away in an old wooden desk. I smiled as I watched it, thinking it looked similar to my *mamm*'s old desk.

Music came up as the image of the man's hands faded away. Then the screen went black and the credits rolled.

Lexie, James, and Giselle both burst into applause, startling me. As the lone *Englischers* in a room filled with Plain folk, their reaction wasn't exactly something we were used to. Applause could lead to pride, so it wasn't often doled out. But then Marta joined in as well, saying, "That was lovely, Zed. Just lovely."

He gave her a modest smile and then moved to Frannie's side. He took her hand. "What did you think, *Mammi*? Did you like it?"

She closed her eyes, and for a moment I thought she had fallen asleep. But then, with her eyes still closed, she said, ever so softly, "Thank you, Zed. You have brought us full circle."

I could feel myself choking up, so I moved away from them and looked around at everyone else. It was interesting to listen to the various conversations that had begun to rise up in the wake of the movie. Ella and Lexie were talking about their beautiful wooden boxes and how much they treasured them. Giselle was asking Zed technical questions about the making of the movie. Alice and Will and Ada were talking about the desk that had been used in the final scene. Apparently, they had one much like it in their home too. I wasn't surprised, as I had a feeling it was a fairly common design, at least back in the 1800s when *Mamm*'s had been built.

"Oh, yeah. *That* desk," Will was saying to his grandmother with a laugh. Then, turning to Ada, he explained, "I thought I was the only one who had discovered it had a secret compartment in it. When I was on *rumspringa*, I kept my driver's license and my one set of *Englisch* clothes hidden in there."

The three of them laughed. It was hard to even picture the fine and upstanding Will Gundy sneaking around on *rumpsringa*.

"*Ya*," Alice said, "then your dad found it and was none too happy with you."

"What happened?" asked Ada, her eyes sparkling as she clearly enjoyed hearing about this side of her husband.

"He wrote me a note and stuck it in the pants pocket. I didn't find it until I was out with friends, and of course it made me feel terrible. The whole night I was dying inside that he'd found out and was upset with me."

Will and Alice shared a smile, remembering.

I thought again of the similar desk in my home, which had been passed down through my mother's family. Then I gasped.

"Izzy?" Ada asked. "Are you okay?"

I shook my head. I caught Zed's eye and waved him over.

"What is it?" he asked, coming closer.

Turning to Will, I said, "Repeat what you were just saying about the desk."

He looked a little confused, but he did as I asked. "We were just commenting that the desk you used in that final scene is similar to one we have at home."

Zed said that style was fairly common.

"But there's something unique about Will's desk," I prodded.

Zed's eyebrows raised as he looked over at him.

"Oh," Will said. "It has a secret compartment behind the lower left drawer."

Zed didn't seem to catch on, so finally I spelled it out for him.

"A secret compartment. In a desk. *Mamm*'s desk is that same style. What if hers has one too? What if the missing pages of the chapbook are hidden in there? It's been in the family for years, you know."

"Which desk? The one in the living room?"

I nodded.

"It wouldn't matter, Iz," he replied. "That desk can't be more than a hundred years old, and it's certainly not from as far back as Abigail's time."

I understood what he was saying, but something inside of me wouldn't let it go. "It's worth a try, don't you think? Even if it didn't exist back then, who's to say that one of Abigail's descendants didn't use it, years later, to hide the rest of the chapbook?"

"Why would they bother? Abigail would've been dead by then—"

I reached for the hem of his sleeve and held on. "I don't know. Why did they cut the rest of the pages from the chapbook?"

He looked at me for a long moment. "Because they wanted to hide the truth about her story?"

"Exactly. We don't know why yet. We only know that they did. What if there's a secret compartment in our desk too—and the missing pages from the chapbook are in there?"

"We need to look at your desk," I told my *mamm* as Zed and I burst in through the door. The house was strangely quiet, and I realized that everyone else was already in bed, save for her. She was in the living room working on *Daed*'s bills.

"Whatever for?"

He went to take a look as I explained. "We just found out it might have a hidden compartment in it. If it does, we're thinking maybe the rest of the chapbook is inside."

She and I followed Zed into the living room, where he was on his knees in front of the desk.

"That's impossible," *Mamm* said. "It was built long after those chapbooks were printed. The desk dates back to after the Civil War."

Zed pulled out each drawer in turn but found nothing. He looked at me, disappointed, but I stepped forward and reminded him what Will had told us.

"You pull out the drawer, and once you think it's all the way out, you pull some more. It has a fake back panel, but then there's room behind that for a little extra space."

"I did that already," he said, but at my urging he tried again, starting on the right side as I tried the drawers on the left. He was right. There were no false backs to any of them.

"Let's pull them all the way out," I suggested, tugging and wiggling the top left drawer until it was completely loose. I set it on the floor and studied it carefully, but there were no hidden surprises anywhere.

I was about to return my attention to the desk and pull out the next drawer down when Zed got the one on his side loose and placed it on the floor next to mine. With a gasp I realized that my drawer was a good six inches shorter than his was.

Our eyes met, and we shared a wide grin.

Heart pounding, I turned toward the desk, still on my knees, and peered inside the dark cavity where the drawer had been. I asked *Mamm* for a flashlight, but before she could respond, Zed had turned on the one on his phone and was shining it into the opening.

The funny thing was, it didn't look as if anything was back there. But when we compared the opening on my side with the one on his, it was clear: The back panel of mine was about six inches closer than his was. He reached inside and pressed his fingers against the wood, moving them along the top, back, and sides, but nothing happened.

"There's room here for a hidden space, so there must be some kind of latch somewhere," he said.

"Maybe you get to it from beneath," I offered, gesturing toward the lower drawer. It was bigger and heavier than the top one, so he helped me jiggle it loose and set it on the floor.

Once that cavity was empty and open, we bent down lower and he shone his light inside it, aiming the beam toward the top at the back. Solid wood divided the top drawer from the bottom, so we weren't able to see our hiding place from this new angle—and there was nothing unusual inside here at all. Just to be sure, however, we removed the lower drawer from the right side and compared the lengths. They were equal. Without a doubt a hiding place was in this desk, and it was located behind the top left drawer.

The question was how to get into it.

Zed reached his hand into each cavity in turn, feeling around for some sort of latch or hidden release. When that didn't work, I suggested we move the desk away from the wall to look at the other side. We did so quickly, and as he returned to his inspection of the cavities and the front of the desk, I studied the back, wondering if the hiding place could be accessed by the removal of a small panel.

At first my idea did not look promising, but when I carefully compared the back panel on the left with the one on the right, I noticed one small difference between them…a tiny square slot at the bottom outer corner.

I looked to *Mamm*, who was now holding the flashlight I had asked for. She handed it to me, and I crouched down on the floor and used the light to try to see inside the little slot. It was just too small.

"You need some tools," *Mamm* said, and as she turned to go, I realized she was finally getting on board with our theory as well.

A few moments later she returned with the small household toolbox and handed me a screwdriver. Gripping the round handle, I carefully slid the flat tip into the slot as far as it would go. Nothing happened, so I gave it an extra push—hoping I wouldn't hurt the antique wood—and much to my surprise I could hear the gentle *ping* of what sounded like a release from somewhere inside.

"That's it!" Zed cried, his head popping up like a groundhog from its hole.

I got to my feet and my mother and I went to the other side. Kneeling, I shone my light into the space behind the top left drawer and saw that the wood panel at the back had indeed come open.

Zed scooted away, gesturing for me to do the honors. Hands trembling, I reached inside and swung the little door wide, thrilled to see that behind it had been stashed a very old and yellowed cloth bag. I carefully removed it from the hiding place and brought it out into the light.

"Well, would you look at that," *Mamm* whispered. "What is it?"

The bag had a drawstring top, so I set it on the desk and worked the strings apart. Once I had it all the way open, I peeled back the fabric so we could all see its contents. From what I could tell, we were looking at a very old and neatly folded bundle of buckskin. It looked like Indian buckskin, and it was small and obviously fragile.

Holding my breath, I slid my hands into the bag and pulled it out, hoping the chapbook might be underneath, but there was nothing else there.

"Check the hiding place," I said to Zed. "Is this everything?"

He took another look and then met my gaze. "That's it."

He got to his feet and we were all silent, just standing and looking at the folded buckskin in my hand. A part of me was so disappointed that we hadn't found the chapbook after all, but another part was thrilled just the same. Whatever this was, it was really, really cool. And just the fact that it had been hidden away had to mean *something*.

Zed reached for the buckskin, and he and I were about to unfold it together when my mother stopped us. "Didn't you tell me Frannie's daughter from Europe is an expert in textiles?"

We nodded.

"Well, then, if I were you, I wouldn't do a thing with this except bring it to her to examine. It might fall apart if you even try."

She was right. I slowly slid the buckskin back into the drawstring bag and then clutched it to my chest as Zed and I headed out.

"*Danke, Mamm,*" I called as we flew down the steps.

"You're welcome," she replied, coming to the door. "*Danke* to you too. For the...uh...adventure."

By the time we got back to Klara's, the crowd had thinned. Will had taken the children home, although Ada had stayed with Lexie and James, who could drive her home later. They sat at the kitchen table with Ella and Luke, their hands wrapped around mugs of tea, still talking about Zed's film. Klara and Alexander had gone on to bed. Marta was also asleep, dozing upright in a chair in the corner.

Giselle was on the couch, her eyes on Frannie, who was resting.

"We have something to show you." Zed said, sitting down beside her as I gently pulled the bag open so that she could see the buckskin inside.

"Oh, my goodness," Giselle said. "That looks ancient. I need those gloves just to touch it." She left quickly and then returned a couple of minutes later with the white cotton glove liners on her hands. "I'm thrilled to do the honors," she said, sitting back down on the couch and taking the bag from me.

Slowly she pulled out the buckskin and then carefully began to unfold it. I watched how she did it, and I was paying so much attention to how she was protecting the creases that I didn't even notice something was in the middle. Zed gasped, and then I looked down and saw that it was a packet of yellowed paper. It had been folded up inside the buckskin.

I was thrilled, but Giselle's voice indicated she wasn't. "That can't have been good for the buckskin all these years." There was a discolored area on the leather, but it didn't seem to have been made by the paper.

Giselle pulled off the gloves and handed them over, telling me to put them on. After I did she gestured toward the packet and said, "Your turn."

My heart pounding, I picked it up and sat on the couch on the other side of Zed. For a long moment I stared down at the documents in my hand, hardly able to grasp that we had uncovered the truth at last.

We decided to go through the items one by one, starting with the one on top, which was a letter dated July 1876 and written by someone named Odette Kanagy. That name sounded familiar, and then I remembered seeing her name on my family tree.

"I'll be right back," I said, standing and leaving the packet with the letter on top on the couch. As soon as I was out the back door, I ran to the *daadi haus*, went swiftly down the hall to my room, and grabbed the paper with the chart. Then I ran back to the house and over to the couch.

"What do you have?" Zed asked as I picked up the packet and sat back down.

"A family tree." I followed down the list of my ancestors with a gloved index finger, coming to a stop on *Odette*. She was my great-great-great-great-grandmother, and Abigail's great-great-granddaughter.

Now I remembered. When I was on the bus coming home from Indiana, I had tried to calculate the number of generations in my family that had lived during a time of Indian unrest. Odette was the ancestor who would have been in her thirties during Custer's Last Stand, which I had figured to be the end of the worst of it.

Zed nudged me. "Read it out loud."

"It's not addressed to anyone in particular," I said. I handed him the family tree, held the letter where I could see it, and then began to read.

> *To Whom It May Concern,*
> *If you are reading this letter, then that means you have found the bundle of buckskin and papers I am now about to hide away. My hope is that enough years have passed between my putting it here and your finding it that the world will have changed in the ways that are so troublesome in these present times.*

In truth, I have chosen to hide these things not because I am ashamed of the truth or of the Indian blood in our past, but because I fear repercussions against me and my own children. Though I could not bear to destroy my great-great-grandmother's chapbooks, I have removed the telling parts of the three remaining copies and kept only the fourth fully intact, which I will hide away in the hidden compartment of my husband's new desk. With it I will include the bishop's letter regarding the situation and the buckskin that was my great-grandmother's only remaining possession from her family of origin.

Sincerely,
Odette Kanagy

My eyes fell back to the beginning of the letter. "Indian blood? What does she mean?"

Zed nudged me again. "Look in the packet for the chapbook."

I pulled out the next item. Sure enough, it was an intact copy. I felt a chill just looking at the cover. At the border design and the feather. At the words printed there:

A Reflection of My Experience Concerning the Indians of Long Ago
Abigail Vogel Bontrager

Overcome with emotion, I took off my gloves and handed them to Zed. Seeming to understand, he slipped them on and then took the chapbook from me.

"Read it," I whispered. "So we can find out whose Indian blood she's talking about."

TWENTY-EIGHT

Zed settled back against the couch, and with a final glance at me began to read the chapbook aloud. I couldn't bear the suspense, so I stopped him on the first page and made him flip forward, to where the first half had ended. He started with the last few paragraphs on that page.

> *All along, father insisted to any who would listen that the Conestogas were not involved in the conflict between the settlers and the Indians and that we could trust them completely.*
>
> *How very wrong he had been.*
>
> *In the end, they were involved in the conflict between the settlers and the Indians, through no fault of their own, to tragic results.*

He paused and we looked at each other, eyes wide. This wasn't a story of broken trust between friends. It had only seemed that way until we had the next part of the story. Zed took a deep breath and kept going.

> *The autumn of that year started out with great joy, but by winter a horrible tragedy changed all of our lives forever.*

I married my beloved Gorg in September 1763. He farmed with my father, and besides the uneasiness swirling around the Indians and many of the settlers, our lives were good. For a while, both Gorg and Father had thought it unsafe for me to visit Indian Town, so I had not seen Konenquas for months, though she was often in my thoughts.

Then, on the morning of 14 December of that year, a neighbor came running across our field, shouting at my father that a group of militia had attacked our friends, the Conestoga Indians. Gorg and I had been breaking up the ice in the trough and understood our neighbor's words before Father did. We ran to hitch our horse to the buggy and then took off toward Indian Town as fast as we could.

What we saw when we got there has haunted me to this day.

Six Indians had been in the village that morning, including Konenquas and her husband. Six Indians, and the Paxton Boys had massacred all of them.

Unable to believe my eyes, I rushed to my friend's side, but I knew before I got there that I was too late. I had not seen my old friend in nearly a year, and now she was dead. I collapsed to my knees and sat weeping beside her lifeless body. But as did, I began to hear an odd, muffled sound coming from beneath her, almost like the mewling of an infant.

Stunned, I pushed her body so as to roll her onto her side, and that's when I realized that there was a babe—a live babe—kicking and crying from inside a basket that had been strapped to Konenquas's chest.

With shock I realized my dear Indian friend must have recently given birth. I had not seen her for so long, I hadn't even known she was in the family way. Now, of this whole tribe, the only one here that day who had survived the massacre was this infant. In the chaos of the attack, Konenquas was fatally stabbed in the back and had fallen down, trapping the baby beneath her. If not for the stiffness of the basket's edge, the child would probably have suffocated.

I wanted to cry out to the other settlers who had come to help, but I was afraid of their reactions. Not knowing what else to do, I waited until no one was watching and then discreetly pulled the little one under my cape and rushed away. Father later told me that those in the group who noticed my quick departure thought I was merely overcome with emotion and could not take any more of the horrible sight.

Gorg brought me and the baby home right away. I fed and changed and cleaned her, and then I dressed her in some of the clothes I'd begun to make in hopes of having our own child now that we were married. I stashed away the infant's buckskin wrap, stained with the blood of her mother, in a cedar trunk in the attic. I knew I should destroy it, but it was the only remaining possession of the orphaned infant, and I couldn't bring myself to do so.

Together, we decided she looked to be less than a month old. I named her Helen, after the helenium blossoms Konenquas and I had picked together as girls.

We kept the infant hidden, terrified if the Paxton Boys learned of her existence that they would come and kill her too. Already they had grown more determined and violent, and on 27 December of that year, they killed fourteen more members of the tribe. Thus, Helen was one of the last surviving Conestoga Indians on earth.

On 3 January, 1764, we learned that the Moravian Indians being held for their own safety on Province Island in Philadelphia would be setting out for New York the next day. We decided to give over the baby to an Indian friend, a baptized Christian, who was among those in the group. We took her to our friend on 4 January and he agreed to take the child.

The Moravian Indians set out from Province Island for New York on 5 January, but when they reached New York, the governor refused to let them in. He sent them back to Pennsylvania, and they arrived in Philadelphia on 24 January. This time, they were housed not on Province Island but in the city barracks for their own safety.

The Paxton Boys were still on the rampage, and I was terrified the Moravian Indians, including Helen, would be killed by them as well. I talked Gorg into going into Philadelphia and retrieving the baby from our friend. He managed to do so, discreetly bringing her back home to me. But beyond that we were in a quandary as to what we should do.

Terrified the babe would be discovered and killed, we finally confided in Father's closest friend, Hubert, who came up with a plan. He said that because the infant could pass as white, Gorg and I needed only go away for a year or so and then return with Helen, claiming her as our own.

Zed paused for a moment and looked at me, his eyes wide. "Hubert. That's *my* Hubert. That's my nine-greats-grandfather!"

We were both stunned to learn that he had played a part in this story. "Keep going," I urged.

Though necessary, this was a deception, and all of us were concerned enough to bring it up with our bishop. He promised to think it over and pray about it. He traveled back home, but the next day he sent word that he thought it was the right thing to do. For the sake of Helen's life, he believed this was the best course of action, though he asked that any outright deceit would be that of implication, not direct lies.

On 3 February, we heard a rumor that the Paxton Boys were about to march on Philadelphia, so Gorg, the baby, and I left town the next day and headed south on the Great Wagon Road to stay with an old family friend, a Moravian brother by the name of Gunter, who had immigrated to the Pennsylvania town of Friedenshütten around the same time we came to Lancaster. The friend had moved down to North

Carolina a few years prior and started an apple orchard there, so the story we told our community was that Gorg was going to spend some time working on the farm of this old friend, to learn that man's unique approach to the apple trade.

The Great Wagon Road made for an arduous journey, but when we finally reached our destination and Br. Gunter read the letter we bore from father, he welcomed us into his home and invited us to stay with him as long as needed. Almost right away, we saw that the plan was working, as no one we met questioned if the child was ours or not. Everyone just assumed she was.

Meanwhile, back at home in Philadelphia, tensions were running high. There were false alarms saying that the Paxton Boys had reached the city. In actuality, they only ended up going as far as Germantown the afternoon of 5 February, and then they stopped their advance. Everyone remained at a standoff until later that day, when the Paxton Boys agreed to handle things legislatively. They sent a delegation into Philadelphia to inspect the Indians held there but didn't recognize any of them as ones who had caused them direct harm. They went home, and by 11 February Benjamin Franklin reported that things were finally quiet around the city. Franklin had already published a pamphlet, "Narrative of the Late Massacres," detailing the entire situation.

After that an angry battle ensued among legislators and citizens, and a "war of words" among numerous people arose. In 1764, sixty-three pamphlets were distributed on the topic, both for and against the Indian situation and how it had been "handled" the day of the massacre.

That August, I received word that my mother was failing quickly, so our little family of three took a chance and returned home, arriving just in time to say goodbye before my mother passed. Unfortunately, though Helen was by then about eight months old, we had to pass her off as just four months old. To make matters worse, the child's hair had been growing in straight and black, and though she was still light skinned, a few Paxton-sympathizing neighbors grew suspicious. When one accused us of trying to pass off an Indian child as our own, Gorg, Father, and I knew something had to be done to allay such suspicions.

Thinking quickly, Gorg responded to our accuser by "confiding" in him that we took the opposite position and were in support of the Paxton Boys. In fact, he claimed authorship of several anti-Indian pamphlets that had come out recently under a pseudonym. He said, "Why on earth would anyone in my family have adopted an Indian baby when we despise all Indians?"

After that, suspicions were somewhat diverted, but of course Gorg and I knew we had failed in the bishop's request that we never outright lie.

Despite that lie, rumors persisted. Concerned, our friend Hubert once again stepped in to help. He had already been vocal about his objection to the Paxton Boys, so he, too, joined in with our deception. To reinforce the impression that our family was anti-Indian, he and Father pretended to break up their friendship over the matter, and the war of words for a while went on between the two families. From all appearances, our family hated the Indians and thus would never have adopted an Indian child. The matter was soon laid to rest.

Unfortunately, by pretending to endorse the actions of the Paxton Boys, Father, Gorg, and I took a nonpacifist stance. The bishop knew the truth of the matter—that it was only a cover for the sake of protecting our child—but he had no choice but to excommunicate us.

He spoke to us privately at first, saying that if we would "repent" of our "sin" of endorsing the violent actions of the Paxton Boys, we wouldn't be excommunicated after all. We did *that gladly, as it allowed us to bring an end to our elaborate ruse.*

We raised Helen in peace after that, seeing her to adulthood. God blessed us beyond measure with her, and with her five siblings who were subsequently born to us.

I am an old woman now of seventy-six years, a widow for the last thirty. Before my days come to an end, I had to write this story and let the truth be known to all, especially Helen's daughters. I never told her the story of her origins, afraid the truth might have haunted her, but perhaps in the afterlife, where she has been now for a decade, she has already met Konenquas and learned all there was to know.

Looking back, Gorg and I would have done nothing differently. God knew our hearts. Helen knew our love. Only Gorg and I, and a few other brave souls, knew the lie that was our sin.

Zed closed the little book with a flourish.

"Wow," I said.

"Yeah." He slipped the chapbook back into the packet for safekeeping and handed it to me. "What a story."

I held it tenderly with both my hands. My ancestors hadn't turned against the Indians at all. They had only pretended to in order to save the life of Konenquas's child, whom they made their own.

I pulled out my family tree again and took another look. I realized that, genetically speaking, my eight-greats-grandmother was not Abigail but instead Konenquas. Thus, I descended, in part, from the Conestoga. The tribe who was wiped out by settlers more than two hundred years before lived on in me and my mother and my siblings and their children.

Overwhelmed at the thought, I took back the gloves and pulled out the final document in the packet, unfolding it to see that it was the letter from Gorg and Abigail's bishop, written just before they took the child and headed down to North Carolina. Once again I began to get choked up, so I simply held up the letter for Zed to read aloud.

"The date is 2 February, 1764," he stated. "Just over six weeks after the massacre."

I blinked back my tears as I listened to the words.

> *Gorg,*
>
> *After much thought and prayer, I write to encourage you to do what is right by this infant. A child of the heart can be just as much a part of a person, and a family, as a child of the body. For the sake of the girl's life, do as Hubert has suggested and flee to North Carolina with Abigail and the baby, presenting the little one as your own, which she now is.*
>
> *My one request is that any outright deceit would be of implication, not direct lies.*
>
> *By the time you return, no one will be the wiser. Those in our community will assume Abigail was already somewhat far along with child at the time of your departure.*
>
> *Your servant in the Lord,*
> *Ingemar Joblenz*

"Wow, what a ruse," Giselle said, the first comment she'd made throughout the whole thing. "Then again, that probably wouldn't have been too hard to pull off back then. Women didn't talk among one another about their pregnancies, let alone announce them to the whole community."

I didn't say so, but in our community many still didn't, although our dresses weren't as loose as some might have been at that time.

I read the letter again—thinking that just as Helen was Abigail's child of the heart, Abigail was my grandmother of the heart.

I looked to Zed, and as our eyes met, I realized the bishop's words were true. Zed, whose birth mother had been a woman named Lydia, had been adopted by Marta. I'd never known a mother to love a child more than she loved him. Lexie, whose birth mother was Giselle, had been adopted by loving non-Amish parents in Oregon. And Ada, whose birth mother was also Giselle, had been adopted by Klara and Alexander and had also been loved beyond measure. My sister Sadie had a different birth father than the rest of us siblings, but you would never know. She was my *daed*'s daughter, one hundred percent.

Adoptive or not, those people were their *parents*, in every sense of the word. Abigail was as much my grandmother as Konenquas was.

That's what this had all been about, I realized. Loving a baby whether he or she came from your body or not, loving them as your very own precious, unique, and wonderful child.

My thoughts went to Frannie and the little time we all had left with her. I couldn't imagine what it was like for her family, especially for Giselle, who had been away for so long. I stood and made my way to the hospital bed, realizing as I did that Frannie's breathing was even more labored than before. I raised the head of the bed as much as possible and waved to Marta, who was now awake, to come over.

According to Marta, Frannie hadn't eaten in a few days now, although she was still taking water and they had managed to get a little bit of a protein drink down her the night before.

I'd been hoping to do that again tonight, but when I tried to wake her, she didn't rouse.

Her head tilted to one side, in my direction, and in the dim light from the lamp by the couch, her eyelids were nearly translucent. Her skin was papery—a sure sign she was becoming more dehydrated.

Marta checked her breathing.

"There's definitely more fluid," she said quietly when she was done. She motioned to Lexie, who now stood behind the couch, to come and listen too.

Lexie did and then nodded, the stethoscope still in her ears.

Giselle joined us as well, bending down and kissing her mother's wrinkled cheek. Frannie stirred and her lids fluttered but she didn't open her eyes again. James and Luke came close to their wives' sides, and we stood that way for a long time, each of us breathing for her as we listened to her struggle for air. I waited for the next breath—it seemed a long time in coming. Finally, she took another raggedy one.

I could feel Zed close at my side. I could hear a sob bubble from Giselle's throat. I could smell the wood smoke from the fireplace.

I could see that Frannie was almost gone.

"I'll get Klara," Marta said, and then she headed for the stairs.

A wave of peace swept over me, and I started to softly recite the Lord's Prayer. Lexie and Ella joined me, and Ada took Frannie's hand. Another raggedy breath and then—nothing. I held my own breath as I waited. Still, nothing more came.

"She's gone, isn't she?" Giselle whispered.

"I think so," I said, surprised at how calm I sounded. I glanced at my watch. It was 12:03, Christmas Eve morn.

Marta came back down the stairs, and she must have known by the expression on Giselle's face because she went to her sister first, putting her arm around her, holding her close.

"I'm so glad I came," Giselle managed to say.

"So am I," Marta said.

A moment later, Klara floated into the room, a white robe over her white nightgown and her hair tucked under a nightcap. She went straight to the bed, and Lexie and Ella parted to let her through. She stood there for a moment looking down at her mother, and then she reached out and brushed a strand of hair from the old woman's face.

Klara went to Giselle next. She put her arm around her sister's shoulder and said, "I'm sorry. Not for *Mamm*. For—"

"I know," Giselle said. "I know. I'm sorry too."

For all I knew, that was as much as Giselle and Klara ever spoke about the past. But it seemed to be enough. Perhaps Frannie's passing became a moment for them that bridged the hurt of long ago.

I put my attention back on Frannie. Her life hadn't turned out the way she expected, but she had lived it well, for God. I think that's all she really wanted for her daughters too.

Frannie had died well. And unlike my experience with Verna, I felt privileged to have been by her side when she took her last breath on earth.

TWENTY-NINE

Sleep did not come easily, but somehow I managed to catch a few hours. By the time I woke up again, the sun was over the horizon, and a peek out the front window showed that several buggies were parked outside. Even though it was Christmas Eve day, I had a feeling they belonged to members of Alexander and Klara's district, who would have come to do chores and help prepare the house and property for the impending visitation and funeral.

I dressed and fixed my hair, and then I went to the kitchen of the *daadi haus* for some breakfast. Last night Alexander had said he would leave a message on my parents' machine about Frannie's death, so I expected my *daed* to show up at some point soon. After some yogurt and a few bites of toast, I cleaned my dishes and then returned to my room to pack as quietly as I could. Giselle was still asleep.

Daed hadn't shown up by the time I was finished, so I brought all of my stuff to the living room and stacked it beside the door. Though I knew I should go on to the main house and pitch in with everyone else, I just couldn't bring myself to do so. Instead, I returned to the little kitchen for another cup of coffee and then sat at the table, alone in the quiet, and tried to work through what I was feeling.

Unsettled was the word that came to mind—though not from Frannie dying. I had seen her go in peace. She had been ready, surrounded by those who loved her. I had now faced a death of someone important to me, and I had seen what Marta had told me about, the beauty of the transition.

No, I think what had my mind spinning was Zed. Had he meant what he said last night before the film? Was he really willing to join the Amish church for me? For us? The thought both thrilled me and terrified me at the same time. Such a move would be a sacrifice for anyone, but especially for him. It would mean the end of his education, his film career. His dreams.

My thoughts were interrupted by the sound of footsteps outside and the gentle knock I recognized as my father's. I let him in, holding a finger to my mouth as I whispered, "Giselle's still asleep."

I pointed to my things beside the door, saying I just needed to straighten the kitchen and then I'd be out. As he began carrying the boxes to the buggy, I cleaned my cup and put it away, and then I dug from my handwork bag the bookmarks I'd made for all the women. I placed them on the table, fanned out in circle, and then dashed off a quick note for Giselle and left it there as well. I asked her to please pass them along to Klara, Ada, Lexie, Ella, Marta, and herself as a small token of thanks and love. I hesitated, not sure how to end the note, and then I finally added, "I'll be praying for you and your family. See you at the visitation. Love, Izzy."

Once we were home, I unpacked my things and then jumped into the fray, helping prepare for tomorrow's Christmas dinner. Finally, however, late that afternoon, my *mamm* sent me off for a nap, saying I was nearly asleep on my feet. She was right.

I ended up sleeping through our entire Christmas Eve family time. Linda tried to wake me, but my body felt like lead and I just couldn't get up. I didn't even realize I'd fallen back to sleep until I awoke many hours later, early Christmas morning. I headed downstairs in the pitch dark and lit the lamp. It was four forty-five. I assumed *Mamm* and *Daed* would be up soon. I started the coffee and the fire, and then I looked in the refrigerator to see if *Mamm* had left her Christmas coffee cake ready to bake. She had, so I took it out to warm by the stove.

Next, I gathered tape, scissors, and some brown paper bags and then retreated to my little room to wrap the gifts I'd made for my family, tying each one with a strand of red yarn. As I worked, my mind returned to Zed. He'd said he was willing to join the Amish church, but I didn't expect he would feel that way for long—not once he really thought it through.

Wait. Sighing deeply, I forced myself to surrender the situation, yet again, to God's will, not my own.

One by one, my other family members began to appear. First *Mamm*, then *Daed*, then Thomas and Stephen. As *Daed* and the boys did the chores, *Mamm* sent me upstairs to wake Tabitha and Linda. After *Daed* and the boys came back in, we ate our breakfast of sausage, eggs, and the coffee cake. Afterward, *Daed* read the Christmas story, and then we all went into the living room. I stopped to gather the gifts I had for the others and then joined them, the morning light through the windows brightening the whole space.

We all exchanged our gifts. Tabitha had knitted me a scarf and Linda had made socks to match. Thomas drew me a picture of a bird in a tree, and Stephen made me a pinecone wreath that he said I could hang on my "little room" door. I passed around the cloth bags I'd made and the handkerchiefs I'd embroidered.

Mamm and *Daed* gave the girls new dresses and the boys new shirts and pants. We each got one small, personal item as well, and I opened my box slowly, eager to see what might be inside.

To my surprise, as I lifted the lid, I saw that it contained a book with an illustration on it of an Indian wearing buckskin. Eyes wide, I looked to my *mamm*, who explained, "It covers all the fashions in America during the 1700s. What everyone would have worn. Natives and Europeans. Rich and poor."

"Where did you find it?" I asked.

"I asked at the bookstore. They did some sort of search…" As usual she'd didn't give much of an explanation. She didn't need to.

I was deeply touched, not so much for the gift itself as for what it represented. Their acceptance. Their approval. Their support.

Sure, this family of mine overwhelmed me at times, but hanging out with another family for such a long stretch had taught me much about my own. Maybe *Mamm* wasn't the talker or the nurturer I wished she was. And maybe my sisters, every one of them, were the exact opposite of me. But I knew they loved me. I knew they were there for me. I knew I belonged to them, always.

The next day was Frannie's funeral, which was held at Klara and Alexander's house. The men and women of the family sat together up front, near the minister, beside the pine casket. Everyone else in attendance sat divided, as usual, into their two sides. I was on the women's side, next to *Mamm*, while *Daed* sat with the men.

The service was long and somber. In attendance were Frannie's family, many of their extended relatives, numerous members of their district, and other specially invited guests, such as me and my parents. Just as we were taking our seats, I noticed Ada greet a young couple at the door, and I had a feeling they were Daniel and Morgan, the friends she and Giselle had told me about from Switzerland, who were currently in the States. What a blessing they had been in the country and were able to come today.

The service had Scripture readings and a sermon, as usual. At the end, though Frannie's name had yet to be mentioned, the bishop finally looked down at her casket and said, "Francis Lantz was eighty-four years old." To eulogize her beyond that would be prideful and wrong.

After the service, the pallbearers carried the casket out to the hearse—an enclosed wagon with a black top. I followed as far as the porch and watched the wind whip against their bodies as they slid the casket onto the bed of the wagon. *Mamm* stepped beside me. "Your *daed*'s going to stay and set up the tables," she said. "And I'm going to get the meal ready. Do you want to help me?"

I shook my head, surprised she'd thought to ask. She was offering me an out—but I didn't need one. "Thank you, but I'm fine. I'll go to the cemetery with the family."

Zed and I rode in the back of Alexander and Klara's buggy, which followed behind the hearse. Zed sat close to me on the back bench seat, and though we didn't talk, I reached out and took his hand for a while when I knew no one was looking.

During our short time at the cemetery, Zed angled himself to block the wind. Thankfully, the minister kept it short considering it was bitter cold and growing more so.

This was the part of Verna's service that had gotten to me the most, but now as I gazed at the deep hole waiting in the ground to receive Frannie's casket, I was filled not with terror but with peace. She had lived a good and godly life. She had known the Lord as her Savior. Surely she was now with the One who had numbered all her days.

By the time we returned to the house, the noon meal of soup and bread was ready to eat. The older people dined first, then we *youngie* took our turn. Zed and I ended up seated near Daniel and Morgan. They were so nice and friendly that soon the four of us were chatting away like old friends.

Nearby, Ada and Lexie were talking and laughing like sisters, and once again I was amazed at how close they seemed despite not having grown up together—or in fact even knowing about each other—until they were both adults. How nice it must be for Giselle to see her daughters get on so well.

I glanced around for Giselle but didn't see her.

Conversation turned to Zed's filmmaking, and then to my contribution as a costumer. When Daniel learned I was a seamstress, he asked what other sorts of work I did. As those around us jumped in and began to describe my various creations, he became excited and said he would love to see some of it if he could.

"I'm always on the lookout for authentic Amish handwork. We sell it in the gift shop at the hotel."

Hearing our conversation, Ada leaned over and added, "Izzy's multitalented, you know. She *is* an amazing seamstress, but she's also quite the caregiver."

"Oh, right," Morgan said, dabbing at her mouth with a napkin. "You were the one who cared for Ada's grandma."

I nodded, surprised when she added, "So what's next? You should think about working for Herr Lauten. We've been trying to find someone for him forever. You could come to Switzerland and be his caregiver—and you could do handwork for the shop while you're there!"

"Switzerland?" I squeaked with a laugh. "Sure. Just let me get my things and we can go."

Everyone laughed, but deep inside I had to wonder if the idea was all that crazy. I didn't necessarily have the wanderlust I knew had driven Ada to travel a few years ago, but I did have a deep love of learning and experiencing new things. I also felt I had established a bond with Giselle, one that could only grow stronger if we lived near each other, at least for a while. Perhaps she might even mentor me. There was just so much about fabric and art she could share and that I yearned to know.

Once again, I looked around for Giselle but still didn't see her. In fact, she seemed to have disappeared. I wasn't quite finished with my dessert, but a gentle urging told me to *go*. I feared this day had been a greater struggle for her than for almost anyone else.

After excusing myself, I retrieved my cape and went out the back door to the *daadi haus*, but she wasn't there. Next I headed toward the barn, but on the way a movement down by the creek caught my attention. There was someone there, a woman from what I could tell, though the hair was covered by a hat and she stepped out of view as soon as I started walking toward the willows. On a hunch I kept going.

As I neared the trees, I could hear the sound of someone sniffling.

"Giselle, don't let me scare you," I said. "It's me, Izzy."

She didn't answer so I continued on, finding her with her back against a willow, her face streaked with tears, her eyes on the icy water before her.

She looked exhausted. Defeated.

Tormented.

I took a deep breath and turned my eyes to the water as well. Somehow, I knew this wasn't just about her mother's death.

It was also about what happened to her right here, so long ago, when Lexie was just a toddler and had almost drowned because of Giselle's negligence. According to what Ella had told me, that event was the final straw that led the woman to give up both daughters for adoption and move away.

I stood next to her now, my back also against the tree, and thought about what I could say that might make her feel better. I wanted to reassure her that her decision, though painful, had been a wise one, as Lexie and Ada had both been raised by loving parents in homes filled with faith and goodness. But I couldn't think of how to say it without hurting her feelings.

I remained silent instead, offering only the comfort of my presence.

Finally, still staring down at the creek, Giselle spoke. "A piece of me, the selfish part, hoped they would never get over losing me. Instead, they have both gone on to become wonderful, loving, productive adults without my help at all."

She barked a laugh through a fresh wave of tears. After a long moment, she added, "It's just astounding how so many lives can be changed in an instant, you know? A mother falls asleep. A child wanders off. A creek nearly swallows her up…"

I said a silent prayer for wisdom as I leaned closer to Giselle, our shoulders touching. "God's hand was on it, though," I whispered. "He knew every one of those things was going to happen."

She nodded, taking that in. "I guess you're right about that." She sucked in a deep breath. "*Danke.*"

I nodded, my eyes narrowing in concern.

"I'm okay," she said, wiping at her face with gloved hands. "I just needed some time. This is a good thing, really. I had to come back to this place." I thought she meant Pennsylvania, or the farm, but then she gestured toward the creek, and I realized she meant this exact place, this body of water.

I gazed at the creek, at the clear liquid that trickled between large rocks and frozen slabs of ice as it flowed downstream. It was about average-sized, as creeks go, but for Giselle I knew it loomed large. To her, it was a river. No, it was an *ocean*, one that had come between her and her mother, her sisters, and her children, keeping her away for all these years.

I thought suddenly of that poem I'd discovered on the bus ride from Indiana, by William Penn, and I asked if I could quote a line from it now.

"Sure."

"It says, 'Death is but crossing the world, as friends do the seas; they live in one another still.'"

She repeated the sentiment, and then she smiled through her tears.

"Wow. So true. Me, my daughters, my mom, even my sisters—no matter what, no matter where we are, we live in one another still. We always have. We always will."

Her voice choked on the last word as she burst into a fresh round of sobs. I embraced her then and she hugged me back, not for long but still I felt the hope of healing behind it.

We stayed there together a few more minutes in silence, but sensing her need for more alone time, I left her to her thoughts and started back to the house, my mind grasping at some new truth of my own as I went. I had just told Giselle that God knew what was going to happen back then. And I believed that. He knew that little Lexie would almost drown. He knew that in her grief and panic, Giselle would flee, leaving behind not just her toddler but her new infant too. He knew that someday all three would be together again, and that from that reunion would come great healing.

He also knew about me. He knew I would struggle for a while with the deaths of loved ones. And He knew I would fall in love with Zed and want to make a life with him.

Eyes wide, I realized one more thing He knew. He knew I *wasn't* going to join the Amish church.

Before that moment, such a realization might have caused me to feel regret or sadness or even guilt. Instead, I felt nothing but peace.

"I'm not joining the Amish church," I whispered aloud, just to make sure that the words felt right on my tongue. "I will still love the Lord with all my heart, soul, mind, and strength, but I will do so as a Mennonite instead."

Again, a surge of peace filled my heart. Not only did God *know,* but to my very core, it felt as if He approved.

Movement up ahead caught my eye, and I realized Zed had come looking for me, wearing his coat and cap against the cold. "We need to talk," I said as we met beside the fallow garden.

Without speaking, he took my icy hand in his and led me around the corner of the house to the stand of pines, which gave us some privacy.

"What is it?" he asked, peering deep into my eyes with concern.

I gave him a reassuring smile and then reached up and touched the handsome plane of his cheek. "I don't want you to become Amish," I said softly. "Though your willingness to do so says volumes about your faith and your love for me."

His lips curved into a tentative smile as he waited to see where I was going with this.

"I want to join the Mennonite church instead. I believe it's the right thing for me, and for—"

Before I could say *us*, Zed's mouth was on mine. His face was cold but his lips were warm, sending rays of heat through my entire being. I kissed him back, just as fiercely, then held on tight, the two of us clinging to each other in the frosty stillness.

After our embrace, we stayed there a while, standing among the trees, gazing into each other's eyes, and stealing a few more kisses. Somehow, being here and talking with this man about spending the rest of our lives together felt as natural and normal as could be.

We both agreed we shouldn't get married until after he finished school, so the question was what my life was going to look like between now and then. We considered the idea of me moving back in with Ella so that we could be closer, but then Zed astounded me by bringing up Switzerland as another possibility.

"You never know, Iz. My mom has been wanting to go to Switzerland for years. Maybe the two of you could do it together."

"What about us?" I asked, my heart filled with fear but also excitement.

"You and me, you mean?"

I nodded.

"I still have a year and a half to go before I graduate. As long as you're back by then, I think it would be an incredible opportunity. Think of all you could see, not to mention all you could learn from Giselle about your craft."

My heart surging with happiness, I hugged him tight, thanking God that this dear sweet man wanted and would always want for my life to be as rich and full—of experiences, of learning, of *pushing* myself—as his was.

Finally, the wind picked up and green needles showered over us like confetti, bringing the fresh scent of pine mixed with the cold. Nearly frozen, we had no choice but to head inside and join the others. As we walked side by side, I thought of what Giselle had said, how life can change in an instant. I thought of all the life-changing instances I'd witnessed of late. Frannie's last, peaceful breath. The other deaths in my life. Zed's accident that had thrown me into such a spiral.

My mind returned to Psalm 139 as he opened the front door and then stepped aside, allowing me to enter first. Just as surely as God knew my past and present, He also already knew the many things my future held, my future as Zed's wife, helpmate, and very best friend.

I couldn't help but smile to myself. In that same chapter, the psalmist proclaimed, "Such knowledge is too wonderful for me," and I had to agree. Such knowledge *was* too wonderful. But it also brought great comfort.

And great joy.

Epilogue

I went to Switzerland three months later, in March. Giselle paid my way, and I worked as her assistant and Herr Lauten's aide for more than a year, helping him organize his books and papers, along with daily care, and helping her organize her studio and expand her business. Giselle made regular appearances teaching fabric art, and she took me along for a few of those too. One time she even had me contribute to the class, but I didn't enjoy it.

I preferred working behind the scenes.

Marta traveled to Switzerland with me, much to my parents' relief, and stayed for eight months while her new business partner managed the practice in Lancaster County. It wasn't a vacation for Marta—she taught classes at a birthing center in Bern, just over a half hour away. But her trip was a huge success, and I was sorry to see her go once her time there came to an end.

Daniel and Morgan became my close friends, especially as they were my bridge to the Mennonite faith. They attended a lovely little church in town, and though there was quite a difference between the services there and the Amish ones I was used to, the theology was similar, and that's what was important. I found it to be a good fit, though sometimes I missed the sense of community that seemed more pervasive in the churches back home.

One of my biggest quandaries over there was clothing, because while I was no longer going to be Amish, I was definitely going to remain Plain— yet the congregation there did not observe rules of dress. In the end, it was Marta who suggested I adopt the garb of her district back home, and I thought that was a good solution. With her guidance, I slowly created a new wardrobe for myself, trading the capes and solid colors and straight pins of my Amish clothing for the modest dresses in simple prints, with buttons, of the Mennonites. At my request, Susie sent me several smaller Mennonite-style *kapps*, which she procured from one of her seamstresses.

Together, Giselle and I worked on the costumes for Zed's film, doing the research, weaving the fabric, and sewing the garments all by hand. Otherwise, I used my sewing time to come up with more items for the gift shop, create prototypes, and implement some of Giselle's designs.

Though I didn't use a computer, Zed convinced me that the best way for us to stay close while so far apart was through face-to-face computer calls, so I relented in that one area. We soon fell into a routine and, using Giselle's laptop, I was able to see and talk with him at least once a week, sometimes even more than that, which was wonderful.

He spent his spring semester in Los Angeles, learning screenwriting and visiting the "majors" and "minors," which I learned were just nicknames for the larger and smaller movie studios that proliferated out there. Though he loved the experience, I could see that it helped shape in his mind a better vision of his own creative future. He came to realize that Hollywood held no interest for him as a long-term career goal. He wanted to be an independent filmmaker and focus primarily on documentaries, especially those on historical topics. I thought that sounded perfect. Somehow, I had never envisioned him making popcorn-munching, cineplex-going movies anyway.

Giselle and I mailed the costumes to Zed in May, and then I followed them soon after myself, making it home just in time for filming, which began in June.

Though I would have loved to have spent hours and hours of quiet "down time" with the just the two of us while I was home, we spent almost every waking moment of that one month together, making our movie, *Hidden Motives*, instead.

We were able to wrap filming before I returned to Switzerland, and once I was gone Zed buried himself in what he called "postproduction" for the rest of the summer. That kept him extremely busy, and I didn't hear from him as much during that time, but once he returned to Goshen in the fall for the beginning of his senior year, our regular communication resumed. Together, we decided I would come home again, for good this time, in April, before his college graduation.

I planned my trip accordingly, arriving in Lancaster the week before, to give me some time with my family. Of course, I spent a good deal of that time in my little room trying not to feel overwhelmed by all the activity around me. Living with Giselle had been peaceful and easy. A week with my family left me feeling frazzled. Though I knew I wouldn't be returning to Switzerland, I was eager to plan a future beyond the walls of my parents' home.

I rode to Indiana with Marta, and we arrived the day before Zed's graduation, going straight to the Home Place. There, we greeted Rosalee, Ella, Luke, and little Sarah, the child Ella had been carrying when I was working here for Rosalee. Now Sarah was a year and a half old and had been joined by a baby brother, just one month ago, named Samuel.

Late that afternoon, as Ella and Rosalee fixed dinner in the kitchen, Samuel napped, and Marta and I played with Sarah in the living room, Marta got a call on her phone. It was Zed, and he asked to speak with me. I wouldn't be seeing him until the next day, but it was still a thrill to hear his voice and know he was just thirteen or so miles away from where I sat at that very moment.

"Hello?" I said, trying to temper my smile in front of his mother.

"What are you doing right this second?" Zed asked in a near whisper.

"Making a tower with some building blocks. Why?"

"Because I'm outside. I only have fifteen minutes, and then I have to get back to school for commencement practice. But I couldn't wait to see you; it was killing me. So I got in the car and headed over."

"Aw, Zed," I whispered, my smile no longer containable on my face.

"I don't want to hurt my mom's feelings, but I don't have time to see her now too. Is there some way you can slip out and just come say hello? Why don't you tell her I need you to borrow her phone to snap a few quick pictures out in the orchard for me?"

"Why?"

"I don't know...for a little film project I'm doing? You know how it is. She's used to accommodating all sorts of wacky requests for the sake of my art."

I laughed, even though I felt hesitant to do so. I was dying to run right out and see him, but I wasn't comfortable telling Marta a lie. "Here, you talk to her," I said, and then I handed the phone back to his mother. Of course, as they spoke, she merely rolled her eyes, nodding, and then after she hung up, she handed over the phone to me with a smile and distracted little Sarah while I slipped out the door.

My heart pounding, I moved down the ramp and across the lawn toward the orchard. I couldn't see Zed or his car, but I ran in among the trees anyway, not even daring to call out his name. As I neared the end of a row, I saw glimpses of red between the leaves, and I realized he'd parked on that part of the driveway that wasn't visible from the windows of the house. I kept moving closer until finally I saw him emerge from the next row over. He looked good to me, so good, and so grown up. He was even taller now, his blond hair cut short, with no more bangs hanging in his eyes.

We continued toward each other, moving faster, and then at the last possible moment he flung open his arms and I ran forward and jumped into them. He spun me around, holding me tight, and I held onto him even tighter. He was my love, my future, my best friend in the whole wide world.

"Could we be any cornier?" he whispered, finally coming to a stop but still holding me close.

"What do you mean?"

"Running toward each like that? Ashley and Melanie got away with it in *Gone with the Wind*, but otherwise it's been a movie cliché since *Wuthering Heights*. Cue the Tchaikovsky, why don't we?"

He lowered me to the ground, and I pulled away just enough to look into his handsome face. I didn't get the references, but I had definitely missed hearing his cinematic evaluations.

"I can't believe you're here," I whispered, smiling.

"I couldn't not come. It's like you were a magnet and I was a bunch of iron filings."

Chuckling, I placed my cheek against his chest. "I'm glad to know I have that kind of power over you."

"You have no idea, Miss Mueller."

He kissed the top of my head. Then he took my face in his hands and leaned down for one very sweet, slow kiss on my lips.

Afterward he just pulled back and gazed at me for a long moment.

"What?" I asked, tucking a loose strand of hair away, feeling suddenly self-conscious.

"Aw, Iz, you look incredible. So beautiful. It's like you're exactly the same but completely different, you know?"

I nodded. I did know. I felt the same looking up at him. Oh, how I had missed him!

Our fifteen minutes went by like seconds, and then it was time for him to leave. I wouldn't see him again until the ceremony, but he told me he wanted me to stick around afterward, that there was something special he had planned for me.

The next day we left Sarah behind with Rosalee and piled into the car. Marta took the wheel, with Luke in the passenger seat, and Ella and I rode in back, the baby between us. Ella had an infant car seat she used when they were with *Englisch* drivers, but Samuel didn't like it and cried the whole way.

"He's used to being held," Ella explained, though we all understood. Amish babies always preferred buggies to cars.

The graduation was in the recreation center. When Zed walked across the stage for his diploma, I felt a flutter in my chest. He looked so handsome in his cap and gown.

Tears stung my eyes, and Marta reached for my hand and then for Ella's too. The three of us sat, connected, while Luke held his son. Once Zed walked off the stage, Marta let go of our hands, dug a tissue from the pocket of her apron, and began dabbing at her eyes. Ella shook her head a little. It was funny how she seemed to be growing more and more practical while Marta became more emotional.

Personally, I sided with Marta. She had raised Zed to be a fine young man—kind, generous, creative, and loving. Marta had an eighth-grade education, although her training as a midwife and years of practice certainly counted for far more than her formal schooling. But still, Zed had graduated from high school and now from college too. The cords around his neck proved it. I thought Marta had every reason to feel relief and joy and sorrow and even a little bit of Plain pride. I knew God had guided her, but she loved Zed with an unconditional, best-for-him sort of love that I could only hope I could emulate with my one child, or maybe two, someday.

After the ceremony, as other families snapped photos, we simply hugged Zed. Marta didn't say she was proud of him. Instead, she said, "Good work."

Ella tugged on his cord and said, "Don't let all this go to your head. You're hard enough to deal with as it is."

"*Ya, ya, ya,*" he answered and then winked at me. He took the baby from Luke and held him up above his head.

"I wouldn't do that unless you want to wear his dinner," Ella cautioned.

The baby smiled and a glob of drool bombed Zed on the forehead.

We all laughed, including little Samuel, and Zed lowered him into his arms, still laughing as he wiped at the mess with a fresh tissue from Marta. I had no doubt he would make a good father. Perhaps he'd be able to make up for my lack of maternal skills.

As we walked toward Marta's car, Zed told his mother I would be staying with him for a while. "I'll bring her back in an hour or two."

"Perfect," Marta responded. "That will give us time to make dinner."

We told everyone goodbye, and after they drove off, we headed back toward the middle of campus. "Where are we going?" I asked.

"The library."

"For?"

"You'll see," he told me.

But I had a feeling I already knew.

Once we entered, I followed him back through the shelves and shelves of books, to the room where we'd watched the film a year and a half ago. As he opened the door I almost expected a group of people to be there like before, but it was empty. The room was dim, lit only by the small amount of light that came through around the window shades.

We made our way up front, and then I stood back as he fooled with the computer, pushing some buttons until an image of the Susquehanna River appeared on the screen. Then he pushed another button, the film started, and we sat down, side by side, to watch it.

I expected Zed to put his arm around me, but he didn't. I leaned toward him in my chair until my shoulder touched his. He leaned against me too, just enough for me to feel the press of his muscle against me. I sat statue still.

The river flowed as the title *Hidden Motives* came on to the screen. And then, *The story of Abigail and Konenquas.*

"Oh, Zed," I whispered.

"Shh. Just watch."

So that's what I did. Everything looked so different on screen than it had when we were filming, and at first I was so busy adjusting my mindset that it was hard to pay attention to the story. But soon Zed's masterful skills took over, and I was swept away into the tale that was now so familiar to me, that of my eight-greats grandmother and how she befriended an Indian woman and ended up saving and adopting, in every way but legally, that woman's child.

Abigail was played by Shelly, and though I had been fairly impressed with her acting during filming, now I could really see why Zed had wanted to use her. On the screen, she came across perfectly, a gifted actress who was made for the part. Konenquas was played by the girl from Belize I'd met the year before—her name was Molly—and fortunately she came across great on film too.

The movie ended with an image of the buckskin Zed and I had found in my *mamm*'s desk. As the camera panned in toward the brownish stain that marred the corner of the centuries-old covering, the narrator explained that it was a bloodstain, made the day of the massacre, when Konenquas was fatally stabbed and her blood soaked through to the leather wrapped around her baby.

"DNA testing of the blood has confirmed a direct genetic link between Konenquas and her most current living female descendants."

"That's you," Zed whispered, but I just smiled. I had humored him before leaving for Switzerland, but I hadn't needed some Q-tip in my cheek to tell me what I already knew, that I had come down from a brave and beautiful Indian woman who lost her life at the hands of her persecutors, on land once promised to her and her people by our founding fathers. In the end, the promise had been betrayed.

"Though the Conestoga tribe was, for all intents and purposes, eliminated by the Paxton Boys back in 1763," the narrator continued, "it still lives on in the few who managed to escape the massacre, including a newborn baby girl who survived the killings, was whisked away by a brave Amish friend, and raised without ever being told the truth of her own origins."

The buckskin on the screen was replaced by an image of the chapbook, the camera slowly zooming inward toward the feather drawn in on one corner.

"Now with the discovery of the chapbook written by Abigail Vogel Bontrager, that truth has been made known at last."

After that the film ended, and though I knew I should feel sad, instead the overall effect was quite the opposite. I felt uplifted. Validated. As though I was a part of something bigger than just myself.

I tried to explain that to Zed, but he simply took my hand and gave it a squeeze, saying, "As usual, Iz, for someone who doesn't go the movies, you sure know how to put it into words. That's exactly how I feel when I see a really great film. That I'm a part of something bigger than myself."

As the credits scrolled upward, I read each line, including "Written, directed, and produced by Zed Bayer." Under costumes was listed "Giselle Lantz and Ms. Wabbim."

I smiled. "Who narrated it?" I asked. The voice was so rich and deep.

"A professor I met at Millersville University. In fact, he ended up helping with some of the research. And—" Zed stood. "He wants me to go to graduate school there. He said I can get a scholarship, plus he'll hire me as his assistant."

"That's great."

He nodded. "It's close to home."

"*Ya.*"

"There's housing," he added.

"Oh?"

He was quiet for a long moment, seemingly lost in thought. Then he moved to the computer and turned it off. But he didn't gesture toward the door or seem as though he was ready to leave.

"Zed?"

He turned toward me in the dim light. "I didn't buy a ring. I didn't think you would want one."

I nodded, barely. He was right. Amish didn't wear rings. Nor did this ex-Amish girl.

"Should I go on?" he asked.

I tried to swallow but choked a little. "Could we go outside? I could use some fresh air."

His face fell.

"Honestly," I said. "It's really hot and stuffy in here."

We headed for the door and then made our way silently through the library, toward the front.

"Wait," I said. "Stop here." Among the books was even better than outside, I decided, especially the part where we were passing through, which was completely deserted except for the two of us. "Hold me," I whispered.

Zed wrapped his arms around me and pulled me close. The fabric of his soft cotton dress shirt rubbed against my chin. He was broader and more muscular than the year before, and he smelled faintly of mild soap and spicy aftershave.

He pulled me in even more tightly, fitting me perfectly under his chin. Finally he said, "Izzy, what are you thinking?"

I realized I hadn't been thinking—not at all. I was just "being," wrapped in his arms.

"What you were saying back in there?" I asked, pulling back to look him in the eyes.

His voice had a hint of the old familiar tease. "About?"

"A ring."

A slow grin spread across his face. "So I can ask you?"

"*Ya,*" I answered. "Please."

"Izzy, will you marry me?"

"*Ya*," I answered. "Please."

We wed that August, before Zed started graduate school, at his church—and now mine—in Lancaster. The night before the wedding, I apologized to my parents, again, for not joining the Amish church, but they stopped me before the words were out of my mouth. *Mamm* spoke for them both when she said they could see how right this was—not for everyone, not for any of their other children, but definitely for me.

Our wedding was well attended. Ella, Luke, Sarah, Samuel, and Rosalee came from Indiana. Lexie and James and their new little three-month-old baby came from Oregon.

Ada, Will, and their brood were there—Mel and Mat helped serve the cake and punch afterward, and Christy played walk-a-mile, every Amish teenager's favorite game, with the *youngie*. Klara and Alexander came—as did Giselle, all the way from Switzerland. We were together once again.

All of my family attended too. Sure, a few of the families in our district and distant relatives didn't, but I understood. Perhaps *Daed* felt a twinge of sadness, but he didn't show it. I knew, at least, that he could see the love between me and Zed. It was the same deep, abiding love he'd had for my mother since long before I was born.

Susie came, bringing a beautiful antique tablecloth as a gift. It had been made by our *Aenti* Verna when she was just about the age I was now. For some reason, I thought of Verna a lot that day—and of my grandmother, and of Frannie too—but not in a sad way. Zed and I got to see James and Lexie's new little one, at the reception, and when they told us they had named him Francis, my eyes welled with tears.

But they were happy tears.

Later, I slipped away and found a quiet corner behind a trellis, where I could see but not be seen. Looking out at the mingling crowd, I realized we weren't the only ones present that day. Even those who had passed on were still with us, in a sense. They lived still, in the faces and memories and dreams of their descendants. Even Konenquas and Abigail.

As I watched Zed with the women in his life—his mother, his aunts, his sister, and his cousins—I couldn't help but feel a bond with all of these women of Lancaster County.

Each walked with God in her own simple way. Each pieced her life together, as best she could, covered by His grace. Each survived pain and joy, in varying measures, by drawing strength from the One who created her.

Following their example, I would strive, always, to do the same.

Discussion Questions

1. Izzy is a sought-after caregiver, even when she is personally struggling with the notion of death. What is it about her personality that makes her so gifted at caring for others? How is this shown in the story?

2. Izzy describes herself as a square peg in the round hole that is her family. Why do you think this is? Will this ever change for her, and, if so, how?

3. Why does Izzy have so much trouble accepting death? In her conversation with Ella, she describes her problem with the randomness of tragic events as a spiritual issue. Do you agree? How would you advise her to overcome this fear?

4. One thing Izzy loves about working with the elderly is hearing their stories. Why do you think this appeals to her? Have you ever had any family lore passed down to you that was unique and compelling?

5. Izzy finds herself drawn to the Lantz women and feels more at home with them than with her own family. Why do you think

this is? How is it that a family that has had so many issues and areas of dysfunction can also be a symbol to her of emotional health and acceptance?

6. When Alice visits with Frannie and Izzy observes their close relationship, she wonders why she has no close female friends of her own. Do you believe such a thing is important? What could Izzy do to expand her circle of friends? What impact does her mother's pattern of friendship with others have on Izzy's own choices?

7. Zed aspires to be a filmmaker, and he sees Izzy as an important part of that. How does this work, given that she has been raised Amish and doesn't even go to the movies? Do you see her as a useful helpmeet to him in this way?

8. When Izzy finds the chapbook written by Abigail, she feels compelled to track down the rest of her story. How did you imagine Abigail's story had played out? Were you surprised by the facts once they came to light?

9. Giselle is a complex character with an interesting back story woven throughout this series. Now that she finally returns to Lancaster County, how do you think she will find healing and growth? Does her story play out the way you expected it to?

10. When Abigail and Gorg are faced with a difficult situation, they make some radical choices. Did you agree with their actions? How would you have handled things in their position?

About the Authors

The Amish Seamstress is Mindy Starns Clark's nineteenth book with Harvest House Publishers. Previous novels include the best-selling, Christy Award—winning *The Amish Midwife* (co-written with Leslie Gould), *Whispers of the Bayou, Shadows of Lancaster County, Under the Cajun Moon,* and *Secrets of Lancaster County,* as well as the well-loved Million Dollar Mysteries.

Mindy lives with her husband, John, and two adult daughters near Valley Forge, Pennsylvania.

Leslie Gould, a former magazine editor, is the author of numerous novels, including *The Amish Midwife* and *Courting Cate. The Amish Seamstress* is her fourth book with Harvest House.

Leslie received her master of fine arts degree from Portland State University and lives in Oregon with her husband, Peter, and their four children.

For detailed family trees to the characters in the Women of Lancaster County series, visit Mindy's and Leslie's websites at www.mindystarnsclark.com and www.lesliegould.com.

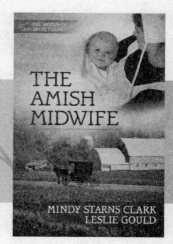

A deathbed confession...
a dusty carved box containing
two locks of hair...
a century-old letter about
property in Switzerland...

Nurse-midwife Lexie Jaeger's encounter with all three rekindles a burning desire to meet her biological family. Propelled on a personal journey of discovery, Lexie's search for the truth takes her from her home in Oregon to the heart of Pennsylvania's Amish country.

There she finds Marta Bayer, a mysterious lay-midwife who may hold the key to Lexie's past. But Marta isn't talking, especially now that she has troubles of her own following the death of an Amish patient during childbirth. As Lexie steps in to assume Marta's patient load and continues the search for her birth family, a handsome local doctor proves to be a welcome distraction. But will he also distract her from James, the man back home who lovingly awaits her return?

From her Amish patients, Lexie learns the true meaning of the Pennsylvania Dutch word *demut,* which means "to let be." Will this woman who wants to control everything ever learn to let be herself and depend totally on God? Or will her stubborn determination to unearth the secrets of the past at all costs only serve to tear her newfound family apart?

A compelling story about a search for identity and the ability to trust that God securely holds our whole life—past, present, and future.

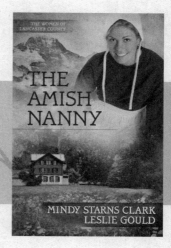

A cave behind a waterfall...
a dying confession...
a secret agreement hidden
for a century...

THE
AMISH
NANNY

MINDY STARNS CLARK
LESLIE GOULD

Amish-raised Ada Rupp knows nothing of these elements of her family's past. Instead, her eyes are fixed firmly on the future—for the first time in her life. Now that a serious medical issue is behind her, Ada is eager to pursue her God-given gifts of teaching at the local Amish school and her dream of marrying Will Gundy, a handsome widower she's loved since she was a child. But when both desires meet with unexpected obstacles, Ada's fragile heart grows heavy with sorrow.

Then she meets Daniel, an attractive Mennonite scholar with a surprising request. He needs her help—along with the help of Will's family—to save an important historic site from being destroyed. Now Ada, a family friend, and a young child must head to Switzerland to mend an old family rift and help preserve her religious heritage.

In order to succeed in saving the site, Ada and Daniel must unlock secrets from the past. But do they also have a future together—or will Ada's heart forever belong to Will, the only man she's ever really wanted?

A fascinating tale of a young woman's journey—to Switzerland, to faith, and finally to love.

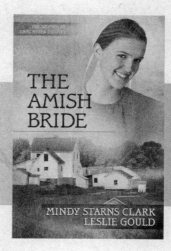

A long-lost painting...
a journal with a secret code...
a father's mysterious return...

Mennonite-raised Ella Bayer has two big dreams: to operate her own bakery and to marry her Amish boyfriend, Ezra Gundy. Ezra adores Ella as well, but his family wants him to marry within the faith.

Hoping some distance will cool the romance, Ezra's parents send him to work on an Amish dairy farm in Indiana. But when Ella's estranged father returns to Lancaster, she heads to Indiana as well—and ends up at a farm linked to her great-grandmother's coded journal. There, her attempts to break that code are aided by Luke Kline, a handsome Amish farmhand.

As Ella makes her way in this new place, she's forced to grapple with the past and question the future. Will she become Ezra's Amish bride? Or does God have something else in mind for the proud and feisty young woman who is used to doing things her way?

A captivating journey of hidden secrets, old love and new love, and discovery of how a life guided by God can be a life of incredible hope and adventure.

To learn more about Harvest House books and
to read sample chapters, log on to our website:

www.harvesthousepublishers.com

HARVEST HOUSE PUBLISHERS
EUGENE, OREGON